Dreams on

Hitler's Couch

Praise for Vitali Vitaliev

'With the charm of Michael Palin and the wit of Clive Anderson, this man is adorable'
TIME OUT

'An ironic and witty commentator on life. He writes with a humanist's appetite, and an outsider's discrimination, for social oddity. There is great charm in this emotional roller-coasting'
SPECTATOR

'Dreams on Hitler's Couch isn't just a memoir of passing interest – "one Russian's personal account of coming to terms with life in the West" – Vitaliev transcends his genre, producing a new travel-writing of the soul, a journey with lessons about what really matters in life. That makes it literature'
LITERARY REVIEW

Dreams on Hitler's Couch

Vitali Vitaliev

Scribner

First published in Great Britain by Richard Cohen Books, 1997
This edition first published by Scribner, 1999
An imprint of Simon & Schuster UK Ltd
A Viacom Company

1 3 5 7 9 10 8 6 4 2

Simon & Schuster UK Ltd
Africa House
64-78 Kingsway
London WC2B 6AH

Simon & Schuster Australia
Sydney

A CIP catalogue record for this book is available from the British
Library

ISBN 0-684-84045-6

Typeset by Palimpsest Book Production Limited,
Polmont, Stirlingshire
Printed and bound in Great Britain by
Bath Press, Bath

To Paul Bernays

Contents

Acknowledgements

I am grateful to *The European*, *The Guardian* and the *Age* newspapers, to Air New Zealand, Ansett Australia, BGB & Associates, Tourism Tasmania, the Royal Literary Fund, the Authors' Foundation of the Society of Authors and a number of other organisations and individuals whose help has made this book possible.

I'd like to thank Lynn H. Nicholas, whose excellent monograph, *The Rape of Europa: The Fate of Europe's Treasures in the Third Reich and the Second World War*, was indispensable in my research.

V.V.

Dreamer of dreams, born out of my due time,
Why should I strive to set the crooked straight?

William Morris

Your emigration is not your own private matter. Otherwise, you are not a writer but just an occupant of a flat. And it doesn't matter where you are – in America, in Japan, in Rostov-on-Don. You have broken out [of the Soviet Union] to tell them about us and about your past. All the rest is petty and irrelevant. All the rest is an insult to your writer's dignity! . . . You have come [to the West] not to buy yourself a pair of jeans and a second-hand car. You have come to tell them the truth . . .

Sergei Dovlatov

1

Dreams on Hitler's Couch

*T*oomas Lembit was born in Tartu, an old Estonian university town, in 1905. As a boy he was an incorrigible hoarder, and his pockets were always brimming with shiny gravel stones, rusty bolts, pieces of mica and other purposeless objects, of which plenty were strewn around Tartu's narrow cobbled streets.

He stored his 'treasures' in a lacquered wooden Palekh box with a galloping Russian troika painted on the lid – a birthday present from his granny who was once married to a Russian hussar. Toomas's parents didn't approve of their son's passion and used covertly to empty the contents of his treasure box into a rubbish bin every now and then.

'He is a real scavenger, this boy,' his father, who was a gardener, would mutter to his taciturn ever-cooking wife. He had no way of knowing that forty years on his blond and blue-eyed boy would become one of Europe's leading art collectors, a high-ranking officer with the Ahnenerbe, a special SS unit dealing with arts and archaeology, and Adolf Hitler's personal curator of furniture and paintings.

God moves in mysterious ways . . .

Nor could the Tartu gardener imagine that his little Toomas was going to die, aged eighty-six, half the world away in

Tasmania, where he would flee after World War Two, and would leave behind thousands of works of art which would be auctioned in Hobart, Tasmania's capital, in August 1991. The proceeds of the auction would go to his distant relatives in Estonia, with the exception of one painting, by the seventeenth-century Dutch artist Johannes Glauber, which would be left to a museum in the Estonian capital, Tallinn.

An interesting detail: Hitler himself was a keen collector of works by sixteenth- and seventeenth-century Dutch painters, and Glauber was one of his favourites.

Among other items in Lembit's collection, mostly consisting of the artifacts looted by the Germans in occupied Europe, were Chinese and Japanese ivory figurines, Tibetan ewers and Biedermeier furniture. The Biedermeier style of furniture-making flourished in Vienna in the first half of the nineteenth century and later spread to other German-speaking countries of Europe. Its main principle was 'plain but comfortable' (bieder means 'plain' in German, and Meier is a common German surname) which in reality implied well-made and elegant yet unpretentious furniture, mostly chairs and sofas, which became quite popular among nineteenth-century European aristocracy.

At this point, the reader can be forgiven for wondering about the purpose of this short excursion into the history of furniture. What is the connection between myself, a Ukrainian-born Russian writer with an Australian passport living in Britain, and the old Estonian collector-turned-Nazi (or Nazi-turned-collector)? The connection is as plain and unpretentious as Biedermeier furniture itself – a Biedermeier couch from Lembit's collection on which I spent a long and restless night in November 1995 during my thirty-fifth, or maybe thirty-sixth, visit to Tasmania.

The freshly upholstered mahogany sofa could have easily belonged to Hitler. He could have slept on it, seeing his recurrent dream of being buried alive, the fate he managed to escape in reality. And, who knows, he might have even shared it with Eva Braun . . . I couldn't help the impression that its upholstery still carried the imprints of the Fuhrer's thin prickly buttocks.

I spotted the couch in the living room of Crabtree House, a

small and plush B&B hotel in the Huon Valley, near Huonville, just twenty miles south of Hobart. It was owned by a married couple of Australianised (or shall I say Tasmanianised?) Italians who had bought it for 2,000 Australian dollars at the above-mentioned auction in August 1991.

'And that couch over there used to belong to Hitler,' the husband said matter-of-factly while showing me around the house.

'Are you sure it was Hitler and not Tamerlane or Alexander the Great?' I smiled. To imagine that a furniture item, whether it belonged to Hitler or not, and even if it had four legs, had somehow covered 20,000 kilometres to end up in Tasmania was a complete baloney.

That was how I first learnt about Toomas Lembit.

As you see, the story starts coming together little by little . . .

Having got a degree in Arts History from Tartu University, Lembit went to continue his studies in Vienna and Paris, where he made friends with Modigliani and Picasso, with whom he used to drink coffee at La Rotonde. Picasso spoke favourably of Lembit's own watercolours and engravings.

When Germany unleashed World War Two, Lembit was living in Vienna, where he had married another Estonian expatriate, Marta. He joined the Wehrmacht (later asserting that he was 'dragged into it'), and became an officer with the SS Ahnenerbe, whose main aim was to prove 'scientifically' the superiority of the German race, using historical and archaeological research.

With the war in progress, the Ahnenerbe was put in charge of pillaging the occupied nations of their cultural heritage. Paintings, sculptures, furniture started trickling into Germany from the invaded countries of Europe. This trickle quickly turned into a stream that soon became a torrent. It was then that the Nazis commandeered Lembit's services in Vienna to restore the paintings they had looted. But his SS career was to reach its pinnacle a couple of years later when he was suddenly summoned to Berlin.

There he was first entrusted with a very important task – engraving German occupational banknotes (his artistic experience obviously came useful). Some German occupational banknotes are still highly valued by collectors.

By that time, some of the top brass of the Third Reich, including Himmler, Goebbels, Goering and Hitler himself, had turned into compulsive hoarders of looted art. Their growing collections needed expert supervision, and Toomas Lembit, as one of the best experts available, was appointed the curator of Hitler's furniture and paintings. This was largely due to the recommendation of Philip Reemtsma, a fellow Estonian, who was also Germany's biggest cigarette tycoon. He was Hitler's personal friend, patron of arts and a generous contributor to the so-called Art Fund, set up by Goering.

Here I have to say that documented proofs of Lembit's work for Hitler do not exist: several months before his death, he burnt all his photos, records and archives. I have reconstructed Lembit's life story from the words of a handful of people who knew him and from my own research. His real name and some of his biographical details had to be changed. So this story has definitely got an element of fiction.

Like most true stories, I presume . . .

Hitler, himself a failed painter, started collecting works of art in 1936, his main interests being Old Master paintings and antique furniture. He was in constant competition with Goering, whose private art gallery was by far the largest and the best in Germany in the late thirties. But it was only with the start of the war that Hitler's collection grew out of all proportion, having surpassed Goering's both in quantity and in quality. It was so huge he had to house it in three different places, Vienna, Linz and Berlin.

During the war Lembit was busy commuting between Berlin and Vienna. He stayed in close touch with Prince Philip of Hesse, a nephew of Kaiser Wilhelm II, who was Hitler's primary agent in acquiring works of art; and with a certain Frau Dietrich, a close friend of Eva Braun, who became the Fuhrer's main provider of paintings from occupied France. Since Frau Dietrich's artistic tastes left much to be desired, Lembit had to sift through her acquisitions, many of which were obvious fakes. Out of 320 paintings, selected by her in Paris, he chose just eighty for one of Hitler's collections.

Yes, Toomas Lembit had his hands full during the war. For his dedicated services to the Reich he was awarded a silver pocket watch with Hitler's signature engraved on it. He was even able to start a small art collection of his own.

When Germany's impending defeat became apparent, Hitler tried to find shelter for his collections, and Lembit played an active role here too. But the Allied forces were progressing too fast and by the end of 1944 the top brass of the Third Reich were more preoccupied with saving their skins than with looted works of art, no matter how precious. After Hitler's suicide in his underground bunker and the capture of Berlin, the witnesses, who had stumbled across Hitler's art caches, unanimously reported that the bulk of his collections 'had been stolen'.

Lembit certainly knew better.

VE-Day found him in Stockholm preparing for his final escape. He rejected South America, to where most of the surviving top Nazis fled, and opted for Tasmania, this 'off-shore island off an off-shore continent', half a world away from Europe. Why?

The first answer that comes to mind is that Tasmania is the world's most remote place, the last piece of solid land before the South Pole, and one can't possibly escape any further. But for Lembit it had another important attraction: Hobart, Tasmania's capital, had the best antiquarian shops in the southern hemisphere. Antiques, brought to the island by the first European settlers, were bound to be inexpensive and well-preserved in such a distant place, spared all the wars and cataclysms of the twentieth century. Also, and this was no less important for Lembit, rich and prosperous Melbourne, with many antiques collectors and prospective buyers, was just a couple of hundred miles away across the Bass Strait.

Lembit was not the only former Nazi to find refuge in Tasmania, this little Europe at the end of the world. Several thousand former Wehrmacht soldiers went there after the war. Work and living space were plentiful, and with White Australia Policy in full swing, they had little problem with entry permits. Their skin was white indeed, though their past was often painted in much darker colours. Most of them, having fled so far, had something sinister to hide.

The Germans mostly settled on the island's northern coast, in the area of Devonport, Tasmania's third largest town, where there is still a German Club with several hundred cheerful septua- and octogenarian members. Overnight ferries from Melbourne docked at Devonport which was also advantageous for Germans who wanted to keep their escape route open. Just in case . . .

It was in the town of Penguin, near Devonport, that I once met Gunter Hinz, a former Berliner, who runs The European Trainworld, a model railway with tiny European trees and stations like Bonn, Kehl and Strasbourg. He was a sprightly, well-preserved man in his early seventies who spoke English with a strong German accent.

I told him that I was born in Kharkov. He got visibly agitated: 'Oh, Sharkow! . . . I've been there during the war . . .' 'You must have visited it twice,' I suggested, having remembered that Kharkov was occupied by the Germans twice, in 1942 and in 1943. 'Yah, yah!' he agreed. 'I came there by motorcycle and had to come back on foot . . . Yes, I was a soldier. What could I do? You couldn't say "no" to Hitler, could you?' he chuckled.

Gunter Hinz went to Tasmania after the war. Having spent almost fifty years there, he returned to Germany only once and didn't like it: 'Berlin is a crazy place: too many people, too much noise. I don't want to go there ever again. *Nein!*'

Yet from the model railway that he had so lovingly constructed, it was plain that he was missing Europe. Model railways have always struck me as extremely nostalgic toys.

While we were talking, the model trains, complete with lit-up windows and miniature seats with minuscule Germans in them, were running back and forth along their tiny tracks. One of them was a cargo train carrying toy German tanks. A soldier is always a soldier, I thought.

But for Toomas Lembit settling in Devonport was out of the question. The only place where he could live in Tasmania was Hobart, with its Salamanca Place, replete with antique shops and art galleries.

He came to Hobart in 1948 and bought himself an old colonial red-brick house in the suburb of Taroona. In all his forty-five years in Hobart, only a handful of strangers were lucky enough to be invited inside. That is not counting three uninvited burglars who broke in during the night in the late seventies. Lembit, already an old man, confronted them with a gun and shot one of the intruders dead in cold blood. The remaining two fled. And this was in the then almost crime-free tranquil Tasmania, where even policemen are not allowed to carry guns (they carry teddy bears in their cars in case they have to pacify a crying child)!

What did Lembit hide in his nondescript and decrepit abode?

Among those chosen few who had managed to have a quick look inside were two Hobart art dealers. Speaking to me, they were unanimous in their appraisal: 'It was like a bloody museum: full of ivory, silver, jewellery, paintings, tapestries, porcelain and antiques.' According to them, among the paintings there were several works by Rubens and Rembrandt, and a couple of canvases by Serov, a famous nineteenth-century Russian artist of the *Peredvizhniki* (Wanderers) school.

How did Lembit manage to smuggle his (or Hitler's?) collections to Tasmania? No one knows the answer. In post-war Europe, like in the former Soviet Union, 'nothing was allowed, but everything was possible'. The only thing that is certain is that the collections came to Tasmania by sea from Stockholm.

In Hobart, Lembit lived the life of a recluse and tried to maintain the lowest possible profile. He first worked in a timber mill, then became a car mechanic with Taroona Body Works, and in his spare time he did some house-painting and restoring.

'He was a very suspicious person and would always scrutinise you for a minute with his bull-terrier's piercing blue eyes before uttering a word,' one of the art dealers told me. 'It looked as if he was always afraid of something.'

Lembit's house was full of fire-arms. And when, after the botched burglary, all of them were confiscated by the police, Lembit went straight to a local gun shop and tried to acquire another set. He went livid with rage, when told that he needed a licence. 'What is licence? I not needs a bloody licence! Police took my weapons and I wants more!' he shouted in his heavily accented English.

Eventually, Lembit did manage to buy himself a new shotgun and a couple of pistols.

It was only once that he was seen seriously embarrassed. Paying for food at a supermarket till, he was groping inside his pockets for some change when a round metallic object fell out onto the floor. Lembit hurried to pick it up, but several people in the queue noticed that it was a massive silver watch with an SS eagle on the lid.

As he was getting older, Lembit grew more and more paranoid and quick-tempered. He pointed a pistol at an art dealer whom he himself invited to look at his collection of ivory. He was furious when asked to take off his shoes and to put on slippers at a house where he was painting. 'I not needs bloody slippers!' he exploded.

Once a month he would drive alone to Richmond, a small historic village twenty miles from Hobart. He would browse through several local antique shops and tiny art galleries and then, with a flask of vodka, he would sit, brooding over his past near a cheerful rivulet, overgrown with weeds. From there, he had a good view of the village, with its roosters and ducks, its colonial log cabins, rustling cedars and gum-trees which one could mistake for willows and poplars from the distance. The place reminded him of his native Estonia which he knew he would never see again . . .

When his wife died in 1989, Lembit hired a burly bodyguard who lived in his house. But he didn't trust even him, and soon sacked him. Several months before his death Lembit burnt all his records and photo albums. 'I not wants people to know anything about me,' he was overheard as saying.

Toomas Lembit died in complete solitude surrounded only by pricey knick-knacks from his (or Hitler's?) collection which, according to his will, was to be auctioned with the proceeds going to his distant relatives in Estonia.

The auction took place in August 1991, and was a huge success. Several buyers came from as far as Sydney, but most of the items stayed in Tasmania. The *Mercury*, a Hobart daily with the somewhat unimaginative masthead 'Mercury Makes a Lot of Sense' ran a pretty innocuous article about this auction with only a tiny hint of Lembit's Nazi past. Nevertheless, the journalist who wrote it told me that she had got a number of hate letters from former Nazis as feedback. This short newspaper piece is the only publication in existence that mentions Lembit, who had certainly succeeded in making his life as inconspicuous as possible.

I stumbled upon the Biedermeier couch from his collection at the small Tasmanian guest house in November 1995 by sheer accident.

As I have said already, this was my thirty-fifth (or maybe thirty-sixth) visit to Tasmania in just five years since leaving the Soviet Union. What was it that attracted me to this remote island in the first place? It was probably its all-permeating nostalgia for Europe that I myself was suffering from while living in Melbourne.

When I first went there, reluctantly, on a speaking tour in April 1991, I was not prepared for the breathtaking beauty of the place. As the plane came in to land at Hobart, I looked through the window and held my breath: I saw a sparkling harbour among gracious green hills. It was a landscape straight out of my childhood dreams: neat houses under red-tiled roofs, quiet streets running down to the River Derwent, the hunched back of the Tasman Bridge. For the whole of my first week in Tasmania, I was breathless, with my mouth agape. It was not only the natural beauty of the island, but also its profound spirituality that stunned me.

Tasmania, with New South Wales, is the oldest convict settlement in Australia. But unlike New South Wales, it was the secondary prison, where convicts were sent for offences while already in exile. For most there was no return.

The first English settlers in Tasmania (which was then called Van Diemen's Land) fell over themselves to recreate their native country on these remote shores. Walking through Richmond, Launceston or Battery Point, the historic centre of Hobart, you cannot help feeling that you are somewhere in Ledbury or Bourton-on-the-Water. The streets are called Cheltenham Place, Marlborough Street and the like. Nineteenth-century village churches imitate their English counterparts; the chimes of the old GPO building in Hobart echo those of Big Ben; Devonshire teas are served everywhere; and pubs have English interiors, exteriors and names, The Fox and Hounds, The Richmond Arms, The Prince of Wales. Roadside inns have bathrooms with separate taps for hot and cold water (very unusual for Australia). Even telephones in Tasmania purred with feline English intonations, or so they sounded to my nostalgic ears.

Arthur Circus in the centre of Hobart is but a toy replica of a London square, its neat colonial houses encircling a tiny park with a wooden bench and a swing in the middle. One wouldn't be surprised to spot a mini double-decker carrying toy, rain-soaked Londoners, cross it.

And you realise with sudden clarity that this is indeed the end of the earth, and you are about 20,000 kilometres away from Soho.

All this couldn't fail to strike a chord with an exile like myself desperately missing Europe. Not any European country in particular, but just Europe, with its smells and sounds, its history and architecture; its wars, troubles, theatres, newspapers and its never-ending excitement.

Nostalgia is one of the most creative human emotions. It is also profoundly cosmopolitan in essence: nostalgia for one country cannot fail to strike a chord in souls nostalgic for any other place.

During my three years in Australia, frequent trips to Tasmania were my cure – indispensable like injections of fresh blood – since there I could easily imagine myself in my beloved England, or almost anywhere in Europe, even in my native Ukraine.

With every visit to Tasmania, my passion for it kept growing. I would grab any pretext to go there on a newspaper assignment, on a speaking engagement or just for a long weekend. Unable to settle in Melbourne, I started to regard Tasmania as my spiritual home and even wrote in one of my columns that I wanted to be buried in Richmond, among the graves of the first European settlers.

This last statement was not just a metaphor. I did mean it, I can assure you.

As it often happens with human passions, my infatuation with Tasmania soon grew into an obsession. During one of my radio interviews, I proudly declared myself a Tasmaniac.

But this last thirty-fifth (or thirty-sixth) visit was special. In autumn, 1995, two and a half years after my marriage breakdown, when I thought I had finally settled in London after three years of transcontinental hopping, I felt I was losing direction. I was broke, desperate and unhappy, and fleeing to Tasmania was the only way out of this seemingly hopeless situation, or so I thought then. I came to Tasmania in search of a missing link in the chain of my existence.

Only this time Tasmania failed me. It didn't offer me any solutions. And could it?

Instead, it offered me, a thoroughly displaced person, a no-less-displaced Biedermeier couch that once used to belong to Hitler.

Coming across a Hitler's couch in the end of the world could mean only one thing – going back.

This is how my tortuous life track crossed with that of Toomas Lembit, who had been dead for more than four years by that time. The difference between us was that he had escaped to Tasmania to hide his dark secrets, and I had come there to re-discover myself.

Also, unlike Lembit, I was still alive, although at times I was having serious doubts about it.

I couldn't tear my gaze off Hitler's freshly upholstered couch standing there, in the lounge of Crabtree House, as if it had never been anywhere else (furniture pieces are like pets – very adaptable). How many amazing stories it must have heard. How many human (and sub-human) bums it must have accommodated during 170 years of its life. If only the couch could talk!

No worries, as they say in Australia: I am not going to plunge into an imaginary interview with the couch. It was only Chekhov who could get away with breathing life into furniture. In the Chekhovs' Taganrog house, where he was born and spent his childhood, there stood a cupboard where his mother used to keep sweets. Passing by this cupboard, young Anton would stop and exclaim with mocking reverence: 'Dear, venerable cupboard!' Later he used this ironic address in *The Cherry Orchard*.

Aldo Buzzi, an Italian travel writer, made an interesting observation on the role of sofas (or couches) in Russian life in his book, *Journey to the Land of the Flies*: 'Dostoyevsky . . . died on a sofa, an item of furniture very often used by the Russians for sleeping . . . and for dying. Even Stalin, according to Molotov, died on a sofa. People often slept without undressing . . ., at times not even taking off their boots or their lapti (clogs). The typical sofa was covered with oilcloth. Sleeping was not a problem. Tolstoy, who was born on a sofa, made himself an overcoat of rough canvas . . . For a pillow he used a big dictionary. And Mandelstam tells of an amputee who at night took off his wooden leg and used it as a pillow.'

Hitler's couch (or sofa) was neither dear, nor venerable (and I was certainly neither Chekhov nor Dostoyevsky: I didn't intend to animate a couch or to die on it – not just yet). Mind you, there was nothing dictatorial or cannibalistic about it either. It was obviously innocent of any crimes against humanity. But its one-time owner had somehow left an invisible, yet ineffaceable, imprint – an indelible stigma, if not on its seat, then definitely on its reputation.

The Austrian-made and Italian-owned Hitler's couch did not belong in Tasmania. No more than a Ukrainian-born Russian with an Australian passport living in London. Neither of us was supposed to be there, but both of us were, there was little doubt about it.

Two lost souls – human and wooden – in the end of the world.

I succeeded in persuading the owners to allow me to sacrifice my double bed in the guest room and to spend one night on the couch, narrow as it was. I don't know why I wanted it so much, but suddenly it was very important to sleep on it. I thought I was bound to have some very special dreams.

Without undressing, in the age-long Russian tradition (according to Aldo Buzzi), I lower myself onto the couch, and the springs of its time-beaten mattress sink under my weight with a heavy senile sigh. Instead of a dictionary, I arrange my rucksack under my head. I close my eyes, and my six years in the West – miserable and happy, troublesome and amusing, misleading and revealing – come back to me in an unsteady kaleidoscopic succession of real-life dreams.

Dreams on Hitler's couch . . .

2

The Illusion Cinema

I dreamt that what I had thought was reality was a dream,
and what I had thought was a dream was reality
                                    Anton Chekhov, *Notebook*

*T*he 'Illusion' was a smallish cinema located on the ground
floor of one of the infamous Stalin Gothic wedding-cake
skyscrapers in the centre of Moscow, near Yauzkiye Gates. It
specialised in showing old (very old) Western movies, and its
tiny auditorium was always packed full. Across the road from
it was an obscure Research Institute of Medical Information
where I worked as a translator in the late seventies.

My boss was a young lawyer called Kostya. With prominent, as if stone-carved, features and a long wavy beard
he looked like a younger version of Solzhenitsyn, or like
the anti-Semitic Saudi Arabian dissident Prof. Al Massari.
Appearances are often misleading. Despite his intellectual
scholarly looks, Kostya was a bully, an alcoholic and a
kleptomaniac. He had an irrepressible passion for stealing
sausages from food shops and mirrors from public toilets. If
apprehended, he would feign utter distress. 'How dare you?!'
he would scream at the top of his voice, and his intellectual
social-democratic beard would start trembling indignantly (he
had an alcohol-induced nervous tic). Then he would run away

carrying his loot under his jacket and mumbling to himself: 'Article 29, part three, of the Criminal Code . . . Up to five years in prison . . .' He was a lawyer after all.

There was nothing much to do at the Research Institute either for a lawyer or for a translator. 'Your first task for today is to get a fire-extinguisher and bring it to the office,' Kostya would instruct me in the morning. 'Fire-extinguisher' was a slang word for a huge bottle of cheap strong white wine, also known as 'biomedicine'.

Having finished with the wine, we would pop out for lunch at the canteen of the neighbouring Institute of Nutrition (the meal was likely to be washed down with more 'biomedicine'), and after that we would go across the road to the Illusion cinema, where Kostya would routinely nod off giving out brief whistle-like snores from time to time.

The Illusion opened a whole new world for me. It was there that I first saw *The Wizard of Oz* and *Singing in the Rain*, *King Kong* and *Gone with the Wind*. It was an ideal place for quiet after-lunch daydreaming.

One grim February afternoon, we went to see John Schlesinger's *Billy Liar*. Kostya fell asleep very soon, and I got totally engrossed with the plot and with the brilliant acting of Tom Courteney. I was amazed to see how many parallels the drab and uneventful life of Billy, an undertaker's clerk from a provincial town in the North of England, had with mine. Like Billy, I was stuck in the stagnant gloomy reality of Brezhnev's Moscow with no prospect of seeing the world, with no hope and no future. Like him, I constantly tried to escape into a wild fantasy where I could realise my dream ambitions. He had his fictitious land Ambrosia, of which he was the supreme ruler. I had my own Ambrosia which was called England and which I knew I was never going to see.

I remember leaving the Illusion cinema that afternoon feeling shattered and spiritually devastated, but also strangely enlightened. It was good to know that you were not alone, that you were not the only compulsive dreamer in this dark, snow-ridden and cynical world.

No other film has ever made a bigger impact on me than *Billy Liar* at the Moscow day-dreamers' cinema, aptly called the Illusion. Now, I only have to close my eyes to see my whole life unveiling in front of me on the tattered screen of time.

Or maybe I am still sitting there, at the Illusion, with plonk-reeking Kostya snoring next to me?

There is surprisingly little time to be one's true self in this life. Every second of our existence is pigeonholed, labelled and put into files.

The moment a man leaves his house, he becomes a pedestrian. He enters the Tube station and turns into a passenger. He sits behind the wheel of his second-hand jalopy, and bingo – he is a motorist. He squeezes himself through the rotating doors of his office and becomes an employee, a worker or an executive. At lunch-time, he plays the part of a pub or restaurant patron. He pops into a shop and immediately he is a customer. Back home he is a husband, a father or a loner. At night, he is a TV-viewer, a lover or a solitary drinker. One can go to prison and become an inmate. Or get sick and be classified as a patient. Or die and be labelled 'deceased'.

There's hardly any time left to be what we all really are – ordinary humans.

It is not true that nobody is interested in someone else's dreams, because it is only in our dreams that we remain completely true to ourselves.

Dreaming (and this includes daydreaming) is the ultimate liberating experience. You can't pretend or cheat in your dream. 'Dreams are the touchstones of our characters,' said Henry David Thoreau. And Jung put it even more explicitly: 'Dreams may give expression to ineluctable truths, to philosophical pronouncements, illusions, wild fantasies, anticipations, irrational experiences, even telepathic visions, and heaven knows what besides.'

What is a dream? It is a state of mind that is hard to define and the exact mechanism of which is a mystery even to scientists. Dreams may occur not only when we are asleep, but when we are wide awake, too. Some people claim that they never dream. This is impossible: they simply cannot remember them. 'All adults used to be children at one time, but, unfortunately, most have forgotten it,' said Antoine de Saint-Exupéry.

Vladimir Levy, a Moscow psychologist, wrote that all humans can be divided into two psychic categories depending on what sort of dreams they have. According to him, introverts always have black-and-white dreams, and extroverts' dreams are multi-coloured. If so, I am definitely an extrovert: my dreams (and I normally have several dozen a night and more during the day) are always in Technicolor.

Dreams are also extremely creative. No one knows how many solutions of seemingly insoluble problems came to people in their dreams. The life-saving Three-Seven-Ace combination was prompted to the despondent card gambler from Pushkin's 'The Queen of Spades' in his dream.

I remember composing a complete three-stanza poem in my dream when I was sixteen. In the morning I simply put it down on paper without changing a single word. It was triggered by the death of my grandfather whom I adored. It was in Russian and it rhymed of course.

> A man goes away
> To get dissolved
> In the early morning mist,
> In the dance of distant city lights.
>
> A man goes away
> To be often dreamt of
> By those to whom he was dear,
> Who he was friends with;
>
> A man goes away,
> But his heart stays with us –
> It rattles in the wheels of fast trains,
> It beats on his son's wrist
> With a smart mechanism of the watch
> That he had given his son as a gift.

I am a strong believer in the creative power of that mystic instant when you are already not asleep, yet not quite awake either. It can be compared to the so-called 'blue moment' which can be observed in winter near the Arctic Circle, when the sun comes out fleetingly for a couple of hours between night and day: neither light nor darkness, neither sleep nor vigilance, but something in between. I saw the blue moment near the Finnish town of Rovaniemi, in Lapland, where I went to interview Santa Claus in December 1992.

It is interesting that scientists are still at a loss as to why we spend twenty years of our life sleeping and dreaming. I think I know the reason: to be ourselves.

An average human being can expect to have about 300,000 dreams in his or her lifetime, or so they say. An avid dreamer, like myself, can probably achieve many more – about a million. My dreams have always been extremely versatile: thriller dreams, romantic dreams, Mills & Boon dreams, travelogue dreams, science fiction dreams, flying dreams (when I fly using my hands as wings – a sign of feeling trapped and willing to move on – I am a frequent flier in my dreams as well as in real life). Many of them – like TV series – run for several consecutive nights. A few keep coming back to haunt me for months and even years. And some of them do come true.

From an early age I dreamt of travelling, of going to the West, to Paris or London, which I knew was never going to happen. And when eventually, contrary to all expectations, I did come to London and Paris, I couldn't help the feeling of déjà vu – as if I had visited these places in the past and could even recognise some of their streets and buildings.

Indeed, I *had* been there before – in my dreams.

During my last five years in the Soviet Union, I had a recurrent dream of taking a lift to the top of the Empire State Building in New York with my close university friend Yuri who emigrated from the USSR in 1980 and settled in America. We corresponded for some time, but then, as it often happens, we lost track of each other. Only I kept having this dream – the two of us in a lift . . .

In 1991, having lived in Australia for more than a year, I placed an ad in *Novoye Russkoye Slovo*, a New York-based Russian daily, looking for Yuri. Shortly, I got a letter from him.

We had found each other after eleven years of separation, and he invited me to come and stay with him in Chicago, where he lived. One day Yuri was showing me around the city, and we took an elevator to the top of the Sears Tower, the world's tallest building. The walls of the high-speed lift, and even the floor buttons were so familiar. My dream came true, only it was set in Chicago, not New York.

Or was I still dreaming? And am I still dreaming now as I am writing these lines? When I look up from my computer screen, I can see a neat row of London chimneys on sloping triangular roofs behind the window – a fragment of a yet another childhood dream.

Is there a borderline separating dreams from reality? In the morning I often feel devastated and emotionally shattered by the previous night's dreams. It takes me a while to recover. And some of the most persisting dreams chase me during the day. This is probably why I can suddenly switch off in the middle of a conversation carried away by an especially assiduous dream or by a flash of memory. Daydreaming is my favourite hobby, although I am well aware of how irritating this can be for the people around me.

'Are you awake or asleep?' my girlfriend often asks me.

I wish I knew . . .

My memory is like a thermonuclear chain reaction: one little flash leads to another, and in no time I am flooded by a torrent of images and thoughts from which I can only escape into my dreams.

I can see my late father pacing away from me briskly along Sumskaya Street in Kharkov. He is wearing a white tee-shirt, underlining the muscular arms of a lifetime sportsman. He is also wearing the peculiar Soviet seal of oppression on his unsmiling face – the expression caused by years of queuing, insecurity and struggling for survival.

I can see myself and my little son Mitya riding our bicycles in the village of Zaveti Ilyicha (Lenin's Bequests) near Moscow where we had our dacha. My wife has sent us to buy some *smetana* (soured cream) for dinner – not an easy task in the late 'eighties. We have to check all three permanently empty village shops, our usual vicious shopping circle. But we enjoy being together. 'We are not afraid of anything, because there are two of us – father and son. We are both soldiers, we are both heroes,' we sing in chorus as we ride.

I can see myself holidaying in the Abkhazian village of Pitsunda on the Black Sea coast in 1986. With my friend Misha Kazovsky, the literary editor of *Krokodil*, we were spending a month at the *Pravda* publishers' sanatorium. After an early morning swim we would go to our rooms and write until noon (I was working on my first novel then), and after lunch we would take long walks along deserted golden beaches. The sea rustled gently against the sand, and although everything around us was calm and peaceful, I couldn't help feeling some inexplicable discomfort during these walks.

I remember closing my eyes one day and, miraculously, seeing dozens of bloated human bodies floating in the water. I opened my eyes – and the corpses disappeared.

'Look, I have just seen lots of drowned men in the sea,' I said to Misha.

He shrugged my vision off as a hallucination caused by too much writing.

Five years later, when I was already in Melbourne and the war between Abkhazia and Georgia was in full swing, I read in a London newspaper about hundreds of corpses washed ashore in Pitsunda.

I can see myself swimming in my own indoor swimming pool in Melbourne and looking at a lemon tree growing in my backyard, behind the window, with lemons on its branches like clots of condensed sunlight.

I can see myself typing away a funny column on my computer while feeling almost suicidal. 'It is hard to write funnily lying under the wheels of a truck that has just run over you,' a fellow Russian writer once observed.

So who am I, after all?

A post-war baby. The only child of a young nuclear physicist and his wife, a chemical engineer. A chubby Kharkov schoolboy, with a compulsory crew-cut, called a semi-box. An *Oktyabryonok* – a member of a Leninist organisation for primary school kids (membership was as compulsory as a semi-box). A young pioneer, with a red kerchief round his neck. An avid reader of science fiction and adventure stories. A learner of English. A collector of maps, guide-books and train timetables. A trainspotter, nicknamed Engine-Driver by his schoolmates. An armchair buccaneer. A radio buff and a BBC World Service covert fan.

A tyro poet. A Komsomol member – both by belief and by compulsion. An encaged dreamer. A university student. A young and premature husband. A university graduate. A young and premature divorcee. A jobless dissident with a stomach ulcer. A 100-roubles-a-month translator at a tiny research institute.

A Muscovite. A second-time husband. A loving father. An interpreter. A freelance writer with an office in a converted wardrobe. A heavy drinker. An award-winning investigative journalist.

A KGB target. A defector. An Australian resident. A newspaper columnist. A TV personality. A household name. A driver. A house-owner. A fatso. An exiled European. A compulsive traveller. A frequent (too frequent) transcontinental flier. A journalist in London. A second-time divorcee. A tenant. A depressed loner. A heavy smoker. A martial artist. A teetotaller. A failed Don Juan. A partner. A bankrupt. A self-confessed Tasmaniac. A tramp. An author of five books. A Taekwon-do blue belt-holder. A Ukrainian-born Russian with an Australian passport living in London.

Yes, like most of us, I've had more than one role to play in this life. At times, I even think that I had already lived through one full life which ended in January 1990 with my defection from the Soviet Union. My six years in the West were so much unlike the thirty-five years of my previous existence that they could easily constitute a totally new life in its own right, with its own birth, childhood and adulthood. Or was it all just a dream?

A condensed life packed into six extraordinary years during which I have gained and lost a lot – without ever realising how and why it all happened or what it was that hit me.

I travelled the whole way from coming to the West with two

suitcases of books, to getting stuck in Tasmania, a beautiful island at the very end of the world that has become my spiritual home away from home (or so I thought), with the same two suitcases, broke, disgruntled and up to my ears in debt. Only some of the books were different, and most of them have commuted several dozen times between London and Australia and back.

It was the end of the line in the true sense of these words. From there one could either go head down over the precipice or turn back. I chose the latter.

The price of living at the breaking point of history.

A dream that I had three years ago while still living comfortably in Australia. I get off the plane in Melbourne, my new home city. Having passed through customs and immigration controls I pick up my luggage – two bulky suitcases – and come out of the terminal. No one is there to meet me. I flag down a taxi and suddenly realise that I have no idea of where to go. I have forgotten all the addresses. I have forgotten the names of all my contacts and friends. I can't even remember a single telephone number. Two and a half years later this dream became reality.

The very day of my birth in January 1954 got stuck in between the epochs – thirty-seven years after the Bolshevik revolution and thirty-seven years before the collapse of the Soviet Union. So I was probably predestined for some sort of a fractured life.

As one of my London friends, an émigré Russian writer, once said, the collapse of the Soviet empire has created a generation of disappointed wanderers who roam the world without any hope of settling down. A disappointed wanderer. This is what I used to be for most of these years.

All dreamers are disappointed wanderers, and all disappointed wanderers are dreamers to a degree.

This book is a look back at my second, Western, life which in many ways was no easier than my first one. But it was certainly much more eventful. My last six years were so heavily packed with events, joys and disappointments that looking back at them is like looking through a kaleidoscope. Or like seeing a dream, blissful one moment and nightmarish the next. My memories are fragmented, multi-coloured and not at all chronological, and certain episodes are so bizarre that I am not even sure whether they really happened to me, Vitali Vitaliev, or to my fictitious hero.

A writer's life, after all, is but a thick book with him as the protagonist, where fiction and reality are intermingled to such an extent that they become almost inseparable – again, like in a dream. But there is one theme, one subject that unites all these kaleidoscopic fragments into one symmetrical story – my continuous quest for Freedom that started many years ago and still goes on.

My six years in the West have so far failed to help me explain what Freedom really is. So this book is just another attempt to try and understand the nature of this curious substance, Freedom.

In a way, I was lucky to have lived two polarly different lives on both sides of the Iron Curtain.

The biggest mistake I made after thirty-five years in the world's cruellest totalitarian state was that I treated Freedom in the same manner an old Bolshevik of my grandad's ilk would treat communism – as a nice-sounding and flexible dream that can be somehow adjusted to a gloomy and down-to-earth reality. I tended to take some Western liberties (like unrestricted travelling, or buying all imaginable books) for granted, like dreams that had suddenly come true. I couldn't get enough of them and, unknowingly, was suffering from Freedom bulimia.

In a way, the West for me was like a thick nice-looking book with a glossy cover, the book that I didn't have a chance to read (and didn't particularly want to). Just admiring its glossy spine on the shelf was enough.

During my first two years in Australia, I subscribed to dozens of British and American newspapers and magazines which to me represented the coveted and repressed freedom of information. I got hold of all existing credit cards. I went on shopping sprees buying ridiculous and unnecessary things by mail catalogues (Freedom of opportunity? Or just a sudden consumerist greed?). Most of my purchases were useless and didn't even work (like a defective car alarm that cost me about 200 dollars), and I would chuck them out without regret. I had a good job, a high salary and a nice three-bedroom house with an indoor swimming pool and Jacuzzi in one of Melbourne's suburbs. My new freedoms were too unexpected, too dream-like, and that was probably why they seemed unlimited. Or maybe I somehow knew that they were not going to last for long?

In the Soviet Union, Freedom for me was like the Moon in the night-time sky, something that you can see, but cannot touch or reach. I had no idea that Freedom – just like the Moon – has a reverse side, invisible from our part of the universe and hence totally unknown. I thought that living in a relatively free society was as easy and natural as driving an automatic car. The car proved to be a manual, and the driver has to stay firmly in control.

I thought that in the West spiritual freedom and material well-being were parallel lines that never criss-crossed. These lines proved to be perpendicular.

Now I do understand that Freedom, if it exists at all, is not so much about rights, but rather about responsibilities, that it is not so much a dream as a hectic and often restrictive reality. There are No Trespassing areas in the West, too. Western Freedom is not in crossing your neighbours' private, even if not fenced off, driveway to shorten the walk to your house, but in choosing to bypass it.

In short, Freedom is not a charity donation. It is rather a bank loan with high interest that keeps building up, the more you borrow from it, the higher the repayments. And if you borrow too much, you may have to pay with your life. The ultimate responsibility of choice comes before freedom of movement, or any other freedom for that matter. This is the most important lesson I have learnt in the West.

I don't want this book to sound didactic. Lecturing people about Freedom is not my intention. Writing for me is not about offering solutions, it is about posing more and more questions, most of which have to remain unanswered.

'Don't be afraid of poverty, don't be afraid of war or plague, but always be wary of someone who tells you: "I know what you have to do."' These simple words of Alexander Galich, an émigré Soviet bard who died in exile, have always been my writer's motto.

Using the terminology of my trains-dominated childhood (in my youthful poems, I used to compare life to a long and bumpy train journey), I can now say that Freedom is probably the station one can never reach but has to try to come close to.

3

Alone on the Road

I am alone on the road,
Deserted track glistens through the mist,
Quiet is the night; the desert is face to face with God,
And the stars keep talking to each other.

The words of the old Russian ballad are floating above
Melbourne. Are they being sung by some invisible and lonely
Russian busker? Or are they simply echoing in my head as I
drag my luggage through dark and deserted streets?

My plane from Tasmania was late, and no one was meeting
me at the airport. I had to take a cab and go to the place where
I thought I could spend the night. There was nobody there, and
the intercom buzz ricocheted deafeningly against the walls of
the empty house before coming back to make my eardrums
vibrate. There is nothing sounding as lonely and desperate as
a late-night door bell in an empty flat.

I had no change to make a phone call and, even if I had,
the nearest public telephone was outside my reach: with two
heavy suitcases and my laptop – all my remaining possessions
– I was unable to go far.

I felt like a stranded snail who suddenly had to carry a
turtle's shell. Or like a patient who wakes up after sedation
only to realise that he had a wrong, healthy, leg amputated

by mistake instead of the bad, gangrenous, one (there was such a case in an American hospital).

A long journey only succeeds if you travel light. But what if your whole life has become an endless journey in search of yourself?

> The Earth is sleeping solemnly and magically
> In her own blue radiance.
> Why then do I feel so much pain and hardship?
> Am I expecting anything to happen?
> Am I regretting anything?

I am humming the familiar Russian lyrics and staring at the bright Australian stars above my head. They might be talking to each other and even calling each other mate, but none of them is willing to talk to me. The city that was once my home now looks so alien and hostile.

Am I expecting anything to happen? Am I regretting anything? No, I am not. Regretting, agonising over one's past, crying over spilt milk are hopeless occupations. Having spent so much time in the gigantic cage of the former Soviet Union and almost six years in the West, I thought I had learnt to appreciate my long-awaited freedom of movement. From an armchair buccaneer with no hope of seeing the world, I turned into a hardened traveller, a wanderer, a vagabond, who felt at home everywhere in the world and was a stranger everywhere in the world, too. I was free to travel. But was it enough?

The price one has to pay for Freedom can be high. I paid for it through my nose, having lost my home, my family and my roots somewhere on the road. An old Russian peasant woman speaking unaccented English in my frequent dream is a sure sign of rootlessness.

I became rootless to the extent that I had to start looking at the mirror every now and then just to make sure that I was still there.

'A good traveller is one who does not know where he goes to, and a perfect traveller does not know where he came from.' I used these words by Li Yutang, a Chinese writer, as an epigraph for my latest book. It was a travel book of course.

'From a homeless tramp,' that was how I used to sign this book to my friends. I was trying to be ironic but forgot to touch wood – and a homeless tramp is what I have become.

> No I am not expecting anything from life,
> And I don't regret my past in the very least;
> I am craving freedom and quiet,
> I'd like to reach oblivion and fall asleep . . .

With an effort, I pick up my luggage and start trudging along the street. Where to? To where my eyes look, as they used to say in Russia.

Having spotted me from the distance, a lonely pedestrian hurries to turn the corner into a side lane. I don't blame him: I probably look like a hapless burglar dragging his loot through the empty streets in the middle of the night. But I have robbed no one. No one apart from myself.

What is it that makes my suitcases so heavy? My five published books in English? Hundreds of newspaper columns? HMV cassettes with my TV documentaries on them? Impressions of more than fifty countries of the globe? A nice red-brick house with a barbie in its backyard that I bought and lost within a couple of years?

Or are they simply overloaded with unfulfilled aspirations? With broken illusions? With ivory towers and sandcastles of which I have built so many? Sand is a heavy substance indeed.

'Every wanderer carries with him a chest of memories,' Dmitri Kedrin, a good Russian poet, once wrote. My memories are too numerous for a chest. That's why I have to carry them in two suitcases, labelled 'HEAVY. BEND YOUR KNEES'.

I bend my knees trying not to break my spine and carry on.

My forehead is covered with sweat. My hands are aching. Yes, yes, I'd like to fall asleep, to escape the inescapable metaphor of the old Russian romance that has become reality – an ultimate writer's nightmare. But not just yet. Not here. Not in an empty street of an unknown Australian city.

Slowly but surely I am stumbling towards another house, the house of friends. And through the sticky blackness of southern night I can already discern a bright dagger-shaped slit of light bursting towards me from under the window curtain. They must be at home. They must be waiting for me. I've got a place where I can spend the night. And tomorrow? We'll see. Morning is wiser than night, as a good Russian proverb goes.

And suddenly I realise how tired I am.

Tired travellers tend to have bags under their eyes. Tired vagabonds have suitcases . . .

> I am craving freedom and quiet,
> I'd like to reach oblivion and fall asleep . . .

The words of the old Russian ballad keep ringing in my ears. 'Freedom and quiet . . .' How little a human being needs to be happy.

How little and how very very much!

4

A Printer's Mistake

On this grim winter morning in July 1991 my pigeonhole in the newsroom of the *Melbourne Age* is brimming with readers' letters of which I receive up to a hundred a day, invitations for different functions and launches (among the events I was invited to open or close were the International Architectural Congress, the National Convention of Teachers of English and Victoria's annual Conference of Pest Controllers) and PR bulletins (for months some stubborn training company, probably misled by my foreign name, keeps inviting me to attend a crash course in 'How to Become a Successful Business Woman').

But today, among piles of mail, there is a neat rectangular parcel with half-a-dozen Queen Elizabeth's heads in the corner. The moment I spot it, my heart starts beating faster, as it only did in my teens during my first romantic trysts with a brown-eyed Kharkov schoolgirl. I know what's in this parcel that has come from my London publishers: a pilot copy of my second book *Dateline Freedom*.

Having one's book published is similar to giving birth. You conceive the idea and let it grow in you for a while before putting it to paper, and then, after months of agony, nausea and discomfort, you deliver the baby (manuscript) to your midwife-editor. There's nothing that can compare with the feeling of holding a pilot copy of your book, your child about to be released into the world. You keep perusing the all too familiar words that look so much weightier in print, you stroke its glossy skin (cover) thinking, Is it really mine? No matter how many books you have written, you can never get used to this feeling.

Publishing a book is the closest a male writer can come to childbirth. Books – like babies – are born in pain.

Dateline Freedom is special. It is my first book written in the West. Describing my last journalistic investigations in the Soviet Union and the circumstances of my defection, it was completed in four months at my first Melbourne flat in St Kilda suburb. I wrote it in my first ever real study (in Moscow I had to write in a wall cupboard for several years), with my first big Western acquisition, *Encyclopedia Britannica*, on the shelf above my desk. I wrote it on my first ever PC that kept swallowing pages and whole chapters and was driving me mad with its compulsive American spelling. It kept winking at me naughtily (like a St Kilda streetwalker) with its ever-blinking screen, it kept grimacing, making faces and teasing me in every possible way. As it turned out later, it was infected with a particularly nasty computer virus.

Running against the deadline, I had to write *Dateline Freedom* during sleepless nights, since during the day I had to be at the *Age* where I worked as a senior writer. I would scribble (or rather type) away all night through until 5 a.m. Then I would snatch three hours' sleep before going to the office. I would come back home at 6.30 p.m. and sleep until 10 p.m. before going back to my desk, piled with newspaper clippings, cigarette ends and dog-eared computer manuals.

The couple of hours before midnight were the hardest: my eyes hurt, I nodded off frequently and only kept myself going by drinking gallons of instant coffee and chain-smoking. But then in the early hours of the morning I would get a second breath, a sudden supply of creative energy from some hidden bodily source, and would be fresh as a cucumber, as they say in Russia. At around 5 a.m., feeling completely drained, I would have a brief sun-worshipping ceremony on my balcony overlooking St Kilda beach. The crimson Australian sun was resting on the flat surface of the ocean like a huge orange on a blue plate.

Behind the wall, Sasha Frukhtman, our neighbour and a recent emigrant from Ukraine, was noisily taking a shower. He worked as a cab-driver and had to have an early start. Was it worth going to the other end of the world only to live on the same landing with Sasha Frukhtman, an elderly Jew from Zhitomir, I sometimes asked myself.

Sea-gulls were perched on the roof of the neighbouring house like question marks on the otherwise blank page of my yet unfinished book.

With the onset of the scorching Melbourne summer, when the temperature climbed up to 42 degrees Centigrade, and the suffocating northern sirocco-type wind would bring the fiery breath of the desert to the city, my task became ever so harder. Our apartment, or unit as they say in Australia, was located on the second floor of an apartment block, straight under the flat black-painted roof which was like a sun-battery, attracting heat during the day and releasing it slowly after dark. My office had no air-conditioning, and I was sitting there in my swimming trunks, sweating like a pig. The temperature under my armpits was probably close to that inside a burning furnace. From time to time Natasha, my wife, would bring in a wet towel, dripping with water, and throw it onto my burning shoulders. I could almost hear a soft sizzling sound of evaporating water the moment the towel touched my skin.

I unwrap the parcel with trembling hands and open the book at random. Oh, no! I am staring at a totally clean page at the end of the last chapter before the Epilogue. No page numbers, no nothing. The page is piercingly, screamingly white and although, as far as I can remember, it contained only four lines of text, these are the last and the most crucial lines of the book. They must have forgotten to print them!

A book without a page. Every writer's nightmare. 'The main thing for a writer is to overcome his disgust of a clean sheet of paper,' Ivan Bunin, a Russian émigré writer and a Nobel Prize-winner, once said. Now I know exactly what he meant!

I am still hoping against hope that it is only one particular copy that is defective. But in my heart of hearts I am somehow sure that this is not the case. My immediate impulse is to call my publisher and find out, but London is eleven hours behind and it is late at night there now.

The tyranny of distance . . .

I keep silently repeating the missing lines, which I know by heart, with a faint hope that this will make them magically reappear on the page: 'And suddenly, the bright sunlight bursts through the clouds and nearly blinds us. Small patches of new green grass are springing out along the track here and there . . . Freedom.'

This was the only time the word Freedom was used in *Dateline Freedom* (apart from the title, of course). I wanted it to be the last word in the book.

These last lines were first written on the train from Moscow to Ostende by which my son, wife and I were escaping from the Soviet Union on 31 January 1990. Until the train crossed the Soviet-Polish border, I was not sure whether we'd make it.

We were fleeing the increasing KGB harassment and the growing uncertainty of life in Gorbachev's Soviet Union. A couple of days prior to our departure I started telling my friends on my KGB-bugged telephone that we were leaving for London for the publication of my first book by plane on 3 February (we all had visas to go to Britain as tourists, and the KGB certainly knew that), whereas in fact we were going on 31 January by train. This little ruse worked. On the extremely cold night of our departure the KGB withdrew their habitual observation van from beneath our windows: they probably decided not to bother.

But we still had to cross the border the following morning.

My son Mitya, who is now fifteen and living in Melbourne, was nine and a half years old then, but he saw and understood much more than I thought he did.

From my son's Australian Citizenship Essay, written in Melbourne in September 1995:

I was soon asleep helped by the monotonous sound of the train moving. It was 11 p.m., and we were on the train headed for Belgium. We were leaving the world's biggest cage and were breaking through the strongest Iron Curtain ever invented. We were defecting from Russia.

My father never liked the term 'defectors'; he did not see himself as a great hero planning the great escape, but he did just that, as any man running for his and his family's lives would.

We were well off in Russia. When I was small we were quite poor, but as time progressed and my father had made some trips to the West, our life reached a higher level . . . of poverty. In Russia, where everyone was equal and no one had anything more than the other person, there were two species of human: the common worker and the common Politburo member. The common worker was also divided into two categories: poor and not-so-poor. Where as the Politburo members and other party apparatchiks were like commandants in a ghetto. But as our leaders told us for seventy years, 'in Russia we are all equal'.

My dad was writing very prolific material about the Soviet Mafia and the KGB and as the two were, no doubt, connected, my dad was a problem to be taken care of. He was approached by the KGB to be recruited, and after many refusals he was told to watch his step. The situation became very clear then, and we had to leave as soon as possible.

At that time I was turning ten. My parents never told me that we were leaving Moscow for good. They were scared that I might slip up and mention this to the wrong person. In those days my parents never told me much of the truth for the reasons of our security. They just had to go along with all the political propaganda I was fed at school and for the time agree . . .

We are about to cross the border. The train is standing at Brest, the old Brest-Litovsk on the Polish border, the place where I would come back four and a half years later from the other, Western, side on the way to make a Channel 4 documentary about my return to Ukraine. By that time, I will have an Australian passport in my pocket, whereas now I have only a hammer-and-sickled Soviet one. Changing of gauge is under way (the tracks in the Soviet Union are somewhat wider than in the rest of Europe).

Half an hour later, both passport and customs controls are over. I can't believe it. They didn't even bother to look into our suitcases where, among other things, were the notes, files, clippings and photographs for my next book. I was worried that they would try to confiscate them, since according to the Soviet customs regulations one cannot take manuscripts, books or newspapers across the border without authorisation. I always suspected that the KGB, just like any other Soviet bureaucratic institution, was not particularly well organised.

At last, the train starts crawling towards the Yuzhni Bug River, along which the border with Poland runs. We are moving past the drab snow-covered outskirts of Brest: depots, log cabins, warehouses with peeling stucco slowly recede. In the distance I can already discern rows of barbed wire, marking the end of the Soviet paradise, and the river behind them.

The sky is cloudy and dull. A skinny middle-aged woman in fur coat and ridiculous hand-knitted cap with two bulging 'perhaps' bags in both hands is trudging through the snow alongside the tracks. Her face is grim and tired, a typical Soviet look. The last human being on the Soviet side. My last, my very last, glimpse of the USSR, where all thirty-six years of my life were spent (by the time of my first come-back in May 1993, the Soviet Union will no longer be there).

Barbed wire. A patch of ploughed 'neutral' land with neat regular furrows, as if the Soviet ground itself is frowning at us. A battered frontier post with the sign 'USSR' on it. A small whitewashed cabin of the border post with big windows facing the track on the bank of the river. A young Soviet frontier guard standing to attention with a Kalashnikov submachine-gun on his shoulder and looking sternly at our train. The brownish gleaming surface of the Yuzhni Bug with a flock of carefree stateless ducks floating on it. A little cabin on the other bank of the river which looks like a twin of the first Soviet one. Only this border post is no longer Soviet: inside there's a drunk Polish railway worker in a dirty orange vest sitting on the floor, smoking.

And suddenly, the bright sunlight bursts through the clouds and nearly blinds us. Small patches of new green grass are

springing out along the track here and there . . .
Freedom.

Until now I can't understand how it happened – on the Soviet side there was winter, and on the Polish side across the river – spring. It looked as if nature itself was welcoming us to the West. The moment our train stopped in Kunowice, the Polish checkpoint station, I uncorked a bottle of cognac we were carrying with us as a gift for our London hosts and had a good swig. Never before (or after) had I had such an acute feeling of Freedom. We were outside the iron grip of the 'evil empire'. We were safe. We were together. We were free.

I opened the window, and pungent smells of the sun and young grass, mixed with those of smoke and tar, burst into our compartment. The smell of travel and adventure, the smell of new life, the smell of Liberty. It was so much unlike the stench of Soviet railway stations, routinely reeking of coals, filthy latrines and human sweat. Yes, even smells in the West were different. Birds were chirping like mad in the trees near the track. 'Free birds,' I muttered to myself and smiled. 'Free trees . . . Free flowers . . . Free mile posts . . .'

A long journey lay ahead of us, and at that time none of us could imagine how bumpy it was going to be. We didn't know that four and a half months later we would be on the way to Australia. We didn't know that three years later another tyranny, the tyranny of distance, would tear us apart and for the rest of our lives we would have to communicate by telephone – through satellite echoes and crackles of space. After several months of hell, when our every step and word had been monitored, we were too happy and too tired to worry about the future.

In my dreams, I often come back to that day – one of the brightest in my entire life.

As to the missing lines in the book, it was just a printer's mistake. The publishers managed to correct it in good time.

5

Snow

*L*iving in Australia, I often dreamt of snow. In my dreams, it was falling silently, almost reluctantly, in translucent star-shaped flakes, melting instantly on my cheeks, cooling me down, and healing my wounds.

From my *Dictionary of Dreams*: 'Dreaming of snow means that the emotions are cold, either those of the dreamer or of someone else. Clean snow signifies innocence. Dirty snow implies guilt.' Nonsense. Snow for me 'implied' and 'signified' only one thing – sweet and quiet nostalgia. For my childhood. For my youth. For my first love. For everything that will never come back.

Snow has been with me all my life. I was born on a snowy January night, and when, five days later, my mother was carrying me in a bundle from the door of the maternity hospital to the waiting *Pobeda* taxi to take me home, several playful snowflakes sneaked under the cotton-wool blanket, in which I was wrapped, and prickled my face gently, welcoming me to the world. I think I can still feel their timid icy touch on my face.

I learnt to ski almost before I learnt to walk. My first skis were brought home by my granny, who was a doctor. They must have been given to her as a gift by one of her patients. The skis were crude and bulky, with primitive bindings, but I was ever so happy. I would go to school on skis. And on

Sundays we sometimes went skiing in Gorky Park with my father, who was an excellent skier and looked so smart and masculine in his unpretentious skiing outfit. We used to glide along the ski-track, dividing the silent wintry forest into two identical snow-covered and glittering worlds.

I see myself sitting on a sledge, dragged by my tireless grandad, Misha. He walks with a slight limp, the result of a leg wound during the 1918–21 Civil War, and because of this – to my sheer delight – the sledge makes little zigzags on the snow. In my hands, clad in *varezhki* – Russian woollen gloves with thumbs but no fingers – I am holding a couple of dog-eared books by Fenimore Cooper. We are going to our local library.

I am not at school, because it is too cold today. Primary school kids are not allowed to attend classes when the temperature falls below minus 20 degrees Centigrade. Every morning I pleadingly look at the thermometer hanging outside the window, trying to hypnotise the dispassionate mercury column into falling a couple of marks further down which will allow me to stay at home, to go tobogganing or to visit my neighbour, Yura, with whom I can play table hockey all day long.

The first snow in our parts would usually fall in early November. It would come as a godsend after a dreary and muddy autumn. It would bring some coveted light and brightness into our lives. Was it on that snowy day that we (I and my grandad) bumped into a couple of navvies digging a trench in the middle of our street? Dressed in dirty overalls, torn tarpaulin gloves and cheap fur hats, they were breaking the frozen asphalt with iron crowbars.

'How old are you, lad?' one of them asked me.

'Seven!' I replied proudly from the sledge.

'Lucky you!' he said. 'You will only be twenty-seven years old when communism comes.'

I knew what he meant. At school we were told that the 22nd Congress of the Communist Party had solemnly proclaimed that 'the present-day generation of the Soviet people will live under communism', and Khrushchev promised in one of his speeches that it would take twenty years to build the society living by the principle 'from everyone according to his abilities, to everyone according to his needs'. This slogan was later officially discarded as one of Khrushchev's 'adventurous mistakes'.

And the trench that the navvies had so painstakingly dug out was strewn with snow and mud in a single night. No one needed it in the first place.

At the age of sixteen I made my first date with a brown-eyed girl from our school. On that day an unforeseen snowstorm broke out in our city. It was something unheard of in Eastern Ukraine where the last snowstorm like that hadn't happened since the Ice Age. All the traffic stopped and one could only move around the city on skis, as did my father who decided to ski to his office which was a good ten miles away from our house.

I was trudging to the tram stop, where we had agreed to meet, sinking up to my waist into the snow every now and then and trying to bypass the torn electric cables, precariously drooping from lamp-posts. A fierce piercing wind was whistling like a hooligan. The streets were deserted. By the time I reached the tram stop, my bones were frozen stiff. Of course, she didn't turn up. I was saved by a strayed lonely tram that somehow made its way through snowdrifts. It was freezing inside as well, but not half as cold as in the street. The clouds of vapour were coming out of the passengers' mouths, as if little internal combustion engines were working somewhere underneath their coats.

Eventually, I did start going out with the brown-eyed girl. I used to wait for her near the music school where she was learning to play the piano, and then we would walk hand in hand through the same snow-covered Gorky Park with which most of my childhood and youth were associated. I would recite my youthful poems to her, and she would listen and look down at her boots as if she was afraid of losing them.

One day, when it was especially cold and slippery, I offered her my hand to help her negotiate a particularly large snow-drift but, instead of supporting her, I stumbled, slipped over the ice, and collapsed head over heels into the snow. Laughing, she extended her thin graceful hand to lift me up from the ground. I wished the frozen earth would open and swallow me up. Never before or after did I feel so profoundly, so deeply embarrassed. Even now, when I remember this small childish incident, I blush involuntarily, ashamed of my adolescent clumsiness.

It was probably this inadvertent fall that triggered our split-up a couple of weeks later. I can see my dark-eyed passion standing on a path in the snow near our Young Guards secondary school and handing me back the book by Erich Maria Remarque that I had given her to read a couple of days before.

'Here's your book,' she told me briskly. 'I haven't had time to read it. By the way, my mother has forbidden me to see you. She says I am too young to go out with boys, besides I've got lots of homework to do. And I think she is right . . .'

I froze, and not so much because of cold. The discarded book slipped out of my hand and silently sank in the snow leaving a dark rectangular niche on the spot where it fell. *All Quiet on the Western Front*. It was my favourite novel then.

We did meet again, eighteen years later, in Moscow, on the day when my first book in Russian was published. I was carrying a stack of my books, tied up with crude flimsy string, across the street. And suddenly I saw her. She hadn't changed much since our last tryst. It was October, but already snowing heavily (not unusual for Moscow) and, to come closer to her, I had to negotiate a dirty snow-pile, of which there were many in the unkempt Moscow streets. 'Watch your step, don't slip!' she called out from the distance and smiled showing her snow-white teeth.

She was divorced and had a teenage daughter. An architect by profession, she was writing poetry in her spare time, and her first collection of poems was about to come out in Kharkov. She told me that she started writing poetry after our short childish romance eighteen years earlier and still keeps all my desperate letters, written within a couple of weeks after our break-up, in which I implored her to reconsider. She had come to Moscow to work on her doctorate, something to do with city environment, as far as I can recall.

And several years ago, already in Australia, I received a copy of her book, which she herself illustrated. One of the sections was called 'Last Snowfalls'. Every poem in this section was about snow. And some of them, I knew, were implicitly addressed to me:

> Snowfall in October.
> Unexpected blizzard.
> What is it – a misfortune or a stroke of luck?
> Snowfall in October. Absurd! Eccentric!
> It has found us at the other end of the world . . .
> It has brought us face to face in a city crowd.
> It patted us on the shoulder,
> This friend of silence in the buzz of the capital.
> Where did it come from?
> How did it find us
> Through all the rains,
> Through all the years since our first date?
> It turned a weekday into a holiday,
> Ignoring all terms, conditions and codes of conduct.
> The world is small indeed,
> And snow is everywhere.
> It means that we'll never lose each other again.

The last line was obviously a hyperbole, a poetic exaggeration, so to speak.

It snowed heavily when I was returning from a journalistic assignment in Siberia and a young local girl, a tyro journalist, unexpectedly turned up at the station with a bunch of flowers (where did she get them in that freezing hole?) to see me off. When the train started, slowly and reluctantly, as if bracing itself for a four-day journey to Moscow, I could discern her small receding figure, dressed in a simple winter overcoat, dissolving in the blizzard. To her chest she was pressing the bunch of flowers which I had refused to accept.

It was snowing on my thirtieth birthday when, having quarrelled with Natasha, I slammed the door behind me and ended up fist-fighting with some hoodlums on the snow, near Clean Ponds restaurant, where I went with a friend and a bottle of pure 'drinking spirit' (96 per cent proof) that I had brought from Siberia. They tried to steal my friend's *shapka*, a hat made of rabbit's fur. My nose was bleeding, and drops of my blood were burning dark wormholes in the snow. They were not red, but claret-coloured in the deceptive light of yellow street lamps.

After the fight, my friend, having pulled down his liberated *shapka* over his eyes (to be on the safe side), jumped into a taxi with a young and agreeable typist from the Kremlin (she had a leather-bound office pass with the word Kremlin on the cover), whom we had picked up at the restaurant, and I was left in the street with the typist's unexpectedly jilted and puzzled boyfriend (they came to the restaurant together), who kindly invited me to spend the night on a folding bed in a nearby room that he rented. It was past midnight, and the Metro had stopped.

I initially agreed, but when I saw his dark littered room, I changed my mind and, having thanked him for his hospitality, found myself in the totally deserted Clean Ponds Boulevard. Snowdrifts were everywhere. They were sparkling under the lamps like protruding breasts of a female circus rope-walker in a spangled glittery dress.

'How strange. I am thirty today,' I thought. And then I remembered that it was morning already and that my birthday was yesterday. It was time to go back home. Finally, I managed to flag down a rubbish-collecting truck, the only car that was roaming Moscow streets at that ungodly hour. For three roubles, a sympathetic and talkative (like all night-shift workers) driver safely delivered me to my house. Luckily, Natasha was asleep and couldn't see me jumping off a refuse truck jauntily, with my nose still bleeding.

Snow dominated my last journalistic assignment in the Soviet Union in October 1989, when I became the first Soviet journalist officially allowed to visit the notorious Perm 35 labour camp for political prisoners, allegedly the last of its kind in the crumbling Soviet empire. On a gloomy October morning I set off towards Camp 35 from the village of Vsesviatskaya, about 400 kilometres from the city of Perm in Western Siberia. The car was moving along a snow-carpeted corridor (winter comes early in that part of Russia) between the fences of labour camps. On both sides of the icy track were unending rows of barbed wire, watchtowers with freezing fur-coated guards on top and dogs barking angrily from behind concrete walls. One camp followed another; there were simply no other structures for miles. It looked as if the whole country, the whole snow-ridden earth was ensnared by some giant villain, shackled, chained and put in irons.

Snow was the last thing we saw in the Soviet Union, a huge labour camp in itself, before crossing the border.

Green Christmas and even greener New Year were among the hardest things for me to endure while in Australia. Celebrating the New Year sitting in a swimming pool with a tinny in your hand under the scorching blinding sun was a complete anathema to me. I remember spending my first Australian Christmas Day in a capacious hired Jacuzzi, in the company of Mike Smith, the *Age* editor, and his relatives. We were sitting in the bubbling tub with our clothes on and drinks on a plastic floating pad in the middle. After each shot we would dive under water to refresh ourselves.

We were luxuriating like this until someone's mischievous child stealthily poured a whole bottle of shampoo into the spa, and the water in it started foaming like freshly uncorked champagne. We had to climb out dribbling like a bunch of Neptunes. Only then I realised that I had been sitting in the spa with a wallet in my trouser pocket. It took the merciless Australian sun just a couple of minutes to burn the contents of my wallet dry.

What a far cry from our habitual Russian New Year, with frost, fir-trees and snow crunching soothingly under your feet. Of course we were missing the European winter. 'Look, Dad, how lucky they are in England having so much snow,' my son Mitya exclaimed one February evening while watching the news on TV. It was a report on the Downing Street bombing in London, and snow was lying indifferently on roofs, pavements and bumpers of flashing police cars.

I remember the so-called Melbourne Winter Festival that was conducted in Toorak Road, one of the plushest Melbourne

streets, in the middle of July. It was about 20 degrees Centigrade, and snow was brought to the venue by a succession of
huge refrigerator vans. Cheerful young lads were throwing it
out onto the pavements with spades, and it would melt before
even touching the ground. As a result, Toorak Road was soon
covered with several inches of sticky slush, and female Scottish
pipe-players, specially invited from Glasgow to participate in
the Festival, were marching back and forth in the mud, mincing
it dutifully with their boots.

Only a very rich country can afford an artificial snowfall
on a warm evening in July.

Looking for snow, I used to go to Tasmania, Australia's
coolest state with an almost European (or rather Mediterranean)
climate. Richard Flanagan, a young Hobart writer, once took
me to Mount Wellington in his derelict old jalopy. The road
was narrow and slippery and we ended up skidding on the
ice. Soon we could see small patches of white, scattered here
and there on both sides of the track. When we finally reached
the top, I was able to make my first snowball since leaving
Russia. It was firm and round, the shape of the globe that I had
crisscrossed and on the very top of which we were standing.

The world was melting quickly in my hands.

On my return to Europe at the end of 1992, one of my
first assignments for *The European* was a trip to Finland to
interview Santa Claus, a typically Christmas feature. To get
to Rovaniemi in Lapland, near the Arctic Circle, where Santa
Claus was permanently residing, I had to take an overnight
train from drab and rainy Helsinki.

When I opened my eyes, alone in my sleeping compartment
in the middle of the night, the train was stationary. It was
dark outside but the compartment was alive with a mysterious
transparent light. Through the window, I could see a station
sign with the word 'Tampere' on it and white heavy flakes
floating in the air. I got dressed quickly and ran out of the
carriage. The moment I stepped onto the platform, my feet
fell through the prickly snow crust. I walked several steps
away from the train and looked back: my steps were firmly

imprinted on the snow as indisputable proofs of my return to Europe, to my childhood, to the real snow-carpeted world.

I was jumping along the platform like a puppy, taken out for a walk after a long day in the house. I was making snowballs and hurling them at passing cargo trains. I was turning somersaults in the snow and giggling like mad. I felt like one African student in Kharkov who, on seeing his first snowfall, burst out screaming: 'White flies! White flies!'

It was the first real snow that I had seen since leaving the USSR. The Soviet Union was no longer there, but the snow was as white, as cold and as indifferent as ever before. This was wonderfully exciting and also a bit sad.

The quiet indifference of nature . . .

In January 1996 I went to America to visit Bill Bryson, a friend of mine and a fellow travel writer. He had just moved to live in New Hampshire after spending twenty-odd years in the Yorkshire Dales which, as he told me, he was missing a lot.

That winter America was struck by a wave of previously unseen snowstorms. Airports and roads came to a stand-still. Washington, New York and lots of other big cities were practically paralysed. For me this was a reminder of the fateful snowstorm in Kharkov on the day of my first youthful date. On my first night, having had dinner at a Chinese res-taurant in Hanover, we were driving across New Hampshire under a heavy snowfall that resembled smatters of Chinese steamed rice, tossed at the windscreen by a white-robed chef of winter.

Snow, like good white wine, can be pleasant and romantic in moderate doses, but it can also become nasty and dangerous if taken in too large quantities.

New England looked deceptively European and even Russian (I mean its nature, not its towns and villages of course). Bill took me to the White Mountains on the border with Vermont where we spent several days talking, walking and snowmobiling in the forest. I was teaching Bill how to ski: he had never done it before but was learning very quickly. For me it was the first chance to ski in almost twenty-five years. But skiing is like swimming, or driving: once you have mastered it, you never lose it.

Again, just like in my childhood, I was gliding, almost flying, along the track, and the wind was throwing handfuls of snow-dust into my face. I thought then that there were few things more wintry, more cosmopolitan and more bizarre than a Ukrainian-born London-based Australian Russian skiing with a Yorkshire-nostalgic American nomad scribe in the White Mountains of New England, USA.

And, somehow, snow was the most wintry, the most cosmopolitan and the most bizarre connecting element in this unbelievably complex and, at the same time, childishly simple amalgam of Freedom.

6

Clickety-Clack

A s a boy and as a teenager I often dreamt of this journey.
I imagined that I would start in a small hamlet, some-
where in the heart of Russia. First, I would travel on a cart,
dragged by a tired horse, then on an equally fast shuttle train.
'Where are you going to, boy?' the locals would ask. 'To
London!' I would answer matter-of-factly.

Our life is like one long train journey. The train of life is chug-
ging forward along the tracks, rattling its wheels – clickety-clack
– on the points of days and weeks. It runs past the whistle-stops
of Childhood and Youth. It slows down at the stations of
Maturity and Old Age, and there, on the hazy horizon, one
can already discern the sad blinking lights of the Terminal.

No matter how dark is the night,
No matter how much soot there is around you –
Just look: the express train of dawn is already piercing the
    darkness,
Carrying the sun on its tail like a signal lamp

So I wrote in one of my youthful poems.

I wanted my imaginary journey to Britain, whose language
and history I had been studying assiduously since the age of
eight, to be long and unhurried. Planes were immediately
discarded as too fast and impersonal: they wouldn't give me

enough time to savour the sweetness of moving towards the place I was longing for.

In my heart of hearts, I was dead sure that this journey would never take place in reality.

As a schoolboy I was a real train buff. I collected maps and train timetables. I treasured a tarred wooden chip that I covertly peeled off a freight car at a railway station. My parents didn't mind, only shrugged. I kept the chip in a special box which I would open and sniff from time to time: it smelled of journeys and adventures.

At school they would tease me for carrying this fancy snuff-box with me and nicknamed me Engine-Driver. I was secretly proud of this nickname.

Playing truant, I used to escape to the nearest railway station where I would stand on a shabby wooden footbridge hanging precariously above the dirty tracks and gape at the passing trains below for hours on end, until my head started spinning and I had the illusion that it was I who was moving, floating in the air above immobile trains.

In the evenings, before falling asleep on my old-fashioned narrow bed, I would knock its nickel-plated leg gently (not to wake up my parents) with my knuckles: *Ta-ta, ta-ta; ta-ta, ta-ta; ta-ta, ta-ta* – to imitate the rattling of train wheels. I was falling asleep to the sweet music of the railroad. *Ta-ta, ta-ta* is clickety-clack in Russian, by the way . . .

When a university student, I chose to work as a sleeper-car attendant during summer holidays. My girlfriend, who was soon to become my first wife, was working with me. After our daily shift, we would make passionate love in our compartment to the same drumming railroad rhythm: *Ta-ta, ta-ta; ta-ta, ta-ta; ta-ta, ta-ta* . . . Only this time the music was for real . . .

Twenty-one years later she phoned me in London (God knows where she got my telephone number from). She was still in Kharkov, twice divorced like myself, and had a small dog-breeding business of her own. ('What do you do?' I asked her. 'I breed dogs . . .' she replied). Her second husband, for whom she had left me, was Vietnamese. She told me he used to beat her up. Then she asked whether there was a way of bringing her to London. 'You must know some old Englishman who needs to be looked after. I will cook for him and do his laundry . . .'

Alas, there was no direct train service from Kharkov to London. Our joint train ride was over. For good.

October 1988. I am already a well-known Moscow journalist, and as a perk of Gorbachev's glasnost I have been magnanimously allowed to travel abroad. Invited by my friend Martin Walker, then the *Guardian* Moscow bureau chief, I am going to Britain. At the age of thirty-four, this is my first ever trip to the West. I still can't believe it's happening – an age-long dream coming true.

Although the procedure of foreign travel has been substantially facilitated, a Soviet-style character reference was still required. When I asked my editor to give me one, he wrinkled his nose: 'I have no time for this nonsense,' he said. 'Why don't you write it yourself and I'll sign it?' This would have been unthinkable a couple of years before.

So I had to write my own character profile using the accepted Soviet clichés: 'Morally stable. Politically literate. Socially active . . . Deserving to go abroad.'

I am travelling by train of course. It is called the East-West Express. My travel companions, with whom I have to share a compartment, are two young lads from Western Ukraine going to visit their relatives in Manchester. It is their first trip to the West, too. We are to spend two nights on this train that will take us from Moscow to the Hook of Holland, from where we'll have to take a ferry to Harwich.

One of the lads immediately confides in me that he is trying to smuggle some cucumber and potato seeds for his brother in Manchester, having hidden them inside wooden matrioshka dolls. 'Don't they have such seeds in Britain?' I ask him.

'Yes, they probably do,' he answers, 'but I want my brother to have genuine seeds from our mother Ukraine.'

The neighbouring compartment is occupied by an elderly Latvian babushka, who was separated from her twin sister during the war. I chat with her in the corridor shortly after the East-West Express leaves Moscow. Her sister is now living in Cambridge, and she is on her way to see her for the first (and last, as she is inclined to think) time in forty-five years.

There are also two very obvious young *putani* (Russian hard-currency prostitutes), with their heavily made-up little faces bearing traces of all imaginable human vices. I used to write about girls like those for *Krokodil* magazine, where I am a special correspondent. They openly boast about going to the Netherlands to have a good time with their 'boyfriends' (they will indeed be met at a station in Holland by two tall broad-shouldered Dutchmen).

Our coach, a moving microcosm of Soviet life, is rattling through the night – *ta-ta, ta-ta* – towards the border.

In my wallet I have £200 sterling, the maximum amount of foreign currency I am allowed to carry. I received it at Moscow's only exchange office after several days of queuing. This sum is supposed to last me for all four weeks of my stay. Apart from surviving on it, I have to buy lots of gifts: souvenirs for my friends, a contact lens holder for my editor's wife, a supply of Alka Seltzers for an alcoholic colleague, a watch for a mildly cooperative visa office clerk (for having processed my application for permission to go abroad with minimum delay), a pair of jeans for Mitya, a sheep-skin coat for Natasha and, if possible, a portable hi-fi system for all three of us. 'If you happen to have any money left, you can look for a cheap video player,' Natasha said authoritatively. She then handed me a dozen matrioskha dolls that I could either give away as gifts to 'any kind people who will help you', or, alternatively, use as a bribe for any cooperative shop assistant who in turn would agree to give me a discount. We were sure that a customer was allowed to bargain in Western shops.

This sounded like a real adventure even for someone like myself who thought that he knew Western ways of life well enough – from books and BBC World Service radio broadcasts.

To minimise my food expenditure, Natasha supplied me with half-a-dozen cans of meat and fish preserves, plus a huge piece of *salo* – pure pork lard – that could be sliced and eaten with bread (each *salo* slice probably had more calories and fat than all the dishes featured in *Delia Smith's Complete Cookery Course* taken together). She warned me against consuming all this food in public which could cause embarrassment and, who knows, maybe even deportation.

I am also carrying presents for my London friends: a loaf of real Moscow rye black bread for Martin, who adores it; an amber necklace for his wife; some wooden Russian toys for their children; a carton of Russian *papirosi* (cardboard filter cigarettes) and a box of Golden Fleece Russian pipe tobacco for any helpful smokers I happen to meet (I myself had been a non-smoker for two and a half years then). No wonder my three pieces of luggage were so heavy that one could be led to believe that I had just robbed a brick factory.

I had to listen to the advice of my omniscient friends who had either been abroad themselves or, more likely, knew someone who had. They told me never to declare my Russianness in public ('They don't like Russians'); always to check the billboard with today's menu and prices before venturing into a cafe or a snack bar ('They will rip you off otherwise'); under no circumstances to use taxis ('They will take you for a ride around the block'); to do all the shopping either on street markets or in second-hand shops ('They sell the same things as they do in the plushest boutiques, only much cheaper') and lots of similar useful nitty-gritty which I dutifully recorded in my notebook.

Having endured the stern-faced sadism of the Soviet passport and customs control at Brest, I and my two travel companions felt a comradely bond, as if we all had been drawn into a perfectly legal, yet somewhat improper, collusion of leaving our great Soviet motherland, even if for a short while. The Ukrainian seed-smuggler was particularly happy to have got away with his little innocent trick.

When the train clattered – *ta-ta, ta-ta* – across the patch of ploughed neutral land which was no longer the USSR – clickety-clack – all three of us felt both relieved and a bit worried: it was good to see that the seemingly limitless empire did have its limits, after all. Yet, the uncertainty of the unknown that lay behind the barbed wire was somewhat unsettling.

We were crossing Poland which already looked so much more Western and prosperous than the Soviet Union. In

Warsaw, an East German dining car which accepted Russian roubles (thank God) was attached to our train. We went there for a meal and were pleasantly shocked by its cleanliness, efficiency and white-aproned waiters. Back in our compartment we drank East German beer that we had bought at the dining car, to the obvious displeasure of two burly stewards who, as we all knew, were part-time KGB agents: public drinking was frowned upon in Gorbachev's Soviet Union, and our car was still part of the Soviet territory, although on wheels.

Polish and later East German frontier guards in differently coloured uniforms kept boarding the train to stamp our passports. They were all withdrawn and coldly polite. We knew they were not important and were bracing ourselves for the encounter with the Berlin Wall – the ultimate outpost of the Soviet empire and the Mother of All Borders, to use Saddam Hussein's terminology.

It was a truly unforgettable experience.

We arrived at Berlin Friedrichstrasse Station at 1 a.m., and shortly afterwards the whole platoon of East German frontier-guards boarded our carriage. They were all young, pimpled and had low foreheads, as if deliberately hand-picked for these particular features. They led snarling dogs straining at their leashes. They were carrying screwdrivers, torches and portable ladders.

And the great search began.

They scrutinised us endlessly with their blank piercing eyes while checking our passports. One of them stared at my face unblinkingly, comparing it with my passport photograph, for such a long time that I started having doubts as to whether it was really me fidgeting nervously under his serial-killer stare. Then they started unscrewing everything that could be unscrewed and opening everything that could be opened in our carriage. One of them was shining his torch on the insides of the toilet.

What were they looking for?

Finding nothing, they eventually got off – all but one – as the train started crawling slowly towards the Wall. The one who had stayed (he was probably the most trusted border guard, with the best character references and impeccable party record) was peeping out of the window to make sure that nobody was riding outside the carriage hanging on by the door rails. Once assured he jumped out.

The system had let us out of its iron grip for a while.

Shocked and mesmerised by the thoroughness of the final check-up, everyone in the carriage seemed glued to the windows. *Ta-ta, ta-ta* . . . Clickety-clack . . .

The darkness of the night enveloped our train.

I was about to get my first ever glimpse of the West. This magic word had a somewhat sinister connotation. The West was that mysterious part of the world, from where crackling noises of foreign radio voices reached us, having bypassed the powerful, yet erratic, Soviet jamming devices (like everything else in the Soviet Union, these devices never worked properly); where whisky-drinking and golf-playing capitalists were constantly plotting something nasty against our country. It was a decadent and pornography-ridden place, from where spies would try to infiltrate our glorious motherland, only to be stopped and arrested by our vigilant heroic frontier-guards with their equally heroic dogs.

The propaganda was so unyielding, so blunt and so strong that even at a fairly mature age, I must confess, I used to experience serious doubts as to whether the Western world existed at all and was not just another KGB invention, a fictitious 'foreign threat' that every totalitarian regime needed to keep its people on the alert.

Four years later, in October 1992, I will come back to Berlin as a London-based columnist to cover the Queen's first visit to re-united Germany. The Berlin Wall will no longer be there, and its tiny fragments will be on sale as souvenirs (10 Deutschmarks a piece) near the Brandenburg Gate. In her speech in Bonn, the Queen will refer to German reunification as a dream that had become reality, and to the forced division of Germany by the Berlin Wall as an affront to history.

But the Berlin Wall was more ominous than that. It was not just Berlin, Germany and Europe that were brutally split in two. The Wall cut through living hearts and souls. Fearing reprisals, millions had to wear a mask of loyalty and obedience at all times, removing it only in the company of trusted friends. The Wall split their personalities, making a mockery of words such as honesty, integrity and dignity, turning its victims from *homo sapiens* into *homo soveticus*.

Those who couldn't accept this vivisection of the human spirit tried to break through. They rammed the Wall with heavy trucks. They swam across the Spree River under the crossfire of Kalashnikov machine-guns. They flew over the Wall in home-made balloons ... Some of them, who will never see the other side of the Wall, are now buried at a little cemetery, called the Crosses, near the Reichstag. The youngest of them is an eleven-year-old girl, the oldest an eighty-six-year-old woman.

They have negotiated the barrier eventually, even if it was after death.

'Here, the free world ends and the domination of the Kremlin starts' – this sign on Checkpoint Charlie on the border of the American and Soviet sectors of East Berlin never failed to send shivers down my spine.

A tiny graffiti-covered fragment of the Berlin Wall, which I brought back from that trip, is lying on my desk as I am writing these lines. It has become a mascot of mine, this piece of the seemingly unbreakable Mother of All Borders, now lying in ruins, that I first crossed in October 1988.

For several minutes our train rides in pitch darkness. And suddenly ... flood of lights. Flags fluttering in the wind. Myriads of gleaming rocket-shaped cars flying in all directions along the Spree embankment.

The lights of the station called Freedom.

When the train stopped at the Berlin Zoo, the first West Berlin station, the platform was empty apart from an elderly couple whom I could clearly see from the window. I shall always remember them, the first ever Westerners I was able to observe in their natural habitat.

The man was stocky, with the ruddy face of a life-long beer-drinker and a big red nose with protruding veins that resembled a map of the Moscow Underground. He was wearing a parka and a pom-pom Tyrolean hat. The woman, skinny and wrinkled, was dressed in a parka, too. She was also sporting a pleated checked skirt and a matching checked headscarf. They were probably just ordinary burghers, returning to their suburb after a late-night party in the city.

Yet there was something very special about them, something that, in my eyes, made them look like creatures from a different planet, visitors from outer space. It was the expression of quiet satisfaction on their faces which were totally devoid of the habitual Soviet 'seal of oppression' – that haunted and worried look, moulded by years of queuing and humiliation, by the daily struggle for survival and repressed emotions, the look that made my compatriots so easily recognisable from the distance, no matter what sort of chic Western clothes they chose to put on. As if they were constantly expecting a blow from behind . . .

A small white poodle the woman was cradling under her parka had the same satisfied Western look, too.

It took me several years of living in the West to get rid of the Soviet I-am-waiting-to-be-hurt appearance. Now I look smiling and relaxed on my passport photos, whereas before I was tense and shrivelled. I look as if the whole world belongs to me – and in a way it does . . . But then, during my first hours and days in the West, I couldn't help feeling that I had just arrived in a strange country, populated exclusively by foreigners. Freedom was written on people's faces. Freedom – that was what they were trying to hide from us behind the Berlin Wall.

Or so I thought . . .

For the rest of the journey I was as if in a trance. We rattled through bafflingly, almost lifelessly, clean and inspiringly dynamic West Germany. We rode through equally sterile, yet sleepy and toy-like, Holland. When the train stopped in Utrecht, I was the only passenger to venture onto the empty platform, only to be immediately shooed back into the carriage by our ever-vigilant steward.

My first step onto Western soil. A small step for a man,

it was completely unnoticed by mankind. But for me it was no less important than Neil Armstrong's 'giant leap' onto the rough surface of the Moon.

At the Hook of Holland we boarded *Queen Beatrix*, a huge cross-Channel ferry which to me looked like a floating Intourist hotel, packed with nice-smelling smiling foreigners. I remember popping into one of the toilets and, overwhelmed by mirrors and smells of deodorants, rushing promptly out, convinced I had wandered into a hairdressing salon by mistake.

I stood speechless and dumbfounded at the entrance to the ship's small and poorly stocked (as I realise now) duty-free shop, not daring step inside. It had many more goods on display than all Moscow supermarkets taken together.

One thing I couldn't resist, though, was buying a fresh copy of *The Times* – my first purchase in the West. In Moscow I had to be happy with a month-old London newspaper from the Intourist hotel news stand (to get there, one first had to gain access to the hotel itself where only foreigners with their conspicuously Western looks were allowed by ferocious doormen, who were also experienced face-readers and had no trouble keeping their compatriots at bay).

During the first hour of the crossing, all the passengers from our East-West Express carriage huddled together and sat next to each other in a spacious sitting compartment below deck. 'What a shame!' the Latvian babushka said in Russian pointing at an unsuspecting punk girl with a ring in her nostril and the clean-shaven skull of a new recruit out of which sprouted an unexpected bush of dyed red hair.

'Isn't it?' agreed one of the Ukrainian lads. 'Doesn't the militia want to do something about it?'

'Don't you know they don't have militia in Britain? They have police instead,' the second Ukrainian explained.

'But still she has no right to look like that,' insisted the babushka.

I was very hungry but, being determined to treasure my precious hard currency, could not make myself venture into one of the ship's restaurants. Instead, hiding behind the backs of my Soviet travel companions (we all took turns doing this) and nearly dying of embarrassment, I opened one of my tins with a can-opener, provided by practical Natasha, and quickly stuffed myself with a disgusting foul-smelling mixture of rice and fish intestines in tomato sauce which was aptly (and somewhat ironically in my case) called Zavtrak Turista (Tourist's Breakfast) – 35 kopecks a can. This was my first and last impromptu Soviet meal in the West. All the other cans and the chunk of *salo* were left untouched.

I was relieved to see that other (Western) passengers were totally indifferent to my shameful repast. Or rather they feigned indifference. I also noticed that conversation and other contact among them was reduced to the absolute minimum (a stark contrast to Russian trains and ferries where fellow travellers readily bare their souls to each other), and no one would occupy a vacant seat next to a stranger if there was another empty seat elsewhere. It was a live illustration of the familiar English expression 'keeping oneself to oneself'.

There were many British students aboard, reluctantly return-ing from the Continent to begin their academic year. Some were sleeping peacefully on the heavily carpeted floor of the sitting compartment. Others slept with their legs draped over the chairs in front of them. Free uninhibited people in their free environment. I envied them.

'What a ridiculous, swine-like way to sit,' commented one of the Ukrainians. 'In our country that wouldn't be tolerated.'

'Such an abuse of public order!' the babushka nodded fervently.

The crossing was rough and long. It took the crew more than an hour to dock in Harwich. For that hour the passengers were standing in the stuffy lobby with their luggage waiting to disembark. Everyone seemed to be getting nervous and impatient. Suddenly a group of students burst into a song, completely obscure to my ear. The refrain went: 'My eyes are dim, I cannot see, I haven't got my specs with me . . .' They sang the chorus again and again. There was so much youthful oomph in their voices that one by one other passengers joined in. 'I haven't got my specs with me!' they all sang.

'But I have got my ears,' grumbled an old gentleman standing beside me with his bulging Samsonite bag. A moment later, however, he too was humming. Then an extraordinary thing happened, my angry compatriots joined in too! The Ukrainians were helping the college kids with their velvety voices. Even the babushka was moving her old faded lips, trying to catch the rhythm. 'My eyes are dim, I cannot see . . .'

I thought it was a pity they didn't understand the words . . .

By the time we finally disembarked in Harwich three hours behind schedule, I was so exhausted – both physically and emotionally – that I almost overlooked a helmeted policeman, a real-life English bobby, who stood near the gang-plank. The first human being I saw in Britain, he was shifting from one foot to the other and yawning, probably bored out of his mind.

It took me a good half-hour to drag my abnormally heavy bags, full of tins and souvenirs, to the immigration area. The handle of one of the suitcases came off and I had to push it ahead of me with my legs (my hands were taken by other pieces of luggage). I was sweating like a marathon runner at the end of the distance, and that was probably why I seemed suspicious to the customs officers.

Having spent forty minutes selflessly helping my Soviet fellow travellers to communicate with passport control officials (it was such a treat, after twenty-six years of learning English, to be actually speaking it in England – something that I thought would never happen to me), I was led aside by a buxom female customs inspector who asked me to open my suitcases.

My train to London was leaving in ten minutes and I didn't want to miss it: poor Martin must have been waiting for me at Liverpool Street Station for a couple of hours already. Out of anxiety, I started sweating even more.

'No drugs, sorry,' I tried to joke, frantically looking for the keys to my suitcases and unable to find them.

I had made a mistake of course. I shouldn't have tested her sense of humour.

'I appreciate it,' the woman said, cutting my suitcase open with a pen-knife.

'And I appreciate your appreciation,' I mumbled. I didn't know what I was doing or saying. This crude intrusion of my suitcase was the last thing I expected to happen during my first moments in the free world.

Matrioshka dolls, my socks, underwear and tins were all piled together onto a low metallic table. By then, half a dozen customs inspectors, having materialised out of nowhere, were busy rummaging through my private possessions.

Who knows how long this humiliation could have lasted, were it not for a man in civilian clothes who was standing nearby and watching the search silently.

'It's OK. Let him go,' he muttered through his set teeth.

And immediately, as if on command (it *was* actually on command), customs people started stuffing my belongings back into bags, patching my hara-kiri-ed suitcases with Sellotape and apologising.

'Quick!' said the woman. 'You will miss your train to London!' And something that could pass for a smile lit up her round emotionless face.

Looking back at this episode now, I realise that I simply became one of the unlikely and undeserving victims of the Cold War paranoia that still persisted in the West.

The moment I puffingly dragged my bags into a carriage of the waiting train, its doors hissed shut behind me. This London-bound Intercity express was very different from East German-made Soviet long-distance trains, but I immediately felt in my element. Trains never failed to calm me down, and soon the unpleasant customs incident was forgotten.

The train was carrying me to London, it was talking to me in the familiar railway Esperanto: '*Ta-ta, ta-ta; ta-ta, ta-ta . . .*'

A whole new world lay ahead.

7

My Glittery Suit

I am standing on a footboard of the Harwich-London train as it slowly crawls under the glass vault of Liverpool Street Station. And here's Martin running towards me with a newspaper under his arm. He has been waiting for more than three hours, poor thing.

'I knew, I knew you would make it!' he keeps repeating.

We embrace.

'Now, stay here and don't move!' he orders and runs away.

The station looks as if it hasn't been cleaned since the Blitz: rubble and debris are everywhere.

In a minute Martin returns with a pint of bitter and a Casey burger in a cardboard box.

'I want you to have your first pint of bitter and your first Western burger here, at the station!' he insists.

Standing up to my ankles in rubbish on the platform, I sip a bitter and tepid drink. I know this is the moment to be remembered for the rest of my life.

My first minutes in London . . .

'Don't you like it?' asks Martin, having noticed my involuntary grimace. 'You will, you will!'

Contrary to Martin's expectations, I shall never come to like bitter which still remains one of the few things in England that I find hard to embrace, let alone drink.

'Is all of London as dirty as this?' I ask Martin as we puffingly (my suitcases are heavy) climb over piles of stucco and pieces of broken scaffolding on our way out of the station.

'The station is under repair,' he explains.

In the street, Martin flags down an old-fashioned black limo – a cross between a vintage car and a hearse. 'This is my friend's first time in London,' he says to the driver. 'Can you drive us around a bit before taking us to Barnsbury Square?'

'Certainly, guv!'

I suddenly realise that we are in a famous London black cab. It gives you an immediate VIP feeling. Only why did the driver call Martin 'guv' which, as I know, is an abbreviation for 'governor'? And if Martin is indeed a governor of something, how come the driver knows it? Or can it be that my modest friend is the Governor of London? No, London is run by the Lord Mayor, not by a governor . . .

All these muddled thoughts flash through my tired brain as our cab fights its way dexterously through night-time London traffic. I wish it were not so dark: I can't see much except for countless shopwindows bursting with goods. And what is this huge moving red box, lit from inside and looking like a giant double-tiered wedding cake on wheels towering above the traffic? Is it really a double-decker bus? Gosh, it is going to grind our cab into dust . . .

Am I dreaming or am I really in London, the city of Dickens, Conan Doyle and George Orwell, the city about which I have read and heard so much? So it does exist, after all!

We drive over Tower Bridge. 'This is the River Thames,' says Martin.

'Jerome K. Jerome. *Three Men in a Boat* . . .' I whisper to myself.

'And this is Big Ben . . .' Yes, of course. I recognise the Houses of Parliament with the famous clock. How many times did I comb the wave bands of my old short-wave radio looking for the sweet familiar sound of its chimes? 'This is London. The BBC World Service. The news is read by . . .'

My head is spinning. My heart is ready to jump out of my mouth. This is getting a bit too much for one day. And two sleepless nights seem to be having their toll. 'Can we please go home?' I ask Martin.

We climb out of the cab. 'This is my house,' Martin says, proudly pointing at a semicircular three-storeyed building with several dozen doors.

'All of it?' I ask in disbelief. In Moscow Martin told me that his house had three floors and a basement, but I could never imagine it was so long and huge. For me a house is something small and detached like a log cabin.

Martin laughs. 'No, not the whole block. Just one little house.'

He unlocks the door and we climb up a narrow carpeted staircase before finding ourselves in a small lounge with a fireplace. The sudden smallness of his house is a disappointment. It is almost like an average Moscow flat, placed upright.

We sit down. I produce a loaf of Moscow rye bread. Martin presses it to his face. 'It smells of Russia,' he mutters blissfully.

A bottle of vodka comes out, the top flies off and here we are drinking and talking. What about? About life, about politics, about our mutual friends. Just like we used to do in Moscow during our numerous Russian-style kitchen sessions. With Martin being the Journalist of the Year in Britain and me in the Soviet Union, we always had lots of things to discuss.

Only now we are in London. Or are we?

Next morning I woke up with a splitting headache and for several minutes I didn't realise where I was. With an effort, I lifted my head from the pillow, looked out of the tiny attic window and saw an endless row of sloping roofs with chimneys sticking out of them like stalagmites from a cave floor. Only then I remembered that I was in London.

I had a vague feeling that I had come to the place that was going to become my home in the not-so-distant future.

While I was shaving, having opened both cold- and hot-water taps, as I would do in Moscow, Martin peeped into the bathroom. 'What are you doing?' he asked sternly.

'I am washing myself. Why?'

'This is not the way to wash. Not in England.' He cooped up the drain with a round rubber plug, poured some water into the sink and closed the taps. 'Now you can wash,' he said.

This reminded me of the memoirs of Gordon Lonsdale, a famous Soviet spy in Britain in the fifties and sixties, that I had read shortly before my trip.

Born Konon Trophimovich Molodiy, he managed to master English to such an extent that he was able to pose as Lord Lonsdale, a member of the London glitterati, for many years until his cover was accidentally blown by his Russian school-mate, who ran into him in a London pub. Molodiy got wonder-fully adjusted to every aspect of the British high society lifestyle, except for separate hot- and cold-water taps in bathrooms.

'The English wash themselves like swine,' he complained and added he was in the habit of locking himself up in a hotel bathroom, opening both taps and washing 'like a normal human being', notwithstanding the risk of exposure.

We took a train to Rye, where Martin's wife Julia was staying with her parents. It was raining non-stop – typical English weather.

Rye, this old English town in East Sussex, was small, pleasant and cosy like my writing closet in Moscow. But what amazed me most were the people – gentle, courteous and ever-smiling. Bumping into each other in Rye's Lego-like narrow streets, they were exchanging not curses, as it would be in Russia, but smiles. They were as easy-going and relaxed as my fellow-Muscovites were likely to be only after several hours in a Russian steam bath.

Because of my meagre resources, I tried to avoid shops and succeeded in all cases except one. A small bookshop in the main street looked so inviting. And there I did something extravagant: I bought a Collins Gem *Thesaurus*, so compact and handy that it was impossible to resist. I once saw a much smaller second-hand thesaurus in a Moscow bookshop. It cost 25 roubles, a quarter of my monthly salary. This one was certainly a good bargain for £1.95. I bought it on the spot, without thinking, fearing that they would run out of stock, if I hesitated. An old Soviet habit: grab it while it's available and think what to do with it later.

The moment I got out of the shop I started feeling guilty. I also felt culpable, delinquent, erring, evil, felonious, offending, responsible and sinful. Consulting my brand-new thesaurus failed to eliminate my guilt, but helped to camouflage its true meaning slightly.

With Martin and his kids we attended a Sunday service at a

local church. 'Welcome, it is so nice to see you!' the priest said to me, shaking my hand as if I were his best friend. I thought he must have confused me with someone else.

Towards the end of the mass, I committed a sin by receiving communion while not being a believer. I couldn't resist kneeling in front of the altar for a free sip of sweet red wine (in my case it was rather a good swig) and a piece of dry bread. And God didn't punish me immediately for such a sacrilege.

We all went for lunch to a country pub in Winchelsea, my first ever experience of a real English pub. It was Sunday, and the pub was full of patrons: local farmers, families with small kids. They were eating their Sunday roast, drinking beer and playing darts near the fireplace. To my surprise, no one was drunk. Having discovered that I was from Moscow, the landlord offered me free drinks for I was the first-ever Russian to visit his pub.

Outside, it was drizzling, and the sheep were grazing obliviously on a nearby lawn. I was slowly but surely falling in love with England.

Next morning we returned to London, and Martin went away on an assignment. I was relocated (courtesy of *The Guardian*) to the Royal Scot Hotel at Kings Cross. Before leaving, Martin talked me into writing a piece for *The Guardian*. My English was fluent, if somewhat old-fashioned, but to write for a national British newspaper was psychologically very difficult. I agonised over the piece that described my first impressions of Britain, writing and re-writing it many times in longhand.

The features desk of *The Guardian*, where I finally delivered my essay, looked like a set from a science fiction movie. Every journalist had a computer of his or her own. They were staring at them oblivious of the world around them, as if expecting to find the answer to the eternal question of the meaning of life on their blinking fluorescent screens.

I had never seen personal computers before.

It couldn't be more different from my Moscow *Krokodil* office where we all sat in separate rooms – three or four in each – and typed our copy on our faithful East German-made Erica typewriters whose keys, when pressed, sounded like the high-boots of the Kremlin guards goose-stepping on the cobbles of Red Square.

Here, dozens of journalists were sitting next to each other, yet the huge room was immersed in silence, strangely enhanced by softly purring telephones and whispered conversations. No one bothered raising their voice. Twice a day a food trolley was rolled into the newsroom by a white-robed young man from the canteen. The journalists bought their tea and sandwiches and consumed them there and then at their desks. When the trolley was about to leave, the young man shouted: 'Trolley going!', at which point the hacks would look up from their computers and chant in chorus: 'Bye-bye, trolley!'

This little ritual was as sweet and spontaneous as only a children's game could be. Can it be that they are all adult children who have forgotten to grow up? I wondered then.

Sweating with embarrassment, I dictated my piece to a friendly female editor who typed it on her screen. It was published next morning, and not a single word was changed.

The magic of seeing your own words in print. The moment a writer loses this magic, he stops being a writer. This time the words were English which made them somewhat alien. And yet they were mine . . .

This first publication boosted my self-esteem, and in the next three weeks I wrote and had printed five features and reviews in *The Guardian*. Having got myself a tiny bottle of cognac from a vending machine in the hotel corridor (another little Western miracle), I would scribble hastily in my room, to where I would usually return after midnight. I would write on the margins of numerous give-away leaflets, pamphlets and brochures, picked up in London streets. My room was literally flooded with them: I was finding it hard to ignore a glossy piece of paper, provided it was free – another bad Soviet habit.

Before my departure from Moscow the editor of *Krokodil* had asked me to get in touch with *Punch* magazine which was well-known in Russia mostly from its cartoons, regularly reprinted in the Soviet press. I visited the magazine's small offices in Blackfriars and was introduced to Russell Davies, then the acting editor, who later became one of my closest British friends. I was impressed by the library which stocked every single issue of *Punch* since it first came out in July, 1841 and by the famous *Punch* table with the initials of Mark Twain, William Thackeray, Giuseppe Garibaldi, Charles Dickens and Margaret Thatcher carved on it. I had a chance to sit at this oval table during the famous *Punch* lunch to which I was invited. A couple of Dickensian tails-clad waiters, a shorty and a giant who looked as if they had come straight from the pages of *The Pickwick Papers*, served us oxtail soup, while we sat around the 'dear esteemed table' (pace Chekhov) joking and bantering. At times I couldn't help feeling that I was sitting at the familiar editorial board table at the Moscow offices of *Krokodil*, even some of the faces were similar: the profession obviously leaves its imprint on one's appearance.

I soon found out that the purpose of these lunches was not just to entertain but to also recruit new authors. At the end of my first *Punch* lunch Russell asked me to contribute a piece on English humour and, if possible, to supply an example of a new glasnost-induced Soviet satire.

The two pieces appeared next to each other in the following issue of *Punch*. One was entitled 'Rye Humour' and the other:

The Speech

Dear comrades! Ladies and gentlemen! Mesdames and messieurs! Signori, signorini and signoriti! Generals and Admirals! Privates! Merchants and marines! Janitors! The Swiss and the Finnish! The Turkish! Workers and peasants! Pensioners and schoolchildren! Poets and counts! Graphomaniacs! Cardinals and Popes! Politicians and beauticians! Morticians! Dear invalids! Citizens and friends! Women and sisters! Sportsmen! I have nothing to say.

Russell Davies invited me to spend a weekend at his Cambridge home, where he entertained me playing a cupboard-size cello, a saxophone that looked like a Honda motorbike bent in the middle and an oil pipe-line-thick trumpet – all custom-made for his eccentric collection.

Another *Punch* character by whom I was befriended was John Langdon, a writer, a radio dramatist and a convinced Russophile who collected Russian obscenities, the ones that would make the rudest of Moscow cobblers blush. His only problem was lack of practice (that was probably why he was so pleased to meet me), and he was in the habit of practising his esoteric knowledge in the streets of London by hurling brief but weighty (and totally undeserved) Russian words of abuse at unsuspecting pedestrians.

'You should be careful, John,' I used to warn him. 'One day you will bump into a Russian and he will beat all this linguistic garbage out of your head . . .' In response he would say . . .

But I've digressed.

Speaking about terms of abuse, I had a chance to hear plenty of them in plain English while watching parliamentary debates from the press gallery of the House of Commons. To my consternation, the MPs were spurting insults at each other. Some cheered and roared after every remark of the Speaker, whereas others were sleeping peacefully on the benches, oblivious of the fuss around them. To me, used to the disciplined serenity and synchronous hand-raising of the rubber-stamp Supreme Soviet (USSR's ruling body), this was a good, even if somewhat noisy, introduction to the procedures of a democratic parliament. And while having dinner with Norris McWhirter, the compiler of the *Guinness Book of Records* at Lockets one evening, I heard the famous division bell. To my disappointment, however, on hearing its piercing sound the venerable diners at the restaurant did not rush out to vote. One of them did get up from his chair and went towards the exit. I followed him with my stare: he disappeared behind the door with a plate 'Lords' on it. A plate on the opposite door said 'Ladies'.

I was also invited to lots of lunches and parties and soon felt at home with all the gossip of London's journalistic world. Or rather with that of the left-wing journalistic world. At that time I had no idea that there was another, right-of-centre, stratum of journalists who seldom mixed with their less conservative colleagues, and that whereas the former would get together at clubs and El Vinos, the latter preferred socialising in pubs.

I had my first encounter with the so-called caviar socialists (or champagne socialists depending on their culinary preferences) – people of rampantly pro-communist views living in plush houses of Hampstead and Notting Hill. One night I was invited to a party to one such house and was stunned to see a portrait of Stalin on the wall.

'What's that?' I asked the owner in disbelief.

'Oh, it's just a joke,' he cackled.

It's interesting that he reacted in exactly the same fashion, when seven years later he was implicated with long-standing KGB connections. 'I thought meeting those Russian guys was a good joke,' he said.

Somehow I didn't find his joke funny.

For the first time I saw that Freedom had its ugly side, too.

But generally I was basking in this atmosphere and was getting used to finding my name in English print.

One thing worried me, though, and that was my style of dress. In Moscow I used to snub dress codes – it was the only realistic attitude in the country where one couldn't buy any decent clothes anyway. Before going to Britain, however, I made an effort and after seven hours of queuing got myself a stylish (or so I thought) Hungarian parka which extracted some positive comments from Martin and some of my new London friends. But under the parka . . . Well, I didn't bring a decent suit. To be honest, I didn't bring any suit. Simply because I didn't have one.

Absence of a suit was not a problem at parties and journalistic gatherings where everyone was casually dressed. This came to me as a surprise. The stereotype of an Englishman, disseminated by the Soviet media, was that of a gentleman in a traditional bowler hat feeding pigeons in St James's Park. All Soviet newspapers periodically ran photos of these living anachronisms. Heaven knows what dusty archive files they were taking them from. Not that I was expecting to see lots of bowler hats and top coats in the streets of London, but I was rather unprepared for the democratic informality of Londoners' every-day attire.

The following little episode led to a decision to get myself a decent suit after all.

Bill Webb, the obituaries editor of *The Guardian*, invited me for lunch at his club. I think it was the Travellers' Club in Pall Mall. Or maybe the Athenaeum, I can't remember.

From my first days with *The Guardian* Bill had kept persuading me to contribute to his section and to write an obituary of Sergei Mikhalkov, a tame Soviet poet who once concocted the lyrics (if one can call this hooray-patriotic doggerel lyrics) for the Soviet national anthem: 'The unbreakable union of free republics was brought together by great Russia. Long live the Soviet Union, created by the will of the people . . .' And so on.

'I'd be genuinely delighted to do it,' I would say to Bill. 'But there's one little problem: Mikhalkov is still alive and seems to be in good health.'

'Never mind,' Bill would insist. 'Sooner or later he is going to die and we'll have the obituary ready.'

I was playing with the idea of telephoning Mikhalkov on my return to Moscow and saying: 'Sergei Vladimirovich, *The Guardian* asked me to write your obituary. Would you mind answering a couple of questions?'

I found out later that preparing the obituaries of public figures in advance was a normal Fleet Street practice. A colleague at *The European*, an old Fleet Street hack, told me that he had had a chance to read his own obituary and had even edited it slightly. Is mine also waiting for its turn on a computer disk somewhere, I wonder?

Anyway, when we arrived at Bill's club, I was refused entry for one simple reason: I was not wearing a tie. I always hated ties, which made me feel like a prisoner, a convict about to be hanged. Eventually, a sympathetic doorman had to lend me a piece of silk which was probably used as a tie in Dickens' time. Having put it round my neck, on top of my sweater, I stepped into a dining room where the lucky members were enjoying their steak and kidney pies and red wine. I was shocked to see among them one youngish fellow sporting a stylish collarless shirt under his jacket. He was not wearing a tie!

I was insulted. Why was someone else allowed to be tieless? 'Look,' I said to Bill angrily, 'the guy over there is not wearing a tie either, yet no one seems to mind . . .'

'Yes,' answered Bill, 'but he is a bishop.'

Next morning I went shopping for a suit. I thought it wouldn't be a problem. But being broad-shouldered and overweight, I soon discovered that it was hard, if not impossible, to find a good fit. 'You are too strong for this suit,' the shop-assistants would comment diplomatically watching my futile attempts to squeeze myself into yet another outfit. Finally, when I was about to give up, I saw *it* in the basement of a seedy menswear shop in Soho. The suit was standing out on the rack like a single birch-tree in a forest of conifers. It was silently screaming at me: 'Here I am! Buy me now!'

It was glittery, almost spangled, and I could see my own distorted and puzzled reflection in its lapels. It fitted perfectly, although I was slightly baffled by the price – £50.

When later in the day I turned up at *The Guardian* proudly sporting my new acquisition, they all gave up working and flocked around me. Everyone was speechless. Reflections of sunrays were dancing on my trousers, and some female secretaries tried to adjust their make-up looking at my sleeves. 'Where . . . where . . . did you get it?' they were all asking.

I couldn't understand whether they were really impressed or just teasing me.

I didn't come across anything like my first London suit for the next couple of years until one day, already in Australia (where one hardly needs a suit at all, by the way), I saw a Hollywood comedy thriller. The main baddie – a Harlem drug-dealer – was wearing exactly the same glittery suit.

One of the last pieces I published in *The Guardian* proved to be a real scoop. It was a feature on the Dnepropetrovsk Mafia, based on my investigations in the Soviet Union. They ran it on the cover of the Review section. On the day of its publication, I was approached by Clarissa Rushdie of A.P. Watt Ltd who offered to act for me as a literary agent. I was aware of KGB agents, CIA agents and Gosstrakh (the state-run insurance company in the USSR) agents, but a literary agent? It was something totally new.

To start with, I had to come up with the outline of my would-be book and I didn't feel like writing it. My time in Britain was running out and I still wanted to see so much. But

Clarissa had to literally (and literarily) chase me day and night and finally I succumbed to her pressure. I wanted the book to be called *Special Correspondent* – my official job title in *Krokodil*. Clarissa was quick and promptly sent the proposal to several publishers. She came back to me on my last day in London, saying that two publishers wanted to meet me. 'I have no time,' I protested. But she insisted. So I had to put on my new glittery suit and go to see the publishers. Leaving the offices of the second one, I stumbled across a stair and fell upon a slim diminutive young woman, who was passing by, crushing her fragile frame against the wall. She was to become my book's editor. Looking back now, I can't understand why my glittery suit didn't put the publishers off my book. They must have thought it was a peculiar Soviet style of dress.

On the same day I was able to witness Clarissa's bargaining over the size of my advance on the telephone. I couldn't believe it was happening: *my* literary agent discussing the terms of *my* hard-currency advance for *my* first book in English, that hadn't been written yet.

Another dream coming true . . . By the end of the day, I had a signed contract in my pocket.

I was sad to be going back. Never before have I felt so much in my element, so much at home as I did in London, chatting with my new friends over a pint or simply wandering around aimlessly through the thick sticky light of yellow street lamps. I wanted to dissolve myself in London crowds. The ultimate sense of belonging . . .

But I was also missing my family and my home. I had to go back.

8

An Evening in Soho

M y last evening in London. Four weeks flashed by in a jiffy. Tomorrow I have to go back to Harwich and then to Moscow.

It was like a dream. In fact, it was much more than I could ever dream about.

I had done all the sights of London. I visited Oxford (twice), Cambridge and Rye. I published five articles in *The Guardian* and one in *Punch*. I attended a football match at Wembley, a famous *Punch* lunch and the launch of *Soho News*, a glossy magazine that collapsed after the first issue. I was invited to a couple of plush Pall Mall clubs. I went on the beat with London and Oxford policemen, researching a piece for *Krokodil*. I interviewed the son of Alexander Kerensky, Russia's first prime minister of 1917. I was interviewed by the BBC World Service, by London television and by LBC and took part in an *After Dark* live TV show, where we drank and talked in front of the camera into the early hours of the morning. I got a contract for my first book from a prestigious London publisher. I got myself a literary agent. I earned quite a bit of money which allowed me to buy not just all the intended presents and souvenirs but also a coveted video player. I shocked Natasha by calling her up in Moscow from the car of a new London friend of mine (later she told me she didn't believe I was calling from the

car and thought I had simply had one drink too many). I fell
in love with London and with England which proved to be
exactly what I thought (and dreamt) they would be, and much
more. I inadvertently started smoking again while demon-
strating to some friends at a party how to smoke Russian
papirosi that I had given them as a souvenir. I'd written to
Prince Charles inviting him to come and stay with me in
Moscow (heaven knows why).

In short, I had a ball.

There is only one thing I haven't seen so far – a strip
show. 'You can't say that you've been to the West unless
you saw striptease,' my male Moscow friends used to tell me.
Theoretically, of course, I could claim to have seen striptease
without actually seeing one – let them go and check – but I
wanted to be honest to myself.

So far my only impressions of striptease were gleaned from
the Soviet foreign correspondents who, in their ideologically
correct reports from the West, never lost a chance to enthuse:
'How disgusting these strip shows are!'

I was mature enough to realise that to make sure of how
disgusting they really are, I had to see one. 'I can resist
everything except temptation,' wrote Oscar Wilde. I tended
to agree with him, although he probably meant something
completely different.

I managed to talk my two *Guardian* friends (Martin was
away travelling) into accompanying me to Soho (for some
reason, I was not prepared to go there on my own) on my
last evening. It was to be a proper finale to my first visit to the
West. To my considerable surprise, they hadn't seen striptease
before either (or claimed that they hadn't) and were probably
secretly interested. It took them a good half-hour each to get
telephone permission from their wives (I didn't have to bother:
my wife was miles away, in snow-ridden Moscow). After that,
we called a cab and went to Soho to burn a bit of nightlight.

Totally inexperienced in matters of striptease, we entered at
random the first strip club promising a live show. The entrance
was £5 per person. I produced a £20 note (I still had some of
my unexpected London earnings left and assured my friends
magnanimously that all the expenses of our wild night out would

be carried by me, to which they naturally didn't object) but the charming scantily-clad girl sitting at a small bureau near the door smiled disarmingly and didn't give any change. Mesmerised by her invitingly promising (or promisingly inviting?) manner, we stumbled into the dimly-lit den of vice and passion.

Inside, we found ourselves in a small room with four tables. At one of them, a middle-aged Chinese gentleman was dozing drunkenly. There was no one else. I ordered a bottle of wine that cost £30, ten times what it would cost in an off-licence. The wine proved to be de-alcoholised. 'These clubs must not be licensed to sell alcohol,' my knowledgeable friends explained.

Sipping sour, tepid and lousy-tasting 'wine', we sat in the room for an hour and a half. Our queries as to when the promised live show would start were answered by waitresses in black leotards with a short and evasive, 'Soon.' When our patience was running out, we were at last invited downstairs to a basement room. The Chinese man followed us, nodding as he walked.

In the basement there were also four tables but, unlike the brightly-lit room upstairs, this one was immersed in intimate semi-darkness. There was a small stage, just a platform in one corner. The toilet doors with 'Gents' and 'Ladies' signs could be discerned on the walls. We spent an hour sitting in the basement, and I had to order another bottle of the same monstrous wish-wash we had just enjoyed upstairs. The Chinese guy kept snoring gently at his table.

Suddenly a loud telephone ring came from somewhere behind the stage. The call was answered by one of the young leotarded waitresses. We couldn't see her but could clearly hear every word: 'Ah, is that you John? . . . No, no, not tonight . . . I can't . . . Why? Well, first of all I'm at work and secondly I'm drunk . . . Yes, these idiots are sitting here waiting . . . I just won't be able to make it . . . sorry . . . bye.'

I thought she probably had a point when referring to us as idiots.

When we were on the verge of despair, a young black girl stealthily entered the room. She was dressed in a modest, almost puritanical way: a long tweed skirt, which covered her knees, and a black turtle neck. She mounted the platform and asked conspiratorially: 'Are there any ladies here?' (as if she couldn't see for herself). At the sound of her voice, the Chinese man woke up and squeaked: 'No, just yourself.'

Click, a tape-recorder was switched on behind the scenes and the room filled with deafening music. The girl made several modest dance steps hither and thither to match the tune – one-two, one-two – then stepped down from the platform and solemnly announced: 'The end of the show!'

'What?!' the four of us cried out in chorus.

'The end of the show!' the girl repeated with angry metallic tones in her voice and retired. The music stopped, and the sudden piercing silence made our teeth ache.

Once we had overcome the shock, one of my friends dashed upstairs to get the club-owner, a squib of a man with a pot belly and darting eyes. He didn't want to come and was beating the air with his plump little legs as my tall and muscular friend dragged him down the stairs to our table.

We demanded an explanation.

'Yes, chaps, it was bad luck for you,' he said apologetically, spreading out his little hands in faked distress. 'The problem is that our soloist has a sprained ankle.'

'Then give us our money back!' we clamoured in unison.

'Sorry, lads, this is not possible.' The affected distress on the owner's round face was now reaching tragic proportions and turning into utter grief, as if he had just buried his own mother. 'We have already sent our takings to the bank . . . but . . . but, no problem, I can lead you to another club where you will definitely see what you want.'

We followed the squib into the street. 'Have a good trip!' the leotarded waitresses sang mockingly behind our backs.

We passed several Soho blocks and arrived at a club which looked like the twin of the first one. 'These blokes are with me,' the squib said to a bouncer standing in the doorway, but the mere fact of being with him didn't spare us the entrance fee. And again we didn't get any change.

Yet, a certain progress was felt here. We were immediately taken downstairs to the basement where we saw the ubiquitous 'Ladies' and 'Gents' signs facing the audience. And there was some audience indeed, even a couple of women, which we took as a good sign.

In an attempt to deceive fate, we ordered not wine but beer. No chance: it was non-alcoholic too and tasted like flat lemonade, only much worse. This 'beer' cost us £10 per pint.

'Enough! I can't stand this any longer!' one of my friends exploded. 'I am off to my club for a real drink!' And he retired.

As soon as he left, two girls – one black and one white – who were sitting at a neighbouring table stood up and came over. Without asking permission, they sat down at our table, took out cigarettes and lighters and started puffing for all they were worth. Here we go! I thought with trepidation.

The white girl kept scratching herself all the time, which was a little disconcerting.

'Where are you two beauties from?' my remaining friend inquired.

'I am from London,' the white one replied coldly while scratching herself fervently. 'And she is from the West Indies.'

'And what are your names?' I asked, having gained some courage.

'You know what, guys?' the black girl said, smiling. 'We don't answer any more questions until you buy us drinks.'

A waitress was already hovering above our table. The drinks on the offered menu were from £40 each.

'No!' my stoic friend roared all of a sudden, 'we have already wasted a fortune!'

Unsurprised, the two girls shrugged and returned to their table.

After a while, a strange girl dressed in a raincoat and carrying a big shoulder bag ran (or rather fell) into the room. She darted through the door with 'Ladies' on it and shortly reappeared without her bag and overcoat. Instead, she was sporting a sparkling harness made of stainless steel and leather, which made her look like a freshly bridled young horse. Having mounted the platform, she started quickly and matter-of-factly relieving herself of her heavy apparel, throwing items of the garment around the room, in a brisk and business-like manner. One heavy piece of her clothing hit me on the knee – quite painfully.

The show lasted about three minutes and was over so

quickly that I didn't understand what had happened. The girl, now in her birthday suit, jumped down from the platform and made a quick racing tour of the room to collect her harness. I asked if I could keep the item that had hit me as a souvenir but she snatched it angrily out of my hands and disappeared behind the toilet door.

In a couple of minutes she re-emerged, fully dressed, with her bag, and, clattering her little hoofs on the stairs, galloped away. She probably ran to another club with a striptease licence; I was told afterwards there were only four in the whole of Soho.

'When is the next show due?' we asked the waitress warily. 'It will be a very long time,' she said through clenched teeth. After we refused to buy drinks for the hostesses, she lost all interest in us. She reminded me of a saleswoman at an average Moscow vegetable shop – rude, untidy, underpaid and likely to hurl a potato at you if you become too demanding.

With our heads heavy and our (especially mine) purses light, we went out into the street. Soho was living its seething night-time life. The sounds of rock music came from restaurants and clubs. Youngsters crowded round discos and neon lights were dancing in their smiling wide-open eyes. An old man with week-old bristle on his cheeks was selling roasted chestnuts on the corner.

We felt duped, a very unpleasant feeling. The only con-solation was that now I could repeat, after the know-it-all Soviet foreign correspondents: 'What a disgusting sight this striptease is!'

Indeed, Soho proved to be all tease and no strip.

This particular part of Western freedom had eluded me so far . . .

On my last morning in London I went to watch the changing of the guard at Buckingham Palace. Standing behind a massive railing huddled together with hundreds of other onlookers, I was peeping from behind someone's back and vainly trying to see what was happening.

The only thing I could discern was the top of a guardsman's fur hat. There was no chance to get closer as policemen were blocking the way.

'I am with the press,' I told them. 'Can I come closer?'

'Sorry, sir, the rules are the same for everyone,' the policeman said.

Suddenly the huge gates of the palace opened to let in a small bus. A dozen people got out of it and started watching the ceremony from inside – a luxury vantage point! I felt furious. My Soviet sense of social justice, moulded by thirty years of queuing, was deeply insulted. What kind of big shots were they? But then I had a better look. These were not big shots but small, mentally retarded children with their teacher. The guards were pacing intricately across the yard. The children were looking and holding hands. The policemen were explaining something to them. I was ashamed of my fury and moved almost to tears.

In Moscow, one rarely bumped into a disabled person in the street, and yet there were millions of them. The system was simply ignoring them. They lived on miserable pensions, they lacked wheelchairs, artificial limbs, even crutches. But most of all they lacked sympathy and help. That was why, for the most part, they had to stay at home (provided they had one of course), both ashamed and unable to go out.

The thing that struck me most on my first visit to Britain was not the well-stocked shops (not being much of a consumer, I hardly noticed them) and restaurants but the sheer numbers of disabled people in the streets and on trains, in museums and stadiums. Special toilets, lifts and other aids for them were everywhere. And they didn't look miserable or deprived. They were no less smiling, self-confident and free than their able-bodied compatriots.

The initial culture shock. Or was it a shock of Freedom?

'Are you carrying Bibles or pornography?!' a rodent-like Soviet customs inspector shouted at me in Brest. After four weeks in Britain where people seldom raised their voices, it was especially irritating.

Overwhelmed with all the presents I brought, Mitya fell ill with excitement.

For two weeks after my return I was walking around Moscow with my head down. I couldn't make myself look up and face the Soviet reality which seemed so much gloomier than before. For two weeks I kept smiling at strangers, getting angry scowls in return.

Einstein was right: everything in this life is relative.

As to my glittery suit, I left it behind in London. But somehow I didn't miss it.

9

Pineapples in Champagne

'*I*n the West they eat fresh strawberries all year round . . .'
One could often hear this disputable remark in Moscow food queues of the late eighties. 'All over the world they eat strawberries every day, but not us . . .' The endless queue for sausages (or was this one for Hungarian shoes? Or for Russian vodka?) was snaking along the snow. I was shifting from one foot to the other trying to read a newspaper. I didn't want to get into conversation with these strawberry addicts who wouldn't believe me if I said that there were places in the world where people didn't eat anything at all every day . . . I didn't blame them. Daily consumption of strawberries for them was an important (and unachievable) human right, much more essential than the right of free expression.

Freedom of sausage (or of strawberries) comes first, freedom of speech follows.

My first pineapple. I had it at the age of ten at my friend's birthday party. His father had just returned from an assignment in Moscow where he bought this exotic tropical fruit from a street vendor after several hours of queuing.

We had never seen a pineapple before, only read about it in the poem by the great proletarian poet Vladimir Mayakovsky which was compulsory learning in our school curriculum:

Gobble up pineapples and munch hazel-hens –
Your time is running out, you vicious bourgeois!

We all knew this poem by heart.

Pineapples in the Soviet Union were as rare as snowstorms in the Sahara Desert and as exotic as an Eskimo in the streets of Abu Dhabi. The pineapple looked like an enlarged pine-tree cone. Or like a *limonka* hand-grenade, popular with heroic Soviet partisans during the war (and hence unpopular with the Germans). We had a picture of it (the grenade, not the pineapple) in our school history manual. The fruit's rough spiky skin smelled of rainforest and of sunsets in the tropics, so colourfully described in a book called *Captains of Frigates* by Nikolai Chukovsky.

The magic 'bourgeois' fruit was cut into a dozen thin, almost transparent, slices – one for each guest at this boys only party (at ten, we still snubbed girls). I will never forget the taste. How shall I describe it? Blissful? Divine? I didn't know the word 'orgasmic' then.

A sweet and astringent taste. Our lips were stiff with it for hours to come. Was it our first taste of Freedom?

I had my second pineapple twenty years later, in 1984, when on a journalistic assignment in the town of Blagoveshchensk in the Soviet Far East, a ten hour flight from Moscow. Blagoveshchensk was a curious place. It was situated on the bank of the Amur River along which the border with China ran. The Chinese city of Sahalyan was on the opposite bank. From the room of my Yubileiniy Hotel facing the river I had a clear visa-free view of China, just a couple of hundred metres away across the Amur. I could see ramshackle houses with small blast furnaces on the roofs – the aftermath of the Great Leap Forward when every Chinese household was forced to melt iron. It was seven years since the death of Mao Tse-tung, and the Cultural Revolution effectively was over. That's why there were no slogans on the buildings, and the countless finger-shaped chimneys of the useless in-house furnaces were sticking out into the sky like peculiar phallic obelisks on the mass grave of human stupidity.

I could even see the people – all dressed in dark-blue or

dark-grey fatigues and riding antediluvian bicycles. My first ever glimpse of the world outside the Soviet Union. And although visa-free, it was not particularly inspiring.

The shops in Blagoveshchensk were as bare as everywhere else in Russia. Probably even slightly barer. Practically nothing was on sale. But . . . A couple of weeks before my arrival, a stray foreign freighter had been stranded in the local port. She was carrying a load of Vietnamese pineapples which were starting to rot. There was little choice but to unload all several hundred tons of this sensitive cargo in Blagoveshchensk and sell it through local shops. That was how the God-forsaken Far Eastern town overnight became the pineapple capital of the Soviet Union, if not of the whole world. A sudden tropical windfall.

Pineapples were sold on every street corner. They were piled in the windows of all the town stores, even bookshops. Humid, oxygen-lacking air was smelling of rotting pineapples, which became the main (and often the only) component of the locals' menu. Schoolkids were having pineapple sandwiches for their school lunches. Alcoholics in parks and gateways were munching on pineapples (in a truly 'bourgeois' fashion) after downing glasses of vodka – a substitute for herrings and pickled cucumbers, not seen in Blagoveshchensk since the fifties.

Well, when in Rome, do as Romans do. Whether I wanted it or not (and remembering my childhood gourmet experience I certainly did, initially at least), I suddenly had to eat pineapples three times a day.

After a couple of days of this enforced tropical diet my tongue felt rough and rigid as a piece of sandpaper stuck into my mouth. I was suffering from a permanent thirst which was impossible to quench: due to the breakdown of the town's plumbing system, only boiling water was coming out of both taps in my hotel bathroom.

It was then that the title of a collection of poems by Igor Severyanin, a turn-of-the-century Russian symbolist poet, came to my mind – *Pineapples in Champagne*. Igor Severyanin's poetry was branded decadent and anti-social by Soviet officialdom. To add apples (or in this case, pineapples) to oranges, he was an émigré who left Russia in 1918, shortly after the revolution. In all the seventy-odd years of Soviet power only a couple of his books were published. They immediately became bibliographic rarities.

Pineapples in champagne . . . It did sound decadent, anti-social and hence irresistible. I decided to diversify my bour-geois pineapple diet by adding a touch of decadence to it. The immediate problem was champagne which was not just unseen but also unheard of in Blagoveshchensk. Instead, I had to satisfy myself with a bottle of cheap sparkling plonk which I put into a permanently empty fridge in my room.

The fridge did a good job, and by the time I was ready for my ultimate decadent experience, the wine was frozen stiff, and I had to keep the bottle on a white-hot window-sill for a while to let it melt.

I chopped a pineapple into small rectangular lumps and tossed them into the glass. The plonk immediately started bubbling and foaming like crazy. You can observe a similar chemical reaction if you drop a piece of chalk into a cup of vinegar. The chemical composition of the plonk was probably close to that of sulphuric acid.

Without waiting for the foaming to subside, I gulped the glass down, choking simultaneously on the wine and on a pineapple chunk.

When I stopped coughing, I felt as if I had just swal-lowed an ice-cold grater, made of stainless steel. Nevertheless, I heroically, with a truly Soviet stoicism better known as obstinacy, continued my 'decadent' experiment until both the wine and the pineapple were gone. In fact, they didn't disappear completely (in full accordance with the preservation of matter law, allegedly discovered by the great Russian scien-tist Lomonosov) and continued their boisterous struggle in my stomach throughout the night. By the following morning, their struggle had reached truly revolutionary proportions.

A civil war between two incompatible substances was under way inside my body. I had also lost my voice and was suffering from the severest cold I had ever had. Lying on my bed, I was sweating and moaning silently.

I was saved by the editor of a local newspaper who popped in for a courtesy chat. Having appraised the situation with one quick glance at the mess on the table and at my wriggling supine body that continued to be mutilated from inside, he asked briskly: 'What have you drunk?'

'Pineapples in champagne,' I whispered.

'Don't move!' he barked and rushed out.

His command was superfluous: I couldn't move even if I wanted to.

Five minutes later he returned with a bottle of vodka and a huge leaking packet of table salt. He poured vodka into a glass, added a generous handful of salt, stirred it violently with his rough, nicotine-stained index finger (I nearly threw up at the sight) and handed it over to me.

'Drink!'

I tried to protest but he literally forced the glass down my tormented throat.

A flash of lightning pierced my brain. A Krakatoa volcano erupted in my body. I don't remember how I reached the toilet.

Two hours later I was cured and felt as fresh as the proverbial Russian cucumber, and strong enough to carry on with my journalistic task. Looking through the window at the hardworking Chinese across the river, I couldn't help feeling that they were laughing at me. They obviously had no idea of what 'decadence' was about.

Now you will understand why, when living in Australia, I had no problem resisting the mind-boggling displays of tropical fruit in shop-windows. My pineapple experiment was a success after all. It proved that good things (like exotic foods and other Western freedoms) could be enjoyed only in moderation. The moment you start taking them for granted and overindulging, they can become explosive and even life-threatening.

So whenever I see a pineapple on a London fruit stall, I am reminded of Mayakovsky and his warning to the bourgeoisie. As for himself, he committed suicide in 1930.

But I think I know exactly what he meant.

10

A Flat for Prince Charles

F orce breeds counterforce . . . Newton's third law of motion which I learnt at school.

There were numerous ways to defect from the Soviet Union.

Belenko, a Soviet military pilot, flew his MiG fighter to Japan, where he asked for political asylum in the mid-seventies. He died under mysterious circumstances several years later. And earlier, in the sixties, a foolhardly captain of a Soviet submarine nearly succeeded in taking his underwater vessel – complete with guns, navigation equipment and crew – to Sweden. Nearly . . . Tom Clancy wrote a book about this incredible deed which was later made into a Hollywood action thriller, *The Hunt for Red October*.

One reckless engineer from Leningrad went skiing in the forest, crossed the heavily-guarded Soviet-Finnish border, but didn't give himself up until he reached Sweden: Finland was in the habit of sending Soviet defectors back to their great motherland to face the notorious Article 64 of the Soviet Criminal Code which qualified 'failure to return' (i.e. defection) as high treason punishable by a brief encounter with a well-practised firing squad. Significantly, in 1997 this Article still existed in the Criminal Code of the new 'democratic' Russia.

A 1994 headline from an independent Moscow newspaper: 'Should we Shoot Defectors or Should we Not?'

Imagine: you have a British passport and go to Australia to

visit your relatives (or just to look around). You like it there so much that you decide to stay. You might have stumbled upon a better job, fallen in love with a local, or just taken a liking to the climate. Without notifying the British government of your 'treacherous' intentions, you stay. After a year or so you become disappointed with the place. The job turns out to be a temporary one, your new sweetheart proves to be married to someone else, and the climate makes you ill. Unsuspectingly, you return to your 'motherland', only to be grabbed by the police at customs and, after a brisk show trial, put in front of your friendly native firing squad.

So much for the Universal Declaration of Human Rights and the Helsinki Accords, of which both the Soviet Union and (later) Russia were signatories.

There were rumours that one Leningrad mushroom-picker, having got lost in the wood, inadvertently found himself in Helsinki. He didn't intend to defect and went straight to the Soviet embassy where his story was dismissed as a scam: he was taken back to Leningrad and imprisoned. Several years in a labour camp made him so anti-Soviet that on his release he decided to defect in earnest which he did after another mushroom-picking expedition.

One resourceful Ukrainian peasant bought himself a tour of North Korea only to dash across the buffer zone separating the socialist paradise from the reactionary South and was nearly shot dead by the vigilant North Korean border guards with Kim Il Sung badges on their lapels. Nearly . . .

A sailor from Novorossiysk crossed the Black Sea to Istanbul on an inflatable mattress, with nothing but a plastic bag with chocolate and vodka to sustain himself during the voyage. And another escapee managed to get from Karelia (in the North-West of the Russian Federation) to Finland through a drainage-tube, having covered his naked body with oil to facilitate the sliding (he kept his clothes in a rubber bag, tied to his ankle). The only reason for his defection, as he explained later, was that he had a dream of circumnavigating the globe in a yacht, but the Soviet authorities didn't allow him to realise it.

And a pilot of a Soviet cargo ship (who was a good family man) smuggled his wife to England in a chest for dirty linen that he kept in his cabin which gave a completely new meaning to the good old English expression 'to wash dirty linen in public'.

A university friend of mine who used to work as an interpreter on board a Soviet cruise ship told me how a girl he knew (her name was Katya) who was a stewardess on the same vessel jumped out of a porthole in nothing but a red bikini while the ship was cruising past Australian shores. She turned up in Sydney as she was – in her red bikini – and was immediately branded 'the red bikini girl' by the Australian press (they still remember this incident well in Australia). She later moved to America and made a fortune by posing – this time without her red bikini – for *Playboy*.

Of course, defections from the Soviet Union were not always successful. In fact, only very few of them were. The price of failure was high. Article 64 was prominent in the official verdicts on the inmates of Perm 35 labour camp for political prisoners that I visited as a Soviet journalist in 1989, shortly before my own defection. One of them, Smirnov, got a lucrative job offer while on a visit to Norway and decided to stay. When, six months later, he went to Moscow to pick up his family, he was arrested by the KGB at Sheremetyevo airport and was sentenced to fifteen years in a labour camp. And the story of our family friend Yuri Vetokhin is even more tragic. A naval officer and a rowing champion, he was accused of trying to flee to Turkey in his rowing boat while practising in the Black Sea, off the coast of the Crimea. He was promptly diagnosed 'insane' and sent to a psychiatric prison where he died several years later.

Force breeds counterforce indeed. The stronger the cage, the harder those inside try to break free.

Our defection from the Soviet Union in January 1990 was relatively smooth, apart from some rolling and pitching.

Having got off the East-West Express in Ostende, Belgium, we boarded a Dover-bound P&O ferry. Due to the extremely rough sea, the crossing, which was supposed to last four hours, took seven and a half. After the first three hours, half of the passengers were prostrated with seasickness. Several dozen Hong Kong schoolkids in bright green uniforms (they were returning from their holidays in Europe) were huddled together in the main lounge and their faces were gradually acquiring the colour of their school shirts. The carpets were covered with vomit, and the stench was becoming unbearable. I thought I was pretty immune to seasickness, but soon I was nauseated too, to say nothing of Mitya and Natasha who were both pale and sick. As a compensation for the 'inconvenience', a free movie was shown in the ship's cinema. It was *Ghostbusters II*. Hoping for a distraction from rocking, we crawled in to watch it. Since then, whenever I hear the word Ghostbusters, I start feeling pangs of nausea.

Was this stormy crossing an omen of rough times ahead of us? Whatever it was, we preferred to overlook bad premonitions and to strive for happier ones. And there was no shortage of them from the moment we stepped onto British soil.

'Aren't you the Russian gentleman from the Clive James show?' an immigration officer asked me while stamping my passport. 'I think you were very funny. Welcome!'

'Ha! I've seen you on telly,' a customs inspector said with a grin. Contrary to my expectations, this time they didn't bother to look into our suitcases.

The perks of sudden fame. They came as a complete surprise.

It had all started at the end of 1988, shortly after my first visit to Britain. One morning a phone call from BBC Television in London came through to my Moscow flat. They suggested that I become a regular on *Saturday Night Clive*. And although I had a rather vague idea of what kind of show it was, I was flattered. Even now I don't know exactly why they chose me. Several of my London friends claim credit for being the first to have tipped Clive's researchers off to my existence. But the truth, I presume, is much simpler: the considerable media exposure that I received during my first visit to London.

The producers of the show were rather naughty in the beginning. They told me it was going to be a serious political interview, so I put on my jacket and tie and a sombre Soviet look and went to the studio. But after the first questions I smelt a rat: they didn't sound serious. I changed my attitude and went back to my usual ironic self.

I was sitting in the studio in front of a tattered, fly-blown picture of Red Square (to create an illusion of being in

Moscow, when in fact I *was* in Moscow), with a prickly little earphone like a hearing aid. The helpfulness of the device was minimal: the technicians on both sides had lots of problems with sound and kept losing the satellite (or maybe it was the satellite that was losing them, I am not sure).

Unable to hear much, apart from crackling noises, I frantically tried to guess what Clive was asking me.

'Is it true that people are constantly watched in the Soviet Union?'

'I am not so sure about the Soviet Union, but dead sure I am being watched in Britain at the moment.'

My London friends told me later that I was the first smiling Russian on British television. 'You don't realise what an impact you had. The day after you spoke about shortages of condoms in Leningrad, say, half of Britain would repeat your jokes in pubs.'

As it turned out, my jokes were duly appreciated not just in Britain and Australia, but at the KGB headquarters in Moscow too . . .

At Dover we were met by my friend Alan Rusbridger, then the editor of the *Weekend Guardian*. He was holding a freshly printed book in a red glossy cover. It was the pilot copy of *Special Correspondent*, my first book in English that had just come off the press. It was somehow reassuring to see the bulk of my Soviet life (this is what *Special Correspondent* was about) condensed to a neat rectangular volume. It implied finality and, as I thought, boded well for the future.

Alan drove us to his house, where we were to stay for several days until . . . Until we decided what to do next. One thing was certain: there was no going back to the Soviet Union.

There was a letter waiting for me at Alan's place. It was from Clarissa, my literary agent, informing me that she had just sold foreign rights for *Special Correspondent* to Germany, France and Japan. I refused to believe our luck.

'We are now rich,' I said to Natasha.

I was wrong: we were neither rich nor safe. The Soviet Union was still there, and London was swarming with KGB agents posing as diplomats, journalists and foreign trade officials. I was well aware of the plight of Georgi Markov, a Bulgarian dissident journalist, who thought he had found a safe haven in London before he was stabbed with a poisoned umbrella tip in October, 1978. We had to either get a secure status in Britain (our tourist visas were valid for six months only) or proceed to any other country which would be prepared to harbour us. But for a moment we felt comfortable – not a little thing after the long months of our Moscow nightmare.

Alan took me to see a lawyer, whose verdict was simple: the only chance for us to stay in Britain was by asking for political asylum. Somehow I was not prepared to do this: we still had close relatives in the Soviet Union whose lives would have been endangered had we undertaken such a step. Looking back now, I realise that we had other options. But the lawyer preferred not to disclose them: political asylum cases were the most profitable, both for his fee and for his prestige (if successful that is).

From my son's Australian Citizenship Essay:

> Our 'holidays' began in London where my father had plenty of contacts: he had already published one of his books there. We were desperate to find a country that would accept us. We tried New Zealand, South Africa, Israel, USA and many more. In the Canadian Embassy we were told to go back to Russia and apply from there. By the way, the penalty for defecting from Russia, is death . . .

To correct my son Mitya, who was only nine years old then, I have to say that we didn't try New Zealand: it sounded too distant and too exotic. As to South Africa, I was seriously thinking of visiting its embassy in Trafalgar Square, but the round-the-clock picket, manned by protesters with anti-apartheid posters, around it made me change my mind: I didn't want us to end up in another totalitarian state which would mean swapping an awl for a soap, as we used to say in Russia. As to the Canadian embassy, Mitya is exactly right: having spent half an hour explaining our situation to a dispassionate woman in the embrasure of a reception window, the only thing I got from her was a piece of paper with the address of Canada's Moscow embassy in Kropotkinskaya Street. 'You should go back and apply from there,' I was told.

With Israel it looked much more promising in the beginning. At the embassy we were given the address of the Aliyah (immigration) office in Finchley Road. We were subjected to a thorough check before we were allowed inside, and Mitya looked with fascination at his own image on the monitors of several closed-circuit security cameras. It was the first time he saw himself on a TV screen.

'No problem. You can go to Israel tomorrow,' a sympathetic lady assured us, having thrown a quick glance at my Soviet internal passport with the word *Yevrei* (Jew) under 'Nationality'. It was harder with Natasha who had a non-Jewish mother and who had chosen to be classified as 'Russian' in her passport (for obvious reasons). By Israeli laws, she was not Jewish. Nor was Mitya. 'Your son might have problems in Israel being non-Jewish,' said the woman. 'But nevertheless you can all go . . .'

She was kind enough to supply us with a description of an 'absorption centre' where we were supposed to live and study Hebrew for the first year. It sounded pretty much like a prison. One was not allowed to leave its heavily guarded territory without permission, and everything – from pillows to tea-spoons (one per inmate) – was strictly rationed. Having thought this option over for a couple of weeks, we decided against it.

I also remember having a meeting with a Third Secretary of the Irish Embassy in London. I knew that Ireland was always willing to accept writers and asked him whether I had a chance to emigrate to Ireland with my family. 'Yes, we like writers,' said the Third Secretary, a lanky loose-jointed Irishman. 'But we don't like journalists.' With just one published book which was in fact a volume of journalism, my chances of being recognised as a writer by the Irish government were close to zero. I wanted to tell him that a writer was simply a journalist who hadn't been able to get his copy into print for a while, but thought better of it.

Our future was hanging in the air.

Random memories:

We go shopping at Brent Cross. I give Natasha some cash and send her to Marks & Spencer's to buy herself a pair of shoes while I take Mitya to a games arcade. Half an hour later we find Natasha standing in the middle of the footwear department crying – overwhelmed by the abundance and unable to make a choice.

Meanwhile, *Special Correspondent* was officially published. After a launch party, I had to go on a promotion tour around the country. Mitya and Natasha went with me. We visited twelve cities in England and Scotland in just ten days. I was lecturing at universities, attending publicity functions and book-signing sessions. Mitya took a liking to pushing luggage trolleys at airports and railway stations. He did it with real gusto and wouldn't accept any help.

The book was selling well, had excellent reviews and even appeared in bestseller lists briefly. But this couldn't solve our immediate problems, one of which was that we no longer wished to inconvenience Alan and had to look for a place of our own to live: no one knew how long we would have to stay in London. And we wanted Mitya to start school.

While I was giving interviews and writing, Natasha was looking for a flat. One day she phoned me at *The Guardian*, her voice trembling with excitement: 'You know, I've just found a wonderful flat,' she said. 'I wouldn't be ashamed to invite Prince Charles there!'

Her last remark was not just a figure of speech.

During my first visit to Britain in October 1988, I had written a letter to Prince Charles inviting him to come and stay with us in Moscow. Why did I do this? I don't know. Maybe it was a way of expressing my gratitude to the country that was so welcoming and hospitable to me. I was not seriously expecting to get a reply, although at times I liked to play with the idea of Prince Charles arriving to our tiny Khrushchev flat with all his valets, equerries and horses.

For some reason, horses and carriages played a prominent role in this repetitive dream of mine.

Several months later, on a Sunday afternoon, I got a phone call from the British embassy. 'We've got a letter from the

Prince of Wales for you, sir. Would you prefer to collect it personally or for it to be delivered to your house?' Had it not been for the caller's impeccable English, I would have been dead sure it was a joke of one of my *Krokodil* colleagues (we liked framing each other from time to time, especially on April Fool's Day).

I asked for the letter to be delivered.

Several weeks passed, but the letter did not arrive. I phoned the embassy, but they pretended ignorance and spoke to me in a condescending manner which British diplomats are so good at. I started thinking that it had indeed been a joke after all when one day the editor of my department at *Krokodil* handed me a neat envelope without a stamp, yet with a Highgrove House emblem on the back. Until now I have no idea why the letter was delivered to my office rather than home and why it took so long. Can it be so that it was intercepted by the Soviet authorities? Or by MI5? Or was it just another case of the British Foreign Office inefficiency?

> Dear Mr Vitaliev, [it started in long hand]
> I am afraid I only received your letter after you had left the UK, but I did want to say how touched and grateful I was to receive it. I have indeed come across some of your pieces. I saw you on *Saturday Night Clive* and thought you were wonderful! You made me laugh a great deal, and I needed a good laugh, I can assure you!
>
> Your kind invitation to visit Moscow is much appreciated but, I fear, a bit difficult at present. If I ever do manage to come to Moscow you will be the first person I want to meet! If you come to the UK again in the future I would very much value meeting you.
>
> This brings you my very best wishes.
> [In long hand] Yours sincerely
>   Charles

The letter was full of genuine warmth and true human emotion emphasised by frequent exclamation marks – rather unusual for the English style of letter-writing. There were several spelling and punctuation mistakes in the typed part of the text, and they were all duly corrected in Charles's own hand. I was aware of his long-lasting crusade for better literacy in Britain and of his complaints of having to correct spelling and grammar mistakes of his own secretaries. A living illustration of this was lying in front of me. And the signature – 'Charles' – added to the feeling of sincerity. It was obvious that the letter was written by a nice and warm person.

Our correspondence lasted for a couple of years and continued after I moved to Australia. I kept sending him copies of my new books as they were coming out. And although I have never had a chance to meet Prince Charles in the flesh (I did meet his parents and his estranged wife), for all these years I couldn't help feeling that I had a good friend at St James's Palace, a friend whose life was probably no less hectic and dramatic than mine. Prince Charles finally did visit Russia in late 1993. Only we were no longer there and thus were unable to entertain him at our tiny Moscow flat.

An unrealised idea for a comic novel developed together with Derek Kartun in 1995:

It is 1999. The millennium is coming to an end and, East and West, it's back to basics again. The House of Windsor has declined further into low farce, and Prince Charles is still the fall guy. Princess Di is on a public relations high, and Prince Philip is negotiating his own deal with Bloomsbury. Charles has frankly had enough.

In the East, the Russian mess is quickly degenerating into disaster. The nationalists are on the rampage; there's fighting down south and the President is drunk. Someone has collected the million signatures needed for a referendum to promote a change in the constitution. The big idea: to bring back a Tsar of all (or nearly all) the Russias.

But where to find the right man?

Some high-level fool in Moscow thinks of Prince Charles. After all, he looks great in uniform, isn't too opinionated, is distantly related to the last Tsar, and he's in deep post-marital (and constitutional) trouble. Maybe he'd go for the challenge: the greatest ecological mess in the world to clear up; 800 miles of North European Plain between him and his father; and a chance to make a fresh start with a nice (and undemanding) Russian girl . . .

Intermediaries are sent. They mediate. The Prince takes advice from those whose dodgy counselling has led to trouble in the past and does a crash course in Russian.

Meanwhile remnant Romanovs, known and hitherto unknown, explode in an international family row: who is the rightful heir? How can they beat off the usurper in St James's Palace?

By chapter 4 we are in the Kremlin with Tsar Karl I. The nationalists, 'reformed' communists, Mafia and drunkards are fighting to get their snouts in the royal trough. Our story takes the reader through the hilarious misunderstandings, disappointments and cultural blind alleys of the new Tsar's reign.

Why no polo ponies? No organic farming? And what are these demands for punitive expeditions to crack open skulls in Chechnya, Moldova and Dagestan? 'Little Father,' goes the old cry, 'tell us what to do!'

'Well, it seems that stringing up a dozen Chechens as a signal to the others would not be, you know, quite what one might see as the best solution . . .'

And then again, does a latter-day born-again Rasputin emerge from the steppe? Maybe poor Charles, just like his hapless predecessor Nicholas II, ends up in a cellar in Ekaterinburg waiting to be shot?

I can't remember who said that history usually repeats itself twice: first as a tragedy and then as a farce . . .

The flat, found by Natasha, was impressive indeed. Situated on the ground floor of an old Victorian house in Muswell Hill, it was full of paintings and antiques and was furnished in a plush, although eclectic, fashion. It had two bedrooms – red and blue – and a spacious, yet permanently dark, sitting room with a real fireplace and a balcony leading into the garden.

The walls in the flat were painted dark green and dark red which later prompted a friend to call it a mausoleum.

The garden was truly stunning. It seemed huge, almost like a small park, with a well-kept rectangular lawn, lined with flowers and trees, among which there were several birch trees. To Mitya's delight, there was a swing in a far corner. My London friends who saw the garden were unanimous that it looked very East European which was unsurprising considering that the landlady was an elderly Polish nun. After our Moscow cubby-hole, it was a real palace. And the rent was affordable.

This North London flat was to become my abode and a pied-à-terre for several years to come. Altogether I lived there for about three years – more than in any other place in the West. Even now I often go there just to have a nostalgic look at the house with a red dragon on the roof where I spent some of the happiest and some of the most miserable days in my life.

We were gradually adjusting to our new Western existence. Having overcome her initial embarrassment, Natasha would routinely go shopping in Sainsbury's and Marks & Spencer's. I would type away features and articles for *The Guardian*, *The Observer* and for *Punch* on an ancient typewriter, borrowed from a friend. Mitya started attending a primary school down the road. It was a Church of England school, but it didn't matter. He was enjoying his new class and soon was chatting away in English for all he was worth. I liked picking him up after classes and waiting for him at the school gates together with other parents. It gave me a sense of belonging to a community, something that all three of us – homeless and stateless – desperately needed. And here he was running towards me and looking deceptively Western, even English, in his school uniform and with a satchel on his back.

His only initial complaint was that compared to his disciplinarian Moscow school they were playing too much and were not doing enough learning. The tasks they were given were simple enough for four-to-five-year-olds. He was also amazed at how easy-going the rules of behaviour were. They were allowed to talk to each other during lessons and could address the teacher without raising their hands first as they must in the Soviet Union. But soon he got used to it all and started enjoying his school even more.

Freedom is both easy and natural to adjust to, especially for a child. Walking in Woodside Avenue now, I can almost see my son's little satchelled figure running briskly along the pavement towards his first Western school, towards his own little Freedom and, sadly, farther and farther away from me.

On weekends we would fly a kite in a nearby park and I would teach Mitya to roller-skate. Natasha, always a bit of a stay-at-home person, was happily cooking us dinners and basking in the previously unknown conveniences of a modern kitchen. We were happy and didn't feel like leaving this house, this city and this country that we had come to love, but our visas were running out and something had to be done to secure our future.

I am often asked why I didn't stay in Britain in the first place and why I chose to take my family to Australia instead. This is a difficult question. To start with, I didn't know anything about loopholes in the British immigration rules. Also, my main contacts at that time were left-wing journalists who were saying in unison that the British Tory establishment would never give me permission to stay (I was also noticing that their attitude to me was changing: it looked as if they were not entirely happy with our decision to defect and some of them would have preferred me to stay in the Soviet Union as a sufferer and a martyr).

Much later I discovered that staying could have been relatively easy. Many of my former countrymen with much flimsier grounds have managed to do so. I had a name in Britain, I had friends, I had reasons not to go back to the Soviet Union. On top of it all, I started getting job offers. The first one came from the *Inverness Chronicle* whose editor volunteered to travel to London to discuss the terms with me. He never made it: on the day of our meeting there were heavy floods in Scotland, and all trains came to a stop.

The unforeseen intervention of Nature . . .

I had an offer of a contract from *The Guardian*, too. But the most serious proposition was put forward by Tony Watson, the editor of the Leeds-based *Yorkshire Post*, who offered me a decent salary and free accommodation for the three of us, had we decided to move to Leeds. This sounded very lucrative to me. Moreover, I had a friend in Leeds, a woman from Kharkov with whom I had studied at the university. Also, we had visited Leeds during the promotion tour for *Special Correspondent* and came to like it. But by the time the *Yorkshire Post* proposal came through, it was already too late: we were firmly on our way to Australia.

From my son's Australian Citizenship Essay:

. . . just by chance we happened to be walking past the Australian High Commission one day when my mother offered to step inside. We were in doubt as hardly any of us knew anything about Australia and we knew that to be able to emigrate to Australia you first had to pass on points.

We stepped inside. My father went up to the booth and took our Soviet passports out. He began explaining our situation.

'You're the Russian Clive James man, aren't you?' happily interrupted the young red-headed girl sitting in the booth.

'Why, yes,' my father answered.

'All of us have seen you on television,' she shrieked again with her strong (it seemed so at that time) Australian accent.

There was something about that girl that made me think different about Australia. Was it her liveliness and cheerful expression, or was it just the way she talked like there was nothing in the world bothering her? She looked as if she had made peace with everything and everyone. Whatever it was, I had already generalised that all Australians were like that, and I began to like it a lot . . . My vivid imaginations of Australia were dark red people walking around in large Mexicano hats. Everyone lived in a straw hut and all they did was swim at the beach or sleep . . .

*   *   *

My son's 'vivid imaginations' proved to be not that far from reality in the long run.

My knowledge of Australia was only somewhat better than Mitya's. In the late seventies I was working as an interpreter for a succession of delegations of Australian museum curators and gallery directors negotiating exhibition exchanges with the Hermitage Museum in Leningrad and Pushkin Fine Arts Museum in Moscow. It was from them that I got my first notion of Australia, my first lessons in Aussie slang, or Strine, my first Australian books. They were all smiling, happy and relaxed which made them stand out in Moscow streets as if they were creatures from a different planet. And in many ways they were . . .

As to my first glimpse of Australia, it happened much earlier when watching an Australian film called *Abba* in a shabby Park cinema with plywood walls in my native Kharkov. The plot was simple, if not to say primitive: it was just footage of Abba's tour of Australia, hastily edited into an hour-and-a-half-long melodrama. What struck me most was the Australian crowd that consisted exclusively of leisurely suntanned people with open and friendly faces that carried the famous 'no worries, mate' expression on them.

This is paradise on earth, I thought then.

I was not familiar with the expression of Malcolm Fraser, Australia's former Liberal Prime Minister, who once poignantly called his country 'fools' paradise'.

Shortly before the defection, I was invited to work as a researcher for *G'Day, Comrade* – an Australian Channel Nine documentary on perestroika – and made good friends with the crew.

Monica, the woman in the Australian High Commission booth, confessed to me later that she immediately recognised me as Clive James's Moscow man when I muttered into her window: 'I need a non-formal approach . . .'

'In the window you looked exactly like you do on TV,' she said.

The High Commission immigration officers were lovely people. They embraced us from the start and gave us the impression that they really needed us. I was offered a rare 'special skills' status which excluded the normal procedure of points scoring. They even decided to forgo the routine police clearance which in my case would have meant a green light for emigration to Australia from the Interior Ministry (read KGB) in Moscow. It would have been like asking a hungry wolf to give a blessing to an escapist lamb. 'You are the best migrants I have ever had to work with,' Joe Rodigari, an Italian-born head of the immigration department, used to tell us. He even kept our family photo on his office desk. While our documents were being processed, I would routinely pop into the High Commission for a tinny or just for a friendly chat. And a group of immigration officers once came to our Muswell Hill flat for dinner.

We no longer felt like outcasts whom no one wanted. Only the distance that we were supposed to cover to get to Australia was a bit of a worry. I tried to avoid looking at the map: the mysterious diamond-shaped continent we were heading for seemed (and was) half the world away.

The High Commission was getting ready to give us a special farewell. They issued a press release alerting the Australian media of our arrival. Our visas were to be granted to us at a special ceremony by the High Commissioner himself in the presence of Clive James.

At that time I was approached by the BBC with an offer to write and present a *Byline* TV documentary on my impressions of Britain. I chose Little Ben, a small and unnoticed monument near Victoria Station in London, as my symbol of an unknown toy-town Britain. *My Friend Little Ben* was the film's title. The last couple of weeks in London were very busy: I was making *Little Ben* with a BBC crew, and a Channel Nine TV crew from Australia was filming me making the BBC film (they were preparing a TV feature on our migration to Australia). For the first (and last) time in my life I was simultaneously filmed by two film crews from two different countries. We finished filming *Little Ben* one day before our departure. The film still had to be edited and cut, and for that the BBC agreed to fly all three of us back to Britain from Australia in a month which somehow helped to reduce the uncertainty of our adventure.

For some reason, I couldn't help an uneasy feeling, as if I was about to do something tragically wrong. This feeling was enhanced by a chat with Igor Pomerantsev, a London-based Radio Liberty correspondent, writer, poet and a Russian émigré of many years' standing. 'I've never been to Australia, Vitali,' he told me. 'I wish you lots of good luck. But I also want to warn you. Several of my Russian friends who had gone there to live came back with one and the same complaint: spiritual heartburn. This is a peculiar sensation: everything seems to be in place and yet something very important is missing. They couldn't tell exactly what it was . . .'

Spiritual heartburn . . . If I only had known how right he was.

The visa-granting ceremony took place in the High Commission's chandeliered assembly hall. We were filmed by Channel Nine walking down the Strand and entering the building. The High Commissioner made a speech and so did Clive James. I said a couple of words of gratitude in reply. Cameras were whirring. Australian hacks were scribbling hastily in their memo pads. There were tears – tears of joy – in Joe Rodigari's honest Italian eyes.

Six years later we shall come to this very assembly hall with fifteen-year-old Mitya, visiting me – his estranged Dad – from Australia, to listen to the performance of the Young Voices of Melbourne choir where Mitya's girlfriend will be a soloist – thus closing the globe-engirdling circle of our lives.

'Top Soviet Journo Opts for a Land of Smiles' – such were the headlines of many Australian newspapers the following morning.

Nightingales were singing in our Muswell Hill garden all night through. It was the end of May, the start of our beloved European summer. We were heading for the Australian winter, for Freedom, for our new life. When you run for your life, you don't look around. You look straight ahead.

We were full of hope, and I had no way of knowing that I was about to commit the biggest mistake of my entire life.

11

This Flying Feeling

How sad, ye gods, how sad the world is at evening, how mysterious the mists over the swamps. You will know it when you have wandered astray in those mists, when you have suffered greatly before dying, when you have walked through the world carrying an unbearable burden. You know it too when you are weary and ready to leave this earth without regret; its mists, its swamps and its rivers; ready to give yourself into the arms of death with a light heart, knowing that death alone can comfort you.

Mikhail Bulgakov, *The Master and Margarita*

Flying is the most common of all my dream topics. According to my *Dictionary of Dreams*, such visions frequently signify a desire to have new experiences and willingness to view the world from a different standpoint.

In plain words, one dreams of flying when feeling trapped.

In my dreams, I first levitate above the ground waving my hands frantically – fledgling-like – and then turn into a human glider hovering freely among the clouds. What a feeling!

'You will commute between Melbourne and London and will write on the plane,' Clive James assured me during one of our first meetings. He proved a good prophet, but even Clive couldn't anticipate the sheer number of intercontinental flights that were in store for me.

Melbourne–London (or London–Melbourne) is the longest commercial passenger flight in the world. And the most expensive too. For most people a flight like that is the ultimate journey to be undertaken once in a lifetime. I have flown to and from Australia nearly fifty times in the last five and a half years, having covered almost a million kilometres – two and half times the distance between the Earth and the Moon (and this is not counting dozens of shorter flights within Europe and America). And, contrary to Clive's assurances, only in a couple of instances the flights were freebies.

No matter how many times you have endured a twenty-four-hour flight, it is impossible to get used to. Especially so if the flight is a non-smoking one and you are a heavy smoker. A non-smoking long-haul flight for a smoker is like a non-urinating long-haul flight for a drinker. In any case, after the first ten hours you turn into a flying vegetable, almost inseparable from your seat with all its basic life-support systems. You can't read, you can't sleep, you can't think straight. To say nothing of writing . . . The only thing you can still do is watch the movies without understanding a single word.

After many long-haul flights you inevitably learn some little tricks that help you to make your journey if not pleasurable then at least endurable. I make sure I wear a shirt with a capacious breast pocket, where I can put a pen (to fill in landing forms), a boarding pass, mints and cigarettes (if the flight is a smoking one of course). I know exactly how to stretch my legs without inconveniencing those who sit next to me and always try to get myself an aisle seat not to disturb my neighbours when going to the loo.

Once in America I came across a book with an intriguing title: *Guerrilla Book of Airline Travel* (or something like this). It was full of advice on different things you can do to beat the boredom of a long-haul flight, from how to irritate a stewardess to how to make love on the plane.

I am sure the author has never been on a London to Melbourne flight.

After ten or twelve hours of non-stop flying, the plane lands for refuelling at some sterile oriental airport, be it Bangkok,

Hong Kong or Singapore, half-way to (or from) Australia. The cabin crew gets changed: they are not allowed to fly for more than ten hours in a row, only the passengers are. You smoke five cigarettes in succession, stumble through endless duty-free shops and gape sleepily at the miniature local women looking mysterious and amazingly sexy with their slanting eyes and compact skittles-like legs.

Asian women remind me of a girl I knew when I was eighteen. They also remind me of my very first flight. These two happen to be connected.

She was Korean (there were many Koreans in the Soviet Union living mainly in Kazakhstan and Eastern Siberia), and we met in Kiev where I was spending a week with my relatives, having successfully passed my university entrance exams. She was a cleaner at their flat (in England she would be called 'a woman who does'), and I couldn't tear my gaze from her slim curvaceous figure dressed in a flimsy and baggy track-suit when she was bending down to wash the floor. She was my age but much more mature.

On my last day in Kiev, having summoned all my courage, I suggested a date and took her to the Moscow Hotel restaurant. I felt wonderfully tall (she was diminutive) and adult in her company – a real man on the threshold of an exciting university life and no longer a schoolboy. We spent the rest of the night on a park bench kissing and hugging one another with the passion and energy that only eighteen-year-olds are capable of.

That night on the bench, her feminine smells and sweet mutterings kept me from sleeping back in Kharkov. My university life started with a month we freshers had to spend in the country helping collective farmers to pick potatoes. Meanwhile, my parents went away on holidays, and having hardly returned from the country, my libido greatly enhanced by a month of strenuous and healthy collective farm exercise which involved carrying sacks of potatoes on my uncomplaining back, I got myself the cheapest train ticket to Kiev and set off to see my sweetheart.

She didn't expect me. In fact, she was avoiding me. I had no money and had to spend two nights at the railway station. During the day, I aimlessly wandered the streets of Kiev and went to sleep in the cheapest movie theatres. On the third night, I was waiting for her near the hostel, where she lived, in Darnitsa, a new development area on the left bank of the Dnieper River.

She got out of a cab at 3 a.m. She was drunk. While I was freezing outside the hostel, exhausted and hungry as I was, she was having a good time with someone else. 'I didn't ask you to come,' she said dryly. I could feel the ground sliding away from under my feet. My whole romantic world built on dreams and poetry was shattered like a Wendy house, struck by a bomb.

Youthful traumas are always the most painful since your soul hasn't hardened up enough yet.

Having briefly contemplated throwing myself into the Dnieper River from the nearby bridge, I discarded this scenario as too pathetic. Also, it was cold as hell and the very thought of jumping into the dark hostile waters gave me the creeps. Instead, I decided to do something no less risky – take a plane back to Kharkov. I had never flown before.

Here I have to explain that Aeroflot then was as unreliable as it is now. Maybe even more so. The only difference was that plane crashes were never reported. Under socialism accidents were impossible – that was the impression the all-permeating Soviet censorship was trying to create.

When official information sources are lying or unreliable, rumours come in their stead. We all knew that planes did crash, and one day many residents of Kharkov were able to see a Moscow-Kharkov jet breaking in two above their heads and its fragments tumbling down onto the suburban Lesopark forest. This plane happened to carry Victor Chistyakov, a famous Moscow comedian who was to perform in Kharkov. His official obituaries in Moscow papers mentioned 'tragic death' and nothing else. So, in many people's minds flying Aeroflot was as safe as playing Russian roulette.

I flagged down some crazy night bus and went to Zhuliani airport. On the bus I got into talking with a young Kharkov tractor factory worker who was also on his way home. I told him my tragic love story, and he was moved almost to tears. 'Look, buddy,' he told me when we arrived at the airport, 'I've got a bottle of excellent moonshine that I wanted to take to Kharkov. Never mind: your grief needs to be cured. Let's drink it together right now!'

We went to the airport cloakroom, offered a shot to a sympathetic attendant and for that he allowed us to drink the opaque stinking liquid hiding behind piles of suitcases. He was even kind enough to supply us with a tainted cut-glass tumbler. It was five o'clock in the morning. I hadn't slept for three nights and had had almost nothing to eat. The home-brew was strong as hell. We finished the bottle and my insides were burning as if I had just swallowed a red-hot frying pan. I also had double vision – for the first and the last time in my whole life. My brain was working properly, and yet, when a yawning militiaman came up to examine my papers, I honestly asked him: 'To whom should I show my passport?'

The plane was small and its wings were patched like a pair of old worn-out socks. I felt sick the moment I stepped on board and kept throwing up throughout the whole bumpy flight. Luckily, it lasted only one hour, most of which I spent in the toilet. When we landed, I felt as if I had been disembowelled, with all my intestines taken out to dry, turned inside out and then shoved back into my stomach in total disarray.

This experience was enough to put me off flying for the next five years or so. I didn't mind being grounded. I was a train buff, after all . . .

Certainly, when an interpreter and then a journalist in Moscow, I had my fair bit of Aeroflot flights with their traditional cold and anorexic chicken and tepid mineral water in an undisposable plastic glass, carrying imprints of previous users' teeth. I would routinely board a plane in Moscow and fly for ten hours non-stop, with my knees stuck in the back of the seat in front and someone else's sharp knees stuck into my back from behind ('Prop my back and I'll prop yours' could be Aeroflot's official logo), only to disembark in precisely the same country, in an almost identical city somewhere in the Soviet Far East, with exactly the same buildings; the same newspapers, full of the same inflated lies; the same food queues; the same downtrodden people with bleak expressionless faces. It was mind-boggling.

Speaking about logos, Aeroflot is probably the only airline that never needed one. Its name used to speak (or rather to scream with awe) for itself. As the Soviet Union's only airline it had no competitors, but nevertheless had a logo. 'Fly Planes' it ran laconically. Had it not been for this logo, the poor Soviet citizens would have probably flown cucumbers, kettles or fountain pens (this would have certainly been much safer). But after the April, 1993 incident, when the captain of a Hong Kong-bound Aeroflot airbus left his fifteen-year-old son and twelve-year-old daughter to pilot the plane (the kids quickly sent the jet into a nose-dive and it crashed killing everyone on board) while he chatted up some female passengers in the saloon, Aeroflot could do with a new one: 'Fly Aeroflot – the world's first DIY airline!'

Or it could borrow the Air Mauritius logo that used to be prominently displayed on a billboard on the way to Melbourne International airport – 'Go Straight to Heaven'.

A Qantas frequent-flyer card-holder, I boast of the world's largest collection of Qantas grey and blue economy-class socks, only occasionally interspersed with the bright spots of white business-class socks of Air New Zealand which make you look like a turn-of-the-century Odessa gangster.

I like Qantas and not only because its planes have never crashed (fingers crossed). It is also the world's only airline where they call you 'mate' rather than 'sir', and a hostess offering you a can of beer is likely to ask: 'Do you need a glass?' In their safety instructions they kindly remind you to extinguish your cigarette before putting on your oxygen mask. It would be interesting to see what happens to someone who tries to disobey (which is impossible simply because all Qantas flights are non-smoking these days).

Qantas cabin crews have nice open smiles. Having flown lots of different airlines, I've had my economy-class share of punctilious and conventional British Airways smiles which looked rather like curved stiff upper lips. I've tasted broad, but empty, PanAm grins. I've caught soft and cold as jellyfishes smiles of Lufthansa hostesses. None of them looked as genuine and spontaneous as Qantas ones.

Flying to and from Australia, one travels not just through space but also through time. On the flight from Los Angeles to Melbourne, say, you lose a whole day of your life. You leave LA at 10 p.m. on Thursday, fly non-stop for fourteen hours and land in Melbourne on Saturday morning. Friday goes down the drain, disappears in the dark time loophole never to be seen again (I don't mind, especially if it is Friday the 13th). And on the way back, you gain time and arrive in LA several hours before you left Melbourne!

It is like depositing one day of your life into a savings bank of time and reclaiming it later. An interest-free time loan . . .

I remember my flight from Adelaide to Kangaroo Island on board a Czechoslovakian-made Cessna 402 four-seater plane. Sitting next to the pilot in a tiny cabin I kept imagining myself in the role of West German youngster Matthias Rust, who landed his Cessna in Red Square in Moscow in 1987. Not that I particularly wanted to land in Red Square.

It was raining heavily. Streams of water were hitting the cabin from all sides, and at times it was not clear whether our Cessna was a two-engined plane floating in the sky above the sea or a little submarine submerged into that very sea under the grey rain-soaked sky. 'When landing on the water, you may be required to remove shoes,' I read in the safety instructions and quickly removed my shoes – just in case we were already in the water. What's the reason for taking off one's shoes after a sea landing? I was thinking. If you have to dive underwater, you wouldn't care about keeping your shoes dry, would you?

Finally the pilot began slowly pulling the joy-stick towards his chest as if trying to hug it, and the plane started landing. I looked down, and to my horror could not see either an airfield or even an airstrip. The waves were pounding the rocky coast of the quickly approaching island and breaking into heaps of bubbling foam. We were landing straight onto a dirt track. I closed my eyes getting ready for a crash, but the miniature plane was already bouncing along the ground splashing mud from under its wheels. It came to a stop straight in the middle of a huge, almost lake-sized, puddle.

I did get my shoes wet, after all.

I like airports, which always strike me as being part of an alienation zone, where you are not yet airborne, but no longer firmly on the ground either. You have one foot in the air, so to speak. Boris Pasternak once called a railway station 'a safe of my separations and re-unions'. I can say the same about airports. There's nothing like the sight of a loved person emerging from the Arrivals lounge with this peculiar I-have-just-arrived-and-don't-know-where-to-go expression on the face. The loved one becomes even dearer when lost or confused.

There's nothing sadder than watching this person disappearing behind the automatic alienation zone doors leading to a different continent, a different season, a different time zone. Or disappearing behind them myself. These doors separate autumn from spring and summer from winter. They separate day from night. Having negotiated so many frontiers, I still find it hard to cope with the Departures area turnstile – my Western life's saddest border.

Flying in itself is much easier. It is an unparalleled feeling, when my whole world is limited to a reclining chair, packaged food on plastic trays and 'No smoking' signs glimmering in the darkness of the cabin like a reproachful guiding beacon for an inveterate smoker like myself; when the captain is my only God and the smiling flight attendants my guardian angels; when on a big map on a video screen I can see our plane slowly – almost reluctantly – crossing the globe.

'Please fasten your belts. We are flying through a slight turbulence area.' Unlike on the ground, turbulences in the air are always slight. No wonder Gods chose to live up there.

I am flying above continents, seas, deserts and snow-capped mountains and the earth looks so placid and quiet from the skies. It is hard to believe that down there people are arguing, suffering and murdering each other. Perhaps, if the world's population could be accommodated in one vast aeroplane, there would be an end to poverty and wars.

Only where would we all fly to?

Such Utopian thoughts invariably flash through my jet-lagged brain on the plane from London to Melbourne. One is bound to start daydreaming at some point during this enormously long flight. This is how Clive James describes his hallucinations on the way from London to Australia in his *Postcard from Sydney*: 'Queues for the loo stretched down every aisle. It was somewhere between Bombay and Perth that the vision hit me. Our enormous aircraft, the apotheosis of modern technology, was filling up with gunk! Converted into chemical inertia by the cobalt-blue reagent in the flushing water, the waste products of our skyborne community were gradually taking over the plane!'

My *Dictionary of Dreams* stays mum about the meaning of this particular vision.

After dozens of flights between Europe and Australia I have gained one important piece of knowledge: our planet which seemed so incredibly huge from the cage of the Soviet Union is in reality very small indeed. Or maybe it is my new Freedom of movement that makes the world look smaller? I wish I knew . . .

And yet, with all the attractions of flying, I still prefer trains. And although it is somehow possible to have a parcel biked from Melbourne to London (and back), you can't take a train from London, Euston, to Melbourne, Spencer Street.

What a pity!

12

Sydney Diary

*I*n my memories and dreams I often return to Sydney, where we spent our first Australian month. I kept a diary during that month, and now I am leafing through its pages, covered with my hasty scribbles, often unintelligible even to myself.

'Director of First Impressions' was written on a business card I once saw at a real-estate office. This is what every writer should aspire to be. First impressions are important in helping you to mould the image of a place which will remain with you for a long time. The shock and fascination, joy and grief of those first days in the strange country which had harboured us come back to me from the pages of the diary I kept between May and June 1990.

DAY ONE
The day of arrival. The Qantas flight was wonderful. The saloon looked and smelled like a first-class restaurant. It was our first experience of a Western airline. For several hours we were flying over the Soviet Union, and I couldn't help thinking of an emergency landing (in London I had nightmarish dreams of such a landing on the way to Australia which, for us as defectors, would mean certain arrest, prison and maybe even death).

When the plane entered Australian airspace, nothing but wild red desert could be seen for more than five hours: red sands and barren brown mountains stretched to the horizon – a mesmerising view. The famous Ayer's Rock was a huge basalt stone visible even at this height. It resembled a nipple pointing up at the plane. Is this really our new mother country? I kept asking myself.

Shortly before the scheduled landing in Sydney, the timidly smiling hostesses started spraying the interior of our Boeing with aerosols. Funny. And a bit frightening. This is the closest one can come to a flight to a different planet. What European viruses were they trying to kill? Was it only rabies, or something else as well? Only time will show . . .

As soon as we stepped down onto the tarmac, I started looking, subconsciously, for snakes and spiders under my feet and was very surprised there were none. 'You must be very careful!' Clive James said in his valediction. 'There are lots of creeping and biting creatures round there . . .' On the plane I was reading his *Unreliable Memoirs* which he had presented to me in London. Indeed, a big chunk of the first chapter is devoted to descriptions of his childhood fights with snakes and spiders. But in the fifty years which have lapsed since, Australia must have changed, whereas in Clive's imagination he must still be living in old Kogarah.

To my pleasant surprise, we were met by a number of people: a representative of the Commonwealth Bank with his wife holding a huge toy koala, several journalists (or 'journos' as they are called in Australia), and a Channel Nine TV crew who were filming us emerging from the Arrivals gates (Mitya was pushing the luggage trolley of course). They tried to shoo everyone else away from blocking their cameras.

First impressions of Sydney were depressing. It was raining. We saw clumsy mud-brick huts with peeling stucco and tiled roofs on the way from the airport. They looked like badly kept beehives. Quite a shock after London. 'Where are we?' Natasha kept asking. I had an impression that I was some-where in Kislovodsk, a provincial spa resort in the south of Russia.

The trees on the roadside were alien – crooked, wet and scrubby, as if they had just been taken out of the drier of a huge washing machine.

DAY TWO

The tennis players are jumping day and night beyond the windows of our temporary flat overlooking the wet and slippery White City tennis courts. We are all suffering from jet lag, and also from some other lag which has no name. It's not nostalgia, but something heavy and unpleasant – indeed like heartburn. Or rather a burning soul. Igor Pomerantsev was probably right. Only isn't it a bit too soon?

Friends took us out to see the city. The harbour was beautiful, but the Opera House looks better on postcards than in reality. It's like an eyesore: wherever you look, it's there. At last I saw the Coat Hanger. I learnt this Australian slang for the Sydney Harbour Bridge in Moscow many years ago, being dead sure that I would never see the bridge with my own eyes. And here I am. That was probably the first moment when I began to realise that I was indeed in Australia.

The ocean is tremendous. I have never seen open ocean before. Seas are different. Here you can see the real power of wild nature. And the colour – aquamarine. Now I know exactly what it means. The surfers on the waves look like twisted periscopes of unidentified submarines.

The prostitutes in Kings Cross stood almost naked in the rain. What a miserable sight! It is sometimes difficult to say whether they are male or female, but irrespective of gender, they look pitiful.

Had a visit from Australia's top literary agent (that was how he introduced himself). He burst into the flat with his secretary and immediately offered to find me a job on the condition that I would pay him one fourth of my salary as his commission. 'As far as I know, we don't have children between us,' I told him. Twenty-five per cent of an income is the size of alimony in the former Soviet Union. Besides, I have already got a couple of alimony-free job offers.

DAY THREE

The tennis players are driving me mad. This must be some enigmatic symbol of Australian life. But what exactly they symbolise escapes me so far.

DAY FOUR

The *Sydney Morning Herald* office where one of the job offers came from. Very similar to *The Guardian* in spirit, in computers and in people. I bumped into a couple of journalists who looked like twins to my *Guardian* friends.

New Era Bookshop. It made me feel so much better: the selection of Russian books is unbelievable. It's like being at the Beriozka hard-currency bookshop for foreigners in Moscow (by the way, it's just round the corner from the Australian embassy), only here I have the right to buy anything. My first big purchase in Australia: a facsimile edition of Dahl's Russian-Russian dictionary in four volumes – my age-long dream. At least one dream has come true.

The city itself looks drab and unimpressive. The skyscrapers are ugly, pretentious and out-of-place. Lots of porno shops. The foodstores are plentiful, probably even more so than in London, but something is still missing. The cardboard boxes of food are piled on top of the counters, and the items on sale are in disarray. Sainsbury's and Marks & Spencer's in Britain have less choice, but look more attractive. This is probably what is meant by general culture, or rather by the lack of it.

A well-known radio journalist died. His photos were displayed at the news stands all over Sydney. A friend of mine from the *Sydney Morning Herald* who knew him very well patted the portrait gently when we were passing by, and said: 'Poor bugger!' His eyes grew red and he dropped a tear. This is a good sign if people in Australia can still cry and laugh spontaneously without trying to contain their emotions like they often do in England.

The evenings are long and dreary. But the thing that is literally killing us is humidity. In short intervals between showers the air is soaked with moisture and full of sickeningly sweet suffocating miasmas. One can almost eat the air, like a stiffening jelly. And the smell is similar to that of a decomposing corpse.

Last night I discovered a huge black cockroach in the bathroom of our flat. It was actually discovered by Natasha whose piercing shriek made me rush into the bathroom. I've never seen an insect of this size before. It probably felt well in this climate and was stirring its long antennae contentedly. For us this cockroach became a symbol of Sydney weather. Obviously, had we come from India or Thailand, we would have probably found Sydney not humid enough. But being northerners, used to the ravishingly clean and crisp air of Russian winters, we are finding it physically hard to adjust. Well, everything is relative, isn't it?

I wonder whether this cockroach is marsupial? Our first touch of Australian fauna, so to speak . . .

DAY FIVE

Wrote my first piece for the *Sydney Morning Herald* sitting on the balcony of our flat, to the accompaniment of the *pok . . . pok . . .* sound of tennis rackets. This sound, unexpectedly but logically, became a sort of a refrain for the whole piece which was about Australia and the Soviet Union, about our feelings and immediate concerns, about the tennis players, freedom and the New Era Bookshop:

Pok . . . Pok . . .

Where am I? The tennis players, clad in white, are jumping behind the windows of my Sydney flat. They are playing day and night. Oblivious of everything, they do not notice me standing on the balcony with the smoking cigarette in my hand.

My mind tells me that I am in Australia, but I refuse to believe.

Pok . . . Pok . . .

To write it was easy, since the words were coming directly from my soul, I simply had to put them down on paper.

It rained all day, but nevertheless we went for a walk through the city. Downtown Sydney reminds me of Manhattan, though I have never been to New York. Chinatown was full of steady and persistent foreign smells. In fact, Sydney smells differently from all the places I've visited before. There's something sweet and tropical in the air. The light is also distinctive: brighter and more transparent than in Europe. And the clouds seem to be much higher in the sky, which makes you feel somewhat uneasy.

DAY SIX

Delivered my first piece to the *Sydney Morning Herald*. A woman journalist was almost crying after she read it. Another proof of my point on Australian sentimentality.

A strange man greeted me in the street: 'Hello, Vitali.'

'I don't know you,' I said.

'But I know you. I've seen you on TV. Good luck and welcome to Australia!'

Now it was my turn to cry, but I am a European and I couldn't.

Met some Russians from the first wave of Russian emigration. They came here from China after the war and have never been to the Soviet Union. They were speaking an amazing, old-fashioned Russian, the language of Tolstoy and Turgenev, using lots of obsolete words. But it sounded like music to my ears.

It's interesting how a language can be frozen for so many years – just like a chicken in the freezer.

DAY EIGHT

My first piece appeared today on the front pages of the *Sydney Morning Herald* and its sister paper the *Melbourne Age*. In the *Herald*, it looks well but the headline they wrote is a disappointment: 'Weep, My Mother Russia!' I may well be sentimental, but not to such an extent! I cannot imagine something like 'Mother Russia' dropping from my lips. Or from my pen. It sounds like a hysterical wail, and I try not to whinge. At least not aloud.

The headline in the *Age* – 'From Russia to Australia: a journey of joy and grief' – is much more to the point. And the lay-out is more professional. Maybe the *Age* is just a better newspaper?

Met a recent Russian-Jewish emigrant. He already looks like a Westerner, and his face has the inexplicable touch of Freedom. 'Australia is not very good for spiritual growth,' he said. I feel that spiritual growth is something that largely depends on a person, rather than surroundings. But I may be wrong.

It's funny how in the papers here they call our European autumn 'Northern autumn'. This really makes you feel the distance.

Visited Sydney fish market. Riot of colours and smells. Hard to believe that the sea can harbour so many weird and colourful creatures. Couldn't help remembering the famous Privoz market in Odessa, also a seaside city, which now hasn't got a single fish on sale. The totalitarian system, as it turns out, is capable not only of killing people, but of decimating fish as well. It was a revelation for me to learn at the market that female crabs are kept separately from the males. Are they protecting he-crabs from she-crabs or vice versa, I wonder?

DAY NINE

The *Age* published a piece 'An Open Letter to the Man Of Glasnost' by its veteran political columnist Peter Cole-Adams. It was triggered by my '*Pok . . . Pok . . .*' article.

> Dear Vitali Vitaliev,
> Welcome and thanks. Your piece is as fine as anything I have read in several long months, and, as I shall explain, its timing is exquisite [it started, and continued on a slightly different note]: But I worry, Vitali, I worry. What will you make of us a year from now? Will the land of smiles and eternal tennis have proved a mirage validating that nursery nightmare of sharks and crocodiles? When the honeymoon ends and you have discovered us for what we are, will you be able to forgive? What, in particular, will you think of Australian attitudes to people like you?

He then dwelt upon some burning political and economic issues of Australia. And in the end – again: 'Enjoy, Vitali. And if that becomes impossible, try to forgive. In either event, keep writing.'

It looked as if Peter Cole-Adams was trying to warn me against something. And what's this whole 'forgive us' thing about? At the moment I feel nothing but gratitude towards

Australia. This is the second vague warning (the first one was from Igor Pomerantsev in London) that I have received in the last couple of weeks. There must be something behind them, but what exactly? I wish I knew.

Was interviewed on SBS, a state-run 'ethnic' TV channel, for *Face the Press*. Competent presenter. Good questions. SBS seems to stand miles apart from the rest of Aussie TV where they have 'It's the taste of Australia!!!' or some other noisy and primitive commercial every five minutes. Watching a feature film becomes like a Chinese water torture – waiting for 'It's the taste of Australia!!!' to fall upon my poor head from the TV screen.

DAY TEN

My '*Pok . . . Pok . . .*' piece seems to have struck a chord. Letters are flowing in to the *Sydney Morning Herald*. People keep approaching me in the streets asking whether it was I who wrote that article (it was illustrated by several photos). It is very flattering of course, but the most reassuring thing is that the readers' letters are very similar to the ones I used to get as a journalist in Russia: open, emotional and sincere. This gives me some hope that I shall be able to adjust to Australian life after a while.

In Paddington, where we are living, there was a hostage crisis. A bloke quarrelled with his girlfriend, and out of despair attacked a young policeman, taking him hostage. The whole area was cordoned off by the mounted police. The crisis was resolved quickly, but it left an unpleasant aftertaste: it didn't look Australian to me. American, maybe, but not Australian . . .

DAY ELEVEN

Was interviewed by *Good Morning, Australia!*. Similar to *Good Morning, Britain!* or *Good Morning, Moscow!*.

Lunch at ex-servicemen's club. Very informal and different from the plush Pall Mall clubs in London. No need to wear a tie. Fisherman's basket on the menu turned out to be a real basket with heaps of seafood in it.

Anti-kangaroo bars on the bumpers of some of the cars

evoke wildlife scenes in the outback. I must go there myself
one day.

Warm and sunny day. Men sporting wide-brimmed hats
in the streets. The hats immediately make them look very
Australian in my eyes.

DAY FOURTEEN

Went to Woy Woy (what a name!) with friends. Had lunch in
a restaurant on the bank of a river. Pelicans water-landed in
front of us, cutting the river's surface like gliders. This must
be Australia, after all!

In the evening went to see a family of Jewish emigrants
from the Soviet Union who have lived here for ten years.
Their children speak Russian with a heavy accent. Isn't that
terrifying? Will Mitya speak like that in a couple of years?

At some point in the evening, together with our hosts'
kids, he went out to chase a brightly painted musical ice-
cream van circling around the block and playing some quiet
melody, like a music box on wheels. A children's fairy-tale
coming to life.

Sometimes, mixing with Russian emigrants, I start feeling
even more rootless than I already am. Just to imagine that I
am an emigrant myself. What a chilling word – emigrant.

DAY SIXTEEN

Got an official job offer from Fairfax Newspapers incorpo-
rating the *Sydney Morning Herald* and the *Age*. I am supposed
to write for both. They are the country's biggest newspapers.
The press in Australia is organised very much along American
lines: the highest-circulated newspapers are local by definition,
although some of them (like the ones from the Fairfax stable)
are read nationwide. There is only one national newspaper –
The Australian – but it is pretty small compared to either the
Age or the *Sydney Morning Herald*.

If I understand my contract correctly, I am free to choose
where to live – in Sydney or in Melbourne. The salary sounds
like a real fortune. It will be split between the two newspapers.
I am supposed to start in about a month and a half, after
our return from Britain where I still have to finish my BBC

documentary. Meanwhile, I wrote another piece – this time on Yeltsin – for my future employers. Everything seems to be working out nicely, although we still find it hard to cope with Sydney and its provincial suffocating atmosphere. Sometimes it feels as if after many years in Moscow I have come back to live in Kharkov. Natasha often cries of an evening . . .

DAY SEVENTEEN

On the seventh floor of the John Fairfax building there's a small shop run by Bob Dawson, an amiable middle-aged man with friendly wrinkles on his sun-tanned Australian face. Here you can buy sweets and cigarettes, have a haircut, have your photos printed and your dry cleaning done – all without leaving the building. A Jack-of-all-trades. 'I like to serve people,' Bob said cutting my hair.

Had a wonderful meeting with Barry. He works at the National Gallery of New South Wales as a curator. Ten years ago he was in Russia with the exhibition of Australian art and I was his interpreter. He hasn't changed much, only his red beard has got a touch of grey. He gave me a photo of the two of us in Leningrad ten years ago. We are standing on the snow in fur hats. 'I have been thinking of you all these years,' he said.

DAY EIGHTEEN

Got our Medicare cards. They seem to have a very comprehensive system of health care in Australia. I am unable to say whether it's efficient or not as yet.

Unexpectedly, received a letter from my best friend Sasha, a fellow train buff. We were inseparable as children and teenagers. He now lives in Czechoslovakia with Dana, his Slovakian wife.

. . . I think I understand what emotions are overfilling you now: a curious mixture of hopes, doubts and apprehensions. Sometimes I feel that I experience this gamut of emotions together with you and I think you have made the right decision. You must have your fate firmly in your own hands. You must do everything for your son to grow up a free man, who knows his own value and relies only on his own strength. For you and Natasha tarnished by your Soviet past it is going to be much more difficult . . . You are very far away now, but I am sure we'll see each other many times more. Let's strive for that as really free people. To stay in Russia, to carry on living like slaves, to be under constant KGB scrutiny was no longer possible for you. Also, you couldn't leave your son as a hostage there . . . Good luck to you, you will need it, old chap! Be courageous and keep your chin up!

Good old Sasha . . .

DAY NINETEEN

Got our Australian Certificates of Identification (travel documents) with an emu and a kangaroo on the cover. Mitya now has his own 'passport'. He is very excited about it (in the Soviet Union you only get a passport at sixteen).

Saw some newly arrived and constantly quarrelling Soviet emigrants at the Foreign Affairs Department. They must have been so embittered in their previous lives that they find it hard to calm down even now.

In ten days we'll have to go to Britain for a couple of weeks, courtesy of the BBC. On the way back we decided to visit my friend Martin Walker, now the *Guardian* bureau chief in Washington, DC. It doesn't make much of a difference money-wise to fly back via America, and I haven't seen Martin for a long time. Not to mention the fact that none of us has been to America before.

With our brand-new CIDs I went to the American consulate to get the visas. There was a queue of about three hundred people there – the first queue I saw in Australia. Eventually, when I approached the counter, they gave me a form with lots of stupid questions to fill: complexion, height, colour of eyes and skin. In the last space I wrote 'pink'. There was also a space for 'special identification marks'. I wrote 'none'.

The clerk at the stand was very surprised: 'Haven't you even got a small scar or anything?'

'No,' I said. She was watching me in disbelief as if I were an ET.

'So you have never been operated upon?'

'Nope!' (I wanted to add: if you don't count a KGB operation, but thought better of it). She shrugged her shoulders, rather reluctantly took the forms and the CIDs and told me dryly to come and collect them tomorrow. I have a bad premonition. If I only had a scar!

DAY TWENTY-ONE

They denied us American visas! After standing in the queue for the second time, instead of a visa I received a crumpled piece of paper saying something to the effect that the US government has the grounds to treat me and my family as 'intended migrants' (what on earth can that mean?). To reconsider our case, they require confirmation of our residency, bank statements, a letter from my employer and a number of other things. And this is America, the stronghold of Freedom! At least they don't ask for proof of my 'nationality', and whether I have relatives abroad, otherwise the parallel with the Soviet Union would be complete. Well, what can I say? Freedom is a relative concept, it really is. A friend from the *Sydney Morning Herald* says that this is the fault of the American Congress being paranoid about illegal migrants. I don't actually care whose fault this is. After all, what can one expect from the country which has recently introduced quotas for the immigration of Soviet Jews? As soon as the Iron Curtain was lifted a wee bit in the Soviet Union, the Americans (as well as many other Western countries) lowered it from their side of the fence. I was told in Moscow that the embassy form for the people going to France includes the question: 'Are you going to beg while in France?' As if anyone would tell them, even if he was.

There seems to be only one Western country with a more or less humane immigration policy left – Australia (although it is rather 'Southern' than Western). I have just learnt of the decision of the Australian government to grant residency to 20,000 students from mainland China, the ones who took part in the Tiananmen Square uprising. Whatever the critics may say, this is a humane decision. And a noble one. Prime Minister Bob Hawke was shown on TV crying on the shoulder of a Chinese student. He often cries in public. In Russia we would say that he has his eyes on a wet spot. But I think that it is much better to have an ever-crying prime minister than an ever-grinning president.

DAY TWENTY-FIVE

Just returned from Melbourne where we spent three days at the invitation of the *Age*. We all liked the city at first sight. It was a feast for our eyes to see the yellow leaves tumbling down from the familiar European trees. It was not humid, and we suddenly saw the whole palette of autumn colours in the streets, something that you won't find in Sydney where most of the trees are evergreen. Bookshops were open until late and had a much better selection than in Sydney. The centre looked graceful and convivial. I especially liked the trams: they made a strangely soothing impression on me.

In short, we decided to move to Melbourne after we come back from overseas. Today I announced this decision to the editor of the *Sydney Morning Herald*, much to his consternation. Yes, the choice was there, yet, in his words, it was the first time when Melbourne was preferred to Sydney. My first encounter with the age-long Melbourne-Sydney rivalry about which I have heard a lot. I can only hope it stops when the interests of the two sister papers are at stake ('It is not as easy as you think,' a *Sydney Morning Herald* colleague told me. I wonder what he meant . . .).

Piles of friendly readers' letters were waiting for me at the office. As we said in Russia, it's better to have a hundred friends than a hundred roubles. I think this stands true with Australian dollars too.

We are gradually adjusting to Australia. Natasha, who was desperate in the beginning, is now feeling much better. We've discovered that the main asset of the country is its openness, lack of pretence and genuine friendliness of the people. The land of smiles indeed . . . As to the laid-back attitude to life . . . Well, nobody is perfect . . .

DAY TWENTY-EIGHT

Today we are leaving for England and America for a month. Yes, the American visas have come through eventually, after my new employers wrote a letter to the consul. So we are going to get a taste of our new freedom of movement. The Americans may not worry: we are not going to stay there. We'll be coming back to Australia, only to Melbourne, not Sydney.

Got into talking with a cab-driver who was taking me to the office this morning. He was a Russian-Jewish emigrant from Odessa. 'I keep telling myself how right I was to come here, though it was pretty hard for the first two or three years,' he was saying. 'You must realise that now you are a free person, and you may say and write whatever you want.' How wise these taxi-drivers are! That probably goes with the profession. It is pretty hard to believe that I am a free person. Who said that the door to Freedom opens inside your soul – not outside? Freedom does not dawn on you overnight. You don't fall asleep a slave and wake up a free person. It takes a lot of time. To remember Chekhov, one must squeeze a slave out of oneself drop by drop.

Drop by drop – that's how it happens . . . After five months in England and one month in Australia, I feel I have already managed to shed a couple.

Our journey continues. Last visit to the bathroom before we go. Who is that tired grey-haired man in the mirror? Oh, my God, it must be me . . .

13

A Shock to the System

More than a hundred years ago the steamship *Great Britain* sailed from Liverpool to Melbourne bringing early settlers to Victoria. Some of them were hoping to find gold, others were looking for a new life. Victoria – what a powerful name! There is so much hope in it. The journey took several months; babies were born, some of the older passengers died and had to be buried at sea, love affairs sparked off, and killjoys were writing angry letters to the captain:

> Sir,
> May I draw your attention to the fact that some young couples are getting too intimate while walking on the upper deck. This shameful practice must be contained at all costs and I should be grateful to you for your assistance . . .

A weekly newspaper – *The 'Great Britain' Times* – was published on board. Details of dinner dress-code were announced daily. *Great Britain* was like a floating microcosm of prosaic nineteenth-century life that had rebelled against this very prose of existence and set out on a long and difficult trip to Australia in search of poetry and adventures.

To the Editor of the *G.B. Times*
Medical Report
Sir,

    I am sorry I have to report since my last note, the very sudden death of Charles Wortman, aged 6 years; through a fall from the upper deck into the engine room. The health of the ship is good. Capt. Gray has so far recovered as to be on deck for a short time daily. This morning Mrs George Shaw Wycherley, intermediate passenger, gave birth to a daughter – both doing well.

          A. Alexander
1st December, 1865

Standing on the embankment near Melbourne Port and staring intently at the flat and empty surface of the ocean, I could almost discern the outlines of the *Great Britain*'s funnels on the hazy horizon. Who is she carrying this time? I could almost see myself standing on her deck dressed in a dinner jacket and with a Russian fur cap on my head.

I was looking into my own eyes from the distance . . .

Curiously, Melbourne's windswept beaches with miles of sand and patches of wild grass reminded me of Odessa, the city port on the Black Sea, the home town of many of my favourite Russian writers. Emerald lawns, familiar trees and gracious Victorian buildings with sun-beaten facades and ornate little balconies overlooking the ocean, and the trams, these moving wrinkles on the city's open Australian face – all these made Melbourne look homely and almost European.

And, of course, the Queen Victoria market, one of the last surviving great markets of the world, with the hub-bub of bargaining voices and cheerful faces of different skin colours and eye shapes, all merging into a bright palette of Melbourne life.

As a child I often dreamt of living in a big city port near the ocean. My native Kharkov was deep inland, it didn't even have a decent river.

It's common knowledge that moving into a new flat is equal to an earthquake. If so, moving into an unfurnished flat and having no furniture to put into it can be compared to a small thermo-nuclear explosion. In a striking contrast to our lavishly decorated Prince Charles's flat in London, our first rented flat in Melbourne was unfurnished. 'A house is built for the sake of the emptiness in it,' says an old Chinese proverb. This might be true, but we didn't feel like starting our new life in Australia in an empty flat, so buying furniture became our first priority.

Never before had I realised how many little but indispensable objects inhabit our households, from brooms, dustbins and window curtains to saucepans, ashtrays and chandeliers (if you can afford them of course). To get any of these in the Soviet Union was an ordeal, a mixture of a thriller, a horror story and an annual fiscal report all in one volume.

My relations with furniture in Russia, long before my Tasmanian encounter with Hitler's couch, were complicated enough to resemble courting an arrogant and stupid lady who is in love with someone else. I remember how for two years I had been trying to buy an armchair. Not a luxury one, so deep and soft that it negatively affected the sitter's sense of self-esteem, but just an ordinary armchair, any armchair at all, to recline in after a busy day: to watch our heroic tractor drivers heroically harvesting the unseen crop 'for our Motherland's granaries' on the TV screen and try not to think of where all these crops and harvests disappear to after being shown on television (no one had ever seen these mysterious granaries overflowing with grain in real life).

To tell you the truth, I saw several armchairs (about a dozen altogether) in Moscow furniture shops. But no matter how many roubles I had, I could not buy them. They could only be acquired by hard currency or by special coupons, given to shock workers (exemplary workers) at Moscow factories. Roubles were not a hard currency, in fact they were almost as soft as the armchairs in question. As for the shock workers whose toil-hardened behinds were worthy of resting in armchairs, I couldn't qualify as one of them, although I was in the state of continuous shock caused by the Soviet reality.

Being a shocked journalist – as opposed to a shock worker – was not good enough to sit in an armchair.

At last in Australia, with our mouths agape, we were scouring Melbourne furniture shops where everything, and I mean it: everything, was on offer. Look at these sofas – soft, enticing and pink as a frightened nymph's thigh. Look at the tables – long as Chile, sturdy as stallions and stable as the International Monetary Fund. Look at the chairs standing at attention like cadets at a military parade.

And beds . . . Oh, those beds, where we are born, where we love and die (pace Guy de Maupassant). Not only birth and love but even death would look attractive on their wavy spring mattresses. The salesman at one of the bed shops was describing the merits of king-size beds as opposed to queen-size ones, with such a zeal and with so many esoteric details that I was dead sure he had a PhD in applied bedology. By the way, formerly I had been inclined to think that only hamburgers and cigarettes could be king-size. How ignorant I was!

But the best thing about this furniture heaven was that you could buy everything not for some mythical 'hard currency', but for good old Australian dollars, provided you had enough of them.

Old habits die hard. Looking at all this abundance, my wife kept pestering me with one troubled question: 'Are you sure that they won't run out of stock and we'll be able to come back tomorrow and buy something?'

'Natasha,' I answered, condescendingly and gravely, as if I were telling off an obnoxious child. 'Natasha,' I repeated, 'just calm down and trust me. Don't you understand that this is capitalism, the market economy, if you wish? Stock is regulated by demand, you see? If there's demand – there's a bed, a table or . . . or' (here I paused to make my point ever so solid) 'an airplane. No worries, as they say in Australia.'

I was very proud of my own eloquence.

'Yes, I know all about market economy,' my wife answered meekly. 'I know that in principle there can be no shortages, but I am still worried, I can't help it . . .'

I hurried to dismiss Natasha's doubts as one of many sad aftermaths of our Spartan Soviet existence.

Next morning we were the first customers to enter a big furniture shop in one of the Melbourne suburbs. Too much choice is as puzzling as no choice at all, so it took us several hours to choose a beautiful dining table to be used as a desk in my new study. We also selected some chairs to match the table. It was not easy with so many things to select from. We happily approached the sales counter and gave our list to the assistant, who scrutinised it thoroughly and somewhat suspiciously as if it was his own bank statement with negative balance. Then he started playing with his computer.

'You see, electronics everywhere,' I whispered to my wife in fascination.

The man behind the counter was looking at his computer screen with utter disbelief as if he suddenly saw a Russian four-letter word on it.

'Sorry, folks,' he said. 'We don't have the tables you want.'

Since we kept staring at him and didn't react, he decided to make himself clear. 'Finished,' he repeated slowly, as if expecting us to be reading his lips. 'Out – of – stock!'

For me it would have been less of a shock to get into Lenin's mausoleum in Red Square after hours of queuing only to discover that Lenin's mummy had been stolen.

'Can't we have the one which is on display?' I mumbled.

'Yes, you can, but it is no good. Very, very wobbly.'

My wife was watching me triumphantly.

'If they have no tables,' she intervened dryly, 'then there's no reason to buy chairs. They were supposed to match each other, weren't they?'

'No worries, ma'am,' the salesman commented. 'We haven't got the chairs either.'

'So what happened to your favourite market economy?' Natasha asked sardonically when we left the shop. 'They seem to have their own ups and downs. And shortages too.'

14

Fame is a Widow

'*I*t is shameful to be famous,' wrote Boris Pasternak. It was only after my first year in Melbourne that I was able to understand the full meaning of these words. I was largely unprepared for the immediate success of my *Age* column. Since the publication of my very first '*Pok . . . Pok . . .*' piece hundreds and thousands of readers' letters had started flowing into the *Age* offices in Spencer Street. It looked as if I had suddenly won hundreds of new friends: 'Welcome to Australia, Mr Vitaliev, congratulations on your writing and if you are ever in Canberra allow me to buy you a drink . . .' '. . . If you are ever at Torquay, which is just south of Geelong, this household will be honoured to have you as a guest . . .' No wonder I was swept off my feet by my sudden fame. Who wouldn't be?

I couldn't physically reply to all my correspondents and would answer the letters collectively, through the paper, every so often. I kept them in a special tarpaulin sack at home. The sack was getting fatter and fatter and was soon blocking the doorway of my office. I couldn't make myself throw the letters out. Apart from letters, readers were sending me flowers, parcels with small souvenirs and food: sweets, pastries, packets of tea, bread and salt in an envelope (in Russia there's a tradition where guests are welcomed with bread and salt) and tins of Vegemite – all of which mostly came from old ladies who, for some reason, were sure that I was permanently hungry. One morning I was stunned to receive (to the sheer amazement of the whole editorial department) a plastic crate with about twenty kilograms of fresh kangaroo meat in it. It came from a disgruntled owner of a 'small kangaroo-processing factory' (as he himself put it) in New South Wales. When I opened the crate, my first terrifying thought was that the pieces of flesh had come from a slaughtered human. The whole load was immediately sent to the RSPCA. The flow was interrupted only after I appealed to the readers from the pages of the *Age* to stop sending me food.

The geography of my mail was expanding too. As a local newspaper by definition, the *Age* was mostly distributed in Victoria and Tasmania, yet I was regularly getting letters from all other Australian states and territories and from overseas – Britain, United States, Germany, Spain. The real pride of my collection was a letter from Mexico, where, as it turned out, the *Age* was also read.

Not that I was not getting any hate mail. But hate letters were few and far between and all of them were anonymous. Since most of them contained Russian curses, I suspected they stemmed from recent Soviet migrants who were probably jealous of my success. Some of the rumours they were spreading about me would reach the *Age* from time to time. The prevailing one was that I was a thoroughly camouflaged KGB agent (who else could have mastered English to such an extent that he was able to write in it?) and that my columns were written not by me but by a Moscow-based team of specially trained KGB writers (some of these rumours had even reached Moscow and ricocheted to Melbourne from there).

It was probably these gossips that triggered a phone call from ASIO, one of the three Australian Secret Intelligence Services, to my *Age* office one morning. A polite male voice explained that they were investigating the KGB penetration of Melbourne's Russian community and suggested a meeting. And although I was warned by the Australian High Commission in London that I would be approached by the Australian Special Branch at some point ('just for a routine interview, you know . . .'), I was puzzled in the extreme. The memories of my KGB persecutors in Moscow were still too fresh. On the other hand, I thought that my new duties as an Australian resident didn't allow me to avoid such a meeting – another Soviet-induced brain aberration.

'Australian Secret Intelligence Office' – it sounded as paradoxical and bizarre as 'Soviet Free Market' or 'Czechoslovakian Navy'. We agreed to meet for lunch in one of the city's restaurants on the following day. Still in doubt, I popped into the editor's office and told him about the call.

'Call them back and cancel the meeting immediately,' said Mike Smith without looking up from the papers piled on his desk. 'Whether you want it or not, you are now a public figure, a celebrity. You don't want to be spotted by our competitors in the company of ASIO and give them a nice front page story, do you? Besides, you don't want them starting a file on you which they will have to do after a meeting. ASIO agents have a reputation of being lazy and incompetent, so it's best to avoid them.'

'What if they come to my house?' I asked.

'Don't let them into your flat! Throw them out!'

This was the first and last order I received from the editor in more than two years at the *Age*.

I dialled the number left by the morning caller, and cancelled our lunch appointment. He was not in the least surprised (he was probably used to such a reaction). This was my only communication with the Australian Secret Intelligence Service. There was still a big difference between ASIO and the KGB: the former was much easier to get rid of.

I could understand why Mike Smith's first concern was about the competitors. At the time the *Age* had three rival daily newspapers in Melbourne and my new column which had attracted enormous readership and given the *Age* a circulation boost was a real thorn in their side. They never lost a chance to have a go at me. Luckily, all these digs were exercised in a classical tabloid fashion and actually added to my column's popularity.

The most common device the competitors used was to lampoon me as a permanently drunk uncouth Russian in a fur hat who downs his vodka and 'eats the *Age*' afterwards. Here's a relatively mild example of a 'Vitali is Not Vital' sort of an article:

> The *Age*'s little chunk of literary glasnost, that writer's block off the Berlin Wall, Vitali Vitaliev, has certainly kicked on since he parted the Iron Curtain and headed west.
>
> As much as he tries to encourage through his writings the view that he is simply an innocent abroad, goggle-eyed and gobsmacked by the wonders of Melbournian capitalism, Vitaliev, in private business life, is learning fast.
>
> We were able to confirm this week that like Graham Kennedy, Ronald Macdonald and Lindy Chamberlain before him, Vitaliev places his affairs in the hands of Harry M. Miller. He is also said to have three London-based agents working his words around Europe.

What can I say? My first encounters with wild Western tabloids were real eye-openers. Does freedom of expression also mean that some rags can print outright lies and get away with it? I was thinking.

I don't know what sources the above-quoted tabloid had, but I had never even thought of 'placing my affairs in the hands of Harry Miller'; nor had I had three agents in London (one, Clarissa, was enough); nor had I ever learnt to have any order in my 'private business life'. I was the most hopeless businessman if not in the whole world, then definitely in the whole of Australia.

My first instinct on reading such publications was to draft an angry letter to the editor threatening litigation and demanding apologies, but Mike Smith would always stop me: 'Just ignore them,' he would say. 'All they are trying to do is to drag you into polemics. No matter what you write to them, they will use it to their own advantage . . .'

It took me a while to realise how right he was. With time I learnt to react to libel with sang-froid. Several years later, when one little Melbourne newspaper went over the top, I sued it and won.

The other tactic used by the tabloids was to interview some visiting Soviet journalistic functionaries who would state in chorus that they had never heard of me. One of them, a man from *Pravda*, whom I knew only slightly, called me once at the *Age* and said: 'I came here to carry out your death penalty – ha, ha, ha . . .' Then he hastily hung up.

The tabloids were unaware of the simple fact that all those privileged few who were allowed to travel to the West from the Soviet Union were strictly banned from having any contacts with emigrants and especially with defectors. The visitors simply didn't want to jeopardise their careers by saying that they knew me or by expressing any opinions – good or bad. But the denial of one well-known Moscow editor who posed as an ice-breaker of glasnost and who knew me very well (I used to contribute to his magazine regularly) was painful. In the end, though, he was caught in his own trap. When at some literary function he said again: 'Vitali Vitaliev? No, I have never heard of him . . .', he was confronted with the collection of stories from his magazine (which he himself selected and edited!) that had just come out in London in English translation. Three stories in this collection were written by me whereas all other contributors had one story each. He went purple with embarrassment and didn't know what to say.

Another revelation was the gradual change of attitude to my column (and to me personally) in the *Sydney Morning Herald*, the *Age*'s sister paper. The paper's hierarchy could never forgive me for having preferred Melbourne to Sydney. Several months after we settled in Melbourne, the *SMH* stopped running my columns on the grounds of them being 'too Melbourne-oriented' (which was not true at all), thus disappointing many of my Sydney-based readers. But the paper didn't stop there and, on a par with the Melbourne tabloids, started attacking me in its gossip column. Once they called me 'a Russian in search of a queue that could provide him with a pair of shoes of the same size and some vodka to help them fit'.

Such animosity between papers that had the same owners and shared a number of overseas bureaus looked ridiculous to me. This was my first real encounter with the so-called great divide, the age-old rivalry between Sydney and Melbourne, that had reached ridiculous proportions.

Luckily, the *SMH*'s position didn't deter my Sydney readers who simply switched over to reading the *Age* on the days when my column appeared. In the end, I didn't lose anything, since the *Age* happily picked up my whole salary package, and the *Sydney Morning Herald* only punished itself, having lost some of its readers.

In my features and columns I tried to provide the readers with a scale of comparison by looking at different sides of Australian (i.e. Western) life through the prism of my Soviet background. I thought that was my mission at the time. For an average Australian, life in a totalitarian state was mysterious and obscure. And whereas most of them would skip a heavy-weight political analysis story, they were likely to go for an amusing human-interest narrative on the life of an ordinary person.

The subject that interests people all over the world is the plight of their fellow human. By giving the readers a scale of comparison, I was trying to enable them to appreciate things from their every-day lives that they were likely to take for granted. The ability not to take life's big and little joys for granted makes one into a happier person.

Contrary to the unwritten rules of Western journalism, my columns were personal and always involved my writer's ego. It was very much in the traditions of Russian (and East European) writing to put all events through the author's soul. By trying to destroy individuality in all its manifestations (simply because individualism inevitably leads to initiative and hence to free thought), totalitarian regimes unwillingly high-light the significance of a human personality. When people do not have enough outlets of expression within a society, they go inside themselves. 'Where's the author's stand in the story?' my Moscow editors would ask me.

I always believed in the Socratic dictum of my favourite Russian writer Konstantin Paustowsky: no matter what you write about, always write about yourself, since yourself is the only thing in this world that you can claim some knowledge of.

I was trying to explain to my Australian readers that the 'I' in my stories did not necessarily mean Vitali Vitaliev. As to my background, it was always with me and kept popping up in the most unusual circumstances.

One of my first assignments at the *Age* was a feature on the hundredth anniversary of the *Great Southern Star*, a small provincial newspaper published in the Victorian town of Leongatha. A centenary of anything is quite an important date in Australia, a 'teenage country' which is just over two hundred years old herself. Two hundred years for a country is like fifteen to sixteen years for a human. By some strange coincidence, the dictaphone tape that I was using during this assignment was the one that I used during my last journalistic trip in the Soviet Union – a visit to the labour camp for political prisoners near Perm in the Urals. It still carried the voices of the poor inmates mixing with the cheerful baritone of the camp's supervisor, Colonel Ossin, saying something to the effect that they were all traitors and dissidents. And muffled barking of guard dogs in the background . . .

How alien and bizarre these half-forgotten voices sounded in the tiny offices of the *Great Southern Star* when I was testing my tape-recorder before switching it into action. They were mixing with a kookaburra's cackling cry from behind the window.

Distant voices in a new world.

On another occasion, I was sent to Canberra to write about a new annual budget session of the Australian parliament. The paper put me up in a nice hotel room which, among other things, had a well-stocked mini-bar. This was my first experience of a first-class Western hotel, and I was overwhelmed with all its comforts: a spare TV set in the bathroom, snow-white bathrobes and a vast double bed, although I was travelling on my own. It was a huge difference to an average Soviet hotel (of which I had seen hundreds) with bare squeaking floors, battered walls, cockroaches, stale smells of disinfectant and unwashed human flesh. On top of it all, one was usually supposed to share a room with complete strangers (of the same sex of course).

The mini-bar in my Canberra hotel room had a special attraction to me. For some reason, I believed that the price of all drinks in it was included in the price of the room (I knew that breakfast was). So, when it was time to go, I thought it would be a shame to leave behind all those nice-looking compact mini-bottles and, after some hesitation, relocated *all of them* into my suitcase.

'Have you used anything from your mini-bar, sir?' a reception clerk asked me when I was checking out.

'Yes,' I answered. I was a bit surprised by such intrusion of my privacy.

'What did you use?'

'Er . . . everything actually . . .'

He gave me the special sort of a 'stuff you' look that hotel receptionists and waiters are so good at, but didn't say anything.

I suddenly understood that I had done something wrong. I could feel my face acquiring the colour of the cherry brandy contained in one of the mini-bottles in my suitcase. I realised that one had to pay extra for drinks and was bracing myself for a painful showdown with the *Age* on my return. But it didn't happen: the drinks were probably written off as my travel expenses. My expense account (another totally new thing unknown in the Soviet Union) entitled me to reference books and newspapers, taxi rides and occasional meals out – enough to make my poor Soviet head spin.

To be really free in Melbourne, one needed a car. I had never driven before: owning a car in the Soviet Union was a rare privilege (only one of all my Moscow friends had one) on a par with owning a personal jet in the West. And when Mazda Australia offered me a free brand-new car for six months and an instructor to teach me to drive, I was overcome with joy which was marred only slightly after I hit a fire hydrant during my first driving lesson.

The wisest of all English sayings, 'There is no such thing as a free lunch', still sounded obscure to me . . .

I was recognised wherever I went and was routinely

approached for autographs or just chats. Australians are extremely friendly and easy-going. They addressed me as 'mate', and I liked it a lot. Invitations to be a guest speaker at all sorts of functions – from school social hours to launches of congresses and conventions – were flowing in every single day. Initially, I accepted all of them, but then realised that too intensive public speaking didn't leave me enough time for writing and learnt to say no.

I certainly couldn't refuse the honour of delivering a Norman Smith Memorial Lecture in Journalism at Melbourne University, a privilege reserved for the country's top journalists and politicians.

I refused to take part in celebrity races when you had to run from one pub to another with a glass of beer in your hand, but couldn't resist drinking a bottle of vodka in front of a TV camera with the presenter of a popular TV chat show (the presenter had to be massaged back to life during a commercial break).

I met and became friends with Peter Ustinov, who was in Melbourne with his one-man show. For some reason, I was asked to introduce him at the Melbourne Press Club at very short notice – a couple of hours. The rationale of the hosts was simple: we were both Russians. They were probably unaware of the fact that Peter Ustinov had only been conceived in Russia, from where he 'defected' inside his mother's womb.

I was totally unprepared for meeting (to say nothing of introducing) one of the greatest artistic personalities of our times. But the proposition was too lucrative to refuse. Dressed in my habitual denim suit, I went to welcome Peter Ustinov, whom I remembered from the Hollywood movie *Spartacus* which I saw a couple of dozen times while playing truant as a schoolboy in Kharkov. I knew its script almost by heart.

The man I saw at the Press Club was a far cry from my image of Peter Ustinov, who had just been knighted: aloof, grey-haired, self-important and arrogantly aristocratic. Of all these attributes he had just one – grey hair. But even this, in his case, was not the sign of exclusivity or venerable age. It was the grey hair of a young man who had suffered a tragedy. Strangely enough, it made him look younger.

As to arrogance, which could well have been forgiven in someone who was a member of all existing academies and the winner of all existing artistic awards, he was totally devoid of it. Not the slightest trace of pomposity could be observed. That was why I found it hard to call him Sir Peter and addressed him by his name and patronymic – Piotr Ionovich – which in Russia signifies warmth and respect.

One evening Peter Ustinov came to visit me at my Melbourne flat. He spotted my brand-new Mazda 121 parked in the courtyard.

'What a lovely little car you've got there! I have never seen a car like that before!' he commented.

He had a great passion for cars and even collected them. (As I found out later, he also had his own personal jet, but I am not sure whether he collected jets too.) My Mazda was one of the first models of its kind to hit the streets of Melbourne. Tiny, bright yellow and shaped like a bubble (or a diminutive plump female, as one of my macho Australian friends suggested), it was spacious inside and extremely roadworthy.

'I'd like to have a ride!' said Piotr Ionovich.

I found it hard to share his enthusiasm. It was only one day before that I had got my driving licence, and my collision with a fire hydrant, the memories of which were still fresh, did not bode well for my driving future. Besides, I had never driven a car on my own, without an instructor.

'I want you to drive me to the restaurant in this lovely car!' Peter Ustinov insisted. We were supposed to have dinner in one of Melbourne's Russian restaurants later in the evening. I tried to talk him out of this fool-hardy whim of his. I told him what an awful driver I was. I told him about the tragic fate of the fire hydrant, but he was not easily deterred.

He squeezed his huge bulk inside my small Mazda – knees first, and the small car sagged under his weight. I climbed onto the driver's seat – and Mazda's metallic belly touched the ground. Off we drove striking sparks from the asphalt. I was sitting behind the wheel trembling like an aspen leaf. If something happens, I shall go down in history as the man who killed Peter Ustinov, I kept thinking. For some reason, I also remembered his recent joke about his new passport that was to expire in 2002: 'My main task now is to try and not expire before my passport.' As you can imagine, it was not conducive to safe driving . . .

By the time we reached our destination – Matrioshka Russian restaurant in Dandenong Road – I was covered with cold sweat and had totally lost my appetite.

'Your driving was perfect!' Piotr Ionovich reassured me as he slowly levered himself out of my Mazda. Thank God, he had survived the experience, and his genius had been preserved for humankind.

Later he bought a Mazda 121 for one of his daughters. Now, every time I see a car of this make in the streets of London, I get a reminder of my precarious ride around Melbourne with Peter Ustinov as my first ever passenger.

In the several years following, I used to meet up with him in many different parts of the world. We would each write a column on the same page of *The European*. This friendship was destined to play a big role in my future life. But then, after our first meeting and a couple of meals together, he presented me with his book *My Russia* with the following dedication:

> For Vitali – Brother; Nephew; Son
> in Spirit; in Laughter; in Rotundity
> And in tranquil earnestness of purpose.

I don't know why he took a liking to me. His wife Helene said once that I reminded him of the way he himself used to be (and to look) when he was my age ('rotundity'?). Whatever the reason, this friendship was one of the biggest gifts of fate I had ever received. And it was received in Australia.

As you see, I was popular and busy enough to be totally happy. Yet, after the first six or seven months, I started feeling that something was missing. Precisely as Igor Pomerantsev had told me in London, I couldn't quite understand what it was. I presume I started feeling somewhat isolated, as if Europe, England and the whole real world, with its wars, troubles and worries, had ceased to exist. Newspapers didn't carry much news about it; local radio stations were totally immersed in their own comfortable little milieu, and I had to wait until midnight, when I could tune to the BBC World Service, to hear some real news and to get a reminder that there was life outside Australia after all. The BBC World Service was retransmitted during the night by a Melbourne radio station for the blind.

The sight of numerous travel agencies offering trips anywhere in the world was reassuring, but the price of these trips was an immediate deterrent. Yes, Australia had her own Iron Curtain. Only, unlike the metaphoric Cold War Iron Curtain, this one was real and was made from dollars which, in a strange way, made it even more impregnable than the Soviet one.

I was coming to understand what 'tyranny of distance' really meant.

Several years later, a German lady who came to Australia from Europe after World War Two told me that there were only two options for a European migrant: one was to forget about Europe and to start enjoying the quiet comforts of Australian life; the second one was to go back.

I was finding it increasingly hard to forget about the outside world. I subscribed to half-a-dozen British and American periodicals that started arriving in heavy bundles (usually a couple of weeks late); I became a radio freak, just like in the Soviet Union, and would spend hours combing the air waves in search of European radio stations which was a hopeless business during the day due to bad reception (and to the distance of course). Crackling noises of space: rustling of ocean waves and whistling of winds were the only things that could be heard.

One of the first bells of alarm was sounded by Ruby Wax, the American comedienne living in London whom I had never met. I was appearing live from Melbourne by satellite on *Saturday Night Clive* and Ruby Wax, Clive's studio guest, was asked to comment on different items of the show, including the interview with me.

'Do you think Vitali will settle in Australia?' Clive asked her.

'No way!' she replied with her heavy American accent,

thick and rough as an army blanket. 'Australia is not for him. Mark my word: he is going to leave soon.'

What a load of rubbish! I thought then. How dare she assume I won't last in Australia! But in my heart of hearts I somehow knew that she was right.

Two years later, in London, I had a chance to shake Ruby's hand at the *Spectator* lunch to which we were both invited.

'You know, you were the first to foresee my departure from Australia,' I said.

'It was obvious from the look of you,' she replied. 'As we say in America, it didn't take a rocket scientist to figure it out . . .'

Ruby's opinion was soon echoed by Nancy Banks-Smith, *The Guardian*'s TV reviewer. Reviewing one of my *Saturday Night Clive* pieces from Melbourne, she wrote that I looked 'a shadow of [my] Moscow self . . . We must take him out of there as soon as possible,' she concluded. By 'shadow' she obviously didn't mean my increasingly blubbery look.

Mitya and Natasha were happy and were coping well with the unexpectedly drab and cold Melbourne winter (we had to sleep with our track-suits on, since our flat, like most Melbourne households, didn't have central heating). Mitya was going to his primary school (this time it was not a Protestant school, like in London, but a Roman Catholic one), and his English (or rather his Australian) was improving by the day (his Russian was deteriorating at the same rate). Natasha was attending English courses and basking in the pleasures of carefree Australian shopping. We were thinking of buying a house.

Yet, in a funny way, I felt that the bond that had kept us so close together during our last months in Moscow and in London was slackening. Maybe it was because I was busy at the *Age* and was writing my second book after office hours, so we could hardly spend time with each other. Or because our life was getting ever so comfortable.

Going through hardships together makes families stronger, whereas comfort and cosiness often take them apart.

In our previous life, we were used to unending problems,

big and small. We had learnt to derive pleasure from coping with them. A problem-free life was a meaningless abstraction. We did not know how to cope with our sudden carefree affluence.

I was certainly not coping well with my own success.

One of the reasons was probably that, unwillingly, I was getting more and more carried away by my fame which, in a funny way, often made me feel lonely and out of place. What the hell am I doing here? I would think while opening ('launching') or closing yet another meaningless function. This feeling was not helped by the most frequent question I was hearing from my readers, viewers and listeners as well as from my numerous interviewers: 'Why did you come to Australia, Vitali?' – the question (or rather the self-induced inferiority complex that it reflected) that was eventually to drive me out of Australia.

I was trying to tell these people how wonderful their country was, but they refused to believe me.

'Lady Fame is not a wife, but a widow,' said Nikolai Dorizo, a Moscow poet. I always liked this expression and used to quote it a lot without understanding it fully. With every new month in Australia, the hidden meaning of Nikolai Dorizo's words was becoming clearer to me.

15

My Books

My old books ... Some of them have just arrived in Melbourne by sea from Moscow. I can't believe that we are together again. All my joys and sorrows, all my ups and downs are in them, and our reunion means that, despite enormous disruptions, my life still goes on.

When leaving Moscow in haste in January 1990, we were unable to take many books with us, although I did take several. We left home with three suitcases of our basic belongings, two of them full of books. These were mainly dictionaries, atlases and other reference literature (for some reason, I thought that they were exorbitantly expensive in the West), but the bulk of my home library remained in our tiny Khrushchev flat. I thought I would never see my books again.

In accordance with the strictly rationed state-imposed information diet, good books were very hard to get in the Soviet Union, although Russian classics of the nineteenth century were published regularly with ubiquitous introductions explaining how they were exposing the sins of tsarist Russia. On the black market one could even buy a collection of Akhmatova's or Pasternak's poems or the stunning novels by Mikhail Bulgakov, priced by shameless profiteers at a hundred roubles or more. Intellectuals were ready to throw away a month's salary to buy one of these books which were printed in very small numbers, mainly intended for export to the West. They were also on sale at special hard-currency Beriozka bookshops where Soviet citizens were denied entry. Despite this, the coveted books were obtained by hook or by crook and were kept by the most avid readers in the safest places of their cramped flats together with the family silver (if any). People were so book-hungry that it was not unusual for them to copy whole volumes by hand.

I've got my own little theory as to who or what eventually brought down the seemingly impregnable monolith of the communist system. Contrary to popular belief, communism in Russia was first undermined and then destroyed neither by external pressure nor by internal contradictions, but by – books. I don't just mean the works by Solzhenitsyn and other dissidents, or the secretly distributed *samizdat* (mere possession of these could have resulted in imprisonment, the risk of which perversely added to the pleasure). No, I am talking about officially published classics which, although hard to get, used to be printed in millions of copies. 'It is amazing that so many wonderful and potentially dangerous books kept coming out under Soviet rule,' said one Western literary critic.

Indeed, the Bolsheviks' biggest mistake was not to ban classical literature straight away, even though attempts to deny the whole of Russia's cultural heritage as a 'relic of the tsarist past' were repeatedly made in the 1920s and 1930s. This was the time of anti-Christmas rallies under the slogan 'Down with Christmas trees!' and of compulsory affection for Comrade Stalin, the Soviet Motherland or one's tractor.

Even some of the traditional Russian female (and male) first names were replaced by the likes of Lenina, Stalina, Industrialisation, Power Station and Gear Wheel. I have even heard of a man whose first name was The 23rd of February – Red Army Day. Just imagine: The 23rd of February Vitaliev!

While this nonsense was proceeding unchallenged, Russian and foreign classics were not banned, only 'retouched' in the most sensitive places. Pushkin, Gogol, Turgenev and Tolstoy, together with Homer, Shakespeare, Dante, Cervantes, Dickens and Flaubert, were fighting the Soviet regime from the pages of dog-eared and heavily annotated books. They were preaching love, faith, honesty and honour – values wholly the opposite of the prevailing dogma. They were moulding our outlook and mentality much more effectively than *Pravda* or volumes of leaden leaders' speeches which no one, even the leaders themselves, bothered to read.

In school literature lessons we were supposed to use special manuals in which all classical works were explained. We were all expected to say that Eugene Onegin was a typical representative of the 'lost generation' of Russian nobility, and Tatyana, his passion, almost a revolutionary; that Tolstoy was an adamant supporter of the proletariat; that Turgenev's Bazarov, a confused philosophising youth from *Fathers and Sons*, was a rebel against the capitalist system; that Gogol's and Chekhov's stories were satirising the tsarist regime, not traditional Russian sloth and corruption.

The classics are capable of speaking for themselves, though, and very few of us believed this scribble. All good books, even if seemingly innocent love stories, were profoundly anti-Soviet in their essence, since love and Freedom are intertwined. Real literature is anti-totalitarian by definition.

Literature was our short cut to Freedom and a mortal time-bomb for the system.

We couldn't help noticing how clumsy, empty and pompous the speeches of Brezhnev and Gorbachev were compared with the lucid, colourful prose of the nineteenth-century Russian writers. Comparisons lead to conclusions, and conclusions lead to decisions – something that our totalitarian rulers always failed to understand.

Even Soviet literature in its best manifestations was important in beating the system. True, the most courageous writers who openly tried to defy official dogma were mercilessly crushed and their readers could face prison. But there was no better publicity for a book than banning it officially by putting it on the KGB-run state censorship agency's monthly updated blacklists.

We read banned *samizdat* editions of Orwell and Solzhenitsyn at night, since the next morning we were to pass them on to the next one in line. Honest reading as well as honest writing always had an element of danger in the Soviet Union. (That's probably why now, when the danger is gone, people in post-communist Russia have largely lost their interest in serious literature, and Moscow bookshops are bursting with pulp and pornography.) Even the more cautious Soviet writers delved into the world of euphemism, analogies, hidden meanings and *double entendre*. The writers were writing between the lines, the readers were reading between the lines – and both understood each other perfectly.

Reading in the Soviet Union was almost as creative as writing itself.

In 1966, when I was twelve, we were asked at school to write an essay on our favourite literary hero. Instead of writing (as we were all expected to) about Pavel Korchagin, the clichéd protagonist of Nikolai Ostrovsky's primitive pro-Soviet novel *How Steel was Tamed*, I wrote about Ostap Bender, 'the smooth operator' from the satirical novel *The Twelve Chairs* by Ilf and Petrov, a brilliant pre-war pair of Moscow humourists.

The Twelve Chairs was a hilarious and vitriolic parody of Soviet officialdom and bureaucracy. It is still a mystery to me that Ilf and Petrov were not banned and purged by Stalin – another gross mistake of the system. The book sparkled with caustic and, yes, very anti-Soviet humour. I, like many of my compatriots, read the novel dozens of times and knew it almost by heart.

But then, in 1966, my grandfather (I was living with my grandparents at that time), an old Bolshevik and a revolutionary in his youth who became profoundly disillusioned with communism by the end of his life, was summoned to the school headmistress, a blue-stocking and virago, and was reprimanded for his grandson's 'dangerous literary tastes'. He came back home very upset. But instead of telling me off (as I expected), he said: 'I am ashamed for your teachers. They want you all to like the same books. They want you to have the same tastes and thoughts. If this is what we fought for in the revolution, then I am ashamed for myself, too.'

I will remember this first real lesson of literature, taught by my grandfather, for as long as I live.

And here they are, my paper jewels in battered cardboard frames. They have crossed the ocean and found me in Australia, and I have found them. We are re-united against all odds. I keep stroking their time-beaten covers, their yellowish pages, permeated with the peculiar smells of childhood and home. I keep re-reading old dedications in faded ink: 'To my dear little son from his grandad, with love'; 'From Dad on your birthday'; 'To Vitali in memory of successful completion of his first year in school'.

Each of the books is memorable to me, each has a story to tell.

Here's *Conversations about Poetry*, published in Moscow in 1970. This little book has a rather sinister history. I tried to quote it in my university diploma paper in 1976, unaware of the fact that its author, a brilliant Russian scholar Yefim Etkind, emigrated a couple of years before and by that time was a professor of Russian literature at the Sorbonne. Books by emigrant authors, notwithstanding the subject, were a strict taboo in the Soviet Union and were to be confiscated from libraries and second-hand bookshops. To mention such a book in a diploma paper would mean automatic trouble. Luckily, my tutor noticed it in time and the reference to Etkind was changed into a vague 'certain scholars think that . . .'

The subject of my diploma paper, by the way, was connected with Russian translations of Henry Longfellow's lyrics. This was triggered by one of my newly arrived books, the *Collected Works of Henry Longfellow*, a bulky leather-bound and beautifully illustrated volume, published in England in 1914. I bought it in 1971 from an old woman in Kharkov for just 3 roubles. Longfellow's lyrics fascinated me, and I started translating them into Russian. Who knows, if the woman had offered me Byron or Keats instead, I would have become a fan of their poetry. But she had only Longfellow, inherited from her grandmother. She had to sell old books to supplement her meagre pension.

Old books of any kind were rare in Kharkov, where during

World War Two, when the city was occupied, twice, by the Germans, most of them ended up either in stoves or as parts of a makeshift bridge across the Lopan River which was blown up by retreating Soviet troops – hundreds of priceless incunabula from the local Korolenko Public Library were thrown into the river to provide a temporary crossing.

In 1982, my translations of Longfellow's poems were published by the prestigious *Literaturnaya Gazeta* in Moscow in commemoration of the hundredth anniversary of the poet's death. The editor preferred them to those of older and more experienced translators. The editor's name was Oleg Bitov. Yes, the same Bitov who mysteriously defected to Britain in 1984 and no less mysteriously re-appeared in Moscow a year later, creating a good deal of speculation in the British media. No one, apart from Bitov himself, knows what had really happened to him, but, whatever it was, I remember him as an intellectual, a polymath and an extremely knowledgeable editor.

What an amazing chain of reminiscences an old book can provoke.

Stalin: The History of a Dictator – this rumpled thick paperback by Montgomery Hyde I bought from a drunk in Moscow in 1981. The seller turned out to be a former high-ranking Soviet diplomat, sacked from his post for excessive drinking. I was pushing a pram with my baby son in it in a Moscow street and reading an English paperback as I walked, when this man approached me and offered this book for 15 roubles. He then invited me to his flat which was full of banned books, smuggled by him from the West. I couldn't buy any more: the prices he was asking were much higher than I could afford.

To get this book – *Twenty Letters to a Friend* by Stalin's daughter Svetlana Aliluyeva – I had to go to Malakhovka, a village not far from Moscow. I bought it from a bearded young man who looked like an archetypal dissident. And he was one, by the way. He showed me all the works by Solzhenitsyn, which he kept openly in his one-room apartment. Possessing Solzhenitsyn's books was a criminal offence at that time, to say nothing of reading them. I remember a short hairy fellow in Kharkov who kept popping into every bookshop in the city asking, specifically, for the sixteenth volume of Solzhenitsyn's collected works. He was mad of course, otherwise he would have certainly been arrested.

Or maybe he was a well-camouflaged agent-provocateur?

And here are the books of my early childhood: a ragged copy of *Robinson Crusoe* with drawings by Jean Grenville, a 1959 gift from my father; a book called *The Captains of Frigates* by Nikolai Chukovsky, describing among other things Captain Cook's journey to Australia. I clearly remember how my grandad bought it from a bookstall in Kharkov's Sumskaya Street on the way to the children's hospital. Who could have thought that twenty-six years later I would have to discover Australia for myself?

Down and Out in Paris and London – my first introduction to George Orwell, courtesy of a sympathetic Penguin Books representative at the Moscow International Book Fair, where I worked as an interpreter in 1981. She just took the book from the stand and gave it to me. I will never forget the ticklish feeling of carrying the book in my pocket past the KGB guards: if Orwell, the biggest literary bugaboo for the Soviet system, had been found, I would have had to say good-bye to my job in the very best of scenarios. Luckily, it was just a small paperback.

I remember coming out into the street, opening the book and freezing in my step with delight after reading one of the first sentences: 'It was a narrow street – a ravine of tall, leprous houses, lurching towards one another in queer attitudes, as though they had all been frozen in the act of collapse.' Since then, Orwell has become one of my favourite writers of all times.

I was less lucky with two books by Isaac Bashevis Singer, a Nobel Prize-winning American-Jewish writer, that were presented to me by a man at the American Association of Jewish Publishers stand. On my way out I was stopped by a KGB guard and taken to a small secret room in the back of the pavilion where the books, which he branded 'Zionist propaganda', were confiscated from me. 'You needn't bother turning up to work tomorrow,' he told me sternly. Devastated, I still did. The same KGB man approached me at my stand and said rather amicably: 'You be careful: you are under constant observation.' I couldn't understand his sudden change of mood until he bent over towards me and whispered conspiratorially: 'I've noticed a nice album with photos of naked women on your stand. Could you be so kind and look the other way for a moment and allow me to pinch it?'

Even KGB agents couldn't resist the attractions of a printed volume.

'Good-bye, my friends!' Alexander Pushkin, the greatest of Russian poets, said to his books a moment before dying. These were his last words.

'Hello, my friends!' I am saying to my old books in Australia. 'Life goes on!'

And a beautiful Henry Longfellow sonnet, 'My Books', which I once translated into Russian, keeps sounding in my ears:

> So I behold these books on their shelf,
> My ornaments and arms of other days;
> Not wholly useless, though no longer used,
> For they remind me of my other self,
> Younger and stronger, and the pleasant ways
> In which I walked, now clouded and confused.

I could have easily put my signature under these beautiful words.

16

Three Australian Dreams

ONE

It was a living illustration to George Orwell's *Animal Farm*. And here I was in the middle of it, which for some reason was called the Royal Melbourne Show (or Victoria's annual agricultural exhibition). The main difficulty was to determine whose show it actually was: who were the actors and who were the audience. I was groping my way through the mooing, bleating and barking crowd; I was slipping on countless dollops of manure. I had heard a lot about bullshit, now at last I saw what it really was.

The animals were certainly the masters here. They were looking down at human beings with a good deal of scorn. The horses' hooves were painted red and black, their backs were washed with soap and sprayed with litres of deodorant. They were covered by embroidered blankets and looked (and smelt) better than most of the visitors. Their stables were spotlessly clean and full of fresh odorous hay, whereas their owners were choking on their stinking Four 'n' Twenty Australian meatpies in their stuffy cubby-holes filled with old rags, where they were supposed to sleep during the Show.

The sheep resembled fluffy pillows with legs, the lambs looked as innocent as only lambs can look. The pigs had their own Pigs' Castle, with bedroom, TV set and even toilet, which had immediately become the photographers' main attraction. But the pigs didn't care a pig about journalists; they were sleeping placidly on the floor making soft sucking sounds with their mouths, just like babies.

'Look at that puppy! Isn't it cute?'

'Yes, but it's not a puppy, it's a calf.'

My head was spinning. I had lost sense of reality (one can lose sense of reality even in a dream). Suddenly I had a feeling that we humans were brought to this show in long windowless vans from our home and office stables, just to be watched, appraised and admired (or criticised) by the animals.

'Look at this suckling kid, mummy. Isn't he cute? Grunt . . .'

'Ye-es, and here's his mother. She is called woman. You can easily distinguish women from men by their udders. They are called breasts. Grunt . . .'

These were a pig and a piglet speaking. And then I overheard the lively conversation of two cows:

'How do you find the show, m-my dear?'

'M-mm . . . m-m-marvellous. Very m-moo-rish . . .'

I produced my tape-recorder and approached a sheep: 'I am a Russian journalist. Would you grant me a short interview?'

'Russians are b-b-bastards. Why aren't they buying my wool?'

'Sorry, but they probably have no money . . .'

'B-b-bullshit! They have enough to b-b-back Iraq and Cuba, b-but not me-e-e-e . . .'

I looked around: a huge snarling dog was leading a fat puffing man on a leash towards a Pizza Hut – feeding time! Who said that dogs resemble the people they own? Very true!

On the nearby lawn, two cows were teaching a farmer how to milk them. These humans can really be tame when they grow up. Their babies, of course, are still pretty wild. Unlike some well-behaved lambs standing quietly in their enclosures and having haircuts, they were running around like mad, snatching fodder in showbags from the stalls and yelping bloody murder. One can only hope that they will grow and get domesticated in the course of time . . .

Show! Show! Show! Animals are having their feast. They lead humans in circles in parades, just to see what they are worth. We are not appraising them – it's the other way round. Just look at their faces and you will see that they despise us for our hectic lifestyles, for our ruthlessness and lack of common sense.

Isn't it cruel that after some time all these cultured intelligent creatures are destined to be eaten up by us, who are in many ways inferior to them? Indeed, animals never cheat or doublecross each other, they don't drink alcohol, they never complain and do not hold union meetings. And look: aren't they beautiful?

After an hour, a decision was made: from tomorrow I would become a vegetarian, possibly even a vegan ... By lunch-time my decision grew less firm. The titillating smell of roast beef was spreading above the show-grounds; it was teasing my nostrils. After all, I am only a human being: unlike domestic animals, I haven't got enough stamina to contain my instincts.

'Can I have a burger? Yes, a large one. Yes, with onions and some ketchup on top.'

I was shamefully munching my burger. Cows, pigs and sheep were casting sad glances at me as if saying: 'These humans, they are incorrigible . . .'

In the afternoon I returned to my stable. 'Milking time!' the editor announced. And I started typing, pressing computer keys softly with my front hooves . . .

TWO

I was in Russia the other day.

I went there without a visa. Grim Soviet customs officers did not scrutinise my face with their blank piercing eyes. They didn't even rummage through my luggage: I had none.

I went to Russia by cab. I got out near Government House, Melbourne. The smiling lady guard – a striking contrast to grave and ever-suspicious Soviet border guards – checked my invitation and waved me into Russia. Magnolias were bloom-ing in the garden. The white, gracious mansion reminded me of Prince Yusupov's palace in Arkhangelskoye, near Moscow, one of my favourite nooks. It was the most beautiful building that I have seen in Australia so far, even more beautiful than the Old Parliament House in Canberra.

The Governor of Victoria and his wife had invited me to the reception in memory of four Russian poets – Anna Akhmatova, Boris Pasternak, Osip Mandelstam and Marina Tsvetayeva – all of whom were born around a hundred years ago. These four are not simply the biggest names in twentieth-century Russian poetry, they are also its most tragic figures.

Osip Mandelstam died in prison in 1938. Marina Tsvetayeva committed suicide in exile in the God-forsaken Tartar town of Yelabuga. Pasternak, the Nobel Prize-winner, was viciously harassed, abused and ostracised in the Soviet Union for most of his life. Akhmatova was publicly branded a whore and a bourgeois by Stalin's henchman Zhdanov, and her first husband, Nikolai Gumilev, also a poet, was shot by Bolsheviks in 1921.

Poetry and tragedy always went hand-in-hand in Russia.

Four gems of Russian culture. They came back sparkling in the hospitable Governor's house. The guests were seated in a semi-circle in the bright state drawing room overlooking the garden. The poems were read first in Russian and then in English.

Where was I?

Familiar poems, voices and faces surrounded me.

At times I felt as if I was fourteen and back in my childhood country, in a tiny philharmonic society hall in Kharkov, listening to a recital and holding my mother's hand. I was not particularly eager to attend poetic recitals, at first that is. Like all children of that age, I preferred the Beatles and soccer. But thanks to my mother's gentle persistence (and she could be persistent when she wanted to), I soon became a fan of poetry and started writing my own verses.

It doesn't matter what is happening outside the room, what century, epoch or political system is behind its walls. What matters is that poetry is with us.

Poetry transcends time and space. It also transcends language barriers.

Was it a mysterious sign from above when suddenly, with the first sounds of Anna Akhmatova's lines, the sunlight faded behind the ornate windows, it grew dark and rain-drops – each one looking like a tiny onion dome from the top of a toy Russian church – began to fall on the lawn, and gusts of wind from the ocean threw handfuls of them onto the window glass?

> They took you away at daybreak.
> Half waking, as though at a wake, I followed.
> In the dark chamber children were crying.
> In the image-case, candlelight guttered.
> At your lips, the chill of an icon.
> A deadly sweat at your brow.
> I shall creep to our wailing wall,
> Crawl to the Kremlin towers . . .

Akhmatova's only son was purged by Stalin. The above lines are her reaction to his sudden night-time arrest (they had a sadistic habit of arresting people during the night, when least expected). They are the cry of pain, the mother's innermost shriek of despair.

Lush Australian nature was crying with the poet. It was not wind, but the heavy sobs of the grieving Russian mother; it was not rain, but her clear salty tears.

'Isn't it wonderful?' I asked my mother. 'Isn't it great to be able to hear and feel all this in Australia – of all places? Mother, can you hear this?'

She was thousands of miles away, in dark snow-ridden Moscow; in her tiny one-room kitchenette, where she gave me her motherly blessing to leave, not being sure whether she would ever see me again, and where she was living alone awaiting permission to join me in Australia (which had already been denied to her twice), whilst I kept seeing her often in my guilty Australian dreams. Her eyesight was deteriorating and she couldn't even read my letters. She could only hear my voice in heavily jammed weekly programmes for Radio Liberty which I recorded by telephone from my Melbourne house.

'Yes,' she replied. 'I can hear you. They will never take you away from me at daybreak.' She was sitting next to me in the state drawing room of Government House. I was holding her hand.

THREE

I am alone in one of the men's solitary confinement cells in the old Richmond Gaol in Tasmania. I have shut the door from inside. It is dark and damp in the cell. Dead silence, the silence of a grave, rings in my ears. The air is full of hopelessness and despair, a typical stench of a prison.

Prisons all over the world smell like that.

After a minute of voluntary confinement, I start feeling hot and claustrophobic. The heavy door opens with a squeak. A burly prison warder brings in a lump of stale black bread and some water in an aluminium tub. I want to talk to him, to explain that I am innocent of any crime and have wandered in here by mistake, just to have a look. But I can't utter a word: enforced silence is part of my punishment. A moment later the door slams shut behind him, and I am left alone in pitch darkness.

My beloved Tasmania. Isn't it a sad irony that this beautiful pearl of an island, which for me came to signify Freedom and nostalgia, used to be one vast prison, a forerunner to the Soviet gulag?

Or can it be so that the sweetest Freedom of all is the one that lies straight behind prison gates?

Tasmania was the place where convicts, transported from Britain to continental Australia, were sent for any type of offence – from killing a fellow convict to stealing a shilling – while already in exile. They knew there was no return. That's why they planted their favourite European trees there – chestnuts, oaks, limes, poplars. They built Gothic churches for themselves and English-looking Victorian cottages for their gaolers. As a rule, there was no return for the latter either. There was only one escape route from Port Arthur, the largest British prison colony in Tasmania – to the neighbouring Isle of Dead, whose name speaks for itself.

The Model Prison, as it was also called, opened in 1830

and had a 'silent' or 'separate' policy. Prisoners lived and worked in solitary confinement, in silence and anonymity. They were called out by numbers, just as in German and Soviet concentration camps a hundred years later. The British 'experimenters' went further. They made the convicts wear masks at all times, lest they be recognised by their fellow sufferers in 'airing yards' and at chapel, where each prisoner had his own 'praying box', allowing a view only of the priest and the altar. Warders, not allowed to speak to prisoners, communicated by hand signals.

Cell number four, nicknamed 'deaf and dumb cell', was an equivalent of the ominous room 101 from Orwell's *1984*. Recalcitrant prisoners were placed there for what must have been the most terrifying punishment of all. Not a ray of light pierced the darkness; not a sound penetrated the maze of stone walls. Here the prisoner was kept for up to three days. It was enough. Most emerged raving mad . . .

In the 1850s Port Arthur was frequently visited by inspectors from London who were positively impressed by the colony's methods. In some modern English history texts Port Arthur is still described as an achievement of the British penal system. One thing the inspectors failed to understand was why prisoners in Port Arthur were going insane in growing numbers. A special asylum had to be built in the prison grounds. In 1872 the number of mad convicts reached 111, exceeding the Model Prison's 'normal' population, and soon afterwards it had to close, since there were no sane prisoners left.

This struck me as being the first (though probably unintended) attempt at punitive psychiatry. Before visiting Port Arthur, I was inclined to think that the world's first mental prisons appeared in Bolshevik Russia in 1918. I was wrong.

Port Arthur is now advertised as 'Tasmania's premier tourist attraction'. 'Convict excursions' are conducted. 'Convict restaurants' in the neighbourhood offer 'convict food'. 'Convict shops' sell 'convict souvenirs'. Annual Australia Day celebrations, with fanfares, re-enactments and fireworks, are held there, on a huge lawn. There is something frighteningly bizarre about celebrating Australia's statehood anniversary on the ruins of one of the world's most horrific prisons.

There was something weird about the popular evening 'ghost tours' of Port Arthur. True, there was no shortage of ghosts in this haunted place. Ghosts of the horrific past should not be disturbed. I couldn't sleep for three nights in May 1996 when I learnt in London about the Port Arthur bloody massacre, when a schizophrenic gunman went on the rampage among the prison ruins, having shot dead thirty-five people.

Ghosts should be treated gently. They don't like fuss and fanfares. They rebel against idle curiosity. They crave well-deserved rest. And quiet memory.

A fresh spot of blood on Tasmania's diamond-shaped map. What a horrible dream!

17

Of Paradise, Polls and Dogs

I cross the Jordan River and head towards Bagdad. The landscape around is placid, almost pastoral, with no signs of
ongoing battle. And Saddam Hussein is nowhere to be seen.

I came to Tasmania to cover the state government elections
in January 1992. Living in Melbourne, just across the Bass
Strait, I would use any pretext to visit the island that I came
to love, and this looked like a perfect one. This was my
first ever encounter with a democratic election campaign.
I did not have much time to adjust to all the realities of
Tasmanian elections and had to plunge into the political whirl-
wind the moment I arrived in Hobart. At the end of the
first day I was dazzled by the mutually abusive pronouncements of the candidates, by stickers and posters calling people
to vote for this or that particular party, by the new (for
me) political rhetoric: proportional representation, the Hare-
Clark electoral system, the Hobson rotating ballot, and so
on.

It was so different from what we used to call elections
in the Soviet Union. There was usually only one candidate,
representing only one party. No campaigning, no abusive
remarks, just 'the overwhelming enthusiasm' and the 99.9
per cent vote in favour. The people were lured to the polls
by stalls with hard-to-get food inside the polling stations. If
you failed to turn up, you were in real trouble, but even so

your ballot paper would have been automatically cast for you by someone else. The ballots were never counted anyway.

I remember how once, in Moscow, in a gesture of despair rather than protest, I didn't drop my ballot into the urn, only pretended to do so, and covertly hid it under my shirt. Having come out of the polling station, I tore the unused ballot into small pieces and threw it into a rubbish bin. If spotted, the risk such a fool-hardy act involved was considerable, and the effect – zero. Next morning both the turn-out and the proportion of votes in favour of the only communist candidate were at their usual 99.9 per cent (0.1 per cent short of 100, which was supposed to give this absurd figure some sort of credibility).

But the sensation was ticklish . . .

It is true that nothing used to change as a result of these strange 'elections'. But isn't it often the case with Western democracies, too? Despite fierce campaigning, hordes of candidates and millions spent on reciprocal public insults, nothing changes when the elections are over and the lucky contenders ascend their political thrones.

So why all the fuss?

By the way, in Australia (and in Tasmania, too) voting is compulsory. Those who do not turn up are fined 50 Australian dollars. The rationale behind this regulation is that, without the fine, no one would bother to vote. Well, with the notorious Australian 'no worries' (or in plain English, 'I don't care') attitude, compulsory voting is not entirely pointless. Even if it smacks of totalitarianism slightly.

'Call me Bob, everyone else does,' Dr Bob Brown, the leader of Tasmanian Greens, the world's first and most powerful Green party, interrupted with a smile, as I mistakenly addressed him as 'Mr Brown'. We were heading for his news conference, held in an old wooden house in the centre of Hobart. Inside, there were lots of pot-plants and 'Clean and Green' posters.

I liked the way Bob Brown spoke. He would look each of those present straight in the eye, shifting his gaze from one face to another, which was aimed at creating an atmosphere of trust, I presume. He talked about how Tasmania must promote tourism and stop building new pulp mills, which in the long run were only going to increase the already high (11.7 per cent) unemployment. He called his main competitors, Liberal and Labour, 'old parties' and said Tasmania was in need of fresh ideas that could be provided solely by the Greens (green is obviously the colour of freshness).

There at the conference I met Mr Geoff Law, a charismatic young Green campaigner. His left hand bore the traces of what looked like a dog bite. It turned out to be just that. During the launch of the Greens' campaign in Hobart Town Hall a couple of weeks before, a stray dog found its way into the building and headed for the stage. Mr Law, who was on the stage speaking, courageously grabbed the intruder and it bit him.

As I could see, campaigning for power in Tasmania had its own hazards. The Green activist was effectively bitten by the very natural environment he was trying to protect.

The media function for Labour, the party that was then still in power in Tasmania (as well as in the whole of Australia), was more informal and had the atmosphere of a family picnic. It was held in the open, on the verandah of the famous Mures seafood restaurant in Hobart docks.

The Premier, Mr Field, sat at a table facing his own Health Minister, Mr White, and two bottles of locally-made Cascade lager, with an elusive thylacine – the extinct Tasmanian tiger – on the label. They were launching the Better Living campaign for Tasmania, with the stress on exercise ('Labour recognises the increasing popularity of cycling') and low-alcohol beer, which Cascade wasn't.

Answering questions, Mr Field called the Liberal assumptions of a secret Labour–Green alliance an 'outrageous libel' and said it was the Greens and the Liberals themselves who 'did a dirty deal'. Then he began his lunch, assembled media watching. I remembered that in ancient China the highest privilege for a commoner was to see how the emperor ate.

It also occurred to me that the political situation in Tasmania might be compared to the archetypal lovers' triangle. For many months G (the Green Party) was living happily with Lab (Labour) until she jilted him, sided with Lib (the Liberals) and, in Mr Field's own words, his minority government became unworkable. Now both Lib and Lab were vying for the favours of capricious G, but she had decided to be fully independent and live on her own.

Tasmanian elections represented a microcosm of a polling campaign in almost any other Western country. In such a remote and seemingly happy place were they likely to be any different? Trying to spot a difference, I undertook a three-day-long drive across the island, having, unwillingly, found myself on a bumpy Tasmanian campaign trail.

I stopped to buy a film at the Bagdad general store. There was only one shop in Bagdad, and it was selling everything, from petrol to lollipops. And certainly I couldn't help asking Wayne, the storekeeper, why this little rivulet – the Jordan River – and this small unremarkable hamlet not far from Hobart had such unusual exotic names.

'Everyone keeps asking this question,' the storekeeper answered with visible annoyance. 'I guess this place was started by an Englishman who had served in the Persian Gulf before coming here. He was probably missing it, hence the names.' The English settler was evidently very nostalgic and not very literate: he missed not only the Persian Gulf, but he had also managed to miss the 'h' in Baghdad.

My next question was naturally about Tasmanian elections. Here Wayne was even more reluctant to voice his opinion. Instead of answering, he went to a store-room behind the counter and re-emerged holding a pile of leaflets and envelopes. 'Here, you can have them all,' he said and added: 'I don't need all this junk . . .'

I sat on the grass at the roadside, in the shade of a gum tree, giving little protection against the midday Bagdad sun, and immersed myself into the passions of Tasmanian election warfare.

In a neatly sealed envelope, discreetly addressed 'To the Householder', there was a pamphlet 'respectfully asking' him to vote for The Duke, a Liberal candidate with a cumbersome name – His Grace, The Most Noble, The Duke of Avram, John', no less. In the leaflet the Duke of Avram, claiming to be a sixth-generation Tasmanian, was referring to himself as 'highly motivated and not afraid to speak up and be heard'. Well, modesty has never been rife among dukes . . .

The second envelope contained a family photograph of yet

another Liberal candidate, Malcolm Cleland, featuring, apart from his smiling self, his smiling wife and his two smiling daughters. His manner of addressing the electorate was in stark contrast with that of His Liberal Grace.

'I am an ordinary sort of bloke, married for 20 years,' the enclosed leaflet ran. 'Jo and I have two lovely daughters, Victoria and Amy. As you can see, I am more comfortable in an open-neck shirt and having my hands dirty – being on formal parade is not usually my style.'

In the photo he was indeed depicted in a democratic open-neck shirt. As to his hands, there was no telling whether they were dirty or not: the photo was a head shot. In the end there was the invitation to call Malcolm Cleland at home and, curiously enough, his home phone number, too. Reading this, one could hardly refrain from crying out: 'Good on yer, mate!' and I felt an irrepressible urge to shake the candidate's hand, even if it was dirty.

Browsing through another half-a-dozen leaflets (all expressing genuine concerns, refraining from making rash promises and castigating the opponents), I was growing more and more sympathetic to the anti-pulp position of the Greens: it was such an apparent waste of paper. Unwilling to do any further harm to the already embattled Tasmanian environment, I carefully put the leaflets into the nearest rubbish bin and drove off to the accompaniment of the lazy Bagdad dogs' lunch-time barking. I had had enough of this Tasmanian mini-Iraq and wanted to get somewhere else.

The elections had visibly transformed the Tasmanian country-side. Grinning portraits of the candidates were attached to the abandoned cars parked at the roadside; they were sticking out from the long wooden poles in the fields like scarecrows (and were probably used for just this purpose by the enterprising farmers); they were winking at me from behind the trees; with a sniper's precision they were targeting my submissive eyes from a long range with their 10-inch shrapnel-like letters. 'Honesty and Integrity! Vote for Ian Braig!', 'Vote for John Davidson!', 'Vote for Eugene Alexander!'

These signs were interspersed with 'For Sale' ones on the colonial country houses, so that for an outsider driving past them along the freeway at 100 kph they would all be merging into one lengthy signpost: 'Vote for Sale!' Indeed, this mysterious Mr Sale was by far the most highly publicised candidate in the Tasmanian elections – a very natural phenomenon for a state where 11.7 per cent of the population had no jobs.

I remembered how a day earlier in Hobart I was inspecting the employment ads on a wooden notice board at the local CES (Commonwealth Employment Service) office. It was not that there hadn't been any. There was a vacancy for a teacher of Japanese in Hobart, a *yum cha* cook in Moonah, a Japanese cook in Somerset, a ski technician, an optometrist – about a dozen altogether. So for someone who couldn't either speak or cook Japanese, who was neither a *yum cha* technician nor a ski optometrist, there was nothing much to do in Tasmania. This explained the almost Soviet-style apathy towards the elections.

I drove for several hours through hills, forests and endless fields. I passed through nondescript little towns, where local teenagers, bored out of their minds, were absent-mindedly tossing stones into rubbish bins in town squares to while away the time. Boredom is the mother of all vices. Wasn't it, among other things, the extreme dullness of provincial existence that made Martin Bryant, a wealthy and mentally unstable Tasmanian youth, pull the trigger of his automatic rifle and kill those thirty-five people in April 1996 in Port Arthur?

'Paradise Junction', said a road sign. I followed the arrow and turned right onto a dirt track.

The road to Paradise was empty.

I drove past a shabby wooden hut with 'Paradise Baptist Church' written in big black letters above the door. Baptists were obviously the smartest lot on the way to Paradise. Paradise itself was just a small dairy farm. 'Is this Paradise?' I asked a bearded farmer with the looks of St Paul. Instead of an answer, he waved his hand, jumped into the cabin of his tractor and chugged away. He was probably used to idle questions of this sort from visitors arriving by accident. I had reached a blind alley and had to turn back. My little detour was not totally useless, though. It was a timely reminder of the fact that paradise didn't exist in real life. Not even in Tasmania.

Shortcut to Paradise. What a good title for a gushy Mills & Boon novel.

Although not in Paradise, I did meet one happy Tasmanian in the end. His name was Roelf Vos, and he was the owner of fourteen supermarkets in and around Launceston, Tasmania's second largest town. I met him in the Swiss village of Grindenwald, the village that he himself designed and built in the centre of Tasmania. It was an exact copy of a hamlet somewhere in Swiss Alps. Mr Vos was a highly successful entrepreneur and a self-made millionaire. He emigrated to Tasmania from Holland after World War Two with not a guilder in his pocket. He supported the Liberals and strongly believed that Tasmania needed more industrial development.

We were talking to the muffled sounds of um-pa-pa music coming from loudspeakers scattered all over the village. Grindenwald looked neat and spotlessly clean, but it was also not very real. A dream village in the land of broken dreams. It looked like a spot of bright paint, left by a careless plasterer on the weathering facade.

I drove on.

Tasmanian landscapes remained strikingly, breathtakingly beautiful, as if nature itself decided to have its final feast on the island where solid land ends to show everything it was capable of. It remained unperturbed by the circus of Tasmanian elections. It didn't care a pin whether Labour or the Liberals won. And neither did I.

Tasmania, the ecologically purest place in the world, the place where even rain water is so clean that it is shipped for sale to Japan, could indeed be the closest proximity to earthly paradise. But paradise and hell are next door neighbours. Shortly after our meeting, Roelf Vos, my only happy Tasmanian, died of cancer. And four years later Martin Bryant blasted the parochial silence of the island with his rifle, turning paradise into inferno.

I will always remember the 1992 Tasmanian elections – my first introduction to the most important Western liberty: Freedom of Choice.

As far as I can recall, they were won by the Liberals.

18

Home, Sad Home

I have become a house-owner.

The feeling is so strange, acute and alien that I find it hard to believe that it's all happening to me in reality. Just another intense heat-invoked Australian dream? I keep repeating aloud: 'I am a house-owner, I am a house-owner, I am a house-owner . . .', but it does little to prepare me for this sudden capitalist reality. 'Vitali Buys a House' – such was the banner headline on the front page of the *Age* the other day.

I woke up yesterday morning to the cheerful singing of suburban birds, with reflections of sunrays jumping on my face. A festive, radiant light was falling into my room from the window, and there, from the corner of my eye, I could discern the slightly rocking branch of the lemon tree. Have you ever noticed that the voices of birds in the suburbs are quite different from those in the city, louder and more optimistic? And the sunlight is softer and brighter. And the air . . .

Do you realise that a house can breathe? Yes, breathe, just like a human being. It is only your own house that is capable of breathing, by the way. A block of council flats does not have a distinctive breath of its own, and if it does it reeks of cabbage soup and cheap tobacco. A suburban house, especially a wooden one, shivers in winter and perspires in summer. It yawns in the morning and snores at night.

My own first house is far from a palace or a mansion. In fact, in terms of living space it's almost as little as our former flat in St Kilda, which we rented for over a year. But it has an indoor swimming pool and a Jacuzzi, ingeniously built by the previous owner into an extended garage in the backyard. It was the swimming pool that made us buy this particular house.

In Australia, a swimming pool is not a luxury, but rather a necessity. In summer it plays the role a fridge in a European household does. Only in Australia this fridge is used for cooling down people, not food. But for us it was definitely a luxury bordering on decadence. It was a touch of a Hollywood movie coming to life. We didn't know that in Melbourne, with its cold winters and not too hot (by Australian standards) summers, an indoor swimming pool was rather a liability than an asset. It needed constant heating which resulted in eye-popping gas bills. It needed daily cleaning and looking after, almost on a full-time basis. It was under constant risk of rot, black fungi and other mysterious water infections. Its pump and filter had to be fixed and replaced regularly, and all swimming pool plumbers of Melbourne were either mad or greedy. Or both. In short, it was rather a white elephant than a bonanza. As we found out later, because of this very swimming pool the house was often floating on the waves of the real estate market, since no owners could afford maintaining it for more than a couple of years.

On top of this, we (or rather I as the family's only working member) became enslaved by a huge mortgage with fixed (and hefty) interest rates which, even with my high salary, we could hardly afford. Yes, buying this house was a huge mistake, but it took us some time to realise it. The swimming pool with its green underwater lights, the bubbling spa bath, the pebble-stone barbecue ('barbie') in the backyard and the rotating hoist for drying the washing – a major Australian invention – were all impossible to resist.

Just try and imagine yourself in the trampled shoes of someone who has spent most of his life in the so-called communal flats. What is a communal flat? This is a typical Soviet apartment, into which several families are crammed so that they have to share a kitchen, a bathroom and a toilet. It was not unusual for up to twenty families to live together; not just under one roof, but also sharing one and the same dark corridor, where dogs and children played all the time. A communal flat also meant permanent vociferous squabbles in the kitchen and never-ending queues to the only lavatory, with a dozen replaceable wooden toilet seats (one for each family) hanging from nails in the wall like giant horse-shoes in an English country pub.

I remember how, when I was four years old, one of the tenants of our communal flat used to keep his motorcycle in the corridor (we lived on the fourth floor of a drab apartment block, and he had to carry his motorbike up and down the stairs every day). I liked to play with this technological miracle, which was parked next to the doors of our room and gave out a strong smell of petrol. One day the motorcycle suddenly jerked and fell down, burying me under it. Fortunately, my parents were quick to react to my screams and rushed out of their room just in time to save me from the deadly grip of the foul-smelling mechanical monster.

By the way, even the tiny rooms in communal flats did not formally belong to those who lived in them. We were only allowed to rent them from the state. The rent was meagre indeed, but so were the living conditions.

One of the reasons behind our hasty decision to buy a house in Melbourne was that we had had a particularly sad communal flat experience in Moscow only several years before. After a quiet old woman, who occupied one of the rooms in our flat, died we had a new neighbour, a young man, who was the son of a well-known Soviet literary functionary, one of the powerful Secretaries of the Soviet Union of Writers. This youngster led a life of booze and dissipation. As it turned out later, his father, unable to cope with his wayward scion, found him a room in a communal flat for the neighbours to keep an eye on him – a convenient solution. Our life became a constant hell. Every single night there was a boisterous drunken orgy in our flat. The corridor was swarming with alcoholics, speculators and prostitutes who were all using our one and only communal bathroom of course. Mitya, who was still a baby, couldn't sleep because of the noise they made.

Several times I had to call the police, but our new neighbour's influential father always managed to keep his son out of real trouble. It was only when I threatened to write a feuilleton (a satirical article) about his son's behaviour that the father got really frightened (a critical article in the national press could harm even his reputation) and tried to blackmail me by threatening to block my journalistic career (which he could do easily if he wanted to). But since my journalistic name had been well-established by then, he eventually chose to move his feckless offspring out of our flat.

On the other hand, if your neighbours were not drug-addicts or drunks, despite occasional kitchen arguments, communal flats had a certain spirit of camaraderie about them. Neighbours used to baby-sit each other's kids, buy short-supplied goods for the whole flat, borrow chairs and cutlery from each other in case of a party, to which all other tenants would be routinely invited, and so on. When people are forced to live in equally miserable conditions, they are prone to forging close relations with each other.

I remember sharing a communal flat with a family of Soviet Greeks: four adults and two children, all in one room sixteen metres square. On top (literally!) of themselves, they always had visitors from the Caucasus staying with them. Where they all slept in that tiny room was a mystery. But despite (or maybe because of) their predicament, the Greeks were nice and kind people, always ready to help us and to look after Mitya when we had to go out.

We were much luckier to have nineteen square metres for only three of us.

The biggest psychological barrier for me as a new house-owner was the negative attitude towards private property in general which had been meticulously knocked into our brains since childhood. Private property had always been the Bolsheviks' biggest anathema, simply because private ownership of anything requires initiative and initiative, in its turn, leads to free thought (i.e. dissent). At schools and kindergartens we were fed with the image of a fat, greedy and ruthless landlord, merciless and idle exploiter of workers, peasants and other underdogs. We were taught that the only way to deal with capitalists was forcibly to take their properties away from them and divide them equally between the have-nots.

This was quite a noble principle on paper. The only problem that made it totally unworkable was that when it came to the real thing, those in charge of dividing always wanted to reserve the biggest piece of cake for themselves.

Had it something to do with all the beautiful and not so beautiful imperfections of human nature?

While Natasha is working happily in the garden, I keep wandering aimlessly around my new house – from the lounge room to my study and then to the backyard – feeling some inexplicable guilt. And although I have honestly earned every cent of the money with which the house was bought, I feel as if I have stolen someone else's life, which I now have to lead, while this anonymous someone is leading my own life somewhere else.

It was all too sudden and all too quick for me to come to grips with.

Or maybe the reason for my sadness is different? Maybe it is triggered by the feeling of having achieved everything I have ever wanted to achieve (and more) and of not having much else left to strive for?

Sergei Dovlatov, a fellow émigré writer (who died of alcoholism in New York in 1992), wrote in one of his letters from America: 'All my life I had been waiting for something: for my secondary education certificate, for loss of virginity, for marriage, for a child, for my first book, for some minimal material stability, and now, when all these have happened, there's nothing else to expect; the source of joy has vanished . . .'

Have I reached the end of the line, from where it is only possible to go back?

19

Spiders

Despite Clive James's sinister warnings of the abundance of creepy-crawlies in Australia, we hadn't seen many of them as yet. Our closest encounter with Australian domestic fauna so far was that huge black cockroach in our flat in Sydney. I got rid of the beast by blocking the entrance (or was it the exit?) to his bathroom hole with sticky tape. The monster tried to break through, ramming the tape desperately from inside with his antennae. Eventually, he gave up and disappeared, probably went to dwell in someone else's bathroom.

It was only with our move to the new house in the quiet (or rather dead) Melbourne suburb of East Bentleigh that we were able to comprehend what Clive really meant when he called his native Australia 'a land of crawling danger' in his *Unreliable Memoirs*. The second chapter, cheerfully entitled 'Valley of Killer Snakes', abounded in remarks like 'The real horror among spiders was more likely to be encountered in the lavatory.'

Here I must confess that of all 555 medically described phobias with tongue-breaking names – from ailurophobia (fear of cats) and soceraphobia (not fear of soccer, as you might have thought, but fear of parents-in-law) to pantophobia (fear of everything, including phobias themselves, I presume) – there was probably only one by which I remained definitely unaffected: natalophobia: a maniacal fear of giving birth.

As for arachnophobia – fear of spiders – I could list myself among the most obsessive arachnophobes in the world. No matter how hard I tried to pacify myself with the thought that many great writers had felt quite positive towards these horrific insects, and Edgar Allan Poe and Vladimir Nabokov had even been experienced amateur entomologists, the very word spider – or *pauk* in Russian – never failed to send shivers down my spine. This terror of mine was mercilessly exploited by my son Mitya who, during our spell in London, bought a saucer-sized plastic spider in one of those rubbish shops in Soho, and had a nasty habit of planting it on my pillow first thing in the morning.

After a year in Australia, I felt that many locals took genuine pride in their spiders. I've noticed a characteristic sparkle of excitement in the eyes of a person who recounted how the other day he saw a 'bloody awful huntsman'. I have also noticed that a modernistic flagpole on the top of the Federal Parliament House in Canberra had a clearly spider-like shape. Was there some hidden menace in it?

The huntsman is one of Australia's most terrifying spiders: although completely harmless (and probably even useful due to his insatiable appetite for flies), it is the size of a dinner plate and covered with thick fluff (I nearly wrote 'fur'). His sharp and protruding beady eyes rotate and follow your every movement. When climbing up and down the wall, he makes a soft shuffling sound with his legs, like an old man dragging his slippers along the floor. Maybe the abundance of these loathsome creatures was a price one had to pay for enjoying all other abundances of Australian life?

Since we moved to our new house, Mitya's plastic toy spider largely lost its effectiveness as my wake-up bugaboo. More than once I was awoken by Natasha's screams coming from the bathroom. Thinking that she was being kidnapped, I would rush to rescue her, only to find her pointing frantically at the ceiling where a giant coal-black creature, looking more like an octopus than a spider, would be standing motionless, as if hypnotised by her screams. My next move would be to grab a broom and try to hit the octopus with the handle. This would result in numerous broom-inflicted holes in the ceiling and walls which could serve as excellent dwellings (and shelters) not only for this particular (and absolutely unharmed) spider, but for many of his relatives too. I could almost hear him (or her) rubbing his disgusting legs in glee and saying to me: 'Good on yer, mate!'

One gets used to everything, and after a while we got more or less accustomed to our silent creeping neighbours. At least they didn't turn the TV to the highest volume or quarrel vociferously in the middle of the night, as the neighbours in our Moscow communal flat used to do. We stopped shuddering at the sight of an innocent daddy-long-legs on the walls.

Soon I was able to watch quietly a self-important garden orb spider weaving his web under the roof of our swimming pool. The geometrically correct web was more like a piece of sophisticated lace, a real work of art. Having finished weaving, the spider placed himself into the web's centre and started waiting. Next morning he was still there, but the net remained empty. I couldn't help admiring the creature's patience and stamina. It reminded me of the countless hours I spent with a fishing rod on the banks of the polluted Moskva River, where to catch a fish was no easier than for a Melbourne spider to woo a somnambulant Australian fly in late autumn. The spider was there for a couple of days, and when eventually, having despaired of catching anything but cold, he reeled his web off and went to hibernate, we all felt sorry for our *pauk*.

Without realising it, the spider had unwillingly helped us to overcome one of the stereotypes of Australian life.

Cured of arachnophobia (well, almost), I wanted to find out more about spiders and visited a Melbourne company called Exopest Australia, where I spoke to a young entomologist who was one of Melbourne's biggest authorities on this creepy (but no longer chilling) subject.

'General dislike of spiders is provoked by prejudice and fear,' he told me. 'It's amazing how such a little creature [he didn't mean a huntsman or a garden orb, I assumed] can create so much scare. Most Australian spiders are very helpful, and only two per cent of them are poisonous. True, they are not aesthetically attractive [that was a gross understatement, I thought], but this is just their biological means of protection. If a prey looks scary, the predator will be less likely to attack it. Biologically, spiders are very successful: they can move with amazing speed, they can squeeze into the smallest of holes. Yes, indeed, they are not social creatures [thank God!], they are solitary, which adds to their sinister image, but they are not so bad after all . . .'

He told me about a garden spider that could actually throw his web like a lasso (a cowboy spider, I would call him) and about the ones that could catch and eat a whole mouse (wasn't my bathroom friend one of them?).

Frankly, I could still understand the man who, having spotted an innocent huntsman in his car, had it towed to Exopest for fumigation. I was still quite reluctant to repeat after the young entomologist, 'I like spiders.' But I was no longer afraid of them (or disgusted by them). This seemingly trifling change of attitude was significant in my attempts to adjust to Australian life.

When invited one day to open an annual conference of Victoria's pest controllers, I started my address with the following statement:

On the way to the conference room I could observe some of your fellow pest controllers arranging drinks and snacks in the lobby. It is obvious that you are preparing for a feast, and I understand you: it's not often that all pest controllers of Victoria can get together in one place. But while drinking your wine and enjoying your food, while discussing new pioneering ways of eliminating creepy-crawlies from our environment, you should remember that at the same time – in dark attics and cellars all over Victoria – spiders, flies, wasps and other pests are having little feasts of their own, simply because you are all here. They are also having their own conferences to discuss how they can best withstand pest controllers and they are probably thanking you from the bottoms of their little hearts for having granted them one day of peace and quiet . . .

I think my joke fell on deaf ears.

Indian summer came to Melbourne in April (it should have been called 'Brazilian summer' instead), and soft, almost transparent, gossamers sparkled under the last rays of the giant red spider of the Australian sun, like delicate silver threads connecting it with the earth.

We were all caught in the fine cobweb of autumn.

20

Dreaming of Paris

Poets write about spring,
About nightingales, and about Paris:
There, people love each other like in a dream,
And the Seine is licking the muses' heels . . .

I saw Paris in my dream last night.
He was a youth, both friendly and homey,
Strolling along the Seine until sunrise
In an embrace with the Eiffel Tower.

The Tower was clad in a mini-skirt,
And Paris was charming and long-nosed.
Like sponges, their lips have absorbed
The sweet calvados of dawn.

But then large flocks of tourists,
Having not watched their dreams to the end,
Came out to graze with an old Guide,
The unhappiest of all the world's shepherds.

And when the Guide started telling the tourists
What a great and multi-faced city Paris was,
The youth pulled his cloth cap over his eyes
And put up the collar of his jacket . . .

This is the English translation of the poem I wrote in Kharkov at the age of fifteen.

Paris for me – and for many of my compatriots – was not just a city, not just the capital of France brimming with paintings, sculpture and architectural masterpieces. It was a symbol of Western Freedom, an archetype of real-life romanticism and wonderful indulgences, a cornucopia of sweet human decadence.

It was also totally unreachable.

An old Soviet joke:

'I want to go to Paris again . . .'

'Have you been there before?'

'No, but I have wanted to before . . .'

An old tattered map of Paris was the pride of my ever-growing collection of guide-books, atlases and train time-tables. I would stare at it until my eyes started hurting, until I was able to discern behind its threadbare paper the outlines of the Eiffel Tower; until I could smell the aroma of freshly-made coffee in the Champs Elysées. In a self-induced dream-like state I could walk, with my eyes closed, from Saint-Germain-des-Prés on the Left Bank to Montmartre.

At the age of fifteen, already fluent in English, I started learning French with a Belgian tutor, thrown to Kharkov by some extraordinary twist of fate. Soon, these lessons had to be stopped: my parents found out that the teacher was a 'foreign citizen', any contacts with whom could jeopardise my future career and eliminate the chance of being admitted to the university, which meant being immediately drafted to the Soviet Army.

The risk was too big to run.

At the university we were taught foreign languages by teachers (mostly Jewish) who had never been abroad themselves, but some of whom had nevertheless achieved amazing results and couldn't be distinguished from native speakers. One – Beatrice Rogovskaya, who taught us Theoretical English Grammar (one of my favourite subjects) and spoke English with a good London accent – was finally 'allowed' to visit Britain for the first time only after the collapse of the Soviet Union, when she was already in her late sixties. The shock of actually seeing the country which preoccupied her whole life was too much for her: she died of a heart attack on the day she was due to go back home.

'I am dying to go to England,' she liked to say to her students. A tragic symmetry of life. And of death, too.

Recently I read a short story by Mikhail Veller, a Russian émigré writer of extraordinary talent. Entitled 'I Want to go to Paris', it chronicles the life of Dima Korenkov, a man from a God-forsaken provincial Soviet town. As a boy he grew besotted with Paris, France and everything French. He learnt the language on his own and managed (with the help of old records) to develop impeccable pronunciation. As a young man he collected every piece of knowledge about France he could. He was aware of all the latest trends in Paris fashion which he tried to imitate. Working at a factory, he never drank with his colleagues on pay days: he preferred spending all his free time perfecting his unparalleled knowledge of France.

Several times he applied to his factory's trade union committee for 'permission' to go to France as a tourist, but since he was just an ordinary worker his applications were invariably refused: only big shots with spotless party records and mighty pull in high places were allowed to travel outside the Soviet Union.

Dima Korenkov was getting older. He had family, children and then grandchildren, but his passion for France did not subside, although several times he tried to give it up in despair and went on drinking sprees. One year before his retirement, he decided to make one last try. He threatened, he intrigued, he simulated heart attacks and eventually managed to frighten the trade union bosses into giving him permission to travel to Paris. He passed with flying colours the interview obligatory for everyone going abroad at the regional party committee during which he was asked the names of all the general secretaries of the French communist party since its foundation and heaps of other nonsense (failure to answer even one of the questions meant almost certain refusal). He paid his whole life savings for the ticket and the voucher . . .

And here he was in Paris which, as it quickly turned out, he knew much better than their French guide, a French

History student of La Sorbonne. Dima was familiar with every corner, every building and every stone. He was basking in the atmosphere of the place where he clearly belonged. In short, he was having the time of his life . . .

On his last morning before going back, he woke up in his hotel room (which he shared with a KGB stooge, part of every Soviet tourist group abroad) and suddenly realised that he couldn't leave Paris. He did not have all that many years left to live, his children and grandchildren had grown up and didn't need his help any longer. He had nothing to lose. And he decided to stay, i.e. to defect.

He ran out into the street, turned the corner, melted into the cheerful Parisian crowd – and suddenly noticed that everyone in Paris was speaking . . . Russian. He looked around: faded Russian signs were decorating the facades of drab Soviet-style apartment blocks; scruffily dressed pedestrians had a Soviet downtrodden expression on their faces; and the Eiffel Tower, which was just forty metres high, had a stamp of Dnepropetrovsk Steel Rolling Works on one of its rust-eaten supports.

He was trudging through the wings of a huge real-life theatre. The centre of Paris was but a crudely painted canvas, stretched against the drab and painfully familiar Soviet carcass. Cobbled streets and graceful houses, tiled roofs and blooming chestnut trees were all either painted or made of cardboard and papier-mâché. It was nothing but massive window-dressing.

Dima took out his cigarette lighter and set the canvas on fire.

'Paris has never existed. It never was and never will be . . .' – this is how the story ends.

Living in the Soviet Union, it was easier to think that there was no real life west of Kaliningrad and east of Khabarovsk. Until a fairly mature age I myself used to experience periodic doubts as to whether the free Western world existed at all and was not just another KGB fabrication to keep the Soviet people on the alert.

Weren't Western radio stations, whose heavily jammed

call signs reached me occasionally from my primitive Soviet short-wave receiver, operated from a special KGB station, somewhere in Siberia? And weren't all those colourful Western brochures and bulky newspapers, which I was occasionally able to lay my knowledge-hungry hands upon, printed by the special Red Banner of Labour KGB publishing house? As to those lucky ones, who had allegedly visited the West, weren't they all kept for the duration of their journeys at a KGB safe house, somewhere deep in the forest, where they were lectured, brainwashed and instructed as to what to say on return?

I first went to Paris in summer, 1992, when I was already living in Australia, and, frankly, I was unimpressed. Well, I am in Paris at last, so what? I kept thinking. Maybe it was because I had already seen a number of Western cities and preferred London to all of them. Or maybe it was due to the fact that I was travelling in the company of boisterous American tourists (I was the only non-American member in our group) who reacted to everything they saw in a childish way: they burst into applause at the sight of the Eiffel Tower, as if expecting it to curtsy in return. And less than a year later I went to Paris with Mitya and Natasha. It proved to be our last trip as a family before the break-up.

I was hoping that life in the West would cure my irrepressible itch to travel. Life in Australia (which was part of the Western world, at least in theory) did the opposite. Before settling in Melbourne, I had just managed to get a quick glimpse of Britain and America. It was not enough and only whetted my appetite for seeing the whole world. And although Australia was a free country, where one didn't need to get official permission to travel, it was in many ways as closed and as cut off from the rest of the world as the Soviet Union, simply because it was so far away.

One could (at least theoretically) crawl under, fly over or ram through the Berlin Wall, made up of the loosely fitting bricks of communist doctrine. The Dollar Wall, with somewhat unstable, yet totally incorruptible, Captain Buck as its only border guard, was, curiously, even more impregnable.

The tyranny of distance came to replace the tyranny of dogma.

I couldn't help noticing that, just like in the Soviet Union, going abroad was the most popular subject of conversations at many Australian barbies. Even the relatively well-travelled newspaper executives constantly boasted of their overseas pilgrimages at their endless lunches: 'When I was in Europe . . .', 'When I recently went to the USA . . .'

A trip abroad in Australia, just like in the Soviet Union, was often regarded as a personal achievement – on a par with obtaining a doctorate or winning a Tattslotto jackpot.

If you happen to watch the ITV Sunday show *Surprise! Surprise!*, presented by the unfading Cilla Black, you can't help noticing that the most common sort of 'surprise' is an ITV-sponsored re-unification of someone from the audience with his or her relatives in Australia – the first in forty or fifty years. If only fifty or sixty years ago going to live in Australia for a European meant disappearing down a black hole with practically no chance of return, now the possibility of a come-back, although higher, still remains largely hypothetical for a person of modest means. Not too many people would be prepared to cough up their monthly salary or two just for the ticket.

If Australians travel, it is usually in their late teens or early twenties. They spend a couple of years overseas working their way through as many countries as possible and then come back home and do not often venture outside their state, or even their suburb.

Just as many years ago in Kharkov and in Moscow, I started suffering from my childhood disease, dromomania – an irrepressible itch to travel – in Australia. Only this time, its pangs were much more painful and were often provoked by a TV commercial for new Qantas travel bargains or by the windows of the countless Go Away travel agencies in suburban high streets: 'London from just A$1500 return . . .'

The world was so accessible and so near, but, on the other hand, it was incredibly far away.

Again, as many years ago, I was spending hours combing

radio waves in search of some decent world news and trying to tune to the evasive BBC World Service that could only be received in Melbourne after midnight.

Australian sketchy news updates, except for the 6.30 p.m. news bulletin on SBS, a state-run ethnic TV channel, were mostly limited to petty crime, local politics and sport, sport, sport, and I felt hopelessly out of date if I missed the SBS news slot, presented by charismatic Greek news reader, Mary Kostakidis.

A typical news bulletin on Australian television, often interrupted by primitive commercials for sweets and laxatives ('Rectinol! It's music to your rear!'), could be summarised as Prime Minister Paul Keating eating a sugar-free chocolate bar in the middle of a bushfire. On the historic day of German re-unification, say, the main news on Australian commercial channels was the 'unification' of two of Murdoch's newspapers in Melbourne, a tabloid and a broadsheet, into one 'broadloid' or 'tablosheet'.

Freedom of choice, one of the basic Freedoms of Western civilisation, was strictly rationed in Australia.

To make up for this enforced information diet, I subscribed to a dozen British and American periodicals which started arriving in heavy bundles and were usually a couple of weeks old. I read them from cover to cover well into the small hours until bright spots started dancing in front of my eyes and my head was tolling like a church bell at Easter. I was missing my old Europe, especially England, the country that opened for me a window to the West, with such pain and passion that I was sometimes worried about my sanity. Frequent trips to Tasmania didn't seem to help any longer: Tasmania was but a well-made carbon copy of Europe, and going there only increased my craving for the original.

My weekly column in the *Age*, which was now called 'Vitali on Monday', continued to enjoy an enormous following, and the paper's sales on Mondays were considerably higher than on any other day of the week. But I was running out of subjects. Having covered every imaginable aspect of Australian life from maternity units to golf and advanced driving schools, I was increasingly concentrating in my columns on my own spiritual world and on my ever-growing nostalgia, or simply fooled around.

'Cosiness is the worst enemy of a writer,' said a fellow Russian scribe.

Just as during my long years in the Soviet Union, I was living inside myself . . .

In September 1991 a collection of my *Age* columns was released by Random House, Australia. Several publishers were vying to publish it, but Clarissa, my London literary agent, opted for Random House. The book triggered heaps of new readers' letters, one of which was probably the most moving in all my writer's career.

It was from a young Melbourne chap who received a copy of *Vitali's Australia* for Christmas and read it on the plane to Detroit, USA, where his American girlfriend, whom he wanted to marry, lived. His girlfriend's mother was opposed to their marriage, thinking that Australia was too remote a place for her daughter. Having read my book, however, she, as my reader wrote, 'came to realise that Australia was not as far off and foreign as it had seemed'. Her changed view of Australia became a factor in the couple's final decision to marry and make their home in Melbourne. 'I thank you, Vitali, for your assistance and invite you to our wedding,' he wrote. Thus, for the first and last time in my life, I played the unwitting role of Cupid.

Vitali's Australia was soon made into a fifty-two-minute ABC television programme which I myself wrote and presented. In it, Australia was played by a fifteen-year-old girl – blonde, freckled and sportive – whom I spotted quite by chance in the *Age* newsroom where she was having her work experience. I wanted to show Australia as a teenage girl of a country – that was how I was more and more inclined to see it.

My own married life was not going too smoothly.

Feeling trapped and unhappy in our new house, I was finding solace in heavy drinking and hearty eating, for both of which there were plenty of opportunities in Melbourne, probably the most hedonistic city in the world. I took a liking to several Melbourne restaurants and wrote articles about them for the *Epicure* section of the *Age*. These restaurants immediately gained popularity, and I was always a welcome guest there. 'Don't write about this nice restaurant, Dad! People will start coming here in droves, and we won't be able to get in!' Mitya would say after yet another dinner out.

The idea of writing about food, which used to be a complete anathema to me (during my first months in Melbourne I swore never to contribute to *Epicure*), was suddenly quite exciting: the amazing versatility of Melbourne's ethnic restaurants was for me just another substitute for travelling the world.

Lack of exercise (I was too lazy and apathetic even to use my own swimming pool) and the typically Australian obsession with driving rather than walking everywhere, even to a corner shop (or milk bar, as they say), topped up with plenty of drink and food couldn't fail but make me fatter and fatter. I was also smoking more than ever before. A visit to a health farm, arranged by my friends, had but a short-term effect: I gave up smoking for several months and then started again.

Once, during a routine health check, I was diagnosed as having liver cirrhosis which sounded pretty much like a death sentence. Curiously, I wasn't particularly concerned. Natasha insisted I went to see another doctor to get a second opinion. The initial diagnosis proved to be a mistake.

I was not sure whether to rejoice or to grieve. I felt trapped in Australia, and life had largely lost its meaning for me.

'Spiritual heartburn' was turning into permanent hangover.

But there were some brighter moments as well, and one of them was an exclusive interview with Rudolf Nureyev, who came to Melbourne during his farewell tour with the stars of world ballet. He only agreed to be interviewed by one Melbourne journalist, and his manager Michael Eldgeley chose me. It was one of Nureyev's last interviews.

I was rather taken aback when I entered his hotel room and saw the legendary dancer sitting in an armchair, with his thin long-fingered sinewy hands resting on his lap like two tired birds whose life-long flight was almost over. He was a shadow of the Nureyev we all knew: thin and stooped, as if withered and bent by some inhuman burden. His tragic Tartar eyes were filled with pain and that special kind of rueful wisdom that one can only find in the eyes of the mortally ill. They were filled with doom. His voice was hoarse and quiet, almost a whisper.

His face, with hollow cheeks and protruding cheekbones, was the face of a sufferer. It was also the face of a boy from the smoky industrial city of Ufa in the Urals, eagerly watching the trains rattling away towards lands mysterious and unknown.

Yes, just like myself, Nureyev had been a trainspotter and an armchair traveller when a teenager. He told me that he was born on a train and added gently: 'Yes, I am a vagabond . . .'

From childhood he had been fascinated by the sight of a train crossing the bridge over a river in Ufa on its way to Siberia and Vladivostok. 'This haunting sound of the train filled me with nostalgia and longing to see other places . . .'

I could not believe my ears: one of this century's greatest artists was speaking out my innermost thoughts.

When I suggested we speak Russian, he mumbled decisively: 'English'. I didn't blame him. The scar left on the artist's soul by the Soviet regime must have been too painful to touch. He told me how at school he used to be tormented by kids and teachers for his passion to dance.

'Do you know what's in my old school building now? A choreographic school – by sheer coincidence. What an irony!'

I thought then that it was not an irony, but a victory. A decisive victory of sparkling art over drab reality, of dancing as a way of life as opposed to standing at attention and marking time, of talent over mediocrity.

He talked about his 'leap to Freedom' at a Paris airport in 1961, about his life in ballet, about his dancing partners. At the mention of Margot Fonteyn his eyes lit up, then dimmed again.

I asked him: 'Do you have many friends?'

'No,' he replied after some hesitation. 'My best friends are dead, and now I don't have any.'

He had very sad memories of Russia and claimed he was

not nostalgic for the place. 'It hasn't changed. They are the same people. They will never change . . . Russian ballet? It stopped growing a long time ago and hasn't created anything new of late.'

I asked him: 'Are you happy with your life?'

He was silent for a long while and then said: 'I think I have achieved quite a lot, but there's one more thing I'd like to do. Now that my dancing career is over I want to conduct, to become a good orchestral conductor. I think I will be able to do this.'

At the time I was thinking of making a film about Olga Spessivtseva, the famous Russian émigré ballerina of the 1920s. I told Nureyev about it and asked him whether he would fancy playing Nijinsky in such a film, if it ever got off the ground.

'I am too old for that,' he said. 'To play Nijinsky one should be much younger.'

I spent almost two hours with Nureyev. It was time to say goodbye. Before leaving I asked him for an autograph for my son. 'What's his name? Mitya? A good Russian name,' he said with sudden warmth. 'How old is he?'

And instead of just a signature, he wrote a cordial little message: 'Dear Mitya, I wish you all the best in this life and hope you will be happy!'

He was saying goodbye to *this* life.

Next evening I saw Nureyev dance at Melbourne's National Theatre. It was not strictly dancing: he was just slowly walking on stage, but there was so much grace in his every movement. He was playing in Debussy's one-act ballet, *L'Apres-Midi d'un Faune*, at the end of which the mythical Faun dies. There was a storm of applause when the curtain fell and Nureyev's motionless figure disappeared behind it.

He didn't emerge for the curtain call.

I knew I would never see him again.

Less than a year later, on a grey February morning, I was standing near Nureyev's fresh grave, still overlaid with wreaths and fading flowers, at the Russian cemetery in Ste-Geneviève-des-Bois, a sleepy suburban town near Paris.

'DANCE IN PEACE' was written on the tomb-stone.

Meanwhile, passions were running high at the *Age*, which, despite remaining the most profitable newspaper in the English-speaking world, went into receivership and became an apple of discord between two media tycoons, Conrad Black and Tony O'Reilly, who both wanted to buy a 25 per cent share in it, thus effectively becoming the paper's new proprietors. The reason for this was that John Fairfax, the company that owned the *Age* since its foundation, had incurred huge losses in other areas of the business, and the profits brought in by the *Age* were used as a tarpaulin to put out the fire of growing debt. But the moment came when even this was no longer enough.

I first heard the news when on an assignment at a dairy farm in Gippsland where I, for the first time in my life, was trying to milk a cow. Without much success, I have to admit. Why is it so that bad news always comes when you try to do something as mundane as milking a cow, say?

It was a completely new experience for me, still a firm believer in Western freedom of the press. Instinctively, I felt very much against either Mr Black or Mr O'Reilly owning *my* newspaper. I thought that when I said 'my newspaper', or when my readers said 'our newspaper', we put into these words a meaning considerably different from the same pronouncement made by Rupert Murdoch, or, say, Kerry Packer. We meant: 'We like this newspaper, we work here, that's why it is ours.' Whereas they meant: 'We own this newspaper, it brings us profits, that's why it is ours.'

The fact that any potential new owner was only going to have a 25 per cent stake in the paper was not a good enough consolation. It was still going to be a form of servitude. Could slavery be measured? Could there possibly be 15 per cent slavery or 25 per cent Freedom? I doubted it. Freedom was Freedom and servitude was servitude. Both of these substances were volatile and if present in any amount, no matter how small, they were bound to spread over the whole vessel.

Freedom cannot be divided into shares, or so I thought.

Together with my colleagues, I took part in demonstrations

calling for a change in Australia's media ownership laws. Standing on street corners in the city, we distributed leaflets calling for the *Age* to be floated, i.e. owned by its readers and its journalists, which looked like the only fair solution to the crisis. But it didn't happen. After a year of uncertainty and frustration, the paper was finally bought by Conrad Black, and Mike Smith, its brilliant editor, was forced to resign. By that time I was already in London working for *The European*.

One of the hardest things for me to come to grips with in my new Australian life was my sudden material well-being. No, we were never wealthy, not by any Western standards, but we did have some money in the bank (that is before we bought a house). It was a hard test for both Natasha and myself who were so used to living from salary to salary in Moscow and almost routinely had to borrow the proverbial 'three roubles before the next salary' from our neighbours and friends, who, in their turn, would do the same to us, if we happened to have some extra cash. Words like bank account and credit card were as obscure, capitalist and bourgeois as hazel-hens and pineapples which we never saw, but only heard of.

Natasha quickly found an outlet for her repressed consumer appetites by buying all the clothes she needed as well as all sorts of fancy household appliances: a dish-washer, a microwave oven, a powerful vacuum-cleaner. I had never been careful with money. In Russia they used to say that people like me had holes in their hands. This and the inexplicable feeling of guilt, from which I kept suffering, made me into a squanderer. I simply could not hold on to money, as if it was indeed burning through my palms. I would plunge into buying sprees like a bulimic into a binge, like an alcoholic into a drinking bout.

Apart from hundreds of books, which I had no chance to read in my whole lifetime, I was buying things by mail catalogues, thus committing one of the gravest mistakes a gullible Western consumer can make. I bought imitation leather purses that would fall apart shortly after being delivered; I ordered a useless collapsible plastic fishing rod (it did collapse – or rather broke in two – after the very first use); I got hold of a defective car alarm that had a nasty habit of switching on, piercingly and totally unprovoked, in the middle of the night. Most of this trash would end up in a rubbish bin shortly after being unpacked. I didn't care. The money kept burning new holes in my already heavily pierced, sieve-like palms. Thank God, I didn't particularly care about clothes and didn't mind my scruffy looks which were imitated by Australian comedians who tried to impersonate me on TV.

Then came credit cards. The ultimate magic of getting goods 'for nothing', of taking money out of the wall, of buying things without actually paying but simply by flashing a shiny piece of plastic in a cashier's respectful face. It was irresistible. I ordered myself all existing credit cards and proudly carried them in my disintegrating mail-order wallet. The statements started trickling in. This trickle soon grew into a flow and then into a torrent. I had thought credit cards meant Freedom. In fact, it was the other way round – Freedom was a credit card in itself: the more you used it, the more you had to pay; the longer you delayed your payment, the higher the interest.

I was obviously overspending on the credit card of my Freedom, and the penalty was imminent.

At the end of 1991, a young journalist from *Izvestiya*, Russia's biggest newspaper, came to Melbourne for a couple of days. He visited the *Age*, and we took him out for lunch. The man struck me as a bit of a smart alec. And although I didn't ask him, the moment we were introduced he started explaining why he wasn't among the defenders of the Russian parliament near the White House during the three-day botched coup in August. With glib, suave, yet always guarded, manners and darting eyes, he looked like a young Komsomol functionary, the Soviet system's favourite pet, allowed to go abroad – a type all too familiar to me. As it turned out, he did graduate from a prestigious KGB-controlled institute, a well-known haunt for offsprings of the Soviet elite.

He asked me about my life and I honestly told him that we had just bought a house with a swimming pool. After lunch I gave him a lift to his hotel in my second-hand thirteen-year-old Volvo.

A couple of months later I was awoken in the middle of the night by a phone call from Moscow. My former *Krokodil* colleague, a cartoonist from whom I hadn't heard since leaving the Soviet Union, was on the line. 'I am so happy for you, so happy!' he said. 'You have made it! I always knew you would!'

'What do you mean?' I asked him sleepily.

'Don't you know? There was an article about you in *Izvestiya*. A very positive article. The whole of Moscow is talking about it . . . By the way, can you find a job for me in Australia?'

Puzzled in the extreme, I went to Melbourne University Library to look through recent issues of *Izvestiya*. And there it was. The article was called 'It is Hard to be Australian'. It was not about me alone, but about Soviet migrants in Australia in general. The author described some of the hardships emigrants were facing, despite Australia's generous social security scheme. 'But some of our former citizens are doing really well,' he wrote. 'Take Vitali Vitaliev, a well-known journalist, an author of many books in English. He lives in a luxury villa with a swimming pool and owns three brand-new cars . . .' There were some more, no less colourful and no less ridiculous, details of my 'luxurious' life. Where did he get these three cars from? I wondered. And how can anybody in his right mind call our small two-bedroom house a luxury villa?

Then I realised that our recent visitor was simply faithful to the old tricks of slapdash Soviet journalism, where one could get away with almost any exaggeration and lie, provided the piece was politically correct. Since communism in Russia collapsed and I could no longer be regarded as an enemy or a traitor, he decided to say something nice about me, but did it in his old, grossly exaggerated, manner, just to strengthen his point, so to speak.

After that I started to be bombarded with phone calls and letters from the former Soviet Union. They were from all sorts of people: those whom I vaguely knew and those whom I had never met or heard of; from my real distant relatives and from those who claimed to be my kith and kin. 'At last! At long last I have found you, my dear. Now, thank God, we are going to be re-united in Australia after all these years!' That was how a typical late-night phone call from a complete stranger would begin (which was usually enough for me to slam down the phone).

In letters addressed to the *Age*, my newly-emerged friends and relatives asked me to sponsor their move to Australia, to send them an invitation, or at least to find them an Australian wife (or husband). Some enclosed their head-shots, probably for their future Australian passports that I was expected to provide.

It looked like half of the citizens of the former USSR were suddenly mysteriously related to me. And all of them wanted to come to Australia. I had to change my home phone number, and ask the *Age* switchboard operators not to disclose it to any random callers. Especially to those from my poor motherland.

Just as I had dreamt of Paris many years ago, they were now desperate to go to Australia – at a time when I was desperate to leave. I wish I could have reminded them of the words of Dima Korenkov from Mikhail Veller's short story 'I Want to go to Paris' which I myself was ready to believe: 'Paris has never existed. It never was and it never will be.' But at that time the story hadn't yet been published.

It was roughly at that time that, on the editor's suggestion, I started exchanging open letters with my friend Robert Haupt, the Fairfax Newspapers' Moscow correspondent. These letters were published in the Features pages of the *Age*.

Few people had such an impact on me as Robert. He was one of the first to welcome me and my family to Australia. On our second day in Sydney, he burst into our flat, tall and loud-mouthed, and immediately filled it to the brim with his jokes, his roaring laughter, with his amazing human magnetism. Our flat was too small for his larger-than-life personality. I realised at once that I had a new friend.

A son of a New South Wales miner, Robert had had a brilliant career in Australian journalism – from humble reporter to senior writer, columnist and editor of a national newspaper. By the time we met, Australia had become too small for him, too. Hungry for new challenges, he was desperate to go to the Soviet Union, from where we had just escaped: his journalistic intuition was telling him that it was there that the main story of the decade was unveiling.

The Fairfax Newspapers didn't have a Moscow bureau then, and Robert started bombarding the executives with pleas to open one. I did my best to introduce him to the confusing Soviet realities, and Natasha gave him his first lessons of Russian. In his turn, Robert helped me to come to grips with Australian journalism and with the Australian character of which he himself was a typical example. He let me use his newspaper office, and my first Australian pieces were written on Robert's personal computer.

Soon he went to Russia as the Fairfax Newspapers' first ever Moscow correspondent, and we moved to Melbourne, but our friendship continued.

'Winter has begun oddly,' one of Robert's first letters from Moscow began. 'The cold came early, but the freeze is delayed. We oscillate between mud and ice, ice and mud. The countryside is under snow, and the little village houses with their intricately decorated windows have adjusted to it happily, chimneys smoking and doors tightly shut. But in Moscow we don't know where we are, and this adds an edge to the prevailing moodiness . . .'

Robert fell in love with Russia straight away. His reports were full of poetry and of genuine affection to the place. He quickly became a familiar figure in Moscow, trudging through the snow to yet another press briefing in his enormous *shapka* and with an unfading broad smile on his face. A fair dinkum Aussie, he was fascinated by the Russian winter, and often wrote in his letters about *sneg* (snow). He was also very critical of Australia. 'We (Australians) are a people who look at the world through a letterbox slit, never quite knowing whether the shadows moving back and forth in front of us belong to lions or grasshoppers. It seems to me unlikely, Vitali, that living in Australia you will be able to remain an internationalist,' he wrote in one of his last letters.

By that time I already knew how right he was. But coming from Robert – an Australian to the core of his bones who regarded his own background as an obstacle to becoming an internationalist – this warning sounded especially convincing. Robert himself never came back to Australia. After his four-year stretch in Moscow, he turned into a globe-trotter, like myself, unable to settle anywhere in the world. Having started from polarly opposite points of the globe, we both ended up covering the same route.

On a rainy morning in Prague in September 1996, I heard the news of his premature death. He was only forty-eight. He did become an internationalist in the end. A displaced Australian, he died suddenly in New York where he had just delivered his first book to his American publishers. The book was on Russia of course.

I am sure that as a child in a small Australian miners' town Robert also dreamt of Paris.

21

Palm Island

*T*hey don't take tourists to Palm Island, Queensland.
        I found myself there quite by chance, or rather by accident. The island was not on the itinerary of my 'familiarisation trip' around North Queensland island resorts in May, 1992. As I had already started to discover, unscheduled detours and deviations from fixed itineraries were likely to provide the most revealing impressions.

This trip, one of my many journeys around Australia as the *Age*'s roving columnist, had a bizarre start. When I arrived at Melbourne's Tullamarine airport to pick up my tickets at 6 a.m., the clerk at the ticket collection window told me that by mistake I had been booked to fly out of Melbourne the day before. As a result my initial flight to Townsville in Queensland and all subsequent flights had been cancelled. 'We can fly you to Brisbane and then you will see,' the clerk said. 'At least you'll be in Queensland.'

I didn't want to go to Brisbane, I wanted to go to Townsville, but there was nothing else I could do.

In Brisbane airport a couple of hours later I was put on stand-by for the fully booked connecting flight to Townsville. They told me to check in my luggage 'just in case' and to hang around until the plane was about to take off. 'How about my bag?' I asked. 'Are you sure it won't fly to Townsville instead of me?' I asked.

'No worries,' a cheerful airport official said and added: 'Forget about your bag, will you?'

I did try hard to forget about my bag, but when the plane took off and I was still 'hanging around' the airport, I suddenly remembered about it and went to pick it up.

The friendly luggage clerk, for some reason, didn't like the look of my red stand-by luggage ticket. 'I'll go and check,' he said with an uncertain expression on his face. He came back ten minutes later and solemnly announced: 'Your bag has gone to Townsville . . . Sometimes it happens the other way round: passengers arrive and their luggage doesn't . . .' He probably wanted to reassure me.

'No worries, mate!' I replied in a truly Australian fashion. 'This will happen to me tomorrow!'

So I had to spend an unscheduled night in Brisbane. I used this chance to dine at the local restaurant called Tsar which, as Peter Ustinov had assured me, was the best Russian restaurant in the world. My peripatetic bag, flown back from Townsville, found me in my Brisbane hotel in the afternoon. It was better-travelled than its owner: it had been to Townsville, whereas I hadn't.

Next morning when I was checking in for the elusive Townsville flight, the check-in clerk looked at his computer screen and said: 'You know, our bosses ordered us to fly you first-class. You must be very important.' There was a slight note of disapproval in his voice – a reflection of the so-called 'tall poppy syndrome', one of the brightest manifestations of Australian egalitarianism (or is it just inferiority complex?) which often makes them regard anyone of distinction with suspicion.

Well, if the cap fits, wear it, I thought. My sudden upgrading was most probably just a form of apology for my mucked-up itinerary and my misplaced luggage. I didn't have enough time to be properly impressed by the first-class flight. The only thing that I remember was that in the course of one hour I was called sir thirty-nine times – more than in all my previous life.

I knew I was in Townsville, Queensland, when I saw lots of men dressed in shorts in the airport building. Even policemen were wearing shorts which made them look like over-grown boy scouts. I was probably the only man in full-length trousers around. Can you expect anything serious from men who wear shorts twelve months a year? Are men in shorts capable of making a scientific discovery or creating an artistic masterpiece? I doubt it very much.

There was only one way to get to my destination now: I had now to fly to Palm Island first, and from there take a boat to the resort of Orpheus Island. I had no idea what Palm Island was. Probably just another exclusive resort, I was thinking.

Apart from myself, there were three other passengers aboard a tiny Cessna aircraft. Three and a half, to be more exact. They were all Aborigines. The half was represented by a smiling black boy, no more than four years of age. He was travelling in the company of a portly Aboriginal granny. She was drunk and heavily reeked of Fosters. In Melbourne, one could hardly ever see an Aborigine outside the specialised Aboriginal Medical Centre in Fitzroy, if you don't count an occasional drunken tramp hanging around St Kilda with a bottle of beer.

There was no airport at Palm Island, just an airstrip on which we landed. Waiting for a bus which was to take me to the jetty, I looked around and all of a sudden realised that I was in a different world. It was no longer the prosperous and laid-back Australia I had become used to. Dark brown kids were playing in the mud nearby. They were all dressed in soiled nappies, nothing else. A half-ruined jalopy screeched to a stop behind the airstrip fence and another dozen bronze-skinned kids jumped out of it. An ancient truck, driven by a stern-looking Aborigine, rattled by in clouds of dust.

Soon the bus arrived. A muscled Aborigine in dirty bermudas and torn singlet was behind the wheel. Next to him stood a black youth, no more than fourteen. He was obviously drunk and kept burping loudly from time to time. It was 9.30 in the morning.

I was sitting next to my flight companions: the Aboriginal granny with the boy, who seemed to be the only sober person on the bus. The old woman produced an unfiltered cigarette and was puffing at it for all she was worth. 'How many people live on the island?' I asked her just for the sake of asking.

'Roughly . . . I don't know,' she coughed out through her clenched teeth without taking the fag out of her mouth.

We were driving past rickety huts on poles, all in different stages of collapse, on both sides of a bumpy dirt road. They reminded me of the house of Baba Yaga, a long-nosed witch in Russian folk-tales who lived in a decrepit forest hut standing on chicken's legs. To call the Aboriginal shanties huts, though, was an exaggeration. They were just clumsy shacks, made of empty cardboard boxes and broken roof-tiles, covered with graffiti. Most of them had no doors or walls. Scruffy dogs were running freely in and out of them.

Around the huts the ubiquitous semi-naked kids were playing among torn newspapers and household rubbish. They all had some sort of an ophthalmic disease, which was evident from bits of pus in the corners of their eyes. The adults squatted outside and watched the passing bus with hostility. Some of them were drinking beer from cans, the others were already dead drunk. Half-ruined jalopies were parked near some of the houses, the only sign of civilisation. Sounds of rock music could be heard from one of the shanties, and a heavy smell of rotting food hung in the hot tropical air.

At the jetty, more kids with suppurating eyes surrounded our bus asking me for 'a dollar, mister'. The boat was already there. I jumped into it, the engine coughed and Palm Island started running away from me quickly. The Aboriginal kids were standing on the shore, and for a long while I could still see them, tiny brown dots on the green background of the bush.

Wandering around the Orpheus Island resort with all its imaginable and unimaginable luxuries I kept thinking about Palm Island, only twenty minutes away by boat. At sunset I stared at its dark, uninviting bulk looming large on the horizon. Not a single light could be seen on it.

Had I really been there? And what was that? A dream? A nightmare? How come that the indigenous people of the 'lucky country', the country that I have embraced as my new homeland and the cradle of Freedom, still lived in stone-age darkness and squalor? Did they really care whether Australia became a republic and what sort of a flag it had? Maybe, instead of wasting energy on debating these meaningless issues, instead of wallowing in uncertain remorse, the white Australians could try to do something for the Aborigines?

I had often heard from my Australian colleagues and friends how complex the Aboriginal issue was and, following their advice, tried to exercise caution and restraint in approaching it in my writing. But 'the issue' itself brutally approached me on Palm Island. It hit me on the head like a boulder and filled me with shame and guilt.

I remembered my Melbourne friends, a married couple of qualified Russian physicians, who emigrated to Australia many years ago but, due to the arrogant exclusivity of AMA (Australian Medical Association) were still unable to get fully registered as doctors and had a conditional registration that had to be renewed every two years. Incredibly, conditional registration allowed them to treat only *prisoners and Aborigines*! Yes, in egalitarian Australia, so proud of its tolerance and cosmopolitanism, in the country where so much lip-service had been paid to the Aboriginal issue, where so many politically correct crocodile tears had been shed over the plight of 'poor Aborigines', whites were supposed (and legally entitled) to be treated by better-qualified doctors than blacks!

I knew that in the 1967 referendum 90 per cent of Australians voted for providing Aborigines with basic human rights. But what about the remaining 10 per cent? And was it really enough – just to cast their votes and retire to exclusive resorts, first-class flights and carefree, 'no-worries' lives, protected by shorts-clad policemen?

'You wouldn't be alive, had you visited Palm Island after dark,' one of the Orpheus Island resort workers confided in me.

And one of the guests, a rich middle-aged woman from Adelaide, said: 'Why did you tell me about this Aboriginal ghetto? You have spoilt my holiday . . .'

We were sitting in one of the resort's heated swimming pools waiting to be called for dinner.

And I suddenly saw more clearly than before why they didn't take tourists to Palm Island.

22

Wind From the Moon

Wind from the Moon,
What are you doing,
Wind from the Moon?
You make girls think they are in love.
You roam around the city,
You mix up my dreams,
You make my head spin,
Wind from the Moon . . .

I first heard this importunate song with a tacky refrain in 1970, when I was spending my summer school holidays at a sports camp near Gaidary, a village outside Kharkov. I went there with my classmates to relax before our final year at school but, to our parents' considerable dismay, we ended up working as dish-washers (or *plongeurs*, to use George Orwell's term from *Down and Out in Paris and London*) at the camp's canteen.

We wanted to prove to ourselves that we were approaching adulthood and were able to earn some money for ourselves. Working before the age of eighteen was not only frowned upon by most Soviet parents, who were usually overprotective of their children ('Yes, we've had rotten lives, but at least our kids will do better . . .'), it was also illegal. Despite this, the camp being in desperate need of dish-washers, we were semi-officially employed for a minimum salary of 60 roubles a month.

At sixteen years of age, we were both naive and idealistic. We loved poetry and craved all the forbidden experiences of adult life. None of us was familiar with the works (or even the name) of George Orwell. I had a dream of buying a tape-recorder for the money I was supposed to earn (with a small contribution from my father).

We had to work every day from morning till night, with no days off. There was no hot water in the camp, situated on the top of an old Scythian mound, and we had to bring it up in huge aluminium tubs from another camp down the hill. By the time we reached our kitchen, the water would have cooled down, and we had to use lots of caustic washing powder to remove the grease from batteries of dirty plates which kept piling up in the kitchen window three times a day. Soon our hands were covered with bleeding ulcers, and dipping them in water had the effect of being struck by an electric current. We had to bandage our hands with layers of rags, but they kept hurting.

Having hardly finished washing up after breakfast, we would run down the hill to an abandoned orchard, pick up a couple of bagfuls of apples, jump into a boat and paddle down the Severski Donets River selling the apples for next to nothing to tourists and hikers.

This simple business venture was prompted by our 'boss', the senior dish-washer called Zhenia, who was already a second-year student and, at eighteen, almost a patriarchal figure in our eyes. He was also an alcoholic, but we didn't know it then.

'Comrade tourists! Would you like to try our delicious apples?' Zhenia would cry out from the boat.

We were oblivious of the fact that even an innocent business transaction like that constituted a criminal offence in the Soviet Union (where any sort of private enterprise was strictly banned), and could easily put all three of us behind bars . . .

By the time we reached the village of Korobov Khutor we had enough change to buy a bottle of cheap red plonk which we drank on the spot before punting frantically back up the river, while the commandant of our camp would already be bursting his lungs out in the loudspeaker: 'Dish-washer boys! Return to the kitchen immediately to carry out your duties!!'

His angry calls were echoing in the hills, which surrounded the river, making us sweat as we struggled with the current. Our only relief was on Sundays when our mothers who came to visit us from Kharkov would replace us in the kitchen after lunch. But evenings were solely ours. We would finish washing up after dinner at around 11 p.m. Then, under Zhenia's expert guidance, we would scour the camp's territory in search of something to drink.

It was then that for the first and last time in my life I drank perfume. It was aptly called 'Russian Forest' and was (obviously) offered to us by resourceful Zhenia one night. We dissolved it with water, and the opaque liquid in the glass was immediately covered with soapy foam. The taste was awful, and for the rest of the evening we stank like three walking barber's shops.

We wanted to try everything in the shortest possible time.

Having fuelled ourselves with any alcohol we could clear, we would proceed to the camp's dancing ground, where the camp's radio operator, nicknamed Matross (the Sailor), was already playing popular Soviet hits of the late sixties.

'Wind from the Moon' was one of them.

We were hoping that our 'adult' status of working guys would be an attraction for the girls. And it probably was, despite the fairly un-aphrodisiac smells of kitchen and booze that we were spreading.

Our ultimate after-dance goal was to lure a girl (or a couple of girls) into our tent for a quick snog and a messy cuddle.

> Wind from the Moon,
> What are you doing,
> Wind from the Moon? . . .

I came back to Gaidary from London twenty-four years later, in 1994, when making a Channel 4 documentary about Ukraine. The hills were still in place and so were the camp buildings. But no one was holidaying there any longer: maintaining the camp became unaffordable for the Kharkov Pedagogical Institute to which it used to belong.

I walked around the half-ruined plywood shed of the kitchen, then stood in the middle of the empty dancing ground and I thought I could clearly hear the familiar tune, played by ever-tipsy Matross:

Wind from the Moon,
What are you doing . . .

The dance of my youth was over, and was never going to be replayed.

It is amazing how catching and evocative simple melodies of your youth can be. Even now I often hum or whistle this primitive unsophisticated tune which for me is still full of innocent teenage lust, awakening libido and radiant youthful hopes. 'Wind from the Moon . . .'

When I feel trapped and lonely, when my life is about to take a sudden change of direction, when I start being ponderous and moody for no obvious reason, when my dreams become mixed-up and elusively nostalgic, it is the Wind from the Moon that must be affecting me.

The Wind from the Moon was blowing through Melbourne in August 1992, when I firmly decided to leave Australia. Or was it just the hot and oppressive sirocco from the Nullarbor Desert? Whatever it was, the wind was suffocating.

I had just returned from a trip to Europe where I was promoting my books. In Amsterdam, I was staggering along the canals as if drunk, overwhelmed by the half-forgotten smells of European summer, and then bought an antique music box in a small Sunday flea market. It was playing a tune that reminded me of 'Wind from the Moon'.

In London, I bought all existing Sunday newspapers and spent the whole day in my hotel room basking in their rich and extremely versatile coverage of European life. I had lunch at an old pub, where you could not only touch history, but eat and drink it as well. I went to gape at our Prince Charles's flat in Muswell Hill and used the whole roll of film snapping the house from all sides. It felt almost like coming back to the house of my childhood. How small, how old and how dear England looked after two years in Australia.

In Paris, in Venice, in Munich, in Lucerne, I felt happy and free as never before. I also felt at home, not in any particular country but in Europe as a whole. I realised that I was European by culture, by upbringing and by fate.

It took me several long years in Australia to achieve this realisation.

Having just read Bill Bryson's *Neither Here Nor There*, I was dying to write a book about Europe, specifically about Europe's smallest states which always fascinated me, but for that I had to come back first.

Just as several years before, when I had been ready to kiss the ground on the other side of the Soviet border, now I was keen to stroke endlessly the rough bark of every European tree, to touch ancient stones of European churches, and almost to lick with my tongue the 'old dirt' of European roads. I came to understand T.E. Lawrence who declared on his return from Arabia in 1921 that he would have happily eaten the very pavement of the Strand.

In Rome, which felt and smelled very much like my native Kharkov, I had dinner with Peter Ustinov and his wife. Halfway through the meal they told me that it was the twentieth anniversary of their marriage. I was extremely moved.

'Listen, Vitali, you must return to Europe,' said Pyotr Ionovich. 'The editor of *The European* newspaper, for which I write a weekly column, is a fan of yours. Why don't you go and talk to him?'

I followed his advice.

I was to fly back to Australia from London, via the United States. The sadness of parting with Europe was somewhat mitigated by a job offer from *The European* that I was carrying in my suitcase. I didn't know what Natasha's reaction to my decision would be like.

Thirty minutes after our plane left Gatwick, some alien rattling sound appeared in the rhythmical buzzing of the engines, as if an invisible giant was sneezing and coughing inside the jumbo jet's iron belly. Having thrown a quick glance out of the window, I could discern little timid flames sticking out of the nozzle of one of the engines and licking the wing gently.

'Ladies and gentlemen, this is your captain speaking. Due to a technical problem, we'll have to return to Gatwick. Please fasten your belts and remain seated.'

At least, he was no longer wishing us a pleasant flight. I looked around. Most of the passengers were calm. Only a middle-aged Irish nun in the row behind me was crossing herself silently, and I could hear her black robes shuffling softly as she prayed. As the plane was making a U-turn in the sky, a chain-smoking Australian lady sitting next to me looked totally unruffled and kept dragging tirelessly at her Benson and Hedges. Is this smoked old hag going to be the last human being I see in this world? I thought ruefully.

'I can't go back to Gatwick! I am to get married in Chicago tonight!' A tall black man jumped up from his seat and was gesticulating frantically in the face of a frightened hostess. Hearing this, several passengers burst into uneasy nervous laughter. Indeed, a plane is not a tram: you can't jump out when in motion, especially if you are seriously willing to get married.

Immediately after landing our jet was surrounded by dozens of blinking and honking ambulances. The maintenance team that boarded the plane almost at the moment of touchdown concluded that one of the engines was defective and had to be replaced. We were to disembark and spend twenty-four hours (at least) in England. Compared to the prospects that had been facing us only a short while ago, this was not so bad after all.

It took us several hours to clear the customs and immigration and reclaim our luggage. The would-be bridegroom was dashing around the airport trying to book himself on an alternative flight. There were none. It was already 7 p.m. when we finished our complimentary dinner at the Gatwick Hilton, where the airline had put us up overnight. After hours of stress and queuing, I decided it would be nice to take a quiet walk around the airport.

The landscape around Gatwick is not particularly inviting. The airport is sandwiched between several roaring highways, and the lawns and small patches of woodland around it are all littered with empty beer cans, torn newspapers and other refuse of our slovenly civilisation. I ventured further from the hotel and all of a sudden stumbled upon a pond in the middle of a small polluted forest, a real European pond, overgrown with weeds and sedge, even with some white water-lilies in the middle.

There was a lonely wooden bench on the bank which reminded me of Onegin Bench in the village of Mikhailovskoye where Pushkin wrote his famous 'life's novel in verse' *Eugene Onegin*. This bench did not spoil the harmony of the sylvan scene. It was naturally integrated into the landscape, like a lonely fisherman on a river bank. I spent nearly three hours sitting there in complete solitude, watching how with the onset of dusk the water in the pond gradually changed its colour from dark green to dark brown and then black. The air reeked of moisture and petrol fumes. A monotonous chorus of frogs was out-shouting the roar of cars on the nearby highway. A flock of wild ducks flew above in a perfectly wedge-like V-formation. Where were they flying to? To Russia? To Australia?

They reminded me of my own peripatetic life.

My fate was that of a migratory duck commuting between continents and hemispheres and unable to settle in one place.

Invisible fish swam under water leaving geometrically correct and quickly disappearing circles on the pond's surface. I was again a little boy in Ukraine sitting on the bank of a pond with a fishing rod in my hand catching prickly silvery perch who didn't want to die and writhed desperately on the hook, then calmed down. I threw them into a bucket with water to take home where my granny would fry them in *smetana* (thick soured cream) and they would crunch appetisingly under my teeth.

I could still hear those soft doomed splashes of the dying fish in the bucket.

I realised suddenly that I was born here, on the bank of this little pond. I belonged here. I was affiliated with every tree, with every cloud in that low satin sky, with every splash of water, with every rustle of this old and polluted forest called Europe. Australia was a beautiful country, no doubt. I was grateful to her for our Freedom, but there I felt very much like a perch, taken out of its habitual environment and thrown into a bucket. I was not that rootless, after all.

Next morning, when we were queuing to board our flight, I saw the hapless bridegroom from Chicago. He was not complaining any longer, just standing in line obediently.

'How about the wedding?' I asked him. 'Your bride must be desperate.'

He shrugged his shoulders and whispered, almost inaudibly: 'Ah, if she loves me, she'll wait.'

When the plane took off, I looked down. There, hidden under the thick foliage, flashed past and disappeared behind the clouds – the quiet pond of my childhood.

It was mid-winter in Melbourne, and the evenings were long, pitch-dark and impenetrable. The days were bleak and short as the final flash of a dying electric bulb. But it was not just the weather that caused shivers and discomfort. It was the all-pervading feeling of gloom that enveloped me as soon as I stepped down onto the tarmac of Melbourne's Tullamarine airport, thus terminating my four-week trip to Europe. The cab-driver who took me home kept rambling about the lack of business, unemployment and 'the bloody mess the bloody government had created'. The streets of the city were wind-swept and empty as an artillery range one minute before the start of shelling practice – in a stark contrast to European cities which brimmed with life and vitality well into the early hours of the morning.

The first thing I learnt at home was that the house of my Russian friend had been robbed during my absence. The burglars took a TV set, some family jewellery and cash. The neighbours saw them and even wrote down the number plate of their car, but the police did not seem interested in pursuing the matter further. They filled a standard form and left without even trying to reassure my friend and his family.

'Will you find them?' he cried out into their receding backs.

'Don't be stupid, mate!' the PCs muttered without turning round. They must have had other, much more serious, crimes on their minds.

What made the case especially sad was the fact that this unfortunate friend of mine, after more than fifteen years in Australia, had turned into a real Aussie patriot, always saying how safe and secure he felt there. The thieves had robbed him not only of some of his treasured possessions, but also – and this was much more important – they robbed him of a fair amount of his faith in Australia. And not because he was not broad-minded enough to dismiss the incident as just another stroke of bad luck (of which he had had plenty), but mainly because of the uncaring attitude of the police, the country's uniformed representatives. It is always painful to realise that your beloved new homeland has stopped caring about you.

His property was not insured, and when, after the burglary, he tried to get coverage for the future from one of the major insurance companies, he was refused on the grounds that he had been robbed already. Who wouldn't be thrown into pessimism?

And he was far from alone. Reading the Australian press, one got the feeling of hopes and beliefs being shattered on a national scale. If in Europe one could see some clear-cut signs of the forthcoming end of recession, and papers were involved in lively discussions about the implications of Maastricht, there was hardly any glimmer of light in the end of the curved Australian tunnel. Even the imminent change of government didn't seem to excite either the people or even the media any longer. What else could one expect when unemployment was over 11 per cent and politicians were engaged in never-ending exchanges of mutually abusive and equally meaningless rhetoric?

The last winter of my Australian discontent . . .

In principle, I should have remained unaffected by this personally: my job was as safe as ever, and my swimming pool was still in place, but was it possible to remain contented while my new country was in the grip of hopelessness, gloom and doom of almost Soviet proportions? The newspapers kept arguing over the best-suited word to describe Australia's deplorable economic state – recession, depression or slump. And while this lively linguistic debate was in progress, Australia kept sliding further and further down into whatever it was.

Every other day some 'mild signs of economic recovery' were proudly reported by this or that thoughtful expert, as if announcing the second coming of Christ, only to be repudiated the next day as premature and over-optimistic by other, no less thoughtful pundits. The country started to resemble a critically ill patient in need of urgent surgery, whereas the surgeons themselves were caught up in an endless argument about what anaesthetic to use.

Like the indifferent constables in my friend's case, the government had turned its back to the robbed (or rather bankrupted) country. 'Will you do anything about us?' the impoverished and the unemployed were screaming into the quickly receding executive backs.

'Don't be stupid, mates. We've got elections on our hands,' the rulers would answer without turning around.

What curse had befallen the 'lucky country', the one that only ten years before could boast one of the world's highest standards of living and strongest currencies; the world's only continent-sized Disneyland, where people valued having fun above anything else in life? Well, it still resembled a Disneyland, only an abandoned one. The rides still operated and the merry-go-rounds rotated cheerfully, but there were no visitors because people couldn't afford the price of a fun ticket.

SBS Radio in Melbourne still broadcast in fifty-nine languages to Victoria's 120 ethnic communities, but the news it offered was mostly gloomy. On television they still advertised 'swimming pool enclosures to fit your backyard design', yet innumerable pool shops were going bust.

What happened to the famous Australian spirit, the one which had built a thriving Western civilisation on bare sand and red rock? Had it completely faded away or just gone into temporary winter hibernation? Or had it been exported to Japan as the last locally-manufactured quality product?

A typical conversation in a Melbourne street that winter sounded almost precisely like a bearded Soviet anecdote about an optimist and a pessimist:

'Life is so awful that it simply can't be any worse,' the pessimist starts moaning.

'Yes, it can! It certainly can!' the optimist exclaims joyfully in reply.

Or maybe it was just the lugubrious Melbourne winter, with its early crimson sunsets, smelling of Cheddar cheese? Maybe it was just the half-forgotten monotonous melody, played by the old music box that I had bought in Amsterdam:

> Wind from the Moon,
> What are you doing . . .

Maybe it was this blasted 'Wind from the Moon' that was making me ever so restless?

New Era, the only Russian-language bookshop in Melbourne, closed down for lack of business, whereas the number of Russian-speaking migrants from the former Soviet Union kept growing by the day. Many of them reminded me of the heroes (or rather anti-heroes) of my *Krokodil* satirical articles: petty crooks and fraudsters from Ukraine and Belorussia who had brought their life-long attitudes of cheating and chicanery with them. They were not interested in Russian or any other books.

It was amazing how few members of the intelligentsia were among those new migrants, although it was also natural: those who treasured their culture were very unlikely to try and voluntarily settle that far away from where their roots were. And those who had tried to challenge the 'tyranny of distance' usually failed. I knew a talented Moscow actor who was quite well-known in Australia, but felt lost and unhappy and kept drinking heavily. His family life was shattered and eventually he had to leave. Exactly the same thing happened to a Moscow film director, a Leningrad bard, a cameraman from Moldavia . . . In Melbourne they all covered the same route: misery, heavy drinking, repressed creativity and as a result – second emigration – to Europe or America.

So, I wasn't the first.

A creative soul needs adrenalin to function properly. It needs to be challenged and tested. It needs constant inspiration, not cosiness. It desperately needs 'worries'. Australia, with its one-time main asset – the 'no worries' and 'she'll be right, mate' attitudes to life – for them quickly became 'a comfortable hell', in the words of a Melbourne-based Russian writer whom I befriended shortly before my departure.

Intelligentsia is a category of history, knowledge and hardship . . .

Could creativity survive in a land where those who were

more successful or talented than the others, those who deserved to be elevated to a star status, were branded 'tall poppies'? Aggravated by the tyranny of distance, this ruinous egalitarian principle had developed into a huge and completely unnecessary chip on the shoulder, cultural cringe, or, as I had come to call it, SIC – Self-Induced Inferiority Complex.

Sadly, many Australians at the bottom of their hearts were sure that really to make it one had to go to Europe or America. And the ones who had actually made it there were greeted as heroes.

I had been trying to prove to them (and to myself) that their country was one of the best in the world, that there was no reason for them always to covertly look up at Washington and London (while constantly denigrating them in the open – 'bloody Yanks', 'bloody Poms' etc.) and to look down at themselves, but they refused to believe. They often reproached me for having a too positive attitude towards their country.

'What are you doing here in Australia?' my Australian friends and well-wishers would ask me. 'Your place is in London.'

They had eventually persuaded me. It is very hard to live and work among people who do not respect themselves.

'Why did you come to Australia?' was the most common question I was asked at my numerous public appearances. It was driving me crazy. Just imagine being constantly bombarded with 'Why did you come to London?' in Britain or 'Why did you come to New York?' in America.

For months I had been trying to persuade the *Age* executives to start producing an international edition of this really excellent newspaper. Their usual response was: 'Ah, Vitali, who needs us there, in the big world?' For months I had been trying to encourage some of my colleagues, truly talented journalists, to offer their copy to overseas newspapers. 'Ah, Vitali, no one is interested in us Australians over there,' they would say. Eventually I had to give up.

Soon I realised that SIC was no less endemic to Australia than its marsupial mammals. It was a fairly complicated phenomenon, comprised of fear, insecurity, xenophobia, convict-style egalitarianism and many other qualities characteristic of a teenager who is not yet quite certain of his real place in an adult world.

When such a teenager goes abroad and finds himself in the company of adults, he tries to attract attention to himself by behaving erratically and obstreperously, failing to realise that he has made himself into a laughing stock instead. Just look at how some Australians behave when overseas, where they fall over themselves to match the stereotype of beer-drinking, loud-mouthed yobbos – the stereotype that they had created themselves.

My first impression of Australia as of a teenage girl was not that far from reality.

SIC permeated all sides of Australian life: media, politics, literature, social thinking. It probably started somewhere in the last century, and at that stage was more or less natural. Australia was a big British gulag, the land of prisons, prisoners and exiles. To get there from 'the big world' took several months. The country was practically detached from the rest of civilisation and had to live a life of its own.

This life was in many ways an attempt to imitate Britain. Money was British; measures, names and language, too. Hyde Parks, dozens and even hundreds of Victoria and George streets in the cities; suburbs called Richmond, Highgate and Kings Cross; newspapers with such names as *Sunday Telegraph* and *Daily Mirror*; clock chimes imitating the sounds of Big Ben – these were the first, but not the last, manifestations of SIC.

Even after gaining formal independence, Australia remained a spiritual colony of the British Crown. And, despite growing republican feelings, this colonial mentality persists even now, when aeroplanes and electronic means of communication have made Australia much closer to Europe and America than ever before.

Only time can cure the country of SIC. Give it another hundred years – and it will be gone. But I didn't have another hundred years at my disposal. One more little episode to illustrate the true meaning of this phenomenon.

'Hi, mate! How are you doing?' The voice on the other end of the line was radiant and buoyant.

It was 3 a.m. in London, although in Melbourne, from where the man was calling, it was already around midday.

I was in Britain on a short visit to promote *Dateline Freedom*, whose publication, curiously, coincided with the August 1991 coup d'état in the Soviet Union. The coup had just been defeated, and I didn't know where to hide from extremely news-wise British interviewers, tormenting me during the day. There was no respite at night either, when Australian media, having had their good night's sleep, would start bombarding me with calls.

I had only just gone to bed after a late celebration of the coup's defeat at Igor Pomerantsev's flat in Maida Vale. Among the guests was Galina Starovoitova, an outspoken Moscow democratic politician. She told me that both our names were at the top of the vanquished Moscow junta's hit list. And then, when I had just started falling asleep, came this phone call from a Melbourne radio station.

'I am fine, thanks, only a wee bit sleepy,' I mumbled.

He asked a couple of traditional questions, such as what I thought of Yeltsin and Gorbachev.

'Listen,' I said, remembering a story in the last issue of the *Evening Standard*. 'What about yesterday's fire at a chemical plant on Coode Island in Melbourne? Have there been any casualties?' I was naturally worried for my family and friends.

'How do you know about the fire?' my restless interviewer asked.

'Why, it was in the news here in London . . .'

'It was in the news in London?! Really?! You must be joking!' His voice was suddenly full of pride and satisfaction. 'But this is great!!'

If you asked me to explain in one sentence what a 'self-induced inferiority complex' really means, I would reply that, among other things, it is the ability to rejoice at a devastating fire in your home city only because it was in the news in London!

Several years later, in an Australian magazine published in London, I came across another powerful definition (or rather manifestation) of SIC stemming from Ron Hitler (sic!) Barassi, the lead singer of TISM, a Melbourne-based rock group which was touring Britain:

> It must be horrible being an Australian in London and faced irretrievably with the fact that Australia's a POX country at the arse end of the world [this expression was actually coined by the former Australian Prime Minister Paul Keating], and you're actually in a city with some sense of literate culture and history behind it rather than the sort of suburban drabness that encapsulates Australian cultural experience. As an Australian, what I'm looking forward to is finding out about my own limitations as a person, purely because of the fact that I'm Australian. For all the ways Australians slag off English people, deep down there is an inferiority complex that I feel is totally valid. Let's face it, when you compare any of Australian literature, drama, history, compared to anything the English have produced, we have failure written all over our cultural faces. From TISM, we'd like to say that we're ashamed of our country and we're going to England to find out something about the real world.

What made this clumsy but passionate diatribe even more ridiculous and SIC-infected was the fact that the Aussie magazine printed this quote on its cover in huge letters!

Barry Humphries, a Melbourne-born writer and comedian, who used to call Australia 'the world's only anti-intellectual country' and 'a koala triangle where people with talent disappear without trace', put it much more wittily and succinctly in one of his 1996 interviews: 'For a writer, living in Australia is like coming to a disco and spending the whole night dancing with your own mother.'

'Do you enjoy Australia?' I was often asked during my first months down under. Since then, the pattern of the question had undergone a slight change: 'Do you *still* like Australia?'

What could I say? I certainly did. It was in many ways a wonderful place. But no longer for me.

It was time for me to move on.

Natasha and I agreed that I would spend three months in

London on my own and, if things went well, she would let our house and join me there with Mitya.

When the plane left Tullamarine airport and started climbing, I opened the letter from one of my closest Australian friends, Tony, a young Melbourne-born intellectual, an Oxford graduate, a traveller and an aspiring writer, who, himself an Australian, was 100 per cent behind my decision to return to Europe. 'Open on the plane' was written on the envelope.

> My dear friend,
> Today is a special day for me: it is the day you have rung to tell me of your victory, that your work permit has been issued and that you are, finally and fatefully, leaving Australia and returning home. This day closes the final chapter on that story which began (or at least one part of it began) unpropitiously by a pond near Gatwick and an overheard mutter 'if she loves me, she'll wait . . .' Well done!
>
> I know this is the right decision. I know that London, and England, and Europe are the proper domain for your investigative and poetic work, and for all your talents. You were not born to become a restaurant critic for the *Age*.
>
> My heart goes with you on your journey and my thoughts and best wishes will be with you in the weeks and months ahead. I am proud, and privileged, to call myself
> Your loving friend,
> Tony

I was about to change the country (and the continent) of residence for the third time in less than three years.

The Wind from the Moon was blowing into my back.

23

Ten Metres From the Past

*A*t 11 a.m. on 21 October 1992, the Queen of England finally walked into the former communist bloc.

Stepping through the Brandenburg Gate, she also stepped through time; through years of lies and propaganda; through mutual extraditions and ultimatums; through sabre-rattling, brain-washing and witch-hunting . . . Two opposite, alien worlds joined together by a diminutive woman in a funny hat resembling a showercap with flowers.

I was there to report the event, my first assignment as a London journalist after several years in Australia. The Queen crossing the border into communist East Germany was a frequent dream of mine during that trip. I would come back to my brand-new Berlin Hilton hotel late at night, after an extensive tour of East Berlin's watering holes in the company of the *Times* columnist Peter Millar, but even then I was finding it hard to sleep.

Imagine someone who was born and spent all his life in a dark cell without getting a glimpse of the world outside. For him happiness is a bowl of thin gruel and a piece of bread. One day a sympathetic warder encourages him to climb up and look through a tiny barred window. The prisoner sees trees, sun and sky for the first time in his life and realises what he has missed. It is then that he becomes really miserable, since, despite his new awareness of the world, he remains in the cell. It would have been better not to know.

Haunted by the tyranny of distance in Australia, I felt very much like a prisoner in a comfortable cell with a view. Having returned to Europe, I crossed the border into a new life, and there was no going back.

'Stay here! I am going to bring *her* around,' Charles Anson, the Queen's press secretary, whom I befriended while covering the Queen's state visit to Australia for the *Age* a couple of years earlier, told me in a conspiratorial whisper during a traditional press reception thrown by the royal couple in Bonn on the first day of their visit to Germany.

I had had a chance to meet the Queen and the Duke before. At a similar press reception in Sydney I got so excited by the opportunity to be introduced to them that, having confused the protocol-dictated forms of address, I ended up addressing the Queen as 'Your Royal Highness' and her husband as 'Your Majesty'. To my great relief, they didn't seem to mind, or more likely, having probably had other things to worry about, they simply didn't notice my awful blunder. The Queen was then whisked away and entered a lively conversation about horses with some of my fellow hacks. At the end of this Australian reception I suddenly found myself face to face with the Duke of Edinburgh.

'Where are you from?' he asked me sternly, having probably spotted my accent after we had exchanged the usual pleasantries. When he learnt that I was originally from Russia, he suddenly got very angry.

'Do you know what the Russian Bolsheviks did to my maternal grandmother?' he asked in an accusatory manner. And although I had very little to do with Russian Bolsheviks and even less with the brutal murder of Russia's royal family in 1918, I felt an inexplicable pang of guilt.

'Sorry, Your Royal Highness, but this tragedy had occurred thirty-six years before I was born,' I said.

'I don't know,' the Duke muttered and added without any connection to the previous subject: 'Moscow is the most awful place in the world!'

I had never been a great admirer of Moscow, but for some reason his words hurt me.

'I am not so sure,' I mumbled, forgetting an unwritten dictum of talking to royals: you are not supposed to contradict them.

At this point, the Duke started fuming with rage: 'But I *do* know!' he roared. 'I've been there! We stayed at the British embassy, and the place was awful!'

By that time, an inquisitive crowd had gathered around us. The Duke continued his offensive: 'You must have already written an article about this reception for your paper,' he said blinking at me fiercely. He knew only too well that the reception was officially off the record. We had been warned about it by Charles Anson more than once.

'I am sorry, Your Royal Highness,' said I. 'But this is provocation.'

I regretted my words immediately. 'A word is not a sparrow: the moment it's out of your mouth you can't take it back', as a wise Russian proverb asserts. I could hear the crowd of onlookers gasp and hold their breath in terror.

The Duke's reaction was totally unexpected for everyone.

'Provocation? Ha-ha. Provocation . . .' he repeated amicably and moved away from me with a smile on his face.

I thought that Charles Anson would be cross with me for my unintended misdemeanor. But he wasn't. On the contrary, when I came to London on a short visit several months later, he invited me to have tea with him at Buckingham Palace. 'It is nice to see a friend in these difficult times,' he told me then. He was probably referring to the marriage of Charles and Diana which had just started falling apart.

There, in Bonn, he kept his word and, having expertly escorted the Queen past the flocks of chatting and drinking journalists, steered her towards me. And then he made a mistake. He tried to explain to Her Majesty my complicated background, bringing Australia, Russia, Britain and even Ukraine into it. From the blank expression on the royal face, I could see that the Queen was utterly confused, and I didn't blame her.

'So you were born in Russia,' she said, and I couldn't grasp whether it was a question or a statement. Also, remembering my unfortunate Sydney experience, I was wary of saying something inappropriate and remained silent.

'So you were born in Russia,' the Queen repeated, and this time, without waiting for me to reply, she continued: 'There have been many changes there of late, haven't there?' I nodded in agreement, and Charles led the monarch away. To my considerable relief, my short audience with the Queen was over.

At least I didn't repeat the *faux pas* of one Soviet diplomat in London, who, when introduced to the Queen, asked her: 'Do you speak English?' He was sent back to Moscow the following morning.

I was renting a modest room in a West Hampstead house belonging to an émigré German poet writing, as he himself put it, 'the poetry of fact'. Having rejected radio, television and newspapers, my landlord looked for inspiration in the back issues of *Scientific American* – no less than five years old. His point was that five years constituted the minimum possible gap between a scientific discovery and its realisation.

In a truly Bohemian arrangement, he lived with his youngish girlfriend, whereas his sick and ageing wife, from whom he was not officially divorced, resided across the road. As a poet he was bound to be absent-minded and forgetful. As a German he was extremely well organised. The house was packed with neat folders and files labelled 'Metaphors', 'Litotes', 'Rhymes' and so on. He had an unparalleled knowledge of London and often took me on Sunday walks across the East End.

The living conditions in his poetic den were a far cry from my Melbourne villa (my room didn't even have a writing table), but I didn't mind. I was spending most of my time travelling, rediscovering my beloved Europe. How wonderful it was to return from a trip to yet another European destination early in the morning, to take a cab from Heathrow and to drive through sleeping London, whose face was still covered with the veil of transparent morning mist, knowing that there were many more journeys and discoveries to come.

Foreign coins were jingling melodiously in my pockets.

The only thing I wasn't looking forward to was the resonant silence of my empty room, where no one was waiting for me.

And Mitya wouldn't run out to meet me with a scream of joy: '*Papa* has come back!'

I was missing my family a great deal.

My first editor at *The European* was Michael Maclay – a polyglot Scottish intellectual and a Euromaniac like myself. We immediately found a *lingua franca*.

'I am not interested in what you think of Russia, Vitali. I'd rather read your impressions of the West,' he would say.

This meant I had a *carte blanche* to explore previously unknown European territories and to write about them. Surrounded by the cosmopolitan, multi-national and multi-lingual staff of *The European*, I couldn't dream of a better working environment.

My intention was to start from the start – to explore Europe from beginning to end. I knew only too well where free Europe began: the ultimate East-West crossing point still lay on the Russian-Finnish border.

I remembered how in the early eighties an armed man broke into the Finnair office in downtown Moscow and, brandishing a gun, demanded that the staff took him to Finland immediately. How he expected the airline clerks to take him out of the Soviet Union remained a mystery. The whole area was quickly sealed off by the militia and the intruder arrested. Instead of his coveted Finland, he found himself in a Lefortovo (Moscow KGB prison) cell.

Naturally, the Soviet newspapers reported the next day that he was mad. And in that particular instance, it could have been true.

Finland had always been a profitable destination for the Soviets as the closest and one of the most affluent Western states. There had been numerous attempts to cross the Finnish border illegally by sea, by air or on skis. All these endeavours, even if they were successful, ended badly for the trespassers: the Finnish authorities, unwilling to irritate the Big Brother neighbour, would invariably return the fugitives to the Soviet Union.

And here I am in Vaalimaa, at Western Europe's eastern outpost. I stand on the patch of no-man's-land at the Finnish-Russian border. There is a little red-and-green-striped border post still bearing the state emblem of the Soviet Union just ten metres down the road. Emblems sometimes outlive the countries they represent.

A no-land's-man on a no-man's-land . . .

The smooth highway on the Finnish side abruptly turns into a bumpy track with holes and puddles immediately behind the hammered-and-sickled post.

All looks quiet, but the seeming peace is misleading. The border, which used to separate two antagonistic social systems, now just separates two different countries – one of the world's richest and one of the world's poorest. One cannot expect a border like this to be peaceful.

A Russian KGB frontier-guard with painfully familiar green lapels approaches the lowered swing-beam from the Russian side. He stares at me with interest, and I stare at him.

He is young, bespectacled, with dishevelled hair showing from under his cap. A couple of years earlier anything but a neat crew-cut would have been unthinkable.

Well, at least something has changed in Russia.

What does he see looking at me? An enemy? A potential spy? Or just a leisurely foreigner, a Western eccentric with a curious passion for border posts? I wonder whether the ineradicable seal of oppression can still be noticed on my face. Or maybe he takes me for what I am – an émigré, a defector, a 'rootless cosmopolitan', who under the Soviet legislation which is still in force in Russia has to be put in front of a firing squad for his 'failure to return'?

Ten metres, only ten metres, separate me from my past, from my poor and ruthless motherland.

Ten metres – and the whole world . . .

What is it that makes these meagre ten metres the world's longest distance? What is the main difference between the cannibalistic, even if somewhat democratised, 'socialist paradise' and the real-life unpretentious capitalism, setting aside for a moment the latter's much praised well-stocked shops and much exaggerated freedom of expression?

As I have said already, the thing that had struck me most during my first months in the West was the humane attitude to the disabled. Standing on the West-East border several years later, I thought I knew the more exact answer.

It lay in just one word – compassion. Or something that Alexander Pushkin, probably Russia's greatest nineteenth-century poet, once called 'mercy to the fallen' – 'For mercy to the fallen I was calling . . .'

Mercy to the fallen is the most characteristic trait of a civilised society. It implies clemency and compassion for our less fortunate fellow beings living on the society's fringe – tramps, beggars, prostitutes, drug-addicts and criminals.

Yes, criminals too, for every felon, after all, is a product of society, its deplorable mistake, its sore point. The community should feel responsible for its stranded sons and daughters, for those who have stumbled on life's bumpy road. It should extend a helping hand to them, rather than push them over the brink and further into the abyss.

A totalitarian (and a post-totalitarian) system has only two approaches to the fallen: ignoring them or destroying them, physically and morally. Does it help? Certainly not. Every criminal, every social outcast is a bearer of some social error or injustice. The easiest thing, it seems, is to wipe out the bearer. But his physical or moral death won't mean that the society's problem is corrected. Its burden will simply be shifted onto someone else's shoulders.

During my many years as a journalist in the Soviet Union, I had plenty of opportunities to visit prisons and labour camps, to talk to homeless tramps and clandestine streetwalkers (prostitution didn't officially exist there), to prisoners on death row. And if all 'normal' law-abiding citizens of the world's first communist state were treated by the system like criminals, then criminals and other 'dregs of society' were treated like animals or worse.

I remember visiting a strict-regime Soviet labour camp in Rostov-on-Don. The forcibly crew-cut inmates were allowed to move only in formation with their hands behind their backs. They were not supposed to sit down – not even for a moment

– during the day, when they were involved in hard manual labour. After work they didn't have the room to stretch their tired legs. They had to take turns to sleep: there was only one bunk for three inmates. The barracks were unkempt and dirty, and iron bars were everywhere. The camp looked like one big cage with watchtowers in the corners. The guards on top of these towers always had their machine-guns ready and aimed at the prisoners.

In the West, the attitude to the fallen differs from country to country, but it is generally much more humane. Western society tries, with varying degrees of success, to treat all its subjects, irrespective of their social status, as human beings. It is here, I think, that the main achievement of Western democracy lies.

I went to the Netherlands, a country with a long tradition of tolerance and compassion, at the end of 1992 (only weeks after my visit to the Finnish-Russian border). While still in the Soviet Union, I had heard a lot about the benevolent treatment of prostitutes, drug-addicts and prisoners in Holland, the reason for which lay in the country's history and geographical situation.

In the sixteenth century, Amsterdam and some other parts of Holland enjoyed a rare status of independence from the foreign rule to which most other European countries were subject. This attracted hordes of skilled migrants – diamond-cutters from Antwerp, Portuguese Jews fleeing the Spanish Inquisition, Protestant Huguenots from France, English dissenters, etc. The Inquisition was never deeply rooted in the Netherlands, where even local Roman Catholics themselves were fighting against it. All these people created a unique tolerance of race, culture and religion which soon became one of the nation's most distinctive features.

Sitting prosperously at the crossroads of the world's main trade routes and boasting two of the planet's busiest ports, the Netherlands has always been a cosmopolitan place with a relatively relaxed (compared to its neighbours) immigra-tion policy. Every Dutch person speaks two or three foreign languages, and their proficiency in English never ceases to surprise visitors. For a small country of 14.5 million people with a little-known native tongue, this has been the only recipe for survival and prosperity.

Tolerance of foreigners involves compassion for the less lucky compatriots too. The Dutch have one of the world's most sophisticated welfare systems, where unemployment benefits are linked to the average wage and are only slightly below it. The health and welfare of all citizens, prostitutes, drug-addicts and gaol-birds included, is one of the country's highest priorities.

In short, the Dutch do not distinguish between their com-patriots of 'normal behaviour' and those who deviate from socially accepted standards.

The 'normal security' prison in Haarlem, about twenty minutes by train from Amsterdam, is one of the town's main landmarks. The circular prison building is topped by a huge glass dome, which makes it look more like a temple than a penitentiary. Inside, right under the dome, prisoners and warders were playing football on an artificial pitch. It was not an inmates versus prison officers match: prisoners and their guards were evenly distributed between the teams, so that it was impossible to tell one from another. It was Christmas time, and the mood inside the prison was almost festive, added to by numerous illuminated Christmas trees.

J.B. van Putten, the prison governor, led me through the immaculate prison kitchen, through a gym where a handful of muscled inmates were pumping iron, through empty computer classrooms and two well-stocked libraries.

'Only once did I have to forbid a book, and this ruined my relations with the librarian,' he said. 'The book was called *How to Make a Bomb*.'

Walls in the brightly lit prison corridors were decorated with paintings and sculptures. 'They are all original works,' van Putten remarked. 'Regulations state that we must spend one per cent of the prison budget on works of art.'

He told me a number of other amazing things. Prisoners were allowed to keep pets – birds and fish – in their cells. They were allowed to make unlimited phone calls and to receive visitors twice a week. During the last year of their sentence they could take six seventy-two-hour leaves and go home. They participated in prison affairs, and could even vote down the governor himself.

In the interests of the prisoners' privacy, members of the prison staff were not allowed to enter the cells, which the governor called residential quarters. And indeed, each cell looked more like a hotel room, with a bathroom, a tiny kitchen, a television set and an occasional bird-cage or aquarium. The one-prisoner-per-cell rule was observed to the letter. There was no communal canteen: each inmate had his food delivered to his room.

But the governor made no excuses for this apparent comfort. 'Being a prisoner is still no fun. It is a huge psychological burden, and we try to reduce it as much as we can,' he said. 'You don't improve people by locking them up . . .'

Despite a relatively high crime rate, the Netherlands locks up fewer people than almost any other country in the world. In 1992, its prison population was about 8,000 (compared with 400,000 in the United States, and more than 1,000,000 in Russia). Apart from maximum and normal security penitentiaries, there are also 'half-open' prisons where the inmates are allowed to go home every six months; 'open' prisons, where the prisoners only stay overnight; and day-detention centres, the name of which speaks for itself. Despite such seeming leniency – or maybe because of it – the rate of recidivist crime in the Netherlands is among the world's lowest. This showed that there was no visible correlation between severe prison conditions and low crime figures, as many are inclined to think.

We entered the prison's artistic studio. On the walls there hung prisoners' paintings depicting their native landscapes: a watercolour of a Turkish village, a lovingly painted sketch of an African forest – there were inmates of more than fifty nationalities at Haarlem. And I realised suddenly that despite all the little luxuries of this prison, despite all these football games, TV sets and computers, the prisoners were bereft of their main human asset – Freedom. And this punishment was enough to make them suffer.

The football match under the dome came to a halt. Prisoners moved to the adjoining assembly hall for the charity concert by a well-known Amsterdam rock-group. Muffled sounds of rock music were floating over the empty pitch.

I raised my head and saw a bright yellow canary, an escapee from a cell, beating desperately against the dome, trying to break through the glass. But prison walls, even if made of glass, were thick and impenetrable.

And there was no escape.

I am standing on a small patch of no-man's-land in Vaalimaa, ten metres from the Russian border. From the Russian side, a row of huge Sovtransavto trucks is waiting for clearance to go into Finland. A procession of Finnish trailers is crawling in the opposite direction. The young Russian border guard, having lost interest in me, disappears inside his wooden sentry box.

I throw a final look at the mist-covered road, winding away into my past, and slowly walk back, towards the West . . .

24

How to Disappear Completely

*H*ow to Disappear Completely and Never be Found* – such
was the title of a book I came across at a bookshop in
Plantsville, Connecticut, some time ago. This 'pseudocide'
manual, written by a certain Doug Richmond, was full of
comprehensive advice on how to remain invisible from whoever might be after you: the police, private eyes, insurance
companies, a spouse etc.

One thing the manual didn't seem to cover was how one
could escape from oneself . . .

Its subtitle was: *Heavy-Duty Disappearing Techniques for
Those with 'A Need to Know'*.

I wish I had had this useful book in May 1993, when,
contrary to all my expectations, I was left alone in Prince
Charles's flat in Muswell Hill and my main (and only) desire
was to vanish into thin London air, to disappear completely
from the face of the earth – anything to stop the gnawing
pain of terminal separation from the two people I loved:
my son and my wife, or rather my ex-wife, as she now
was.

At least sons and daughters can never become 'ex' . . .

It was all so quick and unexpected that I didn't have time
to realise what had actually happened. In January, having
terminated my three-month test period with *The European*, I
returned to Australia to pick up Natasha and Mitya. I thought

we would let our Melbourne house for a couple of years and live in rented accommodation in London. I had arranged for Mitya to attend an excellent state school in Barnet and found a telesales job for Natasha, in case she didn't want to stay at home.

One little episode, a week before my departure to Australia, marred my otherwise cloudless mood. It occurred on the first night of 1993. New Year celebrations were special in the Soviet Union. It was the only public holiday which was totally devoid of ideological context. Families would get together on New Year's Eve, just like they do at Christmas in the West. Living in an atheistic state, we were not allowed to celebrate Christmas, but even the Soviet communists couldn't stop the flow of time. We had a saying to the effect that the way you begin a new year, so you will complete it.

I had always made sure I was back from my journalistic trips in time to meet the New Year with my family. But in 1992–3 it turned out to be impossible: the editor of *The European* wanted me to cover the celebration of the Single European Market which was to come into force as of 1 January 1993. I was told to join a large group of revellers on board a cross-Channel ferry which was to sail from Dover on New Year's Eve and to dock in Calais in time for the French New Year, then go back to Dover (the crossing only took forty minutes) for the English New Year celebrations. The whole thing was made possible due to the one-hour time difference between Britain and France.

It all went well, although I couldn't help thinking of our old Russian superstition about spending a year the way you start it. The partygoers on board the ferry took advantage of their new freedom to bring large quantities of inexpensive alcohol and cigarettes across the Channel. Throughout the journey people were dancing on the decks and the champagne flowed liberally. I knew no one at this boisterous floating New Year party. Am I going to spend the next year on the move and surrounded by strangers? I wondered.

I came up with an idea of 'interviewing' Hitler and Napoleon, both of whom had tried to unify Europe by their own means, in the one-hour time loop on the way back to Dover which, I thought, couldn't fail to attract some ghosts from the past. With the concept of my future piece firmly in my mind, I allowed myself to relax.

Back in Dover the festivities continued. In a hotel bar, where I was drinking in the company of the people from the ferry, I was approached by a man I didn't know. He was drunk. For more than an hour he was pestering me with the story of his recent divorce. He sniffed, sighed and dropped tears into his beer glass. I was sympathetic, but soon started getting annoyed. What am I doing here, far away from my family, listening to the drunken lamentations of a complete stranger?

It was only the thought of my approaching reunion with Mitya and Natasha that stopped me from losing my temper and storming out of the bar, having left the distressed divorcee to tell his story to somebody else.

The way you begin a new year, so you will complete it. The stupid saying was buzzing inside my head like an importunate fly. It had no grounds whatsoever (or so I thought), but I was somehow unable to silence it.

The first thing I learnt on arriving in Melbourne a week later was that Natasha was not too keen to go to London with me. After two and a half years in Australia, she had become so adjusted to her quiet problem-free life that Europe started to look hectic and threatening. She spoke about the imaginary dangers of London life: IRA terrorists, bad weather, rude and indifferent people . . . In the end, she reluctantly agreed to go, but I felt that our marriage was at its all-time low: we stopped understanding each other and were arguing a lot.

The time for our return to London could not have been more inappropriate. It was early February, one of the dreariest on record (I think the English find pleasure in branding every January and February 'the dullest' and 'the gloomiest' ever). The cab we took at Heathrow drove through sticky yellow ganglia, suspended in the air. One could almost scoop the air by handfuls and cut it into pieces. The contrast with the height of Australian summer (February was Melbourne's hottest month) could not have been greater.

I brought them to my West Hampstead flat. The landlord had kindly agreed to move out and let us occupy his two rooms upstairs. But, again, in Natasha's eyes, his flat was not much more than a slum, compared to our Melbourne house. And here she was right. Living there on my own and spending most of my time travelling was one thing; but having it as a family home was different.

She was unhappy with unending rain, with darkness at 4 p.m., with the erratic Tube and crowded double-deckers, with rude supermarket cashiers who didn't bother to pack up the food she had bought. She had no friends in London, and while I was at work, she spent hours on the phone to her Melbourne girlfriends. I would come back home to find her sad and red-eyed.

We were drifting further and further apart.

As for Mitya, he quickly adjusted to his umpteenth school in the West, his only complaint being that the teachers shouted at the pupils for every small misdemeanour.

In a desperate attempt to save our marriage, I took Natasha and Mitya to Paris, where I was sent on an assignment. It didn't help. Natasha remained cold and distraught. She kept talking of her desire to go back to Australia.

When I heard that our Prince Charles's flat in Muswell Hill was vacant, I decided to move back there, hoping against hope that the place where we were so happy three years before could bring about a positive change. The flat was expensive, and I still had to pay the mortgage for our Melbourne house which we had failed to let and simply locked up, but I thought it was worth a try. And, indeed, for a week or so it looked like the situation was improving. Then the paper sent me to Liechtenstein for a week and on my return I found Natasha in the same morose state.

None of us could go on like that any longer. It was decided that we both needed some space, and Natasha would go back to Australia to meet and accommodate her brother who was emigrating there with his family. Since I was travelling frequently and was unable to look after Mitya, he would have to go with her. She promised they would return in several months' time.

I shall never forget seeing them off at Heathrow on a bright sunny afternoon in May. Natasha was unusually cheerful.

'Don't worry, we'll be back soon,' she said with a smile. I was not sure whether she meant it or not. And nor was she. When they disappeared behind Departures gates, I felt as if I was suffocated from within. I wished I could cry to let out the pain. But I couldn't, and this made my anguish almost unbearable.

I knew they would not be coming back.

Alone, I returned to Prince Charles's flat. Only it was not home any longer, for home is where your loved ones are. Deafening silence resonated in hostile walls.

Next morning I went to Manchester to present *What the Papers Say* at Granada TV's studios. They put me up at the Victoria and Albert Hotel where every room bore a *Coronation Street* name. I was making a phone call to Radio Liberty in Munich to record my weekly radio feature in Russian when suddenly the room swam in front of my eyes and I collapsed onto the floor. For the first time in my life I fainted. Having regained consciousness, I stumbled towards the bathroom and stood under a cold shower until I felt alive again. Then I got dressed and went to the studio.

The script that I had written was funny, and the recording went well. When I watch the tape of it now, I find it hard to believe that I was ready to die there and then. Weeks and months dragged on in dreary succession. During the day I was more or less normal, surrounded by my colleagues, writing or travelling. I tried to put off the moment when I had to come back to the empty flat where I couldn't go to sleep without downing a glass of vodka.

Going back 'home' every night, I could almost feel an invisible border that separated my cheerful and confident office self from my depressed and lonely domestic one. The border was somewhere on the corner of Woodside Avenue and the Great North Road, just behind the bus stop. Having got off the bus, I was already in a different world. My self-confidence would evaporate without a trace, and I would turn into a miserable hunched figure trudging gloomily down the street.

In my muddled dreams I was still a father, a family head, and all three of us were together again – walking in the park, watching TV, or having a meal. Waking up was the hardest. A sudden painful realisation of what had happened was like a mighty sledge-hammer blow. Or rather like a series of blows falling upon my head out of the morning stillness of my bedroom. There were times when I wished I had never woken up.

But I had a job, I had deadlines, I had columns and features to write. My readers all over Europe were waiting for them, and I couldn't let them down (that was what I was telling myself in an attempt at self-hypnosis). So I had to drag myself off the bed and carry on. I tried to make my columns as light and amusing as possible. This gave me a life-saving distraction. I still cherished a faint hope that Natasha would change her mind and come back, but even this flimsy hope against hope was shattered one day in November.

I had a lunch appointment to interview John Costello, an American investigative writer, about his new book on the secret KGB archives. Ten minutes before I had to go, the telephone on my desk rang. It was Natasha calling from Melbourne to say that she had applied for separation and was not coming back.

It was too late to cancel the appointment. Robot-like, I went to the restaurant and ordered myself a double vodka. Soon John arrived with his publicist. I switched on my dictaphone and switched myself off. He talked non-stop about KGB conspiracies and Western cover-ups, and I drank vodka and stared at him without seeing anything or anyone in front of me.

A couple of years later I read in the papers about John Costello's sudden and suspicious death on board a plane to America. He was in London researching his next book which, as he claimed, was to be full of striking revelations about British and American secret services. One day before his flight he felt sick and threw up after dinner, having probably eaten a bad prawn. Next morning he was fine, and later in the day he died of a heart attack while flying over the Atlantic Ocean. He was extremely fit and strong and had never had any ailments. I wished I could have been more attentive to what he said during our first and last meeting on that memorable November day.

In December 1993 I was in Edinburgh covering Gorbachev's

visit to Britain arranged by a public relations agency specialising in baseball stars and waltzing dogs. With a handful of
other journalists, I had an opportunity to follow Gorbachev
and his wife Raissa through the exhibition of medieval arms
at Edinburgh Castle and to hear their impromptu verbal
exchanges. They were obviously unaware of the presence of
a Russian-speaker among the hacks.

'Look at these little pistols, Mikhail Sergeyevich, aren't they
cute?' cooed Raissa.

'Yes, they are. Do you think they are real? Do you think I
could fire one?' echoed her husband.

They behaved like a couple of not particularly bright innocent six-year-olds. The only difference was that they addressed
each other by patronymics – Mikhail Sergeyevich and Raissa
Maximovna – in the old tradition of Russian peasants and
Soviet communist party apparatchiks, both of whom they
seemed to represent.

Scouring the deserted campus of Edinburgh University
where Gorby was to deliver the Lothian Lecture, I wandered,
without realising it, into the mortuary of the Medical School.

'Has Mr Gorbachev arrived yet?' I asked a sombre uniformed attendant. He leafed through a thick register.

'No,' he said after a pause. 'The body under that name hasn't
been delivered to us yet.'

It looked increasingly as if I was surrounded by living
corpses. At times I had serious doubts as to whether I was
still alive, myself.

1993 was coming to an end. The memories of my New Year
Calais-Dover rave and of the encounter in the bar made me
shudder: I seemed to have spent the year on the road, surrounded by strangers and coming to the brink of a divorce.

The way you begin a new year, so you will complete it – the
bloody old saying had proved right.

It was there, in Edinburgh, that I learnt about the sale of our
Melbourne family house which I could no longer afford to pay
for. It was sold at an auction at a huge loss of money that we
had – literally – pumped into our indoor swimming pool. 'One
of East Bentleigh's Best Kept Secrets' – that was how it was
advertised on a real-estate billboard. And although I wanted

the house to be sold, the news gave me an acute feeling of loss and homelessness. Wandering the dark streets of Edinburgh the same night, I spotted a tramp sitting on the pavement next to a McDonald's outlet. 'Homeless' was handwritten on a crude piece of cardboard in front him. Well, we are in the same boat, mate, I thought then.

There was one human being with whom I developed a strange form of friendship. He was a Polish gardener who lived in a tiny bedsitter in the same house where Prince Charles's flat was located. My compassionate landlady allowed him to live there for free in return for looking after the garden which he did without much oomph. A former fisherman, he became a gardener after a bad accident at sea which had affected his head (he was hit by a collapsing mast, thrown overboard and spent forty minutes, unconscious, in ice-cold water) and that was reflected in his manner of speaking. Instead of asking: 'Can I offer you a lift to the airport?' he would say, with his strong Polish accent: 'Would you require my private transport facilities to deliver you to the airport?' Instead of saying: 'Would you like to have a meal at my house?' he would inquire, 'What is your attitude towards consuming some nutritious products at my residential dwelling?'

He also had problems with English suffixes and used to call himself a misunderstood intellectualist. 'There are no intellectualists in this country, but there are lots of criminalists,' he would say, meaning Britain, which he stubbornly called 'Brittany'.

He was a kind-hearted fellow, this gardener. He looked after me when I was once laid up with a cold: measured my temperature and brought me medicines. Occasionally, he would cook for both of us a starchy Polish meal and take me shopping to Tesco on Saturday mornings. 'Let us go to Tesco! Let us go to Tesco!' he would chant happily behind the wheel. His driving was terrible (worse than mine), and I kept trembling with fear when I sat next to him in his battered Ford Fiesta.

I was slightly ashamed of him during our shopping expeditions which he himself thoroughly enjoyed: he would dash like mad past the counters (he *was* mad, of course) pushing a loaded trolley in front of him and frightening other shoppers away. Out of embarrassment, I often ended up buying lots of food that I didn't need and had to throw out later.

There were many families in Tesco cheerfully doing their weekly shopping, which made me, accompanied by a mad giggling gardener, feel like a miserable pariah.

'We are both lonelists and must provide assistance for each other,' he liked to say making me feel even more of a 'lonelist'.

Despite this, he could have been tolerable were it not for his two persisting habits. He had a bee under his bonnet about keeping the front gate shut at all times, and whenever I (or anyone else) forgetfully left it open, he would dash out of his bedsitter (where he sat all day watching any potential gatecrashers) fuming and shouting at the offender at the top of his lungs.

His other nasty habit was playing the flute. As he himself told me, he heard a flute melody on the radio while recovering after his accident in hospital and persuaded himself that he had to learn to play it. He would routinely start his flute exercises at 7 p.m. and would carry on well into the early hours of the morning. His clumsy scales tore through my brain and body like toothache and made me look up longingly at a large metallic hook sticking out of one dark green living room wall with no obvious purpose. The 'music' was literally driving me up the wall, and I seriously contemplated the best way of attaching my trouser belt to the hook and putting my poor head through the loop. Depression and loneliness, multiplied by unending flute scales in an adjacent room, plus a good solid hook protruding from the wall, constitute an ideal suicide set. There was no way I could stop him from playing. The moment I raised the subject, he would start screaming and twitching violently.

A couple of years later, when I had already moved out, the gardener grew completely insane and played his awful flute twenty-four hours a day. He stopped looking after the garden (and after himself) and one fine night an ambulance, called by the neighbours, took him to an institution. The neighbours told me that he was clutching his flute in his hands when they carried him out of the house on a stretcher. His lips were covered with bubbling white foam. A coveted silence is now reigning above the house with a red dragon on the roof in Woodside Avenue and its neglected front garden, overgrown with weeds. And the gate stays permanently open. When I saw it ajar for the first time, I realised clearly that the gardener was no longer there. And nor was I . . .

I dreaded weekends and tried to make sure I was away from London on Saturdays and Sundays, but it wasn't always possible. To beat my solitude, I used to throw weekend parties for up to forty people at a time (some of whom I hardly knew). A couple of hours into a party most of my guests would get pissed and forget about me. The carpets would be covered with corks and cigarette-ends. Couples would snog in the bathroom.

Who said that solitude in the crowd was the worst form of loneliness?

One night, after a particularly crowded and long party, I was left on my own to clear up the mess and wash up mountains of dirty plates in the kitchen. I was drunk, having mixed vodka and red wine. Sitting on the sofa in my empty, littered living room, I remembered how one of the guests, a wife of a colleague of mine, referred to my flat as a mausoleum. 'How do you live in this mausoleum?' she asked me, pointing at the grimly painted hospital-like walls and the bulky old furniture.

She's right. It is a mausoleum, I thought. And I am buried here alive. There was nothing but complete muddle in the past. There was nothing but darkness and grief in the future. I realised that I didn't want to carry on. From behind the wall I could hear the gardener tormenting his uncomplaining flute, but this time I thought I could discern a vaguely familiar melody in the cacophony of sounds. It was Chopin's Funeral March.

Had I had some sleeping pills handy, I would have taken them all without thinking. Luckily, I had none. Having grabbed a long kitchen knife, I tried to poke myself in the chest, but had to conclude that hara-kiri wasn't the most comfortable way of committing suicide. I quickly got dressed and was about to dash out of the house (to throw myself under a car?) when I noticed several unopened letters on a window-sill in the corridor. On top of them there was one with an Australian stamp, and the address on the envelope was written in uneven childish letters. I could recognise my son's clumsy handwriting from a hundred yards. This was unusual as he seldom bothered to write to me.

The letter was in broken Russian with heaps of spelling mistakes.

> My dearest Dad,
>
> How are you there, in your dark misty London? I know that you are lonely and I suffer a lot because of that. I miss you heaps and I wish I could be there with you. We could go to Trocadero, as we used to do, and I would play games and you would be angry and hurry me up. And on the way back we would pop into a McDonald's. Soon, very soon, I'll come and visit you and we'll be doing all these and more. I think about you all the time. Sorry for the mistakes.
>
> Bye-bye, my dear, my most beloved Daddy

I spent the rest of the night washing the dishes and picking up cigarette-ends from the floor.

Next day it was Sunday. After lunch, washed down with half a bottle of vodka, I was dozing on the sofa under a thick blanket of unread Sunday newspapers. When I opened my eyes, I saw a huge black cat standing next to the sofa and staring past me into the corner. He must have got in through the balcony door which I had forgotten to shut. I had seen this homeless cat before, scouring the garden in search of food. I knew that a cat was unlikely to enter a strange house when there was someone else inside. But this uninvited feline visitor seemed totally oblivious of my presence. Even when I tried to shoo him away, he pretended not to notice me. Was he deaf and blind?

Or could it be so that he didn't react to me simply because . . . I wasn't actually there? Maybe my whole existence was just a crazy illusion or a protracted dream? Life only becomes meaningful when you are needed and remembered, when people miss you and ring you up to invite you for a meal or for a night out. My telephone had been dead for days. There was no one in London, or in the whole of Britain, who was willing to talk to me and ask me how I was. And in Melbourne it was the middle of the night and the handful of people who still cared for me were probably fast asleep.

I stirred, and the papers on top of me didn't rustle. I looked down: the cat was still there . . .

My disappearance was almost complete, and there was only one living being in the whole world who was still capable of finding me. Myself.

25

November in Norway

'November always seemed to me the Norway of the year,' Emily Dickinson wrote in one of her letters. Developing this fascinating metaphor further, one may safely assume that March is Germany, June is France, July is Italy, August is Spain and May is Japan.

What about February then? Britain of course!

I was spending most of my time travelling around Europe. With an Australian passport in my breast pocket, I was routinely crossing borders and no longer felt intimidated by the blank piercing stares of immigration officers. Once, when on an assignment in Luxembourg, I went for lunch to neighbouring Germany and then had coffee in France. On another occasion, I got lost in the Liechtenstein Alps and, without realising it, wandered into Austria, where I had a glass of beer at a village pub, convinced that I was still in Liechtenstein. It was only when I was asked to pay my bill in Austrian schillings, I realised my mistake and ran towards the nearby border, bracing myself for a painful showdown with incorruptible Austrian frontier-guards.

A huge lock hung on the door of the empty border post. I looked inside, but was able to discern only a poster with the photographs of 'Terroristen' on the wall. I made sure my photograph was not yet among them (just to be on the safe side), and only then noticed a sign above the locked door: 'The frontier post is open daily from 8 a.m. to 8 p.m., except for holidays and weekends.'

Remembering it was Sunday, I gave a deep sigh of relief and briskly walked across the border into Liechtenstein. No one was there to stop me.

A hotel room was one place where I felt more or less at home. At least it was free of painful memories and I knew exactly for how long I was going to stay there. In the overall mess of my existence it gave me a brief feeling of spiritual comfort.

I liked most countries I visited, except perhaps for Switzerland, which was so lifelessly and boringly clean that I came to understand why it had one of the world's highest suicide rates. If we believe Bernard Shaw, who called murder an extreme form of censorship, then suicide is but an extreme form of cleanliness.

I was absolutely fascinated with Venice which reminded me of an ageing but still graceful woman, suffering from insomnia, and shuffling restlessly around the house in her loose-fitting slippers in the night. The soft splashes of canal water against the old Venetian stones were like the shuffle of her slippers against the floor.

I fell in love with Norway when I first came there in November 1993. It was love at first sight. November in Norway is not just a poetic alliteration. It is a succession of crispy morning frosts and transparent sunsets at four o'clock in the afternoon, when rocks and forests are silhouetted clearly against the pinkish satin sky like a huge appliqué work created by Odin, the supreme God of the Vikings called *Allfader*, Father of All. It is an unruffled reflection of ship masts and medieval castles, doubled in the glassy waters of fjords. It is a multiple repetition of the still timid and translucent snowflakes falling silently, almost regretfully, and melting instantly on your face.

November in Norway . . .

The first two people I spotted in the streets of Oslo on arrival were drunks. Boisterous and red-nosed, they looked like a pair of cheerful trolls, fantastical forest characters out of Norwegian folklore. Soon I came to the conclusion that the chance of bumping into a drunk in Norway was much higher than in almost any other West European country, despite (or maybe because of) the strict state monopoly on alcohol. To my considerable dismay, spirits with more than five per cent alcohol content were sold exclusively, at government-fixed prices, by the state-run shops called the Monopolies. A typical Monopoly had a touch of a Moscow vodka store. It was the only place in Norway where one had to queue to get to the counter, but it didn't seem to deter Norwegians. No wonder: forbidden fruit is the most coveted. Prohibition, as history has shown more than once, only leads to heavier drinking.

Was this one of the reasons for my love affair with this Nordic country?

I met a Russian refugee in Oslo who found Norwegians cold and unapproachable. He was obviously unaware of the main law of the Norwegian psyche, the so-called Jante Principle, formulated by Axel Sandemose, a Danish writer turned Norwegian: 'Don't think that you are successful, and if you can't help thinking that you are, at least don't show it.' (I wish I knew it when I lived in Australia!)

For me, Norwegians are among the nicest people in the world. True, they are taciturn and reserved, but also friendly and no-nonsense. They don't waste words and they never fuss. They probably find it hard to be talkative with Norwegian as their mother tongue. Their language abounds in unpronounceable guttural sounds, unpennable letters and threatening high-pitch intonations.

When Norwegians say 'Ya . . . h', they do it in an inimitable gasping manner as if they are about to choke on their own uvulas. That was probably why all Norwegians I met (from a bus driver to an academic) spoke perfect, almost unaccented, English. Maybe they should have adopted it as their official tongue, and reserved Norwegian for quarrels and debates? The only problem here is that Norwegians do not seem to quarrel and argue much.

'The Norwegians are, like their landscape, rather vertical,' a traveller once observed. Quite so. A vertically challenged person like myself felt uncomfortable in this land of fair-haired giants towering above him like snow-capped mountain peaks above a Scythian mound. Door-handles in Norway were set close to my eye-level. I had to jump up to turn the massive handle of the heavy metal-cased doors of the Natural History Museum at Bergen University, and dangled from it for a while, my legs beating the air, before it gave.

My dinner guest at the cosy Chinese restaurant in Oslo kept puffing at his cigarette nervously. 'I started smoking at the re-education camp where they sent me to die in 1978,' he said through clouds of smoke. 'We had to break stones with hammers from 7 a.m. to 6 p.m., and two bowls of rice a day was the only food we had. We all smoked to beat the hunger.'

Do Vahn Thanh, president of the Vietnamese Refugees Association in Norway, ate hastily, as if still expecting someone to tear the plate away from him at any moment. The son of a Saigon banker, he was at university in 1975 when South Vietnam fell to the communists. He was expelled as a 'capitalist element', and when his father was sent to a re-education camp on the Cambodian border Do Vahn Thanh was sent there, too. Listening to his story was like watching *The Killing Fields* over and over again.

'They would beat us up for the slightest misdemeanour, but we had to keep going. An ailment meant certain death. Men and women lived in one huge stinking barrack.'

Despite having lived in Norway for fourteen years, Do Vahn Thanh, now a successful electronics engineer, was still finding it hard to forget. After escaping the camp, he joined 195 people aboard a flimsy twenty-metre boat that took them in August, 1979, away from their mutilated motherland into a new life of uncertainty. Nine days later they were picked up by a Norwegian freighter. He was quick to make a new start. Only five days after arriving in Norway he began studying at Bergen University. He didn't understand a word of Norwegian, yet six months later he was a fluent speaker.

Do Vahn Thanh's story was typical of the 10,000-strong Vietnamese community in Norway, which consisted almost entirely of the boat people picked up by Norwegian sailors in 1979–89. The issue of human rights had always been treated seriously there. The country had never hurried to agree to extradition for escapees from totalitarian countries, as its Finnish and Swedish neighbours often had. The fugitives knew that as soon as they reached Norway they were safe. For many years it had been illegal for Norwegian sailors *not* to take boat people aboard on the high seas. The integration of Vietnamese refugees into Norwegian society is a little-known success story of post-communist Europe, overridden with racist outbreaks and ethnic tensions. Not too many people realise that Norway has become one of Europe's largest refugee havens.

It is hard to find two more different peoples – ethnically, historically and psychologically – than Vietnamese and Norwegians. Orientals and Vikings . . . sand and snow . . . fire and water . . .

'I admire the Vietnamese. We have a lot to learn from them,' said Roald Kristiansen of the state immigration directorate, who had worked with them for many years. A communist sympathiser in his youth, he changed his views under the influence of the Vietnamese fleeing from the communist regime. 'They brought to us their strong family values, their politeness, their concept of friendship and devotion, their will to survive and to sacrifice. They taught us, the traditionally conservative and somewhat cold Norwegians, not to take things for granted.'

Other Norwegians shared Kristiansen's view: 'They have brought some warmth to this cold country,' I kept hearing.

Norwegian admiration for the Vietnamese was reciprocated.

'I feel both Norwegian and Vietnamese,' said Thien Trang Bihn, a young moon-faced woman living in the south-eastern town of Arendal, who spent six months in prison in Vietnam before escaping. 'True, Norwegians are reserved and cold on the surface, but they are warm in their hearts. They gave us Freedom. I haven't repaid them yet, but I will one day. I want to become a good citizen of Norwegian society.'

'In Norway I feel younger than ten years ago in Vietnam,' smiled Loc Dinh Fuong, a thirty-four-year-old interpreter who had learnt Norwegian in 240 hours instead of the allocated 700. 'My biggest dream is to take my Norwegian friends to a new free Vietnam one day.'

So what is a motherland? Is it the place where you were born? Or the country that gave you Freedom? Is it a comfy flat in Oslo or a stiff bamboo bunk in a re-education camp? Perhaps Benjamin Franklin had the answer when he said: 'Where liberty dwells, there is my country.'

Life in Norway was not all milk and honey for the Vietnamese. Not only had they to adjust to a new social order, they also had to come to grips with severe Norwegian winters.

'It's not so much the cold that gets us down, it's darkness and lack of sunlight,' many Vietnamese complained.

And they were also increasingly worried by talk of possible repatriation. Some people in Norway, struggling with their own multiplicity of problems, were inclined to believe that circumstances in Vietnam had changed, and that it was no longer dangerous to live there.

In the village of Sattfjord I spoke to Cao The Thuy, who had come from Vietnam to join her husband only one week before. 'Yes, it is much better economically now but it is still impossible to express your views without ending up in a re-education camp. There's still only one party.'

Racism had never been strong in Norway, but it did exist. The so-called People's Movement Against Immigration, led by Arne Myrdal, was not big enough to be registered as a party, but it still managed to make a lot of noise. Myrdal's rhetoric was not original: migrants bring crime and disease; the Nordic race must be protected from extinction, and so on. Few people, thankfully, took him seriously.

While in Arendal I tried to talk to Myrdal, who agreed to a meeting at first, but then telephoned back to cancel.

'I don't believe you are a journalist from London,' he said (perhaps confused by my name).

'I can show you my press card,' I insisted.

'You could have bought it from someone else,' he snapped and hung up.

I thought to myself: It is good there are still countries where racists are reluctant to talk to journalists.

The next day in Bergen I spoke to Vietnamese teenagers at a Sunday school. They told me about their passion for basketball and skiing, their affection for the Norwegian royal family, their dislike of cold weather – all very normal Western kids. Some of them were products of mixed Vietnamese-Norwegian marriages, the number of which kept growing. They were free citizens of a free country, although their notion of Freedom was, naturally, not as clear as that of their parents:

'Freedom is the possibility to pursue your happiness . . .'

'Freedom is being able to express yourself and do whatever you like . . .'

'Freedom is not to be spied upon by your neighbours . . .'

And, to crown it all, '*Freedom is Norway.*'

26

Of Blondes, Mantras and Taekwon-do

*T*here is something brazen and iconoclastic about London summer. Like a curvaceous bikini-clad blonde who has wandered by mistake into a Pall Mall gentleman's club, summer doesn't belong here, and is generally regarded as a pleasant momentary aberration rather than a legitimate season of the year. Soon she will be gone, thrown out by the grey-clad doorman of early autumn, and the club will return to its normal black-tie routine. But memories of the beautiful visitor will linger in the old boys' hearts for days.

Summer in London ... it ruins dress codes, it shatters stereotypes. The gloomy and rain-soaked image of the British capital gives way to nightingales (or *The Big Issue* salesmen) singing in Berkeley Square, to transparent sunsets, to the pale round moon mooching about in the whisky-coloured night sky, like a pot-bellied drunk trudging unsteadily home after a long evening in a pub.

Some of the habitual London qualities, however, remain unchanged during this short spell of summer warmth.

'Crowds without contact, dissipation without pleasure,' Edward Gibbon said of London. I find this eighteenth-century observation appropriate now. Even on a crowded Tube train commuters manage to maintain a strictly no-touch stance – like in sportive karate – avoiding verbal, physical or any other form of contact: there is always a minute gap between you and your fellow passengers, as if they suspect you of being an IRA suicide bomber infected with leprosy. They mysteriously squeeze past you towards the exit without actually touching you. 'Mind the gap!' loudspeakers at some Tube stations announce every ten seconds. I know exactly what it means.

This no-contact behaviour is in stark contrast with Melbourne. The Australian crowd is characterised by excessive friendliness. They touch you, they shake your hand, they slap you on the back and occasionally punch you in the face – as gestures of friendship and goodwill, of course. They also talk to you, though sometimes you wish they wouldn't. Infrequent verbal exchanges on London's Tube are reduced to 'sorry' (when they tread on your favourite corn) and 'thank you' (when you step off it), accompanied by the peculiar English smile. When someone raises his voice in a London crowd, you can be sure that he is a foreigner.

Like no other city in the world, London has an amazing ability to adjust to your own mood. I call it a Chameleon City. When you are in high spirits, London is friendly, bright and cheerful, and every house smiles at you. When you feel down, London is grim, hostile and uninviting. There is no better place for enjoying yourself and sharing your happiness with. There is no sadder city for those who are miserable and alone.

To me, London was drab and joyless in the hot summer of 1994. One year after my separation from Natasha (or rather her separation from me), there were no signs of recovery.

Living in Australia and writing for the *Age*, I had hundreds of devoted fans. Some of them continued writing to me at *The European*. Among them was a young Australian woman of Serbian extraction. Her letters were especially warm and extremely intelligent: they were full of literary quotes and references. It was obvious that she was well-read and had a good writing style. She told me about her loneliness, about her ex-husband who used to beat her up, about her father who died in a car crash. I couldn't help responding to such openness.

My letters to her were getting longer and longer, whereas hers were routinely no less than ten pages each (she seemed a compulsive writer which worried me a bit). She enclosed some photos of herself: an attractive blue-eyed blonde.

I was finding solace in writing to her, as if I had suddenly acquired a trusted friend. And when she once wrote that she wanted to come over to London and meet me, I invited her to stay at my flat. She immediately agreed, her only problem being lack of money. I volunteered to buy her a one-way (as she had insisted) plane ticket.

Looking back now, I can't help wondering how naive and irresponsible I was to embrace a complete stranger whom I had never seen. Also, after many years in journalism, I should have known better than getting involved with a fan. But solitude and despondency overcame common sense. I was telling myself that due to our common East European background we were bound to click. Also, it was so tremendously romantic . . .

On the morning of her arrival, I dialled for a mini-cab, and, with a huge bunch of flowers, went to Heathrow. I told the driver to wait and ran to the Arrivals lounge. Her plane was late. Pacing the lounge with flowers in my hand and waiting to meet a woman of my dreams gave me a half-forgotten feeling of normality.

The feeling evaporated the moment I spotted her emerging from behind the turnstile and I knew I had made a dreadful mistake. For a start, the blue-eyed blonde photos had been taken some considerable time ago, and what was more, her fine line in literary references flowed straight out of the Dictionary of Quotations. I stood it for eight days. On the eighth I bought her another one-way ticket back to Australia.

The woman's short stay had thrown me into a drinking bout, and I was imbibing on a daily basis. Vodka had never made me really drunk. Instead, it had a soothing, almost sedative, effect. After a usual dose of a couple of glasses, I would sit quietly in the garden, smoking and humming to myself. The 'healing' effect would last for half-an-hour or so, after which I needed another intake to keep it going. I knew that after a couple of weeks of drinking I was bound to have an attack of my stomach ulcer, this internal guardian of my deteriorating health. I realised that if I carried on like this I wouldn't probably last for long.

I decided to cut down on my drinking and smoking and to try and change my diet (I was massively overweight: even a short brisk walk made me sweaty and gasping for breath). But it was easier said than done. I was finding it impossible to break my lifetime habits without support.

It is all in my mind, I kept telling myself. I have to strike a different attitude to life, and I need help.

I made an appointment with a psychotherapist, recommended by a friend, which in itself was a change of attitude: I used to be extremely sceptical about psychotherapists whom I tended to regard as money-grabbing charlatans speculating on their patients' problems. I was inclined to dismiss their popularity as a typically Western form of the chattering classes' decadence.

The psychotherapist was a graceful middle-aged woman with large tranquil eyes. She didn't talk much during our sessions but simply listened to me and made notes. In the beginning I was wondering whether it was worth paying forty pounds for each hour-long monologue of mine, but soon it all started making sense. Having someone to talk to about my problems, even if this someone offered no solutions, was not entirely useless.

The only real treatment she gave me was the so-called 'positive thinking exercise'. She made me repeat hundreds of times a day a special mantra which she had written for me on a piece of paper:

> I am trim, taut and terrific.
> I take control of my life.
> I have a great place to live and work.
> I feel happy and secure being by myself.
> I love and have confidence in myself.
> I let go of the past and welcome the future.
> I make confident positive decisions.
> I totally control my vehicle (mind and body) . . .

And so on . . .

In Russia we had a proverb: 'No matter how often you say

"sugar", it won't give you a sweet taste in your mouth.' No matter how much I was trying to assure myself of being 'trim, taut and terrific', one quick look in the mirror was enough to bring me back to reality: I was fat, insecure and unattractive – and the whole positive thinking abracadabra was no more effective than a gobbledegook doggerel, used by Kharkov kids playing hide-and-seek: '*Ene-bene-ryaba; quinter-pinter-zhaba . . .*'

Having concluded that my life's 'vehicle' was still firmly out of control, I stopped seeing the psychotherapist.

'Morning! I am calling from the Metro Goldwyn Mayer film studios.' The voice in my telephone had a thick American accent, as if my interlocutor had a small Capitol building in his mouth.

Here it comes. At last . . . I thought with trepidation, which was largely the result of a severe hangover. I was not exactly sure whether I was already awake or still asleep.

'Mister Vitaliev, we need your help, sir. We are developing a multi-million-dollar movie about the Russian Mafia, and you were recommended to us as an expert. Would you consider collaborating on a script for a modest fee of a hundred thousand dollars?'

Who? Me? No, thanks . . . Sorry, I wanted to say: 'Yes, of course!'

'Great! One of our top producers will be coming to London next week. Will you be able to meet him at the Savoy Hotel for a quick vodka?' (He said 'vadka' – in a truly American fashion.) I had heard that a cup of coffee at the Savoy was £20. I couldn't even imagine how much a 'quick vadka' could cost.

Preparing for the meeting, I discarded suits and ties as too conventional and opted for an open-neck denim shirt which was supposed to emphasise my unorthodox bohemian soul. Then I phoned a couple of colleagues just to say: 'Sorry, mate, I can't come to the office this afternoon. I've got a meeting with one of those Hollywood fat cats. They want to commission me to do a movie script . . . At the Savoy, where else?'

When I entered the Savoy lobby bar, the producer was

already there sipping his vodka (sorry, vadka). He was a little podgy fellow of Polish descent (no, not Roman Polanski).

'Let's have a drink,' he said. 'I love Russian vadka. I love Russia, although I've never been there. We gonna make a great movie! But let me tell you how I see the screenplay. First of all, I want lots of Georgians in it!'

I choked on my vadka: 'Why Georgians?' I asked.

'I don't know . . . I just love Georgians. Also I want gypsies, Cossacks and lots of horses. Hundreds and hundreds of horses. And fireworks of course . . . Just imagine all those gypsies and Georgians galloping away across the steppe pursued by Cossacks under the velvety Russian sky punctured with fireworks . . .'

'I thought . . . I thought the film was about the Russian Mafia,' I remarked meekly downing my glass.

'Sure thing!' shouted the producer. 'The Georgians are going to steal heaps of Red Mercury from the Russian Mafia and hide it in the Moscow Underground where it will be found by a young Cossack who will turn out to be a Jew and will be crowned as the new Russian Tsar in the end. I have already spoken to Mel, and he is dying to see the script! I can hear all of them chanting "Volga Boatmen" in the final coronation sequence at a Moscow Underground station as credits start to roll!'

And he burst into singing 'The Song of the Volga Boatmen' in a high-pitched drunken falsetto.

I suddenly realised that he was dead serious.

'I am sorry,' I said replacing my glass. 'I think you've made a mistake: my name is Vitali Vitaliev, not Harold Robbins.'

I could see a flock of green US bucks flying out of the hotel's rotating doors and heading south, towards the Thames.

'Give my regards to Mel,' I said and went out into the Strand, along which – manoeuvring among black cabs and red double-deckers – gypsies and Georgians were galloping pursued by whip-wielding Jewish Cossacks in *yarmulkas* under the fireworks-ridden London sky.

Such was the end of my brief association with Hollywood.

I don't know what would have happened to me, had it not

been for a small hand-written ad I spotted once on a notice board near a Tube station. It advertised a Taekwon-do class – the Korean martial art of self-defence – and promised 'fitness, self-confidence and new friends'. In normal circumstances, I wouldn't have paid any notice to an ad like this: I had had a brief experience of learning karate in Moscow.

Teaching martial arts in the Soviet Union was a criminal offence, since, as the USSR Criminal Code bluntly put it, they 'preached the cult of individualism'. Individualism in all its forms was an anathema to the Soviet rulers whose illegitimate power rested solely on a 'collective mentality' which made any sort of individualistic behaviour an immediate threat to them as a short cut to free thinking. Nevertheless, lots of young people practised martial arts (mainly karate) in a number of clandestine outdoor classes.

The one which I attended in the mid eighties was run by Tadeusz Kassyanov, a martial arts instructor for the army and the KGB, the only Soviet organisations that were allowed (and possibly even encouraged) to cultivate 'individualism' within their ranks. We had to practise in a small forest near Kolomenskaya Underground station. During the class, we all took turns as scouts to give an advance warning of an approaching militia patrol. The militia, with dogs on leashes, routinely scoured the forest in search of illegal martial arts enthusiasts. At the sight of a patrol, a scout would give out a cough, at which point we would pick up a football and start kicking it around under the militiamen's sceptical eye. They certainly knew what was going on, but proving it was too much of a bother. The moment they left, we would resume training. I remember feeling much fitter after a couple of months of attending the class, which was soon dispersed by the militia, and Kassyanov himself was arrested and put in prison, allegedly for his connections with the Moscow underworld.

'Fitness, self-confidence and new friends' – this sounded like a panacea to me, the more so as the class was conducted in a school gym, just round the corner from where I lived. I spent the next month conducting a silent argument with myself (after a year of solitude, I started talking to myself pretty often which in itself was a bad sign):

You have to take up Taekwon-do. This is your last chance.

But I am too old and unfit. I also drink and smoke . . .

This is exactly why you have to do it – not to kick the bucket before the end of the year.

But I will look ridiculous in a kimono. They will all laugh at me. I can also have a heart attack . . .

You certainly will, if you carry on as you are. Stop complaining, pull yourself together and go. After all, you have always been a fighter. You've even managed to beat the Soviet system . . . Don't be a chicken!

OK. But not tonight. Next week perhaps. And now I'd rather order myself another vodka . . .

In my disgraceful rumpled track-suit, I came to the gym one evening. I had a drink before leaving my house – to boost my spirits.

The instructor was a woman. She was wearing a black belt on top of her kimono. There were a dozen or so students, mostly very young, at the class. All of them had coloured belts, from yellow to red.

I felt totally superfluous and out of place among these healthy and cheerful youths. Beltless and breathless, I stood at the very end of the line during the warming-up. My stiff joints gave a loud crackle every time I tried to raise my leg. And when we were told to do some stretching, my body nearly broke in two. Torrents of sticky warm sweat were pouring down my face. I was dying for a cigarette.

The good thing was that both the instructor and the students, instead of making me into a laughing stock, were trying to help me. 'Take it easy, don't strain yourself too much,' they would say. I liked the atmosphere in the class, friendly and not too competitive.

In the end, I surprised myself by having done thirty press-ups with relative ease. I always had strong hands, like my father, and could do twenty-five push-ups on the horizontal bar when I was sixteen, twice as many as any other boy in my class.

'You are going to be OK,' Mary, the instructor, reassured me. 'You've lost your form, but it can be helped.' She said she used to be very unfit herself until she had taken up Taekwon-do nine years before.

I stumbled out into the dark street. Every inch of my body was aching. But the pain was not unpleasant. I felt calm and elated – something I hadn't felt for years. My head was light and clear, as if I had just downed a good glass of vodka. No, the feeling was much more natural than the vodka-induced one. I suddenly realised that during the whole class I hadn't thought for once about my broken dreams and my loneliness. For the first time in many months my soul had had a coveted rest.

That night I was able to fall asleep without my usual vodka nightcap.

27

Going Out with Miss World

'*H*i, Vitali! Are you free for dinner tonight?'
   'I'm afraid not. I am dining with Miss World at the Park Lane Hotel.'
   'Give her my regards, whoever she is, ha-ha . . . How about tomorrow?'
   'I am going to the races at Ascot with Miss World, sorry . . .'
   'Will you stop pulling my leg? Just tell me you don't want to see me!'
   And the caller slammed down the phone.
   I was indeed going to spend a couple of days with Yulia Kurochkina, Miss World 1992, whom I first met in December 1992, for a quick interview.
   I had 'flu, and Yulia's manager would heroically throw himself between her and me at the first signs of my approaching sneeze, like a faithful adjutant protecting his commander from a sniper's bullet.
   'What is beauty? And why do people deify it? Is it a vessel with emptiness inside, or a flame burning in this vessel?' I mumbled these words by an obscure Russian poet, Nikolai Zabolotsky, as I elbowed through the throng of fans and photographers. The tall beauty queen, with a charming smile on top, towered above the mob. For a fleeting moment she smiled down at me, and I felt like a snowman under a warm ray of sun: I was melting.

There's a Russian saying: 'She looks at you as if she's giving you a rouble.' Owing to the dire state of the Russian currency, the rouble should have been a dollar, or according to the 1992 exchange rate, 398 roubles. Yulia's smile instantly made me into a rouble millionaire.

An eighteen-year-old from a Moscow suburb of Shcher-binka (which, ironically, means 'a small pock-mark'), Yulia won her title in a tough competition in Sun City, South Africa. There were no pock-marks on her beautiful face. She told me she had just entered the Moscow Institute of Finance and Economy.

'I am only eighteen, you know, and I'd like to have a normal profession,' she said.

Good girl, common sense too, I thought then. Beauty is transitory, but economists are always in demand, especially in Russia.

As a Russian-speaker, I had an advantage over other journalists trying to interview Yulia, who hardly spoke a word of English then. That was probably why there was an immediate rapport between us.

'Does beauty involve responsibility?' I asked her.

'Of course. Looks, after all, are not so important. Beauty is more than that. It's largely what's inside you. Your inner self is capable of influencing your looks . . .'

Had she read Zabolotsky? I doubted it. But she struck me as being honest and bright. She had both the vessel and the flame. I sincerely hoped that her flame would keep burning.

A year and a half later a phone call broke the silence of my solitary London abode. It was Yulia. She said she was in Britain on a short visit and wanted to see me. She suggested we had dinner and asked whether I could accompany her to Ascot the following day. I was so depressed and insecure about my looks that I nearly turned her down. What an unseemly couple we would make . . . I was thinking. In the end, I agreed, of course. No man is able to refuse an invitation from Miss World (even if an ex-one). I decided to treat her call as just another episode in the overall absurdity of my London existence. At least I wasn't suffering from 'flu. But I had toothache instead. What a miserable old wreck!

Waiting for Yulia in the Park Lane Hotel lobby, with a box of Panadol pills in my pocket, I looked at the mirror, and what did I see? A short pot-bellied man in his late thirties, with one cheek slightly bigger than the other (I was developing an abscess).

I turned away from the mirror in disgust and started studying the photo on the opposite wall: 'Mark Veasy, House Porter. Employee of the Month.' He looked much smarter than I did. At least both his cheeks were of the same size.

I had never been a great success with the opposite sex. When I had my first date with a girl from our school twenty-three years before, a rare snowstorm meant she didn't turn up. Miss World, however, did. She smiled at me – and my teeth stopped aching. She extended her hand, and I had to raise mine: Yulia was eighteen centimetres taller than me. I only felt better when we sat down at a table in the hotel's brasserie. Miss World ordered lasagne and an ice-cream (her English had improved dramatically since our last meeting). I ordered a hamburger.

'They will never understand us!' Yulia said (in Russian of course).

Don't get me wrong – what she meant was that the West would never understand Russians. She had had plenty of opportunities to feel this lack of understanding on her own exquisite skin.

Almost all British newspapers had managed to distort her name by calling her Kurochinka (not Kurochkina). Having watched dozens of Yulia's interviews with London hacks, I could testify to the fact that most of them asked just two questions: 'Is it true that you live in a one-bedroom flat?' and 'Aren't you going to get a new flat now, being Miss World?' Yulia would answer 'yes' to the first question and 'no' to the second one, immediately becoming Miss Bored.

'They measure everything by the number of bedrooms in their flats here,' she told me, wrinkling her marvellous nose. 'My life hasn't changed a bit since I won the title. I keep studying at the Finance Institute, and walking my dog in the morning. My popularity in Russia is minimal: they all think I am a millionaire living on a Caribbean island and don't expect to bump into me on the Moscow Metro.'

In the West Yulia was also asked what she thought of Bill Clinton or John Major. To this she usually said: 'We've got heaps of our own problems in Russia.'

A brilliant answer, though I had once had an impression that she was not sure who John Major was.

Here they had the first ever Russian Miss World, a genial and open character, ready to share her innermost thoughts, and the only thing they wanted to know was how many bedrooms her flat had. What a shame!

Yulia told me a lot.

How she was bullied at school because of her height and was nicknamed 'Stick'. How her parents, modest engineers from the Moscow suburb of Shcherbinka, found it hard to cope with having a beauty queen for their only daughter. How the Russian press wrote nonsense about her after she won the Miss World title ('I even wanted to sue them, they're simply jealous'). How she raised 125,000 US dollars for homeless kids during her trip to Colombia, where she was also robbed of her Chinese necklace. How she helped a Russian boy with some serious intestinal problem to get medical treatment in London. How she didn't have a single real friend, because she was afraid of attaching herself to anyone too closely. How she dreamt of having kids and a loving husband. How she deplored (together with her conservative father) the loss of traditional human values and national pride in post-communist Russia.

Miss World was a real Miss Word to anyone who was prepared to listen. But the British media chose to treat her as Miss Weird instead.

At coffee Yulia said that she wanted to talk to me in private and rolled her eyes up towards the ceiling in the manner so familiar to me from my life in the Soviet Union. It meant she didn't want us to be overheard. I suggested we could talk in my flat and she agreed. Reluctantly, I got up from my chair and, trying to keep a three-metre distance from Yulia for the difference in our height not to be so conspicuous, led her out into the street.

And here she was sitting in the sofa in Prince Charles's flat, having scattered her abnormally long legs all over the living room. I tried not to look at her shapely legs, but it was impossible: they were everywhere.

She told me that some shadowy Russian Mafia types were trying to fleece her of her prize money. They threatened to disfigure her and to kill her parents. 'The Mafia rules Russia at present,' she confided and added: 'They said I had to pay for my future.'

She was asking for my advice, and I gave her some of my old and still reliable militia contacts. In 1987, I had been the first journalist to start writing about the Soviet Mafia, and Yulia knew this, having read some of my stories.

Her wish was to stay in England, but she was not sure whether she could find a good job: 'My managers keep telling me that I am too tall to be a model . . .'

I was looking at her and couldn't believe my luck: one of the world's most desired women was sitting on the sofa in my flat, lighting up its grimly-painted interior with her radiant presence. Only for me she was not a woman. She was a confused teenager, almost a child, who had come to a journalist in search of advice and protection. It was late. With a sigh, I poured some more tea into Yulia's cup and reached for the telephone to call her a mini-cab . . .

'Do you have hats like this in Russia?' a BBC interviewer asked Yulia next morning.

We were at Royal Ascot, the most fashionable race meeting in the English social season. It was raining cats and dogs. It was raining hats and frocks too. Women's hats could easily pass for umbrellas and their umbrellas could be mistaken for hats.

The only hat which did not look like an umbrella was Yulia's. Designed by David Shilling (and worth much, much more than just a shilling), it was made of a handful of pheasant's feathers which kept dropping off as she was parading in front of the cameras under the rain.

Walking on tiptoes, I was holding an umbrella over her head (or over her hat, to be more exact). I was openly admiring her and was struggling with the desire to tell everyone at Ascot that this gorgeous young woman had had tea with me in my flat last night.

'The ground is now officially soft,' came the announcement. And Yulia was now unofficially soaked.

What a hell of a job it is to be Miss World, I thought, remembering half-a-dozen photo-sessions and twice as many interviews Yulia had already had that morning.

We were having lunch at a restaurant next to the racecourse. I was sitting next to a woman nutritionist who looked disapprovingly at Yulia eating a big piece of chocolate cake. The nutritionist was plump.

Yulia was sitting next to a tall young man in a bowler hat, a London bond-broker (whatever that could mean) who had been selected to be her *official* escort for the day (I was an unofficial one – a much more glamorous role). 'I just decided to see whether there are some bonds to broke here,' he joked when I asked him what he was doing at Ascot. No one laughed.

No, I was not treating him as my competitor. His role was that of Sancho Panza: carrying Yulia's hats and umbrellas. As for me, I was probably taken for her bodyguard. How can you otherwise explain the fact that my weighty shoulder-bag, which could easily carry a bomb, was not checked at the entrance, whereas everyone else's (Yulia's included) were rummaged through?

What about the horses? Which horses? Ah, horses! Of course, both Yulia and I knew that Ascot was somehow associated not only with hats and lunching but with horses as well. We hadn't seen any though, despite the fact that Yulia specially went on to the balcony to try and spot one. There were none, apart from those on the restaurant's TV screen where we could see them running somewhere – probably for shelter from the rain. Or for lunch. My only consolation was the expression of a Russian poet who said: 'We are all horses to some extent.' I reminded this to Yulia, and she smiled. And I remembered another Russian writer, Isaac Babel, who said that as a teenager, the whole world in his imagination looked like a large lawn with women and horses on it.

I was standing on a big lawn at Ascot with no horses in sight, but next to the world's most beautiful woman, the misunderstood Yulia Kurochkina – my new friend.

It was raining . . .

I am looking at a huge coloured photo of Yulia and myself occupying the whole front page of the *Élan* section of *The European*. It was taken on that memorable day at Royal Ascot. Podgy, overweight and dressed in a rumpled Marks & Spencer's suit, I am looking up at Yulia with a smile. She looks absolutely stunning in her red Versace outfit. 'Vitali Vitaliev (1.69 m) takes Russia's Miss World (1.87 m) to Royal Ascot,' reads the caption.

This photo was later reprinted in many countries, including Russia, and my colleagues at *The European* started calling me Cover Boy.

The last I heard of Yulia was that she got married and lives in Moscow. I hope she has found her ideal loving husband. In my wallet I still carry her business card which says simply '*Yulia Kurochkina. Miss World.*'

Somehow, I find it hard to throw it out.

28

Cricket

*I*n the summer of 1993 I went to Mount Athos, the medieval monastic republic in the north of Greece, where I spent several days visiting monasteries and talking to monks. Once, after a particularly tiring day, I fell asleep in my guest cell in the Abbey of Vatopediou and had an amazing dream.

I was on a Moscow shuttle train on the way to our little dacha in the village of Zaveti Iliycha. An unknown woman with the most beautiful and spiritual face was sitting in front of me. In fact, we were the only passengers on that train. All my life and all my thoughts were reflected in her warm dark brown eyes. I stretched out my hands to hold her and not let her go. The very effort made me feel light and blissful. In a moment I'll be holding her in my arms, and this will be happiness . . . At this point, I was suddenly awoken by the rhythmic sounds of *semantrons*, the wooden drums calling monks to the morning liturgy.

The drumming of *semantrons* was like the rattling of wheels of that distant suburban train from my dream. '*Ta-ta; ta-ta-ta . . .*'

I looked out of my cell window: the black-hooded monks were gliding across the monastery yard towards the church, like white-shrouded ghosts in a slow-motion picture, shown in the negative by the erroneous cinema operator of dawn.

On returning to London, I realised that, whatever my Mount Athos dream could mean, my loneliness had to come to an end.

I desperately needed a friend. Sometimes I thought for a fleeting moment that I could spot the woman from the train in the street crowd. And although I remembered her face very well, I couldn't describe it. How can you describe perfection, apart from calling it 'perfection' of course?

A couple of weeks later, I was sitting in my club, the Academy, with my old friend Sasha Kabakov, a well-known Russian writer and journalist, who was visiting me from Moscow. The Academy, a small writers' club in Soho, run by Auberon Waugh, had become my second home. I liked its informal easy-going atmosphere, so different from the pseudo-bohemian pretentiousness of the Groucho. The draft constitution of the Academy said that it was intended to be 'a sanctuary for congenial people in the West End of London, seeking a familiar and welcoming environment . . . Dress will be informal although shoes must be worn,' it went on.

I used to come to the Academy almost every day, at lunchtime or after the office, to read, to write letters or to have my daily intake of several double-doubles of vodka (they kept a special bottle of Stolichnaya for me in the freezer).

Sasha and I had a lot of catching up to do. I was telling him about my solitary life in London.

'What you need is a good woman,' he said authoritatively. 'Why don't you join a dating agency?'

By that time, I had been emotionally prepared for such a step and only needed a gentle push. I had to fill in half-a-dozen long forms with several hundred questions which included: 'What papers do you read on Sunday?' and 'What are your political views – left, right or centre?' The last time I had to fill a questionnaire as long as that was when I applied to the Soviet OVIR (visa office) for permission to spend a couple of weeks in brotherly Czechoslovakia in 1986.

The 'contacts' started arriving in neat Private and Confidential envelopes with two kissing doves in the corner. They could have just as well printed 'From the Dating Agency' on them.

The psychological approach, implied by the form-filling, didn't seem to work. It looked as if the agency was deliberately trying to match me with utterly unmatchable women, all of whom were direct antipodes to my 'preferences', so painstakingly listed by me in one of the forms. Also, since none of my initial contacts was of British extraction, I had an impression that the agency was specialising in foreigners (probably because foreigners were easier to dupe). The mere list of them sounded like a crash course in Geography, from the London-based German social scientist with verbal diarrhoea, through the Vietnamese lady whose intricate name sounded exactly like one particularly nasty Russian four-letter word; the plump chocoholic Lebanese; the Polish grandmother in her early sixties whose son was five years older than I ('Sorry, a computer mistake,' the agency explained when I called to complain); and a young Spanish journalist who kept promising to cook me a paella (and never did) and seemed to be doing nothing in her spare time but washing her knickers ('I am sorry, I have to go now: I've got loads of knickers to wash . . .')

That last lady talked about cooking me a paella so often that it made me wonder whether promising you a paella was a peculiar quality of Spanish women. Or did cooking a paella mean something more than just cooking a paella? Or something less than just cooking a paella (like *not* cooking a paella, say)? Hopefully, one day I will know the answer.

Despite (or rather because of) all these disappointing encounters, my life had become much more exciting and versatile. One thing that surprised me most about Western women (and after a dozen failed multicultural 'matches' I thought I was well qualified to make some timid generalisations), was how self-assured and easy-going they were about matters that would make most Soviet (or Russian) females blush. The Spanish lady was not alone in being quite open about the state of her underwear. 'I am dying to go to the loo,' or 'I am bursting for a pee,' most of my contacts would say without a shadow of embarrassment. Was this one of the manifestations of their innate Western Freedom?

My new life of an intensely socialising man came to an abrupt stop one morning when the envelope with kissing doves, instead of bringing me the phone number of yet another eccentric foreign woman, contained a strict accountant's note to the effect that the dating agency, of which I was a client, had gone into receivership and all its transactions had been stopped. It also asked whether I had any claims to raise.

I was not particularly surprised or upset by the news. I didn't feel like raising any claims, since I thought that the agency had done a good job by providing me with the equivalent of more than a hundred pounds' worth of life experience.

I decided that I was not yet up to starting a new relationship and chose to concentrate on my Taekwon-do. I soon won myself a yellow and then a green belt. Nothing, apart from going away on an assignment, could force me to miss a class. I got so hooked on it that when Peter Ustinov once called to invite me for dinner (he was spending only a couple of days in London), I apologised and said that I couldn't make it because of my martial arts class. (I am sure he didn't believe me.) Despite strenuous exercise, however, my weight had only gone down a tiny bit, probably due to the fact that I kept drinking several times a week (but no longer on the days of my class which in itself was quite an achievement).

It was one of those purposeless London parties, with bad food, plenty of small talk and no place to sit down, the party where conversation mostly rotates around how quickly and by what means of transport everybody had got there; where everyone says: 'Lovely to meet you', meaning 'How boring you are!' and 'We must do lunch one day', implying 'I wish I need never see you again.' I can't even remember how (or by what means of transport) I got there and who the hosts were. One thing I do remember is that I was, habitually, on my own . . .

We were suddenly brought face to face by the party's mysterious maelstrom – me, clutching a glass of vodka (thank God, they had plenty of vodka), she – with a glass of wine in her left hand (she was left-handed). I bumped into her in my usual elephantine manner, and as a result of this collision she spilled some of her wine onto the floor. 'Oh, I am so sorry,' I muttered and looked up . . .

All I could see was a pair of warm and eager brown eyes, eyes in which I could read my innermost thoughts, eyes that reflected all forty years of my life, eyes in which I wanted to drown.

The woman from my Mount Athos dream was standing in front of me with a glass of wine in her left hand.

Like me, she had come to the party by accident. I think she arrived there with someone else, but it didn't matter. Nothing mattered any longer, only being able to stand there, with glasses in our hands, and to look into each other's eyes.

'Would you . . . would you have a drink with me at my club?' I heard myself saying and immediately cursed myself for sounding like a snob. But somehow I also knew that she would agree. It was half-snowing and half-drizzling outside – typical February weather. I flagged down a cab.

We were sitting on a sofa, near the burning fireplace, in the Academy's cosy lounge. It was only there that I was able to look at her properly. She was slim, slightly taller than I, with some early wrinkles on her face that, curiously, made her look younger. I couldn't tear my gaze away from her radiant twinkling eyes, where two little fires were tirelessly dancing.

She was sipping wine, I was downing my double-doubles without getting drunk.

She lived on her own, with two cats and three fish in her garden pond.

She was Dutch but had lived in Britain since she was four.

She liked gardening and dress-making.

She didn't have children.

She worked as a PA.

She didn't read much and liked watching TV.

She enjoyed going out.

I was imbibing every little detail, all of which suddenly seemed very important.

We were definitely attracted to each other, and we both knew it.

I told her about my Mount Athos dream.

I told her about my broken marriage.

I told her about Mitya.

I told her about my Muswell Hill flat.

I told her about the mad gardener.

I told her about my books and films.

I told her about my loneliness.

I told her about my past.

Or maybe we were not talking at all, just staring at each other and not uttering a word. I felt that we didn't need to talk, that we could communicate without opening our mouths, with eyes alone.

'Can I kiss you?' I asked, surprising myself. She agreed silently, with a slight, almost unnoticeable, stir of her slowly parting lips.

The club's lounge was suddenly empty. Where had all the people gone? I looked at my watch: it was past midnight.

And then I nearly ruined it all. 'Do you feel like having a quick look at my garden?' I asked her. It was so stupid and banal that I blushed. And so did she. She looked at me for a moment with wide-open eyes – and we both burst out laughing.

In her sleep, she ground her teeth gently in a child-like way, as if regretting something she hadn't done. For that, I started calling her Cricket.

Of course we were very different. She was a Westerner – I was an 'Eastie'.

She was sophisticated and stylish – I was dowdy and clumsy.

She was easy-going and relaxed – I was self-absorbed and insecure.

She was practical – I was wasteful.

She ate healthy food – I preferred chips and sausages.

She liked wine – I drank vodka.

An unlikely match for any computer. Like Vietnamese and Norwegians, we were seemingly incompatible. Sand and snow . . . Fire and water . . . But just like Vietnamese and Norwegians in Norway, we had one thing in common: we needed each other.

The process of our mutual adjustment was long and painful. We were both mature people with well-formed habits which were hard to change. Several times we split up, but only for a while. There was something in our relationship that would inevitably bring us back together.

That mysterious something was probably called love.

She started with a thorough scrutiny of my wardrobe. As a result, 90 per cent of my clothes ended up in a bin. I tried to protest: 'What are you doing? I've been wearing this jacket for seven years, and it is still as good as new! I remember buying it in Druzhba department store in Moscow after three hours of queuing . . .'

'Tough!' she would reply. 'I can't allow my boyfriend to walk around in this baggy scruffy-looking shroud!'

This would be followed by a shopping expedition to Jaeger or Liberty where I would be persuaded to buy myself a 'decent' jacket for a couple of hundred pounds. Everything in me rebelled against such a waste. 'Just imagine how many good books I could have bought . . . And how many jackets on a street market!' I was whining.

'Forget about street markets!' she would retort. 'From now on you are wearing good quality clothes!'

She would buy me silk ties for fifty-odd pounds (one of them, to my considerable relief, she left behind in a cab).

With nostalgia, I was recalling my mirror-like glittery suit . . .

Gradually, however, I got the taste for good clothes. Under Cricket's influence (and pressure) I came to realise that the way you looked was an important part of your self-awareness and self-esteem. I was enjoying my new jackets, pants and shoes that suited me nicely and weren't coming apart at the seams after a couple of weeks. They were definitely worth the money that I had grudgingly coughed up.

It was the same with food. Cricket was genuinely appalled by my fatty and sugary diet. Little by little, she was introducing me to vegetables and salads, corn-flakes and yogurts, cottage cheeses and other low-fat foods. She also taught me 'Western' table manners of which I had had a very vague idea. Eating with her was not just a physiological act of stuffing your belly – a process opposite to emptying one's bowels. It was a pleasure, a treat, almost a form of art.

It was a bit harder with her innate Western practicism. She would tell me off for walking across someone else's driveway: 'It is private property, don't you understand?' She was also preoccupied with matters of security and financial stability, whereas I, in a typically Soviet way, could not care less about the future. Gradually, under her unyielding influence, my attitudes started to change.

But the most amazing thing that happened to me a couple of months after meeting Cricket was that I gave up drinking.

Not just drinking vodka, but drinking alcohol altogether. And she didn't push me into it. One fine morning (or was it evening?) I suddenly realised that I no longer needed any artificial stimulation (or artificial sedation) of my thoughts and feelings. I wanted to have my mind and soul fresh to be able to enjoy my time with her, and the vodka-induced time-killing effect – when you could almost see minutes, hours and days slipping away from you at breakneck speed – was no longer necessary. Suddenly, every moment of my life was meaningful and precious again and I didn't want to waste it in a drunken (or a semi-drunken) haze.

And one day, having climbed onto the scales which I had just acquired on Cricket's advice, I couldn't believe my eyes: I was twenty-five kilos lighter than I thought I was! I thought the scales were defective and even took them back to the shop, where I was assured that they were perfectly fine. People whom I hadn't seen for a while could hardly recognise me, and I was basking in their compliments of how 'trim and terrific' I looked. Immigration officers at Heathrow were scrutinising my old fat passport photo with a good deal of suspicion. 'You have certainly lost weight, pal!' they would say with respect, having made sure that it was indeed me on the photo.

Even Mitya didn't immediately recognise me, when I went to Australia to see him.

I stopped avoiding mirrors like a bashful vampire (as I had done for a very long time), simply because for the first time in many years I actually liked what I saw in them. And, although it sounds like a cliché, I did feel a completely new man.

'Hey, what's the secret?' I was often asked. 'Is it just the diet, or diet plus exercise, or something else?'

What could I say? Something that all the psychotherapists and all the vodka in the world were unable to do in years was achieved with the help of a loving woman within several months.

It was not long before Cricket and I decided to try and live together. I said good-bye to Prince Charles's flat in Muswell Hill without regret. Tube trains rattled beyond the windows of her North London house – *ta-ta, ta-ta; ta-ta, ta-ta* – making me feel almost at home.

29

Back in Ukraine

I was spending a week in San Marino researching my book on the smallest states of Europe. One day, having come back to my hotel perched on top of Mount Titano, I found a message from BBC Radio 4's *Start the Week*. The producer was wondering whether I was available to go to Ukraine in a couple of weeks' time to do a live radio programme from there. 'Jeremy Paxman, the presenter, wants you to come,' she said when I called her back.

This made me think hard. I knew only too well that I couldn't go back to Russia. Not while the ominous Article 64 punishing defectors by death in front of a firing squad remained in the country's Criminal Code. But what about my native Ukraine, which had become an independent nation? It was probably the same . . . So I refused at first. 'Well, call us if you change your mind,' said the producer.

For the whole of the next day I kept pondering my decision. I wanted to go back to see what was going on in my confused and impoverished motherland. Going with the BBC Radio crew was certainly preferable to going on my own, so it was a good opportunity to break the ice. I called the producer and said that I was ready.

'You can't enter the same river twice,' said Confucius. 'You can't return to a country that doesn't exist any longer,' wrote Joseph Brodsky.

Kiev met me with rain. Our plane was taxiing along the wet bumpy tarmac, overgrown with wormwood, which reminded me of the tiny village of Gaidary where I had turned a quick rouble at the student camp. The pungent and slightly intoxicating smell of Ukrainian wormwood, the smell of my youth: I could almost feel it bursting through the plane's portholes.

'*Pani i panove!* Ladies and gentlemen! Our plane has just landed in Kiev, the capital of free Ukraine.'

The announcement was in Ukrainian, or rather in *surzhik*, a crude mixture of Ukrainian and Russian, resulting from centuries of forced russification. 'Ladies and gentlemen', instead of the customary 'comrades', sounded encouraging, but also somewhat unsettling.

'Ukrainian International Airlines' was written on the fuselage of a small aircraft parked on the opposite side of the airfield.

It was my first visit to the former Soviet Union after almost four years of absence. I was pleased to be back, yet a bit worried. Not so much about potential problems that I might encounter at passport control as a recent defector: my dark-blue Australian passport with an emu and a kangaroo on the cover had been stamped with the Ukrainian visa in London (I never thought I would live to see a real Ukrainian visa: five years before, one could go to prison for simply uttering these two words), and the visa form that I had been given to fill in at the brand-new Ukrainian embassy was unexpectedly short and matter-of-fact, in stark contrast to the Russian questionnaire, still based on the old Soviet principles. No, I was afraid to find my motherland too depressing and didn't want to have sweet memories of my youth (I left Ukraine for Moscow when I was twenty-three) shattered by ruthless reality.

The first time I had been able to see a blue-and-yellow Ukrainian national flag was a couple of years earlier, in Tasmania. During one of my visits to Hobart in 1991, I spotted a rusty trawler with a soiled Soviet flag on her mast (the Soviet Union had just ceased to exist). The Sebastopol-registered ship was in port for a major overhaul, and when I came to Tasmania again several months later, the red Soviet flag was replaced with a makeshift blue-and-yellow Ukrainian one, crudely made out of coloured rags by the sailors themselves. The national flag of my native Ukraine was proudly flapping in the wind above the tranquil beauty of Hobart Harbour, above the dark bulk of Mount Wellington, above Tasmania and the whole world.

Its very colours were a strict taboo in the Soviet Ukraine, and anyone who ventured to wear a blue-and-yellow tee-shirt, say, could find himself in trouble. In 1974 three boys from my university department in Kharkov were expelled for chatting in Ukrainian. They were accused of 'Ukrainian bourgeois nationalism'. What was so nationalistic (to say nothing of 'bourgeois') about speaking one's native language in one's own country? Only God (and, possibly, Brezhnev) knew.

Going back was like bracing yourself for a rendezvous with your former sweetheart whom you hadn't seen for a number of years. What is she going to look like? Wrinkled, ageing and alien? Or dear and almost unchanged, with a familiar youthful twinkle in her eyes?

My first love had lived in Kiev, in Red Army Street, which had probably been renamed. I would come to see her from Kharkov, 400 kilometres away and, not being able to afford a hotel, would sleep on a hard wooden bench at the railway station, from where a bored and sleepy militiaman would periodically shoo me away. I was eighteen, and my dreams were invariably in Technicolor, even when I was sleeping on a station bench.

My other Kiev-based love was Dynamo, the local soccer team. One day in the mid-1970s I came specially from Kharkov to see Dynamo play Borussia Munich in the European Supercup. Dynamo won 2:0, and the whole city went mad with joy for several days. Dynamo fans were hugging and kissing each other on every street corner, as if the victory of their club signified the start of new and happier lives for themselves.

Two stone-faced border guards in green-topped caps stood either side of the gangway. Two more were positioned at the entrance to the terminal, and there were many more inside, their grey Soviet Army uniforms the same as four years before, but something had changed in their appearance: they looked detached rather than threatening.

An oblong dusty mirror hung above my head as I stood,

shifting from one foot to the other, in the narrow passage of passport control. The purpose of that mirror, part and parcel of every Soviet immigration point, had always been a mystery to me. Was it supposed to enable the officer to scrutinise the crown of your head for signs of a wig, or to monitor your dissident thoughts? Or was it simply designed to make every visitor feel like a trespasser?

'Pass on!' the officer squeezed out curtly, hitting my emu-ed and kangaroo-ed passport with something that looked and sounded like a sledge-hammer. I could almost hear the poor Australian animals squeal with pain.

A last step towards my motherland, and here he was, my old university friend, standing in the crowd. 'Vitya!' he cried out.

I had only been called Vitya by my parents and the friends of my youth.

'Tolik!' I gasped. We embraced.

It was raining heavily outside the terminal as we were getting into the car.

'You see, your motherland is crying with joy at having you back!' Tolik said.

Next morning I was woken by the piercing wailing of a tram screechingly turning the corner, and for a fleeting moment wasn't quite sure where I was. But then the sound of the tram, and the soft rustling of chestnut trees beyond the window, and the bright reflections of the sun's rays on the walls, all added up to one word – Ukraine.

I looked around my 200-dollar-a-night room of the Intourist hotel (yes, I came to my native land as a foreigner!): drab tattered furniture; an antediluvian TV set which didn't work; a tiny and smelly bathroom with no trace of soap or shampoo, but with tufts of someone's hair in the bath; a fridge the size of a polar bear, but empty as a stretch of tundra. Home?

'In the Soviet Union we lived like animals in the zoo: encaged, but regularly fed. Now it's like a jungle: only the strongest and the cruellest can survive,' Tolik had said the day before and added: 'Old Karl Marx was right: the rich get richer, the poor – poorer.' A university-educated interpreter (like myself), he was now a businessman.

'What sort of business are you in?' I asked him.

He waved his hand: 'Just anything, you know . . .'

According to him, lawlessness reigned. It was impossible to get anything without greasing the insatiable palms of the new 'democratic' bureaucrats (or were they bureaucratic 'democrats'?). At the newly-established frontier posts with Russia, customs officers would take anything away from a traveller, unless generously bribed.

'Everything is for sale. You can buy a restaurant or a cemetery, a parliament or a country – it's just the question of how much you can afford to pay,' my friend concluded.

It was the same country, and yet it was different. There were no habitual 'Let's Pull Together' slogans on the facades of ornate Stalin Gothic houses with peeling stucco. Khreshchatik, Kiev's main street, was still lined with blossoming, almost foaming, chestnut trees, but it was also lined with countless money-changers openly buying and selling US dollars and deutschmarks. For some reason, they were suspicious of pounds sterling, and my attempts either to exchange them or to offer them as payment were unsuccessful. Yet an old country woman at the famous Bessarabka market readily accepted three 'greens' (US dollars in the local jargon) for a big can of first-class Beluga caviar which could easily fetch £300 in London. At the next stall, the same can was on offer for just two 'greens'.

Street kiosks were displaying 'gentleman's sets' of Marlboro, chewing gum and faked Western soft drinks in plastic bottles, all totally unaffordable for an average local. A long queue for the cheapest fruit ice-cream snaked outside the state-run Gastronom food shop, also stocking affordable but clearly inedible and elderly chickens, which looked as if they had all died of malnutrition. A nearby newsagent's stall was piled high with flimsy yellowish newspapers of all imaginable affiliations from anarchist to openly fascist and pornographic (some of the latter had absolutely explicit advertisements offering sale and exchange of child porn with names, addresses and phone numbers supplied). In the window of the main department store imitation Western trainers were displayed. They cost two average monthly salaries a pair.

A street vendor in once white overalls was doing a brisk trade in *vatrushki* – round cottage-cheese pies that I used to have for my school lunches – and *kvas*, a drink made of yeast, and black bread (he had no drinking glasses, and I had to gulp the brown liquid from an empty pickles container which the vendor would sparingly splash with water after each use). The half-forgotten taste of this slightly alcoholic drink sent youthful pulsations through my body.

A beggar-girl, no more than seven years old, sat on the ground in the middle of Independence (formerly October Revolution) Square. Since coins had long ago gone out of circulation, passers-by tossed practically worthless Ukrainian coupons (paper money) at her, and she was half-covered with these rumpled (and worthless) pieces of coloured paper.

Was this beggar-girl the young independent Ukraine reincarnated?

Next to her a teenage boy with sad brown eyes was playing a trumpet. The melody was familiar: it was an old Ukrainian folk song about heroic Cossacks and their eccentric, but no less heroic, *hetmans* (commanders) – the only touch of real Ukraine in the streets of rootless and predominantly Russian-speaking Kiev:

> There, on the hill, peasants are harvesting,
> And down the hill Cossacks are riding. Hey!

Two dishevelled stray cats dexterously crossed Sophievska Street in front of a moving trolley-bus and headed for the nearby Pizza Bar, their protruding ribs going back and forth under their skin like pistons of an out-dated steam engine.

'Beer factory number one provides customers with beer only on condition that empty bottles are duly returned. Please hand empty bottles over to the bartender,' the sign inside the dark and stuffy Pizza Bar ran. Two street urchins were walking around the tables begging for empty bottles. Citizens of free Ukraine were drinking insipid and tepid beer from hot opaque glasses (at least they had glasses). A young girl at one of the tables was mouth-feeding her squiffy boyfriend with pizza. The floor was covered with sawdust.

And not far from the Pizza Bar, hundreds of busy-looking KGB (now called National Security) officers, whose Moscow colleagues drove me out of the Soviet Union in January 1990, were moving in and out of the huge block of houses in Volodimirska Street. Their expressionless faces, their baggy suits and unmatching greasy ties were the same as four, ten or fifty years ago. What were they up to now? They seemed to ignore the newly installed memorial plaque on the house of Mikhail Bulgakov, a profoundly anti-Soviet writer, in Andriyivsky Uzviz, and books by Solzhenitsyn selling from street stalls for 10 coupons (1/50th of a penny) each. They didn't seem to know that (as it had become obvious to me) the new Ukrainian Criminal Code had no Article 64, according to which former defectors like myself could face a friendly Soviet firing squad. They didn't seem to be aware of the main change that had happened to their country: people were no longer afraid of them.

True, Ukraine was still poor and run down. True, politics were a mess, inflation was running rampant and the government was impotent. True, chaos, anarchy and corruption were everywhere. True, there were plenty of beggars in the streets (not half as many as in London, however). But the expression on ordinary people's faces had become less haunted. The notorious seal of oppression, making any *homo soveticus* easily recognisable from afar, even if dressed in the latest Western fashion, had given way to normal human anxiety. Fear had gone, and the whole place had become a bit more relaxed, a bit more fast moving and, yes, a bit more honest than it used to be before.

The redeeming effects of Freedom . . .

With Tolik we were having one for the road at the Kiev airport's seedy bar, just reopened after a mysterious 'sanitary hour'. Some Mafia-like characters in soiled Adidas track-suits and with round brutish faces, resembling unwashed plates with leftovers of food on them, were hanging around. BMW and Mercedes keys jingled in their pockets as they jerked their heads to down their glasses.

We were eating pale and amazingly tasty Ukrainian tomatoes (clearly, grown in a vegetable garden, not in a hot-house) and home-made sausage, oozing with fat.

'You haven't changed a bit,' my friend told me.

'Neither have you,' I replied. 'The only thing that has changed is our country.'

I nearly missed my plane.

The turnstile at passport control clicked matter-of-factly, shutting me away from my past. I was no longer worried about the mirror above my head.

> There, on the hill, peasants are harvesting,
> And down the hill Cossacks are riding. Hey!

The old Ukrainian song was echoing in my head as our plane made the last circle above Kiev and headed West.

I knew I would be back . . .

30

Chernobyl

You can redecorate the walls and rearrange furniture in the room of your childhood, but you can't change the view from its window.

My second trip to Ukraine took place one year after the first one. This time I went there with a Channel 4 TV crew to make a *Travels With My Camera* documentary in June 1994. Over three weeks, I visited the capital, Kiev, again; Kharkov, the city where I was born; and Chernobyl, Ukraine's inoperable malignant tumour.

In Kiev we were allowed to film inside the local KGB (now calling themselves National Security Service) building where portraits of Dzerzhinsky, the sadistic chief of Lenin's secret police, Cheka, have been hastily replaced with those of the nineteenth-century Ukrainian poet Taras Shevchenko. A woman guide, who was a staff KGB employee, was taking us around the in-house KGB museum. She was falling over herself to speak Ukrainian – in accordance with a new national awareness. In the Soviet Union all minority tongues were mercilessly suppressed and everyone was expected to speak Russian. But her Ukrainian was awful, and this visibly unnerved her. She was stumbling and stuttering at every word, and her forehead was covered with sweat. She was obviously scared of us – an unimportant British film crew.

What an extraordinary twist! I thought then. I had never dreamt of living to see the day when a KGB agent would be literally shivering with fear in front of me. In the end, I took pity on the poor KGB woman. 'It's OK,' I said. 'You can now relax and switch over to Russian.'

With a loud sigh of relief, she promptly followed my advice.

The return to my native Kharkov was like watching a familiar play with an old stage design but with a new cast of actors. It was amazing how little the city itself had changed: same buildings, only somewhat more dilapidated; same landscape, only somewhat more forlorn; same environment, only somewhat more polluted and irradiated; same people, only much much poorer than ever before. Even the KGB, under a different name, followed the old script to the letter and aimlessly trailed our film crew for days on end, bringing back sinister memories from my not-so-distant past.

On this trip I was less emotional and more sober-minded than during the first one. Maybe it was because I was no longer lonely and had firmly decided to settle in London . . . Or could it be that the forthcoming trip to Chernobyl was affecting my mood?

Walking the familiar streets of my childhood I didn't feel like a stranger. But nor did I feel at home. I visited all the three flats where I used to live with my parents. Some of the neighbours were still there. They recognised me and cried, having remembered my late father. Others were gone – to Israel, to America, to Australia.

At the railway station, I stood for a while on the wobbly footbridge, suspended above the track, where I used to spend hours as a boy watching the trains and dreaming of travelling. It felt as if my life had come a full circle. I had criss-crossed the globe many times over only to come back to this bridge, from where my life-long travels had actually started.

My childhood friends were all living from hand to mouth. All their PhDs were suddenly useless, and they survived by petty profiteering of sorts. My old flame, the brown-eyed girl from my school, now a Doctor of Architecture, was in hospital being treated for malnutrition.

'You have become a Westerner, Vitya,' my childhood friends told me.

It was probably my new clothes, bought under the influence of Cricket, that gave me that peculiar 'foreign' look. Or maybe the seal of oppression was disappearing gradually from my face. But the real moment of truth came when I was taking nostalgic photos of our last home in Lenin Avenue.

'Look, a foreigner,' a woman in the street said to her friend, pointing at me. She thought I couldn't understand the language she spoke. To be mistaken for a foreigner in the city of my childhood and youth. And I probably was one, too. I was not sure whether to laugh or cry.

I managed to track down my first KGB interrogator, now retired and an alcoholic. For 20 dollars he agreed to talk to me on the phone. He sounded withdrawn and kept muttering something to the effect that he had to carry out the orders of his superiors. In the end, however, he said that, despite everything, the KGB had been a 'useful' organisation and that if anyone was able to sort out the mess the country was in it was the good old KGB. In short, he was defeated but not repenting.

I couldn't help feeling that I had a part in a sentimental and badly-rehearsed play – *The Return of the Prodigal*. Only my father was not there to embrace me. A nuclear physicist who had to deal with radioactive substances, he was killed by the long-term effects of radiation at the age of fifty-six.

I visited his modest grave in an old Kharkov cemetery, with trams rattling constantly past its high concrete fence, and laid flowers. For some reason, I was remembering us – me and my father – developing photos in the dark communal kitchen of our flat. The red light added mystery to this favourite ritual of my childhood. I would watch with fascination how the familiar features of my relatives and friends came to life on blank sheets of photographic paper immersed in smelly developing liquid. When I stirred the tray slightly, their faces would smile or frown, and this was both amazing and frightening, as if I, a six-year-old boy, were somehow in control of their lives.

The biggest terrifying truth about photos is that most of them are destined to outlive the people they depict. My father's photos certainly did. Here he is, strong and smiling, looking at me from a framed portrait above my desk. Wasn't it I who developed this photo under his guidance (he made our whole photo laboratory with his own hands) many years ago and thus made it, the photo, immortal, but couldn't stop my father from dying? I was twenty-eight and living in Moscow. One Sunday afternoon my mother telephoned from Kharkov and said that my father had died suddenly. I had just had lunch and was putting two-year-old Mitya to bed for his afternoon nap.

Every time I take a photo of someone I love, I get a painful reminder of that piercing Sunday telephone call.

'*Papa oomer.*' 'Your father has just died.' How cruel and how utterly meaningless the sounds of words can be! '*Papa oomer . . .*' Thank God, I am not going to hear them ever again. But Mitya probably will. I don't envy him this future experience.

It was only last night that I saw my father in a dream (he often comes to me when I am asleep). We are watching a volley-ball game together (I am six or seven years old), when suddenly the small open-air stadium and the terraces on which we are sitting start collapsing and falling down the precipice, dragging us down with them. We are falling down endlessly and painlessly like two snowflakes, big and small. Fear and pleasure are very closely mixed in that flight. In the end, I somehow manage to stop my free fall and wake up (for how long?), whereas my young and muscular father stays there (where?) and keeps falling down – slowly and gracefully – with a peculiar charismatic smile on his face.

I knew that one night I was going to catch up with him, and this thought was not at all frightening.

When you start seeing more dead than living people in your dreams, it is a sure sign of getting older . . .

My father's early radiation-induced death gave my visit to Chernobyl a special personal significance. Sasha, a young dosimetrist assigned to our film crew, was making a point of ignoring the radiation and refusing to wear a protective mask. With his every step forward, his Geiger counter showed great jumps in the level of background radiation.

I couldn't tear my eyes from the faded slogan crowning the building next to reactor number four: 'The victory of communism will come!' Several times they had tried to paint this tragically ironic slogan over, but the stubborn white letters were still clearly visible through layers of paint. 'The victory of communism will come!' they were screaming.

Down below, shift workers fished patiently in the reactor's cooling pond. Even the worldly Sasha couldn't refrain from commenting: 'They must be mad! Eat that fish and you'll lose all your hair within hours.'

The sinister theatre of life. And of death . . .

Our small crew had to pay 600 dollars for the Chernobyl tour plus a further 100 for each hour of filming. As well as a chauffeured Chaika limo (usually reserved for top party apparatchiks, this particular vehicle was abandoned in the contaminated zone by some visiting Soviet dignitary: it was too irradiated to be taken back to the outside world), the package included lunch and an English-speaking guide. As I had discovered, the Chernobyl tour was open to any foreigner with a half-decent excuse for being interested. And with plenty of dollars of course. We were granted a brisk interview with an official from the Ministry for Chernobyl (there is such a ministry in Ukraine), who spoke forcefully against the closure of the crippled fourth reactor. No wonder: the Chernobyl disaster looked like becoming one of Ukraine's more important hard-currency earners. The Chernobyl museum had just opened in Kiev, publicising 'achievements' made in tackling the catastrophe.

At the entrance to the ten-kilometre interior (heavily contaminated) zone we were offered sets of baggy 'protective' clothing, which were merely used battle fatigues. We were given face masks called *lepestok* (petal) to protect our lungs against radiation. The guide cheerfully informed us that within the ten-kilometre exclusion zone the level of radiation was a thousand times higher than the accepted safe maximum which made me think that the only outfit that could provide proper protection was probably a complete set of medieval knight's armour, lined with lead. We exchanged black jokes and nervous cackles, made even more uneasy by the knowledge that there had been an even bigger radioactive leak than usual the day before our visit.

Chernobyl, we were given to understand, leaked *all the time*.

Standing there in front of the reactor in my stupid khaki

outfit and with a flimsy white mask over my mouth, I was confrontedagainwiththefrighteningmelodramaofthesituation.

'If there's another explosion here, it would mean ultimate disaster, not only for Ukraine but for the whole of Europe,' the guide announced in a tone of unmistakable pride.

Earlier, at the entrance to the outer thirty-kilometre zone, we had seen a busload of workers returning from their fifteen-day shift at the reactor. The workers were getting off the 'dirty' zone bus and boarding a 'clean', decontaminated, one to take them to the neighbouring town of Slavutich for a fortnight's rest. They literally fell out of the bus, drunk out of their minds.

Many reactor workers, it seemed, started working in a state of mild inebriation and continued drinking throughout the shift in the mistaken but officially encouraged belief that alcohol could fend off radiation. The realisation that Europe's future was in the unsteady hands of these drunken men and women sent shivers down my spine.

There was another old slogan in Pripyat, the nearest town to Chernobyl, half a kilometre away. 'Let us translate the historic decisions of the 27th Soviet Communist Party Congress into life!'

The 'historic decisions' had indeed been translated. Pripyat once housed 50,000 residents, but it was dead and empty now. The explosion at reactor number four, which had affected 55 million people worldwide, was in some ways the last nail in the coffin of Soviet-style communism. The whole of Pripyat was evacuated in one day, thirty-six hours after the explosion, though for most of the evacuees it was already too late.

Kremlin bosses, instructed by Gorbachev, fell over themselves to keep quiet about what had happened. Ukrainian Communist Party leaders busily reassured the population there was no danger, while hastily (and secretly) evacuating their own families from the Kiev area. Had it not been for the Swedes, who noticed a sharp rise in radiation levels in their country and raised the alarm, the truth about the explosion might have been concealed for much longer.

Pripyat was eerie.

The motor of our camera whirred in utter silence.

Flower beds had vanished beneath thick vegetation.

In the city funfair, nestling between abandoned high-rise apartment blocks, the wind slowly propelled a rusty merry-go-round.

The wind also leafed through the pages of the March 1986 issue of the children's magazine, *Merry Pictures*, left beneath a park bench.

Here there was an overturned go-cart; there, a broken LP with 1986 Soviet musical hits trampled in the ground.

'Long live the First of May!' proclaimed the signs in empty shop windows. The disaster happened on 26 April, 1986. They had no time to celebrate First of May in Pripyat, and they never will. Walking around this dead town, you could almost feel the radiation in the air.

I entered an empty pillaged flat on the second floor of one of the defunct apartment blocks – and froze. Its lay-out was the same as my last flat in Kharkov: the same corridor with doorless closets in the wall, the same crudely tiled bathroom, the same tiny kitchen with broken gas-stove and heaps of rubbish on the scratched wooden floor. It felt like trudging through the ruins of my childhood.

I pressed my forehead to the window and looked out.

Silence and death . . . They have ruined my country. They have changed the view from my window.

This is probably what Joseph Brodsky meant by saying that it was impossible to come back to the country that does not exist any longer.

Leaving the thirty-kilometre zone, we passed through several villages now populated by *samosyoli* (self-settlers), the people who had flouted every ban to return, by choice, to their contaminated dwellings. In the village of Opachichi an old wrinkled man offered me a glass of water from his well. I stupidly drank it without thinking, and only then the realisation struck me: what am I doing? I am in Chernobyl.

'Don't you worry about the radiation,' the old man said reassuringly. 'They have pumped it all out.'

Two weeks before, he told me, there had been a wedding in Opachichi – the first wedding inside the exclusion zone. I looked up at the straw roof of his house, where a stork had built a nest – a symbol of procreation, an omen of life. The people who had withstood history's worst nuclear accident, the people who chose to live and marry in the contaminated zone, the people who sincerely believed radiation could be 'pumped out', deserved such an omen more than anyone else.

Through the murky window of my childhood house, I could see timid flowers of hope and life stubbornly breaking through radioactive rubble.

31

What Price Freedom

*T*he average cost of a London-Melbourne return flight is in excess of £1,000. In the four years since leaving Australia I have flown to Melbourne and back twenty-five times, once every two months. The tickets alone cost me over £25,000.

It is good to have this figure in the back of my mind when I try to understand why after six years in the West, after six successful books and five films, after several years of well-paid newspaper jobs, I ended up literally penniless and up to my ears in debts. I was thoroughly unprepared for such a turn of events. Money had never been an issue for me, neither in the Soviet Union (where I didn't have it but nor did anyone else), nor in the West where I quickly got used to a lump sum appearing monthly, as if by magic, on my bank account.

It is not easy to have your life fractured between Melbourne and London, two of the most remote cities from each other in the world. And although I always wanted to lead a peripatetic existence, not even in my wildest dreams could I ever imagine that one day I would end up living half a world away from my son.

I missed him terribly and often, on the spur of the moment, I would book a flight to Melbourne and go there for a week, most of which would be spent recovering from jet lag. £1,000 more, £1,000 less – who cares. It was sheer stupidity, it was madness, but it was also my only way of survival during those difficult years.

And credit cards of course, these treacherous pieces of plastic, making each purchase so easy and so glamorous that receiving a dry, tersely formulated statement comes almost as a surprise. One can easily get addicted to credit cards, just like to gambling or to playing the National Lottery. I read somewhere that a quarter of all bankruptcies are blamed on the profligate use of our flexible friends.

It was simply bound to happen to me. I had to learn this cruel lesson of Western life not from books or movies but from my own personal experience.

In May 1994, I was confronted with two dream projects: making a film on my native Ukraine and writing my book on the mini-states of Europe (which I had finished researching by then), neither of which I could either refuse or ignore. There was no alternative but resign from *The European* and concentrate on filming and writing. I still had some money in the bank, and *The European* gave me a bit of a golden handshake which was bound to keep me going for a while. I was writing my book every day, stopping only for a cup of coffee, and in the evenings would go out with Cricket (she liked good restaurants and so did I). Every now and then I would take off to Australia to see Mitya.

When I was half-way through the book, our London flat was broken into and my PC and printer were taken (luckily, I had copied everything I had written onto a disk which the thieves, mercifully, left behind). It was upsetting of course, but, having given it some thought, I decided that Western freedom of choice must spread to burglars as well: they simply took a liking to my computer (I don't blame them) and chose to steal it. After all, it was just a machine that let you make mistakes faster than any other invention in human history, with the possible exception of handguns and tequila, as one modern American writer put it. So I simply went out and bought myself a new one (which was stolen from me in Melbourne six months later).

My bank account figure was shrinking and melting away irretrievably, like a Moscow icicle in April.

No sooner had I finished the manuscript and delivered it to

the publishers, than the news came from Australia that Mitya was getting out of hand. He had just reached the dangerous age of thirteen and was misbehaving: mixing with a wrong crowd, neglecting his studies and possibly even smoking. Natasha was unable to cope with him on her own. I had to return to Australia for what I thought would be two or three years. Having quickly secured myself a couple of weekly columns in Australian newspapers, I packed up my well-travelled books and, having dispatched them by sea, boarded a plane to Melbourne.

One day before my departure, I was given a blue belt at my Taekwon-do class. I felt extremely proud when all the students bowed to me and applauded. I also got a farewell card, signed by all of them and wishing me well down under.

I had just had an umpteenth reconciliation with Cricket after an umpteenth fall-out. It was agreed that as soon as I got settled in Melbourne, she would rent out her London house and join me there.

I went back to Australia just in time: Mitya needed to be dragged out of the mess he had found himself in. I rented an unfurnished two-bedroom flat in the Melbourne suburb of Brighton, not far from where Mitya and Natasha were living. I had to purchase furniture and every little household item from cutlery to washing machine and to buy myself a second-hand car (life without a car in Melbourne is a nightmare: the distances are huge and public transport erratic). The old Toyota required lots of maintenance. My bank account plunged into an overdraft, so I had to resort to using credit cards even more often.

This time, disappointment with Australia struck me just after a couple of months. I was remembering with nostalgia my trips around Europe and the never-ending excitement of London life. It was harder and harder to find subjects for my two weekly columns. I felt cut off, detached and isolated, just like several years before, only this time the heart-burning spiritual discomfort was much stronger.

Delivering my column to a newspaper one day, I saw Justine, who had played teenage Australia in my ABC film *Vitali's Australia* several years before. She was selling sandwiches in a snack bar at Melbourne's Collins Plaza Hotel lobby. She was now nineteen but still looked childlike and largely unchanged.

Seeing my archetypal Australia selling sandwiches impressed me as highly symbolic. I was again unhappy in the country that I had once loved, in the continent-sized teenage nation that, although full of promises and hope, was stubbornly refusing to grow up.

I thought I was finally beginning to understand what Peter Cole-Adams meant when he wrote in his open letter to me several years before: 'When the honeymoon ends and you have discovered us for what we are, will you be able to forgive?' I had nothing to forgive Australia for (I was still profoundly grateful to it for having given me Freedom) and was only hoping she would eventually forgive me.

There was a timid knock on the door of my Melbourne flat at about midnight. It was my neighbour's teenage son.

'Excuse me, can we borrow your telescope? My mum wants to look at the stars.'

Freckles on top of his nose were trembling slightly as he spoke, like distant blinking stars in the Australian sky. I had bought this telescope for Mitya several years before, when we still lived in our house with a swimming pool. It was one of the few objects that survived all our subsequent moves. A fragment of my former Australian comfort.

Oh, these stuffy Australian summer nights when I lay wide awake in my bed unable to cope with alien nocturnal sounds outside my window, with ubiquitous possums pounding the roof with their little tenacious feet – 'Boom-boom-boom!' Indeed, there was something extra-terrestrial about Australia, with its crooked trees, red deserts and brown Gothic sunsets smelling of Indian curry. This was probably why my Melbourne neighbours liked to look at the stars in the middle of the night: subconsciously, they tried to rediscover the Earth (or themselves?) somewhere in the depths of the Universe.

On a hot and humid morning in February 1995, when the blasted northern wind from the Nullarbor Desert drove Melbourne (and myself) to the point of suffocation, my seventeen-year-long marriage to Natasha was officially terminated. The death occurred in an air-conditioned and brightly-lit courtroom, where a sweating Australian judge sat in state under the national emblem, with an emu and a kangaroo on it. A kangaroo court, I thought and smiled uneasily at my own unhappy pun while the judge muttered something to the effect that he declared our marriage, our seventeen-year-long life together, with all its joys, discoveries, delights and lots of hardship, null and void.

It suddenly occurred to me that both emus and kangaroos were fairly stupid and primitive animals.

Natasha, with whom I remained very friendly, did not turn up at the court and I didn't blame her for that. I was remembering how it all started in a shabby Moscow registration office seventeen years before. We both wore our everyday clothes during the ceremony – no suit, white dress or bridal veil, which was very unusual for the occasion. The reason for that was that we were not sure whether the clerk would agree to register us without putting a stamp in my passport. I couldn't allow my passport to be stamped: it was registered in Kharkov, and a Moscow marriage certificate would automatically give me the right to a coveted Moscow *propiska* (residence permit), but on one condition only: that no adult members of my would-be wife's family should object. My future mother-in-law did.

So my dilemma was as follows: to be registered in Moscow I had to cancel my Kharkov registration first. But as soon as I did that I would lose the right to return to live in my native city if anything went wrong. I was aware of my future mother-in-law's reluctance to grant me Moscow registration: it was well within her powers. This could create a situation in which I might find myself without any registration at all and thus become an outcast and a 'socially dangerous element'. All this sounds totally absurd by Western standards, but for us, who lived in the totalitarian country where absurdity was the main law of existence, the threat was more than real.

The night before our marriage neither Natasha nor I could sleep a wink. Shortly before dawn we came to a decision: to ask the marriage registration clerk not to put a marriage stamp in my passport. That would leave me the possibility of preserving my Kharkov registration if something went out of synch.

In the morning I bought a box of expensive chocolates and we went to ZAGS (the Marriages, Births and Deaths Registration office). It was raining. I gave the sweets to the female clerk and asked her confidentially not to stamp my passport. It was a serious breach of the regulations on her part, but she grew sympathetic and agreed to go along with it. If she hadn't, we simply would not have been married that day. So it was an unusual wedding. But at least it was not typical, and hence something to be remembered, or so we consoled ourselves.

Our divorce, with an emu and a kangaroo presiding over it, was not merely unusual, it was bizarre, just like almost everything that had happened to us during our five years in the West.

Cricket came to Australia and spent five weeks with me in my flat. Being very attached to her home, she didn't like either (the flat or Australia). After she left, I started feeling even more desolate. I didn't see much of Mitya who was now spending most of his time with his mates, although his behaviour had improved considerably since my arrival. Isn't a happy father in London preferable to a miserable one close-by? I was thinking. I knew I would never be happy living without him. I also knew I would be desperate if I stayed in Australia for much longer: I couldn't write there, I couldn't breathe. This time, even Tasmania, where I went three or four times in search of inspiration, failed to provide a cure.

Life was punishing me with yet another unsolvable dilemma.

At least I was sure that my son would never become cannon fodder and would never be sent to die crushing someone else's Freedom (which would have been a real possibility had he stayed in Russia, caught up in a disgraceful and unwinnable war with Chechnya). I knew that if he woke up from a knock on the door in the middle of the night, it would only be his Australian neighbours wanting to look at the stars. And I was grateful to Australia for that, too.

By the time my roving books reached Melbourne by sea, I already knew that I was returning to Europe. Without bothering to unpack the boxes, I sent them back to London!

Another £1,000. And yet another. I sold my recently bought car and furniture for next to nothing. I paid a fine to the real estate agency for breaking a year-long lease on my flat and boarded a plane to London exactly five months after leaving it.

Back in London, I became seriously hard-up. Yes, thanks to Cricket, I had a roof over my head, but work took a long time to start picking up. It is amazing how quickly they forget about you in London. Five months were certainly not enough to be forgotten completely, but just sufficient for everyone to know that I was in Australia. My telephone was dead.

Hemingway once wrote that poverty was good for a writer: it made his eyes sharper. He was probably right. Having no money was a real eye-opener for me, and I was noticing things that I had never seen before. With £10 (and at one point £4) left on my bank account I would start my day with trying to calculate what I could do – go out for a cup of coffee in my area, or venture to the City for some door-knocking and job-hunting. I could afford either a cup of coffee or a one-day travel card, but not both. Soon I started noticing that at certain Tube stations they seldom checked your ticket, so with luck one could get there for 90 pence – the lowest rate. I had to stop buying *The Independent* and had to switch over to *The Times*, the cheapest broadsheet newspaper. Never before had I realised that 15–20 pence could make a difference. But they certainly could. I really began to appreciate the little pleasures of life (like a cup of coffee in a café) that I used to take for granted.

I knew that my poverty was a temporary thing and the fault was solely mine: I had done everything to confuse London editors, researchers and producers as to my whereabouts. I knew that Mark Twain, Edgar Allan Poe, George Orwell and countless other writers had to live from hand to mouth at some stage of their lives. 'Devastating wealth! God save a writer from it!' said Boris Pasternak. But I was not after wealth. I was after keeping my head above water.

Two months after my return, my book on the eleven European mini-states, *Little is the Light*, was launched. It generated a good deal of publicity, and my telephone started ringing again.

The life of a freelance writer and columnist in London was far from easy. To my surprise, however, the main difficulty was not getting a piece commissioned, but making sure you were paid for it. A nasty side of Western morality that I had never known existed was suddenly exposed to me in all its glaring ugliness. Despite my thirty-five years in the former Soviet Union, the country which stood on lies and dishonesty, I always tried to respect freelances and make sure they were paid on time. (In Russian journalistic jargon, freelances were called 'kettles', heaven knows why. Maybe because most of them had long Jewish noses: it was hard for a Jew to get a staff journalistic job.) Of course, they were paid very little. But so were we.

Soon after becoming a freelance (or a kettle, if you wish) in London I started noticing that, with rare exceptions (*The Spectator* and the *Daily Telegraph* among them), my punctiliousness was not reciprocated.

'You have to chase them!' my omniscient freelance friends advised. But the sad truth is that those who commission a piece tend to forget about it the moment it is published. It wasn't always like that. In one of his letters Chekhov remembers how his brother Mikhail, an aspiring writer, got a grand piano as a royalty from one of Moscow's end-of-the-last-century magazines which was short of cash at that particular moment. I wish I could get at least a harmonica from a London tabloid which begged me into writing a piece on Zhirinovsky in 1993. ('We need the copy in two hours. Can you do it for 500 quid?') They ran it the next day but for the next three years I hadn't got a penny (to say nothing of a piano) for that. With money owed to me by a handful of newspapers, magazines and radio stations, I was prepared to put my own signature under the words of Dorothy Parker: 'The two most beautiful words in the English language are "cheque enclosed".'

Another convincing lesson in Western morality was in store for me. One day, leafing through a freshly-published Russia-based thriller in a London bookshop, I was stunned to discover that both its plot and characters were largely 'borrowed' by its author from my two books, *Special Correspondent* and *Dateline Freedom*. In fact, the main hero of the book, a Soviet investigative journalist writing about the Soviet Mafia, was myself (only the name was different). He had the same origins, wrote for the same magazines, had the same awards and even a similar appearance. Like me he lived in a communal flat and had to write in a cupboard. Like me, he was harassed by the KGB. Dozens of episodes and twists of the plot were repeating my real-life investigations to the letter. Real-life Russian people from my two books were turned into fictitious characters, and several passages were simply copied word for word! Altogether, I counted fifty-eight direct borrowings, and the author (quite a successful young London writer) hadn't even bother to credit me in the Acknowledgments.

I didn't know what to do. To say that I was angry would be an understatement. I was absolutely furious. I threatened legal action and received several apologetic (even somewhat sycophantic) letters from the novelist, saying that he was an admirer of my work, that he hoped to meet me one day, and that he was prepared to give me credits in the future paperback edition of his thriller.

This was certainly not enough, but I was running out of steam. The saga had already cost me lots of nervous energy and time. But the final stop in it was put by an amicable Jewish lawyer whom I went to consult (he was kind enough to offer me free advice) in his Holborn offices. He explained that copyright litigation (with no guarantee of victory) could cost me hundreds of thousands of pounds. For reading three thick books alone, lawyers could charge me from ten to twenty grand (they charged by the hour). For me, who at the time of the conversation had a couple of hundred pounds in the bank and plenty of debts, this was obviously the end of the matter.

'In the society where you have come from, there was no justice whatsoever,' the lawyer said when we were parting. 'In Western society justice does exist, but it costs a lot of money, which is still better than having no justice at all . . .'

I thanked him and went to the door, thinking that it was not only justice that was costly in the West. Freedom itself, as I had learnt, was quite an expensive commodity as well.

32

Standing in Piccadilly

*A*pparently, if you stand all day in London's Piccadilly Circus – be you a Londoner, a Mancunian, a Muscovite, or an Eskimo – you'll bump into someone you know. And here I am, hanging around the silly statue of Eros. My plane to somewhere leaves tomorrow, and meanwhile I am desperate to bump into a friend, a relative, or at least into someone I know.

Two hours pass, three hours – no luck.

I am standing in the middle of the square looking at the multi-coloured London crowd, at buskers more and more often appearing in groups of three, four and even five (I won't be surprised if one day I see the Red Army Choir, complete with dancers, musicians and a grey-haired uniformed conductor, shouting 'Kalinka' in a London subway and collecting change from pedestrians into their peaked caps) – but fail to spot a single familiar face.

Soon I start hallucinating. I feel as if I am somehow familiar with every person in the passing throng – with this lanky gentleman in a smart double-breasted suit, with this slim black girl, whose nose is pierced with a silver ring, with this dishevelled smelly tramp pushing a rusty shopping trolley. Only, for love nor money, I can't recall where, how and when I have actually met them all. Human memory is like a rubbish bin, which our brain, this lazy amnesiac dustman, chronically forgets to empty. Einstein was right when he said that the ability to forget was the best quality of our minds. My head is bursting with unnecessary information, firmly stored on the hard disk of my skull – dates, faces, names, dreams, streets, towns, countries.

Curiously, I still remember the phone number of our Kharkov flat thirty-six years ago, when I was six: 3–39–22. We had a facetious relative who would call us up of an evening and bark into the phone in a disguised voice: 'Hello, this is a telephone exchange warning. A thunderstorm is approaching, so please cover your telephone with a wet rag, lest it should explode!' And we did – just in case. Private telephones were rare at that time and we didn't want to run any risks: who knows, what if, indeed, it had exploded.

You can dial this number endlessly now without reaching anyone: half of the subscribers are no longer alive and the dead do not need a telephone, and the other half, including me, having changed dozens of flats and countries, now use different numbers, preceded by long, almost spy-like, codes which are impossible to decipher.

Similarly, I can't forget the name and the patronymic of the dumb and pugnacious kindergarten governess who used to hit us, her little wards, with a spoon when we refused to eat our daily portions of semolina – cold, thick and tasteless like a snowdrift: Nina Nikolayevna. Having forgotten the names of so many good people, I can't help remembering her, this long-handed grenadier-like virago. By the way, isn't it she, in her bright-red overcoat of thick woollen cloth with cotton-wool padded shoulders, barging like an ice-breaker through the soft Piccadilly crowd? No, it is a different lady, whom I don't know, and Nina Nikolayevna is lying quietly in Kharkov cemetery number two, and her grave is touched with white poplar fluff, like with the leftovers of the uneaten semolina.

And isn't this Lyonia Prudnikov, my university professor, coming out of the Dillons bookshop with Muller's *English-Russian Dictionary* (which he had learnt by heart) under his armpit? A polyglot, a bookworm and an eternal teenager, never allowed outside the Soviet Union, he was fluent in eighteen languages, including Estonian, Catalan and Malayalam. No, I can't possibly bump into him in Piccadilly, simply because I know that he died, aged fifty-two, ten years ago. He was brushing his teeth in the morning and suddenly collapsed on the tiled floor of his tiny communal bathroom, and 'Miatniy' (Minty) tooth-powder spilled out and dusted his flabby scholarly body like snow. Or like tender chestnut blooms from the boulevards of Paris, the city which he had failed to see.

A plush and gleaming Audi 100 limo screeches to a halt on the opposite side of the square, nearly colliding with a double-decker. Irina Underwood, a young Russian woman married to a British millionaire, is behind the wheel. I have never met her, only seen her photos in the papers. She looks withdrawn (probably drunk), and a smoking fag is sticking out of her mouth. Even from the distance, I can see her hands tremble. I can hear diamond rings on her tremulous fingers touching each other with a soft clanking sound, like miniature railway carriages when coupled.

A bubbly and fun-loving Moscow girl, she came to Britain to improve her English several years ago. She met her future husband, a fifty-four-year-old widower, at a party. After they got married, he showered her with riches: a luxury car, her own saddlery business, jewellery and fur coats. Suddenly, all the wildest dreams of a simple Russian girl came true like in a fairy-tale. She was living in her 'wonderful Great Britain', she was rich, she was free. There was nothing else to expect from life, nothing else to strive for.

There are two biggest tragedies in life: not to see the realisation of your dreams, and to see it, according to Bernard Shaw.

Unable to cope with her sudden affluence, Irina started drinking. She was stopped several times for drink-driving, served ten days in Holloway and another fifteen in an open prison, but continued to drive while drunk. Her husband provided her with a personal chauffeur, and she had enough cash to afford taxis, but sitting behind the wheel of her Audi gave her an illusion of being still in control of her life. Her car dashed along narrow English country lanes scaring away geese, sheep and tweed-clad village-dwellers walking their dogs along the hedgerows. She drank, she smoked so much that her lips were permanently burnt. One day her husband returned home to find his young wife's body hanging from an electric cord in the old dairy of their country mansion. She left a farewell note saying simply: 'John, I really loved you. Bye.'

Irina failed the test of Freedom, one of the hardest trials a human being, or a country, can be subjected to – probably the second hardest after the trial of servitude. I know exactly how she must have felt since I have nearly failed it myself. I only survived because I was older – and stronger – than her. Irina's tragedy is, in a way, a story of post-communist Russia, unable to cope with her unexpected, even if fragile, democracy and drinking herself into oblivion while balancing precariously on a high-voltage electric cord.

The Audi 100 starts moving towards me. It glides straight across the statue of Eros leaving it intact. It drives, noiseless and invisible, through the crowd. It bumps into me at full speed, but I don't feel the impact of its bumper ramming through my chest. I feel nothing. I see nothing – only a horrific red scar around Irina's neck. The ghost car vanishes into thin Piccadilly air. It was not the sort of an encounter I was hoping for. But maybe unexpected meetings simply cannot be pre-planned or predicted?

I couldn't expect to bump into a girl from my Kharkov school in a Melbourne supermarket six years ago. I couldn't even recall the name of this dark-eyed girl with pigtails – no longer a girl and with no pigtails, but I could clearly see my childhood still reflected in her eyes. We had nothing to talk about, just stood there, at the end of the world among the shelves of a foreign supermarket sagging under foreign exotic foods, and stared at each other silently – two displaced human souls who had had a tragic fortune (or a happy misfortune?) to be born and to live at the breaking point of epochs.

Likewise, I couldn't expect to stumble across Hitler's couch in Tasmania, an even more extraordinary case of displacement.

It so happens that my former schoolmates are now more likely to be encountered in Melbourne, New York or Tel Aviv than in Kharkov's Barachnaya (Barracks) Street, later renamed Culture Street (heaven knows why), where our school was located. Fate has scattered us all over the globe and I have been scattered more than anyone else.

How nice it would be to look out of the window one morning and to see our quiet Culture Street, overgrown with trees, and the group of *siavki* (beggar-boys) near the Tempo food shop, and the old peasant woman selling fried sunflower seeds near Sumskoi market – 10 kopecks a glass measure (and the seeds are hot and are pleasantly warming your thigh through your trousers), and our school, with crude goggle-eyed busts of the Young Guard members at the entrance.

The view from the window of my childhood. Wherever I go, I look at the world through it.

I am also on a look-out for my Culture Street. To my knowledge, no other city in the world, but Kharkov, has a street with such a peculiar name. The closest to it so far – in feeling and atmosphere rather than in architecture – was Rue Princesse in Lille. I went there to look at the house where Charles de Gaulle, one of my all-time heroes, was born. Not too many people in Lille knew how to find it.

'*La France a perdu une bataille, mais la France n'a pas perdu la guerre,*' declared Charles de Gaulle when the Nazis invaded Paris. 'France has lost a battle, but France hasn't lost the war.' These proud words helped me to cope with countless set-backs and disasters in my life.

Rue Princesse was quiet, cosy and clearly provincial, but there was something in it that reminded me of the street of my childhood. Was it the smell of old stucco, peeling off shabby facades of low-built sunburnt houses and mixing with a slightly intoxicating pungent odour of blooming acacias? Or was it a touch of the warm southern sun on my face? Or the tangled balls of grey poplar fluff along the kerb. As kids we used to set them on fire by touching them with a burning match, and they would flare up with a curt crackling sound like magnesium flashes in antediluvian turn-of-the-century cameras. We didn't realise then that our lives were only marginally longer than these momentary frantic flashes.

Standing there, in this French 'Culture Street' next to Charles de Gaulle's house, where the great man's cradle and his white baptismal gown were displayed, I thought that the appearance of Melbourne in my life was not entirely coincidental either. It probably happened thanks to my Kharkov friend Zhenia Bulavin, who decided to avoid being drafted to the Soviet Army by simulating a rare psychiatric condition – dromomania, an irrepressible passion for aimless travelling. He had read about it in a specialised medical journal. Having dutifully turned up for a medical examination at a military recruitment office, he produced a tattered map of the world out of his pocket and began to scrutinise it, greedily and oblivious.

'Are you dreaming of going to Paris, young man?' an experienced woman neuro-pathologist (who had never been to Paris herself) asked him.

'No, I am not,' replied my well-prepared friend. 'I am actually more interested in the stretch of the coastline between Melbourne and Sydney . . .'

Of course, he was immediately pronounced unfit for service: you had to be mentally disturbed to take interest in those remote, almost non-existing, Australian cities, to say nothing of the coastline stretch between them. Well, Zhenia did manage to avoid military draft, but couldn't stop himself from excessive drinking and ended up as an alcoholic. It was I who became a dromomaniac in his stead.

Until recently, there was a place in the world, from where, as I thought, I could see the street of my childhood. It was Tasmania, that small green island off the Australian coast which had stunned me with its nostalgic, almost European, beauty. I used to go there often from Melbourne and was happy to be calling myself a Tasmaniac.

What a sinister connotation this innocent pun of mine has taken on after the April 1996 massacre in Port Arthur.

Yes, Tasmania had a sinister side, which until recently I preferred to ignore, and although there can be no comparison in sheer number of victims, in the history of mankind Port Arthur should be remembered along with the KGB dungeons and the Nazi concentration camps.

The truth is that Port Arthur was grossly overmarketed in a

truly Australian (or Tasmanian) teenage fashion, lacking hind-
sight and depth of vision. Can you imagine Poland advertising
Auschwitz as 'the country's premier tourist attraction' and
conducting its Independence Day celebrations there? Who
knows what sort of effect this continuous irreverent com-
motion in and around Port Arthur could have had on the
already sick and disturbed mind of Martin Bryant, the killer
gunman.

The moment I saw his photo in London newspapers – long
blond hair, bulging glassy eyes – I knew I had seen him once
before. I was buying a sandwich in a small takeaway shop
in Hobart's Salamanca Place when he stumbled in. Tall and
stoopy, he was dressed in jeans and dirty tee-shirt. His long
hair was tussled and unwashed. But what stunned me most
were his blank unseeing eyes – the eyes of a maniac or of
a drug-addict. His movements were slow and arbitrary, like
those of a somnambulant, and his whole appearance screamed
danger and brutal force. How come he was allowed to own
guns? Having looked at me sullenly from under his brows, he
turned round and walked out of the shop. The Port Arthur
massacre was still more than three months away.

Tragic history should be learnt in reverence and silence,
not marketed with fanfares. And a place that meant ultimate
nightmare for so many humans in the not-so-distant past
should not be turned into a fee-charging farcical chamber
of horrors. Ghosts of the grievous past should not be idly
disturbed. Their only legitimate place is in human memory,
not at a Blackpool-style funfair, and the best way to put them
to rest is to leave them alone. Otherwise, they will sooner or
later return to haunt us.

I hope tourists will keep coming to Tasmania – to see, to
remember and to learn from the past. But my Tasmanian
sojourn is over. It ended when I was having lunch with
a Channel 4 film crew (I was making a short travel TV
programme about Tasmania) in the very café in Port Arthur
where six months later Bryant would start his carnage (I can
visualise it as clearly as if I was there on that fatal day, and
can almost feel the smell of gunpowder mixing with that of
barbecued sausages and Tasmanian 'national pies'). It ended

when I stumbled across an antique couch that used to belong to Hitler at a small Tasmanian country hotel and realised that I had to turn back.

I don't seriously believe in omens, but these two encounters were too sinister to be dismissed. When your nomadic trail is suddenly blocked by Hitler's couch, standing next to the site of one of the most atrocious mass murders in human history, it is a sure sign that you've lost your direction.

It's evening. I am still standing in Piccadilly, glittering with what H.V. Morton called its 'feverish epileptic lights searching for something that they will never find'. What is it that they are searching for? Solitude? Freedom? Quiet? Or, like me, a familiar face? Whatever it is, there is still one place in the world where I am always welcome; the place where I can always find peace with myself – Mount Athos, the Orthodox monastic republic in Macedonia where I have a trusted friend, Father Ioannikios, a former communist turned monk.

Mount Athos is one of the few places in the world that does not change with time. For more than a thousand years, the monks of its many monasteries, *kellions* and *skites* (groups of small monastic houses) have been passing their earthly days in prayer and fasting. For more than a thousand years, not a single 'smooth-faced person' (female) has stepped on its rocky, sunburnt shores. Time does not exist on the Holy Mountain where monks still live by the Julian calendar which is thirteen days behind our Gregorian one. Clocks in some monasteries are set to midnight at sunset. In others they are set to noon at dawn which makes the act of making any kind of appointment on Mount Athos a hopeless business, but which does not bother the monks whose only appointment is with God, and His working hours are flexible.

Each monastery resembles a fortified medieval town perched precariously on top of a cliff. At sunset, when the red-robed monk of the setting sun is leaving Mount Athos and heading for the sea, the monasteries' gates are locked for the night. At 3 a.m. *semantrons* start calling the monks for the first five-hour-long liturgy of the day. Nothing can change or interrupt this age-long order of monastic existence.

We were sitting with Father Ioannikios on the balcony of his old *kellion* Ravdouchou, overlooking the Aegean Sea. We drank his excellent home-made *raki* and ate lunch of grilled fish and olives. I was happy to see how much the *kellion*, which is recognised by UNESCO as the oldest residential dwelling in Europe continuously inhabited since the seventh century, had changed since my previous visit three years before.

After my feature about Father Ioannikios and his unique *kellion* was published by *The European* and reprinted by several Greek dailies, the ageing monk started receiving donations for its badly needed restoration. Money came from private individuals and from the Greek Ministry of Culture which offered him 8 million drachmas.

The results were obvious – walls well-plastered, beautifully made ceilings and ivory-laid doors. An eighth-century chapel, the oldest on Mount Athos, was also being restored – quite a difference from three years before when floorboards were rotting, walls were crumbling and bats were nesting in the basement.

Father Ioannikios had hired three Albanians who toiled all day, only stopping to light cigarettes and eat the noon meal of beans and cheese prepared by the monk himself. The clamour of hammering, sawing and the deep voice of the monk supervising, shouting in a heavy mix of Greek, Bulgarian and dog Albanian . . . It was wonderful to see that a writer *can* make a difference, after all.

Somewhere, in a Melbourne suburb, there lives a young American-Australian couple who got married with the help of my book *Vitali's Australia*. And a restored seventh-century *kellion* on Mount Athos – my two biggest 'literary' achievements.

In the evening, after the bean soup and the *reti* wine from the casks below in the dust-covered dark (a red wine which clears the day's work and worries in a single swallow), the monk talked of his past – of his life in Africa, Denmark and Bulgaria, where he worked as a film director, and of his seven years' imprisonment on the island of Yeros. He was worried about not finishing the restoration before he, like his predecessor Father Theodorus, keeled over dead in the *kellion*'s garden.

He chanted his melodious religious poems in Greek, and I read him mine in Russian.

The night was falling on the Holy Mountain like a giant monk descending slowly from his heavenly *skites* and covering the earth with his black robes.

'Remember, Vitali, you've got your *kellion* on Mount Athos where you will be always be a dear guest,' Father Ioannikios told me.

Suddenly, everything around me was full of harmony and meaning. My own life was no longer purposeless and hectic. The grief that I had inflicted on those around me was forgiven, my own suffering was forgotten; and even death itself was no longer frightening.

Maybe it is our world, not the monks', that is unreal? And are we not all living in one big chaotic monastery where we constantly fight each other for worshipping different gods and revering different icons? And although out of three main virtues of a Mount Athos monk – chastity, obedience and lack of personal possessions – I could only boast of the third, I knew if I went there ever again I probably would not come back.

The day's act at Piccadilly Circus is over. (Shakespeare was wrong: life is not a theatre, it is a circus.)

I am standing in the empty square face to face with the Moon, still hoping against all hope to see the one living being whom I want to see most of all – my fifteen-year-old son, who speaks Russian with an English and English with an Australian accent. I would take him to the Trocadero games arcade round the corner, where he liked to play so much when we lived together in London, and on the way back home we could pop into the Academy Club in Soho where I would have a cup of coffee and he a glass of Coke with ice. But this is unrealistic: it is now morning in Australia, and he is getting ready for his Melbourne school – the ninth school in his peripatetic fifteen-year-long life, full of flights and house moves. The Trocadero has lost attraction for him, now preoccupied with more mature games. And the Academy, my own second home, closed down some time ago after a stray truck drove into its ground floor lounge one Saturday afternoon, the very lounge where I sat with Cricket on the night that we met.

A thunderstorm broke over the city of Kharkov, having blown to pieces my old life-line telephone.

3–39–22; 3–39–22 – and no reply . . .

Having left Piccadilly, I trudge towards Oxford Circus Tube station through dark winding lanes of Soho. And then, at last, I see *him* inside a small second-hand furniture store: a sturdy figure, early grey hair, dark shadows under the eyes, obviously a vagabond and a wastrel. He is lying on an antique Biedermeier couch, displayed in the window. He is asleep.

Where on earth could I have met him?

Standing two metres away from the window, I cough gently to attract his attention. He wakes up, gets off the couch sleepily and stares at me in disbelief. Blasted memory . . . I rub my forehead trying to remember where I know him from. And he rubs his. I step forward – and he moves hesitantly towards me.

I come up against the cold glass of the shop-window and – a moment later – disappear completely, without a trace . . .

33

Two Pages From an Old Notebook

I found these yellowish and brittle sheets of paper between pages of an old Russian book of mine the other day. They were covered with the notes I had made during a journalistic assignment in Karelia in the Russian North, the land of white nights, thick coniferous forests and deep blue-eyed lakes, in the summer of 1984 or 1985.

Here they are translated from Russian, these miraculously preserved impressions from my previous life:

Petrozavodsk [Karelia's capital].

Shortly after 11 p.m. the sun suddenly dived out from behind the clouds. I went for a walk along the embankment. Smooth pinkish surface of the Onega lake. On the opposite shore – a dark forest edge. Lilac is blooming for all it is worth (in June!), nightingales are singing. A white motor ship is moored to a distant pier. Dandelions and *kashka* [white clover] spread their sweet odour all around the place. A monument to Peter the Great near the river terminal. Soft rosy light, lots of space. I feel like sailing off along this lake.

What a small town it is! Today I've bumped into two fellow passengers from the train that brought me here from Moscow. With one I travelled in the same compartment. There is nowhere you can hide . . .

I am now in my hotel room feeling reluctant to pull down the blinds: such a waste of daylight . . . But it's late, and I have to sleep . . .

. . . What a wonderful day!

I am on board a hovercraft on the way to the island of Kizhi. The captain invited me to the wheel house on the upper deck where we drank the purest ice-cold water which a crew member had drawn up straight from the lake in an empty milk bottle.

The Kizhi.

I am staying in a tiny cubby-hole of a room on the Kizhi pier. During the day, the pier master uses it as his office. The walls are pasted over with sailing directions and old river maps.

Fishing.

The fish bite almost non-stop. The moment you throw in the line they start biting. Roach, tench . . . V. L., the pier master, ferreted out a couple of rather big gleaming ides. My hands are permeated with a smell of fish. Huge and very spiteful mosquitoes. My face is wet with white stinking Deta [anti-mosquito liquid].

Stunning sunset – I am speechless. From time to time I scoop water from the lake with a faceted glass and drink it. A shabby wooden hut on the shore. Inside – a mouldy smell of poverty.

We are cleaning the fish from our catch straight on the pier. Sea-gulls pick up fish entrails from under our knives. A glass of milk fresh from the cow before going to sleep.

Solonezhskaya Inlet.

The whole flotilla of boats is sailing towards a Kometa hovercraft entering the harbour. Old women are paddling frantically. They have come to meet their relatives arriving from Petrozavodsk and are too impatient to wait for them to step ashore . . .

Morning.

Two motor ships with tourists from Leningrad are moored to the pier. They came in during the night. One is called *Mamin-Sibiryak* [a nineteenth-century Russian writer]. On their decks – flocks of Leningraders with nice soft accents. In droves, they set off to have a look at the church escorted by Lena, a local tourist guide in red kerchief.

I drink cold beer sitting on a concrete platform with my legs dangling over the edge, a couple of inches above the water. Small groups of noisy and ruddy Finns are wandering about. In a moment we are going to eat *ukha* [fish-soup] cooked from our yesterday's catch.

Old houses of the Kizhi.

They are like living beings and look as if they can breathe, yawn and snore. Lena: 'A Kizhi *izba* [log cabin] is very human-oriented. Everything in it is rational and well-measured . . .' The sturdy houses of rich peasants. Wealth created by hard labour. Where has it all gone?

An almost human scream of sea-gulls.

London, 1996

Postscript

THE BIEDERMEIER SOFA in the sitting room of Crabtree House, a bed and breakfast hotel at Huonville, Tasmania, once belonged to Adolf Hitler. Otherwise unremarkable, it is the provenance of this piece of furniture that makes it as incongruous as a wallaby at the Brandenburg Gate. And the same goes for Vitali Vitaliev. A man with his kind of history belongs in Europe, he is surely mislocated in a Melbourne suburb.

The sofa's long journey south to the very edge of the world deserves a book of its own. It is the story of an Estonian, Toomas Lembit, who became a high ranking officer in the Ahnenerbe, the department of the SS charged with looting occupied Europe's art collections and curating them for the Nazi hierarchy. Lembit looked after the Führer's private collection and built up an impressive one of his own. After the war, he fled to Tasmania where he bought a house, crammed it with paintings and furniture, and spent his remaining days in grumpy isolation, standing guard over his stolen treasure with a shotgun. When Lembit died there was no effort to trace the original owners nor any question of handing the booty over to the Israelis. The Australians cheerfully auctioned the lot. The Biedermeier sofa was snapped up by an Italian couple and found its way to Crabtree House, where Vitaliev, erstwhile Moscow correspondent for the Clive James show, writer in the midst of marital and financial crises, and bone-weary traveller, lay down on it one November night in 1995 to sleep, perchance to dream.

Dreams were at that time for Vitaliev the only authentic episodes of his existence. Awake, he was role-playing. Vitaliev had an extensive repertoire to perform: former fugitive from the KGB, journalist, TV personality, husband, father, Ukrainian-born Russian, migrant to Australia, culturally displaced person. But if the daytime was given over to whatever his family demanded, employers had contracted or circumstances might dictate, at night Vitaliev could be himself. He determined to make the most of it:

> An average human being can expect to have three hundred thousand dreams in his or her lifetime. An avid dreamer like myself can probably achieve a million . . . thriller dreams, Mills & Boon dreams, travelogue dreams, science-fiction dreams, flying dreams where I use my hands as wings. Many, like TV series, run for several consecutive nights. A few keep coming back to haunt me for months or even years. And some of them do come true.

Incarcerated in the dreary gulag of Soviet society, a mind fed on classical Russian literature dreamed of escape. Those dreams came true: he did, at last, see Paris and London. But was this 'freedom'? In a dream there is always something powerfully present, yet elusive, laden with promise but just out of grasp – more an atmosphere than anything solid. Freedom is like that for Vitaliev, a concept that belongs in a dreamscape of shadows and archetypes. As Vitaliev, the struggling freelance writer, discovers in the West, the credit-card limit can be as insuperable a barrier to a man's freedom of movement as the Berlin Wall.

The chapters of this book are overlapping vignettes drawn from dreams and from journalistic assignments. They range from Kharkov to Sydney, by way of Soho and include an encounter with a giant spider and lunch, at Ascot, with Miss World. But chiefly they are telling the adventures of his childhood, loves and marriages, hopes and despairs and the awful error he made in emigrating to Australia. He frequently quotes from the works of his fellow countrymen, and one quickly becomes aware of the axiomatic force of Russian literature – there surely cannot be a human situation which it has not distilled into proverb. To be born into such a culture, you'd think, is to be given the chance to lead one's life without ever making a mistake. Things do not work out like that, however, and Vitaliev, like the rest of us, has had to develop his wisdom the hard way.

Readers of *Literary Review* who were members of the Academy Club may remember Vitaliev. He was the roly-poly Russian in the scruffy suit who told improbable stories: the one who disappeared for three months, fell in love, gave up drink, shed three stones and ten years, returning kitted out in Jaeger. But don't get the wrong idea: *Dreams on Hitler's Couch* isn't just a memoir of passing interest – 'one Russian's personal account of coming to terms with life in the West' – Vitaliev transcends his genre, producing a new travel-writing of the soul, a journey with lessons about what really matters in life. That makes it literature. Perhaps now the Academy's door is shut, a new door will open and Chekhov or Dostoevsky will emerge, embrace Vitaliev in the Russian fashion and say 'Welcome to the club, Vitali.' Perhaps, at least, in a dream.

Dennis Sewell, *Literary Review*